Romany Legacy

A NOVEL

Other books by Jo-Anne:

Yesterday's Shadows

A Walking Shadow

Nets of Gold

Keeping Mum

The Emperor's Women

Taking Stock

The S.O.B.

Doin' It

The S.O.B.

The Quandary

No Smoke Without Fire

A Grievous Burden

Check out the web page at
www.joannesouthernbooks.com

Romany Legacy

A NOVEL

Jo-Anne Southern

Primix Publishing
11620 Wilshire Blvd
Suite 900, West Wilshire Center, Los Angeles, CA, 90025
www.primixpublishing.com
Phone: 1-800-538-5788

Published by Primix Publishing   08/23/2021

ISBN: 978-1-955177-35-1(sc)
ISBN: 978-1-955177-36-8(e)

Library of Congress Control Number: 2021920781

Contents

CHAPTER ONE

1879

"**G**et that top field ploughed today," Jake snarled, glaring at his son. Clifford glanced at his mother, Liz, as she set a bowl of porridge in front of him, shaking her head as if warning him not to argue.

"You know that's what I've got on for today, Dad." He kept his voice easy, kept the anger hidden. "No need to order me around."

"I'll pack your dinner," his mother said as she bustled about the kitchen, opened a cupboard, and took out a linen cloth.

"That lad don't need no food, woman, he's got enough to do without stopping for a break."

Liz looked at him and snarled.,"I expect *you* won't want any food at noon either, then." Angry now, she turned to the fireplace.

Jake snorted. "Don't talk stupid, woman, I'll be here at the usual time for my meal."

"Even horses have to rest sometime, Dad," Clifford's seventeen year old sister Betty said, her face wide in a smile. "You allus said they fall down and die," her voice faltered, "if they don't get fed and rested."

"What do you know about animals, eh?" He bawled as he turned on her. "Keep to your hens and dairy, girl. Don't interfere in things that don't concern you."

Betty, her sister Joyce and mother exchanged looks. Jake, it seemed, was in a foul mood, which meant little peace in the house today.

When Jake went to saddle his horse, Liz packed Clifford's meal. None mentioned Jake, but bade each other a good day as Clifford left for the barn. It was just past five thirty, still dark although the distant hills were touched with a tinge of orange. His breath came out in a mist and a chill struck through his boots from the frosty ground.

As he ate his midday dinner seated on the back of the cart, the day was bright with a slight wind. Hungry, breakfast porridge a memory now, he unwrapped the linen cloth. His mother had packed him a meat pasty, four sandwiches of cheese and pickle, and two apples. In the front of the cart, wrapped in wet sacking, was the stone bottle he had filled at the well.

As he ate, he surveyed the partially tilled field, the woods on the slight rise and the distant highs of the Pennines, thinking it a bonny place to live. No doubt about it. He could never recall a time when he had not been happy here, even with his miserable old father, swine that he was, always carping and laying about with his walking stick. Clifford carried many a scar from that stick.

His father, Jake, a large, wellbuilt man, had huge arms developed from years of farming, from that and moving the rocks that dotted their sloping, hillside fields. In a way, Clifford admired him because his hard work and dedication to the land had made it what it was today.

When a lad of eighteen, Jake's father, George, died and left him what, to all intents and purposes, was the ruins of a farm, because organized agriculture never was a science grandfather understood. Fields that were once cleared went wild, the moor gorse invaded ever closer to the farm house, and small trees and brush quickly took over open spaces. Aye, Jake had done wonders with the place, as Clifford knew only too well, having heard the story ad infinitum.

As he ate an apple, he looked around with the satisfaction of knowing that one day this would be his inheritance. Years of toil and care showed in every groomed acre, years of deprivation were exhibited in each well tended copse and spinney. Tears of frustration and exhaustion had watered that white farmhouse where the smoke rose like a prayer from the two chimneys.

His mother often told him how his father toiled from sunup to sundown every day of the year when he first inherited the farm. His scanty education having taught him to read, he devoured every book on agriculture he could find. Now he was a homespun expert on many subjects, and this knowledge he passed to Clifford.

As he chewed, Clifford leaned back his head and squinted against the sun, seeking the fluttering skylark overhead singing its praise to God. The tiny birds were hard to see, even for someone with good eyesight. In the woods he heard mourning doves purling, and the hedgerows were alive with sparrows, grackles, jays and blackbirds. He saw rabbits, mice and voles on their various errands, a grass snake basking on a rock Aye, he enjoyed being here and working the land today.

He appreciated his life apart from one aspect. His father saw Clifford as sole heir, and while he liked farming Clifford did not see it as his only work, not that he could ever have left the land. He wanted to be a veterinarian while keeping the land productive. This was a knotty subject as Jake contended Clifford should take charge on his death and devote himself wholeheartedly to running the farm. Still, that could be a long way off because Jake, a strong man, intended to work until he dropped.

After Clifford drank half the water, he went over to the patient horses who, heads hanging, dozed as they waited. Geeing them up, he set to work on the remaining area, knowing the sun left him only another eight hours to finish.

Jake Wright sat atop his horse looking down the fell to where his son ploughed the lower field. A good boy that, he thought, eyeing the straight furrows. Aye, Clifford was a son to be proud of in many ways and when his time was over, he could trust Clifford to run the place well. The lad had often spoken about being a vet but that was not what Jake had in mind. No, he would farm the land of his forefathers.

Spurring his horse, he rode along the hill top looking down to the farm buildings where he could see one of his daughters hanging out washing, the other tending the vegetable garden. Girls! He snorted. What use were they? Oh aye, someone had to tend the garden, do the housework and look after the small animals, but three sons now, by, that would be grand. As it was, they had two females after Clifford, and, although he had set his heart on having a large family, Joyce's birth had done something to Liz's insides so she could never have more children.

Still and all, Clifford could handle the place, Clifford was smart, sometimes too smart, with his better education and thirst for knowledge. Jake often saw him plough a long furrow with a book on the handles, and if he were taking muck to the fields or fetching hay back, Jake could bet he had a book with him since the horses knew well enough where they were going. Education was a marvellous thing and Jake subscribed to it, although it annoyed him when young Clifford tried to tell him, his own father, how to run the place.

He cantered down the road, surveying his fields, his cows, the sheep grazing on the moor. All his, every inch of it, and to think he had started with a tumbledown farm house and a toppling barn. Hard work, that's what it took, aye, hard work and determination.

Not like the shiftless gypsies. Earlier today that damned gypsy woman with her stupid curse had found short shrift with him. The dirty, bedraggled wretch had come to the door, begging for food and drink. Well, he wasn't having any of that rubbish, wasn't going to feed a single tramp or gypsy because the word always percolated through their tribe, and beggars would soon surround his door. Already he had erased their chalk marks from his fence posts, had knocked over the peculiar arrangement of rocks and stones they placed. He smiled now, recalling how he dealt with her, the ragged scarecrow.

"Find work, get a job," he had told her when she whined of her hunger.

"Please master, a bite of food, something to help me on my way. Maybe a jug of water?"

He regarded her scruffy clothing and matted hair, her dirty claw-like hands. "Don't you go near that well," he warned, taking his shotgun from behind the door and training it on her. "I want no poison in my water."

She looked at him, looked at him long and hard.

"Get away from here or I'll shoot. Go on." He gestured with the gun barrel.

She held out her hands in supplication. "Not a bite, not a drink?

He nudged her with the gun, but saw she was not afraid. "Get away from here. We don't want your kind."

She faced him down, did not move. "You'd not treat your animals this way," she said.

"Bloody right, woman, my animals are worth money to me, but you're worthless, worse than vermin . . . and I shoot vermin. Get off with you."

She put back her shoulders, drew herself up and her voice when she spoke was strong. "Damned be thy house. From this day may thy children sicken and may thy crops fail. Evil will stalk this land," she said, making magic signs with her filthy hands. "Folk who deal with your cursed family will feel the curse, even to the seventh generation."

Aye, he had laughed at her curses, laughed and spat at her feet and she made those magic signs again. Befuddled old cow, ill bred and ignorant. Everyone knew it was a load of rubbish and didn't mean anything. People with weak minds might believe, but not him, oh no, not him. Well, no matter what Liz said, it was all tommyrot. Aye, if it were left to his wife, she'd feed the entire county.

Pausing again to overlook his acres, he admired the crops in his fields, a good crop, a perfect crop. Stupid people, those gypsies, thinking they could scare people, people who knew better.

As he rounded the edge of the beech wood, he spotted two of the farm hands. Supposedly rebuilding a dry stone wall, they sat in the shade of it, chatting and smoking pipes. As the sound of hooves reached them, they scrambled to their feet.

He dismounted and walked over to where they were setting the grey stones atop each other.

"What the hell am I paying you for? This job should have been finished two hours ago." Jake was as angry as they had ever seen him.

Bill Cunliffe said: "Sorry, master,"

"Sorry? Sorry? I'll make you a whole lot sorrier if this isn't done within the half hour." As he spoke, he slapped his riding whip against his leggings, daring them to speak. "To make sure you aren't skiving off again, I'll watch you do it."

Tying his horse to an overhanging branch, he sat on a shady rock and watched the men struggling to lift the heavy stones. Bill and his mate Ken White, eyed each other. Jake knew they worked damned hard for him without complaint, and for years they had worked for a starvation wage, while he and his family lived in comparative ease in their big farmhouse.

Mind you, he had housed them in a one storey, mud floored cottage when they were first taken on, and knew back then they felt themselves lucky. They did all the heavy work, rising at cockcrow and working by lantern light sometimes as late as midnight. Aye, he was not above lashing out with his whip and had an assortment of them, a bull whip, a riding whip, a horse whip, his riding crop.

Ken, a few bricks short of a load, was mentally incapable of action without guidance. Bill had taken care of him years ago when he found him lying in a ditch. The children, cruel as only children can be, had driven him out of their village by pelting him with stones and calling him terrible names when he wandered from his home. He soon became petrified of going back past his tormentors, back to the hovel where he lived with his aged mother, nor did he know where it was.

Earlier Bill trekked from the north in his search for work. The northern lands of his birth were untillable due to the abundance of rocks and shale, and his widower father died trying to scratch a living from a few acres. A cow and one horse were all they could afford, and when father died, Bill gave the cow to their neighbours and the furniture to another family trying to eke out an existence.

After packing his few things, he rode away on the old horse to find his fortune. It was two days into his journey when the horse dropped dead. For four weeks Bill walked. He slept in fields when it was fine, and tumbledown barns if it rained, lived off whatever he could scavenge, potatoes, turnips, apples, cabbages, berries, nuts.

Then he found Ken. The pair of them set out together, and while Bill liked having company, he soon discovered Ken a liability. Ken, although an adult, was childlike and liked to dawdle, liked to stand gazing at the view, to lie on the grassy verges. He was in no way self-sufficient and Bill quickly found himself becoming both mother and father to him.

Aye, he thought now, they had been dead lucky to find this job. Dead lucky the master had sacked two men for playing cards in the barn. Jake was dead set against gambling, (in fact was against dancing, singing, and most anything that made life worthwhile), but for a roof over their head and a small income, Bill jumped at the chance.

Back then he had been content, but now he had come to hate his life tied to this cruel master. Lately Bill had realized they were little more than slaves to Jake's whim

CHAPTER TWO

J ake watched them. They were lazy good for nothing, uneducated, dirty, out for what they could get types. Sitting smoking while he paid them to work, huh!

"Ow!" Ken roared, having dropped a stone on his foot.

"Are you all right, Ken?" Bill asked, adjusting a stone. "What did you do?"

They were on opposite sides of the wall.

"I done droppered a stone on me foot. It hurts awful bad, Bill."

"Sit down a minute and take off your boot. I'll come and look at it."

"Get on with your work, man," Jake ordered. "The man is all right. Come on, get cracking, I can't sit here all day waiting for you to finish."

"Nobody is asking you to," Bill, muttered as he bent to pick up another stone.

Ken started to cry. He was a big baby about anything that hurt him. "Bill? I hurted my foot and it makes me feel funny. Can I go home now?"

Bill quickly placed a stone, jumped over the wall, put his arm around Ken's shoulders and said, "Look, Ken, the master wants this finished. Now be a good chap and help me. Your foot will be all right in bit. Come on now, snap out of it."

Ken wiped his nose on his sleeve and the tears from his face with his filthy hands. He smiled up at Bill.

Jake watched them through narrowed eyes. The man was a bloody moron, not a brain in his head. Why hadn't he seen that before? The man Bill always did the talking as the other stood at his side. Well, he'd have to find another couple of men; he couldn't have idiots working for him, they might do damage.

"Get on with it, you two. Hurry it up. I have work waiting to be done."

"Yes, master," Bill said, as he scrambled back over the wall. Quickly he picked up a large stone and, working as quickly as he could, placed it. Ken hefted stones from his side and Bill manhandled them into place. It took almost an hour to finish the wall. Jake sauntered over to look at their handiwork, pushing here and there, scrunching down on his haunches to look at it more closely.

"It will do for now, but you'll need to take it down and start properly from the footings. You," he pointed at Bill with his whip. "Why did you not tell me that this man is doolally? He has no brains from what I can see. Huh! A grown man crying over a dropped stone."

"I didn't think it mattered, sir," Bill said, "He has a strong back and is willing to work hard."

Jake squinted his eyes as he looked from one to the other. "Is he your brother? I shudder to think I have a family of idiots working for me."

Bill flushed angrily. "No sir, he is no relation. I met him on the road."

"He'll have to go." Jake regarded Ken with malice, as he impatiently slapped his crop against his boots. "I can't employ idiots."

"But master," Bill started.

Jake ignored him. "Get him off my property by day's end. You can stay."

Ken looked from one to the other, his eyes frightened. "No, master," Bill said staunchly. "I won't stay. Ken needs someone to look out for him. If he goes, I go with him."

The blood rose to Jake's face, the large vein in his neck standing out like a danger signal. "You signed a bond, man, you must stay. He made his mark, but I don't want him on my land."

Pale faced and angry, Bill decided to stand up for Ken and himself. "Bond or no bond, I must go with him. You can't do this."

Ken stood like an ox, mouth open, gazing from face to face, obviously puzzled at the shouting, wondering why Bill was so angry.

Jake, who could not abide anyone that refused to obey him, raised his whip and laid about Ken's shoulders like a man possessed. "Get off my land! Get off, you blithering idiot."

Bill pushed the master aside and put his arms around Ken who stood statue-like, his face a mask of fright. He made not a sound, nor did he shed a tear.

Jake untied his horse and, mounting, turned to face the two men, urged the horse forward until he was sitting facing down on them, and raising the whip high, lashed out at their heads.

Bill, unwilling to stand for being whipped, felt such hate for a master who would ill treat Ken. He grabbed the whip and pulled, as Jake pulled back.

"Get your filthy hands off, idiot!"

The horse shied at this uproar, Ken lost his grip and somehow Jake slipped from the saddle, his right foot still in the stirrup. Now skittish, at the change of weight, the horse bolted.

"Oh, my God in heaven," Bill said, "Stay here, Ken. Don't move." He ran after the horse which dragged an insensible Jake along the rocky and gravel lane. Eventually he caught it and, hauling on the free stirrup, slowed its pace until he could grab the bridle.

Jake lay unconscious, but still breathing, and Bill wiped his brow with a shaky hand. Unhooking Jake's boot from the stirrup, he dragged him to the grassy bank, yelled for Ken to stay with the master, and jumped on the lathered horse. He rode to the field where young master Clifford was working.

Clifford and Bill manhandled Jake onto the cart and set off for the farm. Jake groaned loudly and Clifford took that as a good sign. Bill cast anxious glances at the man who lay on the straw and sighed deeply. Ken watched him and giggled at the blood that ran from his head until Bill stopped him.

Clifford assured Bill that, while his father might have a sore head and more than a few bruises, it was not life threatening.

"He'll be around again tomorrow, Bill, laying about with his whip and shouting his fool head off," Clifford said. "Mind you, it depends on what the doctor says. With any luck, he'll make him stay in bed, then we'll all get a rest from his moods."

In the back of the cart, Ken mumbled to himself. He was intelligent enough to know that when the master regained consciousness he would remember what had happened. Bill looked over to where he crouched at Jake's feet, saw him biting his nails, drooling, and wondered what they should do. If the master remained confined to the house, he could leave the farm, take Ken somewhere with a more tolerant master. Aye, that's what he'd do.

The doctor, Doctor Walters, was a grizzled man of nearly seventy. Ill equipped to handle anything more serious than a cut or a cold, he had been their doctor for so long that they always called on him, whatever the illness or accident. He left a tonic for Jake, saying time healed most things and a banged head should cure itself.

The accident changed Jake, and not for the better. Once he recovered enough to walk without dizziness and headache, he set out to find Bill and Ken, the cause of his troubles.

CHAPTER THREE

Jenny Bradley decided she did not like the farm. So much dirt - and it smelled.

She and her mother had come to stay at Uncle Albert Stockton's farm while her mother nursed her sister, Aunt Adele, Uncle Albert's wife. After a bad childbirth and a stillborn baby, Adele, who was nearly forty, lost all her strength and became unable to cope. Uncle Albert wrote to her mother begging for help, and before Jenny could say 'no' she and her mother were on a coach headed for the country.

"Do we *have* to stay here?" she asked peevishly, curling her lip as she eyed the dust on the table where they sat. Fastidious, she dusted off her fingers.

"Yes, Jenny, we do. Remember what the good book says. We must always help those who need our help and Adele is my sister, your aunt. We cannot desert her in her hour of need. She'd do the same for me. Charity, child, comes in many different forms and helping the sick is charity. I'd like to think my daughter was charitable."

At first Jenny helped her mother with her aunt, but it soon palled. One morning she decided to venture outdoors, but, on opening the kitchen door, changed her mind as the stench of the farmyard reached her delicate nose. When she tried the front way, the wind blowing from the pigsties smelled like a midden and she almost vomited.

She was accustomed to town living, where things seemed clean, where life and lots of people made it exciting. The street where they lived was busy with smart carriages, people strolling to the shops. Why she had once seen one of the new horseless carriages, its brass fittings gleaming like gold, preceded by a man with a red flag. In town were more mechanical marvels and many other amusements.

"I could go back and stay with Daddy," she said now, "He'll look after me and we could manage. Daddy must miss me dreadfully, Mamma. Couldn't I please go back now, please?"

"No, Jenny, you'll stay here and help me. Your father is self-sufficient and is out at work most of the day." Eliza bustled out with a tray on which stood a mug of milk and a bowl of beef tea for her sister.

Miserable, Jenny sat on a low bench by the kitchen fire and looked around, thinking even the furniture was horrible, uncomfortable and old-fashioned. It seemed to loom, making the small room even smaller. On the table stood the oil lamps waiting for her attention - her chore was to clean the chimneys and trim the wicks. She glared at the window: small, hardly large enough to allow fresh air to enter - if any air around the farm didn't stink - with tiny diamond-shaped panes terribly distorted. Seeing anything outside was impossible, other than vague shapes or shadows.

Oh, why do I have to be stuck here? she mused. I could be at home with my friends attending the ladies' auxiliary meetings, going to the library, the sewing circle, the book club. Now look at me, sitting in a cramped, dirty farmhouse while my mother sits upstairs in an even smaller bedroom reading to or attending to my aunt. I have nothing to do, nowhere to go that isn't smelly or dirty. This is like living in a prison. How could Mamma expect me to stay here where dirt will soil my gowns, where dust coats everything, where there is no life or sunshine?

She needed to get away from the place and after moving around restlessly like a caged animal, wrapped a scarf around her face and walked as quickly as she could from the house. Somewhere she must find fresh air.

Clifford Wright spotted the young lady as he rode along the top lane. Bill and Ken had left the farm one evening without saying a word to anyone, and now he had two new men to supervise. Not that he had wanted to lose Ken and his pal, but they simply vanished. Probably fearing Jake's wrath, he thought. Once his father was back on his feet, he sought to punish them.

Who was the girl? he wondered, noticing her trim shape, the curling blonde hair that fell almost to her waist, the fancy gown with its many petticoats. She was young, he could see, even from this distance.

Curious, he rode toward her, forgetting the reason for his ride altogether.

"Good afternoon," he said, reining in his horse.

"Good afternoon," Jenny looked up with a smile. This was more like it, a young handsome man with manners.

"Are you visiting hereabouts?"

"At my Uncle Albert's." She gracefully waved a hand down the hill to Mayhurst Farm.

Clifford nodded. "I heard Mrs. Stockton was sick after her confinement. She is improving, I hope."

"She's all right," Jenny said, not caring or knowing. "My mother, her sister, is looking after her. I'm helping to nurse her to health."

The horse edged backwards, knocking up stone and dust, eager to be off.

"Ooh!" Jenny said, stepping upwind. A cloud of dust eddied around and she flapped her hands to prevent it from falling on her gown.

Clifford laughed. "You're not from a country village, I would say. Do you live in town?"

"Yes, we live in Wigan. I hate this place, it's so dirty and smelly." She flushed redly, aware she had been rude.

He smiled as he gentled his mount. "I don't think much smells around this neck of the woods, other than the good smells of growing and animals. As for towns, well, I've smelled them and they really stink." He looked around from his perch and smiled. "I think this is the most beautiful place in the world."

"Huh! You're welcome to it. I can't wait to go home." Again she brushed at her gown as the horse snickered, moving its feet.

"Well, I'm pleased to meet you," Clifford gentled the horse. "What's your name?"

Jenny blushed. "Jenny, Jenny Bradley and yours?"

"I'm Clifford Wright of Hillshead Farm."

With that, he saluted her with a wave, turned the horse and cantered away on his business.

What a beauty she was, he thought, as he galloped up to the ridge. What shining hair, what fine bones, what white skin and clear blue eyes. Clifford felt happy to have met and talked to such a young woman, thinking it too bad she was a townie and leaving soon.

Jenny sat on a stile watching as the horse took to the heights. She greatly admired a man on a horse, and Clifford Wright sat like he was part of the animal. He was a man, not a boy. Look how he cleared that stone wall, how he sat erect, hardly jostled by the horse's movements. He was handsome, incredibly handsome for a farm hand. She closed her eyes and pictured him clad in good clothes and knew he could look presentable. Maybe he was the farmer's son as his mount was a good riding horse, not a farm animal. Hmm, at last the place had come up with something of interest.

CHAPTER FOUR

Clifford stabled the horse and called to the old dog snuffling around in the hay.

"Outside now, Shadow. Out of there, let's be having you."

The border collie came out, tail wagging, jumping up to be petted. Shadow had been his dog from a pup, and was a grand sheep herder. He stooped and rubbed the dog around the neck, turning his head to avoid the tongue licking Shadow dished out. "Good boy, you're a good boy."

"Leave that bloody dog alone and get the milking started," his father's voice roared from the hay barn.

Clifford, sighed, patted the dog one last time and started for the cow shed, Shadow racing ahead.

Drat his father. Since the accident Jake had become even more surly and difficult to please. He had taken to riding around searching for Bill and Ken. Only one thought occupied his mind, to find and punish them. Thankfully they were long gone or he would have shot the pair of them with the shotgun he now kept tied to his saddle.

Even when toddlers, the three Wright children clearly sensed their mother found their father hard to live with because he acted so strangely at times. All shied away from him and Jake, for the most part, ignored them until they were old enough to work. Clifford figured the accident had now scrambled his brains. The girls took to hiding from him because he continually struck out at them, and when a young chap came over to take them to the fair, he chased him off with his gun.

"It's all his fault, you know," Liz said that morning, as she rubbed at her weary eyes. "He turned away that poor gypsy, the one who cursed us. This is only the start of our bad luck."

Clifford put his hand on her shoulder. "Aaw, Mam, pay no attention to the likes of her. That's rubbish and you know it. She put no curse, as you call it, on us. Dad's not right in the head since that accident, not that he was any great shakes before the fall, come to think of it."

No, his father wasn't right in the head and whereas before he had been self-righteous and moral, now he was suspicious of any meeting between a man and woman. He did not trust his daughters or his wife and was ever watchful. His son he treated with disdain, for a healthy young man could be up to no good once out of his sight.

Lately Jake had taken to carrying a long staff and this he used as a weapon, both to poke a miscreant, then to beat them unmercifully. Because of this they lost the two women dairy and poultry workers because he beat them as they lay sleeping of exhaustion on their lunch break. Their days started at cockcrow and they were often at work in the barns, fields or orchard until night fell. Talking to his father, who considered them slackers, proved futile.

Clifford tried to be everywhere at once because of his father's attitude to the workers and tried to protect them. Toil and worry filled his every waking moment, and he became pale and enervated. His mother and sisters helped by doing what chores they could manage, but still Jake laid about with his staff, bruising and breaking, hurting more than limbs.

"Mam, he'll have to be put away," Clifford quietly said one evening as his father lay in his chair snoring. "He's out of his skull."

"Oh, no," Liz, said, "We can't do that. This is his home and here he'll stay. I married him for better or worse and we've had better, now haven't we?"

"No! No, Mam, we have not," Clifford snapped. "You know he's been a cruel bastard all of our lives. I've had more than one beating and so have the girls. To beat girls, I ask you. Mam, you've had more than one black eye and he once broke two of your fingers."

His mother shook her head, unconvinced, he could see that, and after the beating she received this morning, he couldn't fathom her.

"He doesn't care who he hits," Cliff argued, "And now it's worse, much worse. The man is puddled. Better get him put someplace where he can't hurt anyone."

Liz was aghast at the thought, at the shame of it. "No! How could you think such a thing? He's sick, that's all and he'll get better, you wait and see." She moved over to where Jake lay in his chair and stroked his hair gently.

Clifford shook his head. What was wrong with her? Surely she knew as well as he that father was insane? That accident, the banging of his head against the rocks of the rough road had knocked him silly, added to his other mental incapacity.

"Come on now, Mam, admit it, he's puddled."

"Aye, he is an'all," Betty said.

"Yes, Mam, he is," Joyce added.

Liz rounded on them. "What? You'd side with Cliff against your father? Look at you, hardly out of nappies and you try to tell me, your mother, what I should do?"

Betty, the eldest, spoke first, "Aaw, Mam, you know how he's been with us lately. We can't eat at the same table or speak to him. He's laid about both of us with that blasted pole of his too often. Look at the bruises I've got on this leg." She lifted her skirt to show the black and blue marks on her thigh. At seventeen Betty was a tall lithe girl, able to take care of herself, but not against her maddened father.

Liz gasped, but did not agree. Her own bruises were far worse, but the canny old bugger made sure her clothes hid them.

"That'll soon clear, our Betty, and I've had far worse from banging into this table. You can't put your Dad away for something as minor as that."

Joyce, now sixteen, stood silently, afraid to anger her mother. She also hated her father, and terrified of being close to him.

"Put your Dad away where?" Jake came to life suddenly. The women cast anxious glances at each other; they had no idea how long he had been awake. The girls scurried to the scullery and hid behind the wash tubs.

"Wife! Where are you, wife?" he shouted, not looking to see that she stood by his chair.

"Here I am, Jake," Liz said quietly, "What can I get you?"

"Beer. You did make beer?"

"Yes, Jake," she said, hurrying to the scullery and the wooden barrel.

"Mam?" Betty said quietly.

"Stay there, you two, or go outside," she hissed to the girls when they popped up their heads.

Jake slouched in his large wooden chair, his eyes fixed on the embers of the fire. Hunching himself against the chair back, he turned his head.

"Oh, so you've come home, have you?"

Clifford wondered what he was talking about, but agreed.

"Yes, father, I've come home."

"About time too. I can't do everything, you know. The long acres need ploughing and the orchard still must be picked, then there's the barley needs cutting. The gangman will be along soon enough with his tribe and they need watching. Where have you been? You've been away now for over three months."

Clifford scratched his head, what was the old fool talking about? Should he agree or argue?

"Yes, father. It was a long trip."

Obviously he said the right thing for his father sat up and looked him straight in the face. "Was it a good tour? Did you see Venice and Rome?"

This was a mystery. What went on in his father's mind? Still, he seemed composed and was smiling.

"Yes, sir," he said, adding no detail. How could he? He had never left the county.

Jake closed his eyes, nodding. "Aye, yes, a young man's grand tour is the best thing that happens to him in his entire life. Sets him up for his life of work and worry. Every lad of twenty needs to take the tour." He looked back in his mind's eye. "If only my father had allowed me the journey. I wanted to go, you know," He looked at Clifford now, "How dearly I wanted to go with my friends." His eyes misted with tears, though his voice did not waver, "But they were the upper class, and I was but a farmer's son. I grew up with him, you know, Alphonse Gerrard," he spat the words as if they were hateful. "Yet did he care that he left me behind? No sir, he did not. Away he went on his tour while I stayed here working the earth and when he came back, he had changed. Aye, sophisticated, he was, well read and patrician. Yes, lad, the tour is a grand thing, and I hope you enjoyed it as it cost me a fair bit."

Clifford sat flummoxed, what *was* his father talking about? They had never had more then two pence to rub together, and put any profit back into the farm for new equipment or fertilizers. Yet he was talking about grand tours of Europe. What should he say? Arguing with him was useless.

"Aye, it was grand, I learned a lot, father."

Jake got out of his chair and stretched his arms over his head. Yawning, he said, "So you should, lad, learn a whole lot. That tour cost me good money and I wouldn't want to think I'd wasted a penny. Now, tell me about Venice."

Clifford's heart sank. It had been the wrong thing to say. He had no idea what Venice was like, not even from the few books he had read at school. Wondering what he should say, he cleared his throat.

Just then his mother came in with a stone tankard of beer and offered it to Jake. "Here it is, Jake, good home brew."

Jake dashed the proffered tankard from her hand with his staff, not noticing how it splashed everywhere.

"What on earth?" she gasped, shocked, rubbing at her bruised wrist.

Jake rounded on her. "How dare you, woman! You think I'm a peasant? You'll be gone from my service before morning. I'll not have familiarity from servants. To bring me home brew, to call me by my Christian name? How dare you, you bitch!"

Lizzie gasped and looked to Clifford who nodded his head. "Now do you believe me?" he whispered.

"Speak up, sir, speak up. I'll have no whispering in corners." He turned to Liz. "Why are you still in my presence? Get out of here, you wizened old crone."

Lizzie burst into tears so Clifford put his arm around her protectively, moving her out of the room. Jake stood with his back to the fire, smirking at her discomfort. Then picking up his long staff, he flailed it loudly against the table top. Clifford started at the sound, and his sisters whimpered from their hiding place.

"Take mother upstairs," he hissed, "Get her away from him. Go on. I'll talk to him." He cast an anxious glance over his shoulder at his father, who stood in front of the fireplace, flailing with the staff. "It may be only a temporary mood."

Somehow he doubted it, for his father had become gradually worse and this latest symptom scared him.

"Father," he said as he strode into the room as nothing was untoward. "Why are you doing that?"

The women dashed upstairs, frightened out of their wits.

Jake still beat angrily at the table, the pewter plates, tin and stoneware dishes lifting and crashing to the floor, his face white and drawn.

"Who the hell are *you*? What are you doing in my house, sir?"

A cold chill ran down Clifford's spine. "Father, it's me, Clifford, your son. Are you not feeling well?"

Jake drew himself up and looked down his nose, his chin tucked into his cravat. "I feel very well, sir, very well indeed. Where are the servants? This fire needs tending." Clifford listened as his father raved. What should he do? Send for the doctor? Well, that much was evident, but how could he get out of the room to send one of his sisters?

"I don't know what I pay them for," Jake said, his voice sounding strange, forced, "Always skiving off. I gave it to them, though. Oh aye, I dealt them a few blows." Spittle dotted the front of his jerkin and gathered at the corners of his mouth. "Not as many as they deserved, mind. You've got to hold some in reserve, lad, that's the only way to deal with upstart servants. They should know their place. Talking to me as if they were on par with me, the master. I'm in charge here and they should know it. Imagine, a servant woman fetching me beer in a filthy mug, having the nerve to call me by my Christian name! When I get my hands on her, she'll feel the full extent of my wrath." He dealt the table top another fearful blow and more dishes crashed to the floor.

"Where is she now, that woman?" he bellowed, "Why is there no servant here to clean up this mess? What am I paying them for?" He walked quickly from the room, banging the staff against anything in his path and shouting loudly.

Clifford watched him go into the farm yard then ran upstairs to tell Betty to fetch the doctor. She dashed down the stairs and out the front door, moving quickly into the woods.

Meanwhile Clifford must ensure his father did not find his mother and Joyce. Oh God, the man was out of his mind. What was to be done with him?

He walked through the farm yard, checked the stables and outhouses, but could not find Jake. After calling and searching, it became obvious his father had wandered off somewhere. The horses were still stabled which meant he was on foot. Two hands were in the yard fixing a plough share, and after telling them what happened, the group set out to search.

Meanwhile Jake strolled along the path happy, happier than he had been in years. The sun shone warmly, the sounds of nature were all around. Taking to the woods, he watched as a doe and two fauns cropped grass on the hillside close to the bush, rabbits skittered across the path, a woodpecker hammered at the tree above his head and birds sang lyrically in the leaves. He admired the wind flowers and bluebell leaves massed under the beeches, while dog daisies and anemones, the remnants of an old garden, nodded in the slight breeze. It all seemed so peaceful and lovely that he sat on a fallen log to admire it at leisure and within minutes had fallen asleep.

"We found him, Master Clifford. He's in the far woods asleep. At least I think he's asleep," Reg White reported.

"Right, I'll wake him but I want you to stand by. Who knows what kind of humour he'll be in when he wakes." Clifford led the men to the wood. They stood back while he approached his father.

"Father?" He put a tentative hand on the old man's shoulder.

"Aye, lad." Suddenly he was his old self, or so it appeared.

"Come along, father, sleeping on that damp log can't be good for you at your age."

"Damned upstart! If I want to sleep on the log or on the grass, I'll bloody well sleep on the grass. Who are you to wake a man when he's in need of a nap?"

Clifford didn't know what to say and decided food might be the answer. "Your meal is almost ready and mother is wondering where you are. That's why I woke you."

"All you had to do was say so. A man needs a good meal after a long hard morning. Lead the way, lad, lead the way."

Clifford noticed he picked up the long staff and used it as a walking stick.

When they got to the house, the doctor had arrived.

"Well, if it isn't my old pal Jeremiah," Jake said, his face wreathed in smiles, as he extended his hand and forcefully shook Walter's. "Come into the kitchen and take meat with us. You can stay a while, I hope?"

"Certainly, Jake."

Jeremiah stood back to let Jake lead the way and raised his eyebrows to Clifford who hissed, "He fell asleep and woke up normal. Can you observe him for a while? We can talk when he naps."

As Jake later lay snoring in his fireside chair, Clifford took Dr. Walters outside and explained the happenings.

Jeremiah sighed. "He's definitely suffering from some mental aberration, but I don't know what kind. If we could get him to enter the institution in Wigan, we possibly have a chance of determining the cause of his problem. Mental conditions manifest themselves in many different ways, and it takes time and effort to exactly discover the cause."

Clifford shook his head. "He won't go anywhere near a hospital or infirmary, you know that. As for going to the institution in town, that's out of the question, unless you drug him."

"It might come to that, young man," Dr. Walters said soberly, "I'm not going to say differently. Your father is seriously ill and I fear for your family's safety. If this illness takes him in the middle of the night while you are sleeping, who is to say what might happen? You may call on me night or day for assistance. I'm going to prescribe a strong sleeping draft that you must somehow get him to take each night before he retires. It might be that with a sound sleep for a few nights the problem may resolve itself. The mind is a strange thing."

Clifford took the small blue bottle. "'Two teaspoons in a liquid before retiring," he read. "What is it?" he asked. "Does it taste bad?"

"No, it's bland and mixes well with tea or milk, beer or wine. Whatever he drinks before bed will do."

Clifford shook Dr. Walter's hand and slipped the bottle into his pocket. "Thank you, Doctor. You can be assured we'll send for you if anything happens. He's usually a creature of habit, so it's usually easy to keep track of him, but we'll be vigilant."

Jeremiah rode back in his carriage wondering if he should pay a visit on the smart new doctor who had recently set up a practice in Mossvale, a small town about four miles distant. He recognized his own medical knowledge was insufficient to cure anything mental, his field having been family medicine for the last fifty years or more. Still, what he had learned as a boy stood him in good stead for common ailments; anything more serious he referred to Wigan Infirmary.

Obviously Jake Wright was not right in the head and probably never recover. His skull obviously was not as hard as Jeremiah had first thought. Yes, he would consult with Anthony McAdam, a bright lad by all accounts, who used something called ether to put his patients to sleep when setting a limb and now used bandages dipped in Plaster of Paris instead of wooden splints to set a broken bone. A wellread practitioner by all accounts, he had a smattering of psychology, so Walters had heard.

CHAPTER FIVE

Jenny sat on the low stone wall surrounding the grave yard and watched people as they passed. She decided they were all countrified, plump and rounded, broad in speech, and, to her, horrible. Apart from Clifford Wright, she had seen no other person to whom she would deign to talk.

Her aunt didn't seem to improve, but then how could she with that ancient quack treating her? Dr. Jeremiah Walters - even his name was old-fashioned - paid a house call every day fetching small glass bottles of brown medicine, swearing they were a tonic. Jenny tasted the last bottle and found it tasted of peppermint and little else.

"This is a placebo, Mamma," she said. "It will not do aunt much good, although it will put another few shillings in the doctor's pocket."

"Jenny, do not disparage the doctor. He is a learned man and has been the village doctor for years."

"Surely you can see this country doctor knows nothing," Jenny said as her mother served tea. "Uncle should call in someone younger, someone with access to modern methods. Why doesn't he call the young doctor from Mossvale that aunt mentioned?"

"Young men are not good doctors, Jenny. Age is what matters medically, age and experience."

Jenny doubted it and wondered how she could get to Mossvale to visit this new young doctor to ask his opinion. For her age Jenny was audacious, unafraid to approach those other people treated as sacred cows.

As she spotted the vicar coming down the road, she stood from the wall, brushed out her skirt, and, standing in the shade of a huge old oak, watched him approach. Today she wore one of her nicer gowns, a deep green with pale yellow trimming, tight-waisted and full-skirted. With this she wore a small cape over her shoulders in the same green and atop her curls, a green bonnet with yellow ribbons. She had dressed up in case she met a nice young man, or Clifford Wright, whoever came first.

"Good morning, young lady," Reverend Mather said, putting out his gloved hand in greeting.

Jenny looked at the roly-poly Reverend and wanted to laugh. He was a replica of Mr. Bumble in a Charles Dickens' book. Round of face and body, round of eyes and mouth, everything so spherical, apart from his lower legs in their gaiters which looked stick-like. The gaiters made his huge feet look even bigger in their laced boots.

"Good morning, Reverend." She smiled as she shook his hand and bobbed her head.

"Are you living in this parish, my dear?"

"No, sir. We're visiting my relatives at Mayhurst Farm. My aunt is sick and my mother, her sister, is taking care of her."

"Ah yes, I recall one of my flock telling me Mrs. Stockton was unwell. I trust she is recovering?"

"Yes, but I think we need to get another doctor, the old one here gives her bottles of coloured water." Her cheeks became redder as she realized she had been rude again.

Reverend Mather often thought the village needed a new doctor, although Jeremiah obviously was reluctant to retire. The villagers often suggested he take on an locum, someone younger to take the weight off his shoulders, but he wouldn't hear of it. He told anyone who would listen straightforwardly, that if he could work, he would do so, and when he couldn't, then they could fetch in as many doctors as they liked.

"Yes, yes," he murmured, nodding. "As for yourself, you will be attending our church?"

Jenny said the first thing that came into her head. She always did. "No, my father doesn't believe in all that popery. We don't attend any church, even back home."

Reverend Mather smothered a smile. "As a young woman, an obviously intelligent young woman, I expect you can make up your own mind about religion. Church attendance is not mandatory, but it is a way of getting to know your fellow man, of giving something back to the community through charitable works and things of that nature. Also, you will meet people of your own age group."

"Yes, I see," she said, thinking him pompous. "I shall ask mother if I may attend this Sunday." That should appease him, and it made her feel better to know she had displayed a munificence that erased her earlier rudeness.

"Good, good," he passed his hand across her as if giving her a blessing. "I will look forward to seeing you next Sunday. Your name, child, what is your name?"

"Jenny Bradley."

"I see, I see," As if the devil were at his heels, he scurried up the church path and into the vestry, looking to Jenny like some exotic beetle flying to its lair. She grinned and looked down the road with its towering elms and oaks. In the distance, the Pennines looked dark blue against a pale grey sky, and a flock of sheep on the side of the nearest hill reminded her of the polka dots on her new afternoon gown.

Slowly she sauntered along the village street wishing she could find someone with whom to talk, but the few females she saw were homely and looked at her strangely. How lonely she was in this place and how lacking in entertainment. Oh, why could she not have stayed at home with her father? The small houses held no charms, no attraction for her. Their gardens were well tended and the houses themselves well maintained, but all she saw were sub-standard cottages cheek by jowl, lower class and unhealthy with their thatched roofs and tiny windows. The small windows were, she knew, because at the time of building people had to pay taxes on windows. It just went to show what a poor area this was, she thought, proud her own town home seemed palatial in comparison.

Clifford spotted her as he headed for the doctor's house. A small, colourful figure sauntering up the hill from the village, headed toward Mayhurst Farm lane. After leaving the doctor a message, he jumped on his horse and galloped as fast as he could in the direction she had taken.

Jenny heard the sound of hooves before he came into view and wondered who could be riding so hard and why? As she stood underneath the shade of a spreading sycamore, she saw the rider crest the hill and knew it was Clifford. Her entire body lit up with the delight of it. How lucky she had worn a good dress and how lucky today her hair was behaving. She primped, arranged her cape and patted her curls as he neared.

Clifford slid from his horse and dropped the reins.

"So it *was* you, Jenny. I thought so."

His face seemed so handsome, she thought, his strong teeth so white and his muscles, oh his muscles. She could see them through his damp shirt. His jerkin lay across the saddle.

"Good day, Mr. Wright," she said from under her bonnet brim, pretending to be shy.

"Oh come now, call me Clifford, please. I call you Jenny."

"How are you, Clifford? I heard from my uncle that your father is unwell."

"Yes, a result of the accident he had sometime ago. He is not sick, mind you, only confused."

"Oh, so Uncle Albert was correct," she said, thinking back to a conversation on which she eavesdropped when her uncle told her mother that Mr. Wright was mad as a hatter. "I hope he soon recovers."

"He is much better today, and your aunt? How is she today?"

"She's as well as can be expected, considering that old fool Dr. Walters has no idea how to cure her."

Cliff threw back his head and laughed, his strong white teeth contrasting with his tanned cheeks. "Aye, the old man is getting past it, we all know that, but how can you take away the one thing that gives him reason to live? We all know there's a competent young doctor in Mossvale, not so experienced, but he knows all the latest methods and medicines."

"Yes, I heard something about him from the dairy maid." Another conversation on which she had eavesdropped.

They walked a little, leaving the horse to gorge itself on wet young grass. Clifford realized the horse would be uncomfortable tonight and full of flatulence, but did not bother to stop it. Jenny looked so beautiful. She was the most beautiful young woman he had ever seen and the village girls, those with whom he attended school, appeared ugly compared to her fair loveliness.

Jenny realized she had made a conquest. She glittered and dazzled with his every word, making him feel ten feet tall. Clifford bloomed under her frank gaze, felt more handsome. How wonderful it was to walk and talk with her. How marvellous that she and her mother could be here for another week or so. Madly attracted to her, Clifford had thought of little else than Jenny since their first meeting.

If his father were only not so unpredictable, he mused as she chattered, he could spend more time with her, but as it was, he rarely left the vicinity of the farm house in case his father went into one of his strange moods. Old Dr. Walters' medicine seemed useless and his father's condition remained uncertain.

All his worry about the situation vanished from his mind as he looked into Jenny's shining face. She flirted and laughed, touched his arm, his hand. They spoke of the weather, the woods, the farm, about themselves and soon Clifford wanted to kiss her, touch those rosy lips with his own. His body lusted for hers.

Jenny, sure she was falling in love, felt her heart beat faster. Clifford spoke well, she mused, had a good education, almost as good as her own and they thought alike on many subjects.

They looked toward the pit head as the hooter sounded and she saw men coming down the hill side.

"Shift change," he said, thinking the time had flown they talked. "The three-thirty hooter."

"Oh my, I'd better get home before they send someone out to find me," Jenny said, gasping. At four, they had tea, and her mother would worry if she were missing.

They walked back and Clifford grabbed at the reins. The horse lifted its head. "I, too, must go. My mother will think I've had an accident. How the time has flown. It must be the company." He vaulted into the saddle and looked down on her. "Maybe we can meet again, tomorrow if it is fine?"

"Yes, let's," Jenny said, watching as he controlled the restless horse with little effort. "Here beneath the sycamore at two o'clock or so."

"See you then." Clifford galloped away, the horse eager to work off excess energy.

She watched him grow smaller as the horse climbed the hill, her heart churning with affection for him, then turning, she ran toward Mayhurst.

That evening she seemed so cheerful that her mother could not help but notice. Instead of the usual grumbles and gripes, she sang as she scrubbed the dinner pots. A rare thing since Jenny hated housework, contending they paid servants to attend to menial things.

Adele was downstairs tonight and sat in the wing chair in front of the fire. "You have a lovely voice, Jenny," she said.

"I know, aunt," she said, smiling widely.

Liza observed, "My, you are a ray of sunshine this evening. What's come over you?" She moved to bank up the fire.

"Nothing. I had a nice talk with the farmer from the next farm, that's all."

It became crystal clear and Adele nodded. She had talked to Eliza about the handsome Clifford and his sisters. "Oh, and that farmer wouldn't happen to be young Master Clifford of Hillshead, would it?" she asked.

"It might." Jenny smiled joyfully, the mention of his name brought a thrill of shivers through her frame.

"A nice young chap, that," Uncle Albert said. "Allus ready with advice or help if needed. She could do far worse, you know, 'Liza." He puffed on his pipe and extended his hands to the flames.

Eliza waved away his words. What did he know of suitability for a young lady? "Really, Albert, you talk as if they were courting. She's only met him today and the last thing on her mind is wedding him . . . at least I hope so." She stared contemplatively at Jenny, who, wiping pots, gazed into space.

That's all she needed, her child running after a farmer. Still, Jenny was now eighteen, almost an adult so they could not always confine her to the house. Up to now she hadn't shown much interest in young men, always scoffed at their stupidity. Eliza knew every young woman developed her own ideas of her Prince Charming so maybe Clifford Wright suited the naive, unworldly Jenny. She must keep her at home more, she decided, although that might prove difficult if she were tending to her sister. Then, she decided, Jenny must do more of the work. Better to be safe than sorry.

Jake, normal for hours at a time, would suddenly go into a paroxysm from which he did not recover as himself, but the monster they had grown to fear. Completely unconscious of what he was doing when in the grip of one of these seizures, his mind became so deranged he thought everyone and everything was against him, and flailed about with his staff. No matter how they tried, they could not get it away from him. Clifford hid it in the barn one night when he was asleep. Jake found another the next day and continued to make their lives a misery.

The sleeping potion Dr. Walter prescribed put him to sleep for hours. Though getting him to take it was difficult and Liz became proficient at mixing drinks that disguised its taste. Jake, suspicious of any food or liquid she gave him when in his mood, watched her like a hawk, calling her terrible names. Once he caught her adding the medicine to his cocoa and beat her with the staff until Clifford and Betty wrested it away from him.

It was an uneasy household, particularly for the women. They darted quietly between buildings and rooms as they performed the chores. All felt relief when Jake decided to ride out. The youngsters sincerely hoped he would fall off and break his neck.

"I'd have thought that curse would have worked on him faster than this," Betty said to Joyce as they swilled the pigs one afternoon.

"That's a lot of rot. Curses indeed," Joyce snorted, "Father's always been peculiar, you know that. We've always been scared of his moods, but that accident wasn't exactly helpful."

They stood for a moment watching the sow slurp the mash.

Betty sighed. "No, I suppose not, but his mind is confused and we all have to pay for it. I wish he'd come a cropper, and soon."

Clifford took to rising early and starting work long before his father woke from a drugged sleep. This industry paid off as the chores were now up to date and the extra men Clifford had recently hired were busy repairing fences and walls. The crops were doing well this year and all that remained was to pray for good weather while they got caught up with the never ending farm chores, starting with repairs to the cow barn roof.

When Jake took to riding carelessly through and across corn and barley fields, Clifford became infuriated as he could not stop him, and nobody dared broach the subject of his carelessness. Jake lived in a world where everybody jumped to his bidding, but nobody spoke to him. The only thing to do, Cliff decided, was take his father's horse over to Mayhurst and have them stable it. He reasoned that Jake would not get too far without a mount. His mother and the girls discussed this ploy. The story concocted was that horse had died and they had called the knacker to take it away.

When Jake was still asleep, Clifford rode the horse to Mayhurst and put it in the stable. First thing tomorrow he would ride over and explain, and maybe catch a glimpse of Jenny.

CHAPTER SIX

All hell broke lose when Jake heard about his horse.

"If the animal was sick, you should have told me about it." He glowered at Clifford, while Liz hovered near the sink, praying this upset would not bring on one of his turns. "Who gave you permission to sell the body? I wanted to bury him at home on the land. That was my horse and you have no right to remove it."

Clifford tried reasoning. "It's only like you said, father, we can't keep a dead animal around for long when the weather is warm. We could have infected the other animals with whatever ailed him. It was so fast."

Jake pulled at his side whiskers. "Aye, well you get that veterinary over here today as I want to talk to him. He owes me for a perfectly sound animal, so he'd better come up with the money for a new horse or I'll have his guts for garters."

Clifford glanced at his mother. "We didn't call in the vet, father," he said quietly. "The horse was already dead."

Jake rose as if to jump on him. "What? What?" he roared, "The devil you say! Didn't call him in? This is outrageous." Jake started pacing, taking four steps to one side, then the other, his nervously twisting hands clasped behind his back.

"It was the curse, Jake," Liz said without thinking, "I told you not to turn that poor gypsy away. She was starving."

"Horse feathers! Curses don't exist. Talk sense, woman," he shouted.

Clifford stood and faced his mother, who raised her eyebrows. At least Jake seemed sane right then, though angry.

Liz jumped as Jake slammed one fist against his palm. "I must do something about this." Cliff's heart sank. "Get in touch with the knacker and tell him I want to see him. I must find out what killed my horse. This is serious. It could be the start of an equine epidemic."

Clifford knew they were sunk. Next Jake would want to see the vet and talk to other horse owners. How could he have been so silly as to think his father would accept the story? Who would have thought his father could suddenly become saner than he had ever been?

"How is *your* horse behaving? Does it show any signs?"

"No, father." He put a hand on his father's arm as he cast a glance at his mother. "Look, don't worry about this. The horse is probably glue by now and we can't do anything about it. There's no way we can contact the knacker as he was off to Lancaster this afternoon. Why don't you talk to the vet?"

Cliff decided to ride over to Dr. Henry to tell him what had happened. He was a patient and concerned man who would probably go along with the tall tale.

"Fetch him here now! Hurry up, don't dawdle, fetch him quick. I'll check the stables and outhouses for other sick animals."

Cliff patted his mother's shoulder and made his way to the stable to saddle his horse, sure the vet probably could come up with an equine disease that carried them off fast.

As he rode he looked down the fell toward Mayhurst Farm. Earlier this morning he had ridden over to explain the horse to Albert, who thought it a great joke.

"You wouldn't think it so funny if he was trampling your crops, Albert," Clifford said, "I doubt we can harvest much of the barley because it looks as if he was riding round and round in circles in the top field. He's not himself when the mood comes over him."

Albert poked the dottle out of his pipe and sucked on the stem. "Well, lad, take care of him 'cos he's the only father you'll ever have.

I'll tend the hoss, don't you worry none. We won't put him out in the near field but to the back, down the dip where your dad can't see him."

"Thanks, Albert. Is Jenny around by any chance?"

So that was the way the wind was blowing, was it? "Aye, chance would be a fine thing, eh?" He chuckled at the look on Clifford's smitten face. "That young lady is still snoring, getting her beauty sleep she calls it. Lazy-itis I calls it." Albert laughed.

Clifford laughed too. "How is your wife? Is she improving?"

"Oh aye, she's right gradely now her sister's here. Did her a world of good, that bed rest." He scratched his head under his flat cap with his pipe stem. "It's too bad about the nipper. I'd have liked another babbie or two, but that's God's way, sure enough. Adele was feeling lonely for our lads, never hearing from them. Aye, she loves kids, does Adele. Hired on men don't work as hard as kin, and you have to watch them to get your money's worth. The harvest work gang that comes through here is sparse these days. The good ones go over to your farm and I get the leftovers. Aye, it's too bad my sons left home." He sighed as he recalled the terrible times he experienced when both his sons walked out on him. "They wouldn't take to farming at all. Doing well in town now, though. Mind you, we only hear from them once in a month of Sundays."

"Too bad," Clifford echoed. Albert junior, wanted to become a mechanic and left home when he finished school. He was training as a tool and die maker somewhere in Yorkshire. Then the younger brother, Arnold, took off after him and worked as a mechanic at the same factory.

Albert struggled along with two full time farm hands, occasional help and the itinerant harvest workers, but the lack of a dedicated work force showed in the state of the acres. While Albert watched his men they worked like Trojans, but they slacked off the minute his back turned.

Now Clifford saw far more fallow fields than cultivated, and the buildings, house included, looked shabby. Still, Albert had hired on two more men last month and that should make a difference.

Shaking his head sympathetically, he headed back to the farm hoping Jenny would suddenly run out, but she didn't. He longed to see her.

His father talked to the vet who assured him that a horse's sudden death was a rare occurrence, but one never knew with horses. He stayed to eat the noon meal and Liz put a large dose of the medicine in Jake's tea. Soon he lay snoring beside the fire and they knew he would stay that way for hours.

When they met that afternoon under the sycamore, she wore a sprigged muslin gown that fluttered in the breeze. She resembled a beautiful butterfly, tantalizingly close, but unattainable. He sighed with frustration for though he could see she reciprocated his feelings, he knew any hasty moves might offend her. She was that type of female, all wiles and flirtation, unwilling to accept the blame for any untoward attentions.

Clifford had his pick of the local girls as he was personable, handsome and everyone knew he would inherit the farm. He had, of course, dallied with many of them, but always shied away from a commitment. Jenny seemed different. She was not bovine or uneducated and wore beautiful clothes, clothes as fine as any he had ever seen.

"You look beautiful today, Jenny. That dress is wonderful."

"Oh yes, this old thing," she said, belittling it though it was her best Sunday gown. Forbidden to wear it outside, today she sneaked upstairs and donned it while her mother was with her Aunt Adele, wanting to impress him. How she had run to the tree, praying nobody saw her. She even wore the white satin slippers, a terrible thing for they had thin soles and were only for indoor wear but they made her feet look so dainty. "My mother made it for me a year ago. I *never* gain weight," Jenny murmured with a look of pride. She knew she had a good figure, and her mother purchased only the best corsets and waist-cinchers. By comparing herself to other girls of her age, she appreciated how much finer she looked, and too, the admiring look in men's eyes told her so much.

"You look like a spring flower," Clifford said, moving closer to lean with one arm against the tree trunk so his arm touched hers.

Jenny felt a surge of longing run through her at his touch and the colour rose to her cheeks. Excitedly she started chattering of her days: of how she longed to get away from the farmhouse, how bored she was, how she wanted to see the surrounding district, how she wished she had a horse.

Clifford wondered if she were hinting about his father's mount. He listened and nodded, agreeing with her every word, as his mind plotted and planned an outing.

"My father's horse is stabled at Mayhurst, as I'm sure you know, but he's such a brute to handle that even I'm reluctant to ride him. Under no circumstances should you try to mount him. He's no match for a young lady."

"Oh no, not that huge fierce animal. I agree with you. I tried to talk my mother into buying me a horse, but she says no." She sighed, "I must agree with her ruling, though, because we are not going to staying much longer and a horse would be a liability."

He eyed her quizzically. "Maybe you and I could travel out in the trap."

Her eyes lit up and she clapped her hands "Oh yes, please."

Clifford realized she might expect something in the league of a royal carriage. "Now, now, it isn't up to much, only a two-seater affair that's seen better days. Don't get the impression that it's grand."

"Oh, that doesn't matter, if it can take us about to see things. Yet won't it be difficult for you to take off the time? The farm is under your control, is it not, now your father is unwell?" She looked up at him from under her lashes, smiling a secret smile, knowing she had him under her spell. The information about his expectations and his father she had gleaned from Uncle Albert.

"Yes, I do run the farm, but if the chores keep my father busy and he doesn't have any of his turns, we probably could take an afternoon for a short outing. I'll work on it and let you know."

"Oh, Clifford," She practically threw herself into his arms, but held back and, placing her hands on his biceps looked up into his face. "It will be so wonderful, to get away from this place, to see something."

"Aye, well, don't get all excited until I've made some arrangements," he said, knowing he would move heaven and earth to get her alone.

Two days later, they bowled along country lanes, a cloud of dust roiling in their wake. Jenny had fetched a picnic lunch, stolen from the pantry while her mother was upstairs. She left a note on the kitchen table saying she would be back by tea time and not to worry about her.

As the farm lay further behind them, she became ever more animated. They laughed at silly things, talked of everything and nothing, and soon her sparkling personality attracted Clifford even more. This was the girl he would marry, he decided. It never occurred to him that Jenny would prefer to live in town, or that she hated the countryside, for here she was exclaiming with delight at each wood or stream.

"Could we stop now? Look at that lovely glade by the river. We'll eat our picnic right there. Come on, let's stop." Jenny seemed filled with enthusiasm and Cliff didn't like to deflate her eagerness. She would soon learn that sitting near the water meant the constant irritation of midges and flies.

He handed her down from the carriage, passed her the blanket and, after putting down the reins to allow the horse to graze, followed her with the basket.

Being country raised, Clifford did not find eating outdoors by water palatable, not with ants and wasps and other pests. City and town folk, he knew, drove out at weekends to eat their meals under a tree and enjoyed every minute of discomfort.

After they had eaten, she lay back on the blanket and gazed up into the lacy branches. She sighed with pleasure and Clifford looked down at her. Moving closer, he lay back also and took her hand in his.

"Isn't this lovely, Clifford? Do you not love the song birds and that tiny red squirrel who watches overhead?"

Clifford looked up and all he saw were dusty leaves, rotting branches and a chittering rodent who flicked its tail. As for the birds, they were common blackbirds and a sparrow or two. "I think you see things differently. I've lived here all my life. This is all new to you."

She rolled onto her side and put her hand on his chest. "Yes, it is new to me and I like being here with you."

He put his hand on hers and pressed it. Such a soft dainty hand, with shell like nails and white skin. Other hands he had held were work worn and rough. He looked at her and saw she was staring at him, her eyes wide.

"What's the matter?"

"I wondered if you could kiss me," she said shyly. "No one has ever kissed me, and I would like you to be the first."

His heart thumped painfully as he raised himself onto his elbow and moved over her. No lad had never kissed her, and he was to be the first! His heart raced and pounded.

From the moment their lips touched, time stood still. In a fairyland of emotion, he kissed her softly, then passionately and she reciprocated. Before he knew it, her skirt was up to her waist and she urged him on.

Four hours later Clifford came to his senses. What they did was only natural, he told himself, conscious he should have controlled himself because Jenny at eighteen did not understand a man's bodily needs. Then again, she instigated it, had thrown herself at him, ran her hands all over his body and what could a man do but give in to the urge? It was human nature.

"We'll marry as soon as possible," she announced as they started the ride home, her cheeks still flushed and her eyes bright. "You'll have to come to town to speak to my father, of course, as that is only proper. I won't tell my mother until you have father's permission."

Clifford swore, knowing castigating himself was useless. How could he have done it? How could he have taken advantage of an innocent young lady? Not only once, either, but many times. He didn't want to get married, in fact, marriage was the furthest thing from his mind. The local girls knew a tumble didn't mean anything, and brought pleasure to both parties.

"I think a plain ring, one stone. A ruby or an emerald," she said, smiling up at him as she pressed herself to his side.

Cliff looked down into her shining face. Admittedly she was beautiful and he lusted for her, but her good looks and his lust were not enough foundation on which to build a marriage. The local girls liked a romp in the hay and never suggested an engagement. Men did what men did, and the locals accepted that, but Jenny didn't. That much was obvious. She thought their love making was a commitment, so how could he say that he didn't want her? Not after taking her virginity. That she was eager to part with it did not enter the equation because her father would never see it that way.

"We'll see. I don't have much money," he said ruefully. His father did not pay him a wage, only passing him money when he begged for a new coat or boots.

"What do you think your father will say?"

He looked at her surprised. Surely she knew his father was addled. "Do you think I should tell him?"

"Of course, silly." She patted his thigh and smiled. "I imagine he won't be too pleased when he hears you are leaving and coming to live in town. He'll need to arrange to replace you."

"What? Leaving? What on earth gave you that impression?" Clifford felt shocked to his core. Why on earth would she imagine he would leave the country to live in Wigan of all places? How could he earn a living in town?

"I wouldn't want to take up residence in this place." She shuddered at the thought. "It's too far from everything, and what could I do with my time? I couldn't see my friends if we stayed here. We wouldn't travel to the museum or libraries, the art gallery, or attend the theatre. Of course we'll live in town, Clifford. We have gas lighting and heating in our house, and it's so clean and ash free that you'll love it."

"I have a job here," he said, swallowing the lump in his throat. This was becoming too complicated. "What could I do in Wigan? For work, I mean."

Jenny brushed his worries aside with a flick of her wrist. "My father will find you something. He is very well connected."

All this was presupposing her father gave his permission, which Clifford knew was far from likely. He gave her a nervous smile and concentrated on controlling the horses.

How weak he was, to have carnal knowledge of a schoolgirl like this scatterbrained child who had not a thought her head for the consequences. He should have known better because he was older and wiser. Clifford berated himself all the way back, his earlier feelings of euphoria now dissipated.

As they neared the outskirts of the village, he moved away. "No need to give the gossips fuel, is there?"

"I don't suppose so," she agreed, moving further to the side so at least two feet stood between them.

"How stupid this is when we are going to be married," she said, "We're as good as betrothed right now." Stealing a glance at him, she sighed with pleasure. What a wonderful husband he would make. Her mind thought of their future and saw them lying in their own bed to further explore each other's bodies.

While Jenny was a well brought up young lady, and in her home bodily functions were unsuitable conversation, she had read many books belonging to her friends that talked of love making and romance. These awakened longings inside her, longings that came to fruition in Clifford's arms. The books were right, it was wonderful, it was fantastic. She put out her hand and touched his thigh. If he had stopped right then, she would have willingly ripped off her clothing and given herself to him.

"Hey! Suppose someone should see you!" Clifford, taken aback, removed her hand. "Nice young ladies didn't touch men, not in public."

"Silly Billy, I don't see any houses along this road and I don't think that cow minds." She laughed merrily, and he had to chuckle, in spite of himself.

His mind sought a way through the maze of matters that revolved in his head. Deep in the depths of a situation so vast, he hadn't a clue on how to extricate himself and knew nobody he could ask for advice.

Clifford dropped Jenny at the farm lane and passed her the basket and blanket.

"Jenny, don't tell anyone yet, please?" he begged,

"Don't worry, darling, this will be our secret. I don't want to share it with anyone. Tonight I shall dream about our lovely day and of making love with you."

"Jenny, don't talk like that, it isn't proper," Clifford shocked, looked around in case anyone was in earshot.

"Not proper? You a country boy with animals fornicating all around you?" She laughed. *"That* you don't give a second thought, yet our wonderful experience embarrasses you?"

Clifford felt uncomfortable with her direct speech. Surely a lady didn't talk that way? "That's not the same thing at all," he said now, "I don't want to talk about it here like this. I'll meet you tomorrow near the sycamore."

"All right, darling,"

All this 'darling' talk made his head ache and he clicked to the horse who started to move.

"Bye-bye," she called, her voice filled with love, as the carriage moved away. She stood waving her hand saying "Bye" repeatedly, but he did not look back. Disappointed, she walked to the farm.

As Clifford slowly and reluctantly drove home, he formed his excuses. His father would, of course, be furious at his absence for Clifford had not told him he was going anywhere. He had missed an afternoon's work and his mother would be mightily curious.

This morning he had felt happy, but now since making love to Jenny, he felt depressed at her insistence that they marry. He didn't want marriage. If only he had someone to confide in, some other male his own age, but unfortunately he had no close friends. His father had seen to that. Years ago he made it plain that friends were not welcome on the farm, and ensured Clifford did not pal around with any of the village lads even when he was at school. Aye, his father had ruined his younger life, sure enough. He sighed. What was he going to do now?

Suppose Jenny came to the farm and spoke to his mother? His

blood ran cold at the thought. Suppose she told her own mother, who would surely come to Hillshead with fire in her eyes, and demand he make an honest woman of her daughter? He groaned.

If his father were not sick in the head, he might have packed his clothes and run for it. With his lifetime of experience, he would be an asset to any farmer, and where was it written that he had to stay home? He wrestled with the problem and realized running away was out of the question as he could not leave his mother and sisters to fend for themselves. Not with his father acting so crazily.

CHAPTER SEVEN

Jenny ran the last twenty yards, humming merrily. She was in love, in honest to goodness, passionate, physical love. This was better than all the romance novelettes she had read, this longing for him, this yearning to be near him, this need for closeness. She lifted her hand, the hand that had caressed him and, putting it to her nose, imagined she could still detect his aroma, a mixture of sweat, soap and body odour, a smell that made her feel weak.

As she entered the kitchen, her mother looked up from the pastry she was rolling. "Where have you been to this hour, Jenny? I know you wrote you were picnicking, but you have been gone nearly six hours. I was worried about you."

"Oh, it was lovely, Mamma, a glorious afternoon." Putting down the basket, she pirouetted around the kitchen. "The river was so peaceful and I saw swans and ducks."

Eliza watched her. She was acting silly and strangely. What had she been doing? "River? What river? I know of no river hereabouts," Eliza put down the rolling pin. Her voice became cold, her eyes angry. "Where have you been? Who were you with?"

Drat it. Jenny realized she had said too much. Ostensibly the picnic had been for herself alone, or so she told her Uncle Albert. Nobody at the house had any idea she was meeting a young man, or they would have refused to let her go.

She put on a sober face and tried to speak like an adult. "Well, mother, I met Clifford Wright and he took me in their carriage."

Eliza's hands flew to her mouth. "You were unchaperoned with a young man?" She felt a frisson of shock, thinking Jenny knew better than to do such a thing. Maybe they should have kept her in town where, with her father watching, she would have been unable to get into trouble. "What is this about, Jennifer?"

Jenny clapped her hands, her joy evident, her face aglow. "Oh mother, he is nice, you wait and see. He's tall, and handsome, and he has such nice black curly hair."

"I care nothing for the young man's looks. You know young ladies don't take drives with young men without a chaperone. What on earth is your father going to say?" She put her hands to her breast as if to stop her heart from pounding, already picturing the trouble she would have with her authoritarian husband.

"Oh mother, don't worry about father," Jenny said nonchalantly. "Clifford is going to talk to him."

"Talk to him?" Eliza gasped. "What about?"

Eliza knew what about, though. All she had to do was look at Jenny's shining face.

"He'll ask father for my hand in marriage, of course," she said smugly. "Isn't it wonderful, mother? Won't it surprise father?"

Eliza wiped her floury hands. "I'm more than surprised myself. In fact, I'm terribly shocked. You have not been here two minutes, yet now you arrive home to tell me this farmer wants to marry you? You don't even know the man, I don't know the man, and your father surely doesn't."

Jenny smirked and tossed her head. "That is incidental. Oh mother, he's wonderful and he's well educated, considering his parentage. He's hoping to become a veterinarian."

Eliza knew she was wasting her time arguing with the child. Her face grew grim as she thought about what faced her when she told her husband.

"I'll speak to your father when we get back. I do not wish you to speak to him before I do. I want you to promise me that much, Jenny. Adele is improving rapidly and we'll soon be going home."

"But, Mamma, Clifford will go to town to speak to Daddy. He said he would, and I'll tell him tomorrow he should go soon because I want to marry in late summer. We see no point waiting since we are both madly in love, and to wait any longer would be most cruel."

"Oh child, you don't know what you are talking about!" Eliza knew Jenny lived in a dream world, a world of fantasy. She had no idea what life beyond her parent's home entailed. "Love? This is a childish crush, nothing more, and we all feel like that about the first young man we kiss. You cannot possibly know him, and you cannot expect him to marry you. I don't expect your father will take this lightly. He has plans for you."

"Yes, to marry one of his business associates." Jenny sneered churlishly. "That fat old Richard Waithe." She pulled a face and made a sound like vomiting. "Yech! Well, I'm not interested. I've told Daddy often, although he will keep talking about it. No, I will marry Clifford Wright. I will marry for love, and nothing you or father do or say can change my mind."

"You are still a minor, Jennifer," she said sharply. The conversation was going nowhere, she knew, so why bother to continue? "You must obey your father."

"Oh, no I don't." Jenny stood with her hands on her hips, not a particularly refined posture, but one that showed her displeasure. "I'll run away and Clifford will come with me. I don't want to marry the man of my father's choice, I want to marry the man I love, and I will. You wait and see."

She darted out of the kitchen door and stopped dead in the middle of the farm yard, suddenly aware she had nowhere to run.

Eliza wrote a short note to Michael. He must come at once and sort this out, she wrote. She could not chain the girl up, and it was possible that even as she wrote Jenny was running to this farm lad. Going to the stable, she found the young lad who looked after the horses and sent him to the livery office with enough money to pay for delivery of the message.

That evening Jenny moped around the orchard, miserable in her love. If only old people could understand how she felt. What could her mother know of her love for Clifford? Jenny knew from her mother that her parent's marriage was one arranged by her grandparents, that they did not love each other. That much was obvious even to her, so why should she put up with years of misery when she had a lover, a handsome, desirable lover?

CHAPTER EIGHT

After Clifford stabled the horse and trap, he went to the cow shed to see to the milking. Already two of the cows were lowing mournfully from the pain of full udders. His hands moved rhythmically as the milk sussed into the foamy pail. What an rotten ending to an afternoon, he thought, as he rested his cheek against the cow's flank.

Where was his father? Why hadn't someone started the milking, for surely they had heard the cows? It took the best part of an hour to finish the milking, another half hour to clear out the byre and lay fresh straw. He let the cows out and they ambled over to the shade of the beech trees where they would rest.

By the time he finished the chores, he felt famished. The picnic lunch was hardly enough for one, never mind two, and he had a hearty appetite. He scraped the mud off his boots outside the kitchen door and stepped out of them on the door mat, putting on his indoor clogs.

Nobody in the kitchen? He stopped in astonishment. This was strange because his mother was always in the kitchen at this hour and, although it neared supper time, he detected no odour of cooking. Stranger still, the fire was out.

This was peculiar. Oh God, his father. . . had his father done something stupid, he wondered? He searched the house from top to bottom, and found nobody home.

Maybe they had gone out together, but how? He'd had the carriage all afternoon, the cart was with the farm hands in the bottom fields, the plough horses were ploughing the long acres. That only left his father's horse and that was at the Mayhurst stable.

Clifford sat in the cold kitchen wondering what to do. Unable to sit still for the worry of it, he went to search the outbuildings. He found not a soul. The men were still out in the bottoms hay making, he saw them from the second storey of the big barn. Where and why had his family disappeared? Leading out his horse, he quickly saddled and riding to the lower meadows, questioned the men.

"No, Mister Clifford, we wondered where the missus was when nobody brought us our dinner. Have they gone to town maybe?" Alan Smith asked.

"No, how would they get there? There's only the farm cart and the carriage, I had the carriage, and you have the cart. The plough horses are working."

Alan squinted up at Clifford. "Maybe we'd all better start looking. I hate to say this, young Clifford, but your Dad's mighty peculiar these days."

"I know, I know." Clifford rubbed at his forehead, worried. "Come on then, we'll split up and search. We'll meet back at the farm in an hour. Give a yell if you find them."

The three men went their separate ways and Clifford prayed his father had not done something stupid. How strange that the entire family had disappeared.

"Jake?" Liz said, keeping her voice pleasant, "How long are we going to stand here?" She stood, his gun aimed at her midsection, inwardly quaking with fright, outwardly calm.

Jake had erupted into a rage when he learned Clifford had taken the low carriage. It was close to mid afternoon and this spoiled his plans as he planned to take his son rabbit shooting. The blasted ruminants were ruining the crops and breeding too fast.

He pointed his gun at her, telling her to fetch the two 'wenches' from the yard where they were hanging out washing. Betty and Joyce clattered in the back door, their faces blanching as they saw the gun, especially when he said, "How much is this woman paying you to spy on me? What are you doing out there in my yard?"

Betty spoke first. "We were hanging out the washing, Father, this is the first good drying day this week."

Joyce added: "Come on, Dad, let us get on with it. We won't have time to . . ."

"Silence! Who gave you permission to speak? Why are you two bitches in this house doing my washing? Who gave you permission?" The gun wavered between them as Betty and Joyce clung together. "Aye, you'll do well to pay heed. We don't need your kind around here."

Liz edged slowly toward the fireplace, thinking if she could pick up the poker, she could hit him over the head. He was off his rocker and it seemed obvious that she could not jolly him around this time. His face looked different, feral and wrathful.

As she moved into his peripheral vision, he turned on her, grabbing at his staff and moving the gun to his left hand. "What are you about, woman? Get back here." He pushed her with the pole until she was at Betty's side. "Right, I must do something about this insurrection. I don't know who you are or why you're here, but I must remove you from my property." With the gun, he poked at Betty who squealed with fright. "Start moving, put your arms around each other and start moving. I will shoot any one of you that breaks away."

They walked and walked. Strangely enough they saw not one other person as the men were working in the bottom fields. They muttered to each other, whispering as they tried to find a way out of their dilemma.

"What are you mumbling about?" he shouted, enraged. They clung to each other, afraid. "I didn't give you permission to talk. Keep walking, to the right now. Up that path."

Soon they started to stagger wearily for he kept up a killing pace. Where was he taking them? They whispered anxiously. Was he going to kill them? They all felt alarmed, were scared of him. If only they could talk him down again, change his mood.

"Father, I'm getting tired. Can we stop and rest?" Joyce asked.

"Keep walking, woman. You harlots have energy enough when it comes to fleecing a man of his hard earned money."

When he got into one of these moods, he treated all women as prostitutes.

Liz muttered. "Keep walking, you two, we maybe can talk him out of it when we stop. We've managed before and I see no reason why we can't do it this time." Liz prayed his mood would change, and soon.

"What are you mumbling about, woman? Tell me what you said," Jake demanded, butting her in the back with the gun barrel.

"Only that I was tired and my shoes are rubbing my heels," Liz said over her shoulder.

"Kick them off, then. Kick them off. Stupid bitch, stupid old cow who doesn't have any brains," Jake gasped for breath, though he had set the pace.

Liz kept plodding forward. No way was she going to remove her shoes as the path was stony and overgrown by brambles.

"It's the curse, Mam, it's got to be." Joyce hissed.

"Stop yattering, walk faster. Move on," Jake yelled, poking at her with his staff.

Half an hour later they were far onto the moor and nearing an outcrop of black rocks.

Jake laughed maniacally. "Here we are, nearly there," he said, his tone gleeful. "Move along now, to the left. To the left."

Then Liz saw it, the entrance to a cave. They knew of it, of course, had heard stories about it for years. The entire district knew its location. It wound down many miles to an open cavern. Spelunkers often used it and a magazine once photographed the larger cave. Word was that stone age drawings decorated some side caverns and said to be the first type of home decoration.

They moved sideways through the narrow opening and stopped. The darkness blinded them, though as their eyes adjusted, they saw that light from the opening penetrated a short way into the interior. Liz then saw four lanterns at her feet, probably left by the cave explorers.

Jake halted behind them and she risked a glance, noting he still had the gun pointed at them. Suppose he shot them now, Liz thought, who would know where they were? How often did the cave explorers come here? She didn't know, only knew it would not be soon enough to rescue them. They had to find some way of escaping from Jake.

"Jake? How long are we going to stand here?"

"You." Jake poked Betty in the back. "You woman, light the lanterns. Take these matches." He flung a box of sulphur matches at her feet.

Betty was so nervous that it took her a while to light the four lanterns, but then it was done. She tucked the matches into her apron pocket.

"Pick up a lantern each and move on. Make no sudden move or I'll shoot," Jake barked, his voice echoing.

Warily they moved along a short narrow passage and into a wide tunnel, Liz leading with two lanterns. It was slow going as the path was stony and full of huge rocks they must move around or over. Their ankle length dresses were a hindrance and Betty raised her hem by tucking hers into her pinafore waist band until Jake noticed and told her to cover herself like a decent female.

It seemed like hours before he allowed them to rest, although in reality it was only ten minutes. As they moved further inside the cavern, the damp cold struck into them and their breath came in white clouds. They were cold and hungry now, and exhausted.

Betty sighed miserably, and her sigh echoed through the rocky chamber.

"Ooh," she whimpered, her head near Liz's ear. "I'm scared, Mam, so scared. Do you think he's going to shoot us? Talk to him, go on, talk to him. You can bring him around."

Jake sat on a low rock, cradling his gun and staff. They looked at him, their gaze darting around the bleak surroundings, seeking escape.

By this time, Liz felt completely panic-stricken. Jake was no longer the man she had married, he was a stranger. She had forgiven him often since his accident, knowing his moods were beyond his control. He was sick, but to fetch them here, this godforsaken hole in the ground, and for what? She shivered with cold as the damp struck right into her bones.

"Jake," she said, trying to keep the shiver out of her voice. "Can we go back now, please? It's nearly tea time." The thought of food might snap him out of it. "Clifford will be home wondering where we are. You don't want him to go hungry, surely."

His head jerked up and he pointed the gun at her. "Who are you talking about, woman? Who is this Clifford?"

It was useless. He was still in the throes of his delusion.

Betty nudged her. "Get him to talk about something. Sometimes that works."

She cleared her throat. Jake had shut his eyes and was practically nodding off. He must be tired, or his condition was bleeding him of energy. "Jake? Tell me about when you were a young man. It is so interesting."

Jake's eyes opened wide and they knew he was thinking of his youth, when comely young women chased after him, women who wanted to marry him for his prospects. They had heard his highly coloured reminiscences often. Nervously they watched as he fell into a dreamlike state, saw his head slowly nod to his chest, but as his chin hit his breastbone, it snapped him alert. His eyes flickered over them and he licked his lips.

"You woman, you, the one in blue. Come with me," he ordered. A young woman would satisfy him right now, the way they used to when he was young.

"Come over here," he ordered as Betty stood. "You're not a bad wench, maybe overstuffed, a bit too well fed, but comely enough." He looked now at Liz and Joyce. "You two stay there and don't try to move. I'll be watching you." He dragged Betty by the arm into an alcove a short way back.

"Take off your clothes," he said, pointing the gun at her.

"No, Father. No!" Betty knew what was in his mind. How could he do this to her? Her mind raced, maybe if she stalled him long enough the others may come to her defence. He spoke loudly enough for them to hear and surely they heard her refusing?

"Take tha clobber off, woman. If you don't, I'll shoot you." Raising the gun, he pointed it at her chest.

"No, father, don't you know me? I'm your daughter, don't do this."

"Take off those clothes, woman, now!" he came closer with the gun, pushing it into her breast. "Hurry up."

She had little choice, it was either this or death, and she didn't want to die. Dithering, she unlaced her bodice, thinking that he might snap out of it. Please God, she prayed, help me, please help me.

"Come here," Jake said, his pants unbuttoned, his penis springing free. "Come here and service me. You know what to do."

Although Betty was twenty-one, she had no idea what the human sex act involved. Animals she had seen aplenty, but human love making was beyond her.

"Come on, come on. I bet if I was dangling a gold guinea afore your eyes you'd be quick enough."

"Father, I'm a virgin, don't make me. Please don't make me. Don't you know me? I'm your daughter. Please don't make me. Please."

Jake laughed. It was not a nice laugh, but one of evil.

Fascinated, she watched his penis bob around as he laughed. He caressed it and admired it. No daughter should see her father like this, it wasn't right. Bursting into tears, she collapsed in a heap onto a rock.

"A good jape, the virgin and a father, eh? Well this is a new one for me. I like it, woman, I like it very much." He put down the gun and advanced on her. Although she didn't look up, she knew he was standing over her. "All right now, stand up and put your arms around me," he ordered.

She didn't move so he pulled at her arms, his fingers digging in so hard she was forced to stand. He pulled her close to his body and she could feel the rough tweed of his jacket, the buttons, his penis throbbing against her stomach.

"Please don't do this father, please don't," she begged frantically. Her frantic pleas only seemed to make him more excited.

"Feel at it. A rod of iron it is, a rod that will excite you more than any other man's has done. Put your hands on it, woman. Take it into your mouth." Roughly he pushed her to her knees and pulled her face upwards by the ears. "Take it into your mouth and pleasure me."

She felt revolted, but had no choice as he picked up the gun and pointed it at her head.

After he tired of her ministrations, for she had no idea of what to do, he pushed her over a rock and drove himself into her. He hurt her tender tissues because she was tight and dry. Her back felt broken and the sharp stones bit into her arms and legs. When she screamed as if he were killing her, that made him drive into her harder.

Liz and Joyce heard the screams and stood, unsure of what to do.

"We have to save her, Joyce. God only knows what he's doing to her, although I have a good idea," Liz said, grabbing a lantern and moving toward the alcove.

Joyce, afraid to be alone, grabbed at her skirt and accompanied her. Then they saw Jake raping Betty.

"No, Jake, stop that. Stop it. It's a sin!" Liz screamed as she clawed at his back and he roared even as he climaxed. "Stop it, Jake, that's your daughter. You don't know what you're doing." She was hysterical now. "If you had wanted to do that, you should have taken me, your wife."

Jake roared with fury and flung Betty away from him. She had fainted, and as she fell she hit her head and knew nothing.

"Take off your clothes, woman," He pulled at her dress. "I'll show you who's boss around here. I can take both of you harlots on and still be ready for more."

Liz didn't move. "Jake, please listen to me. We need to get home soon. Clifford will wonder where we are."

"Pah! Stop your blathering and get those clothes off, or shall I rip them off you. Is that what you prefer?"

Liz realized that this time he had gone off the deep end. She slowly removed her clothes, feeling the cold damp strike into her bare skin.

Jake raised the lantern and looked at Joyce who was cowering in a fissure. "You, young wench. You're first, I'll save the old cow for later. Take off your clothes."

Joyce raised her chin and defied him. "No, father, I won't. This is wrong, it's immoral and a sin. I will not do it. God will punish you for this."

"Stop your mealy mouthed puling. Are you a nun? Is that how you dress to please the men? I prefer them buck naked. Take off your things." He pointed the gun at her and she cowered back, shaking her head.

Jake became angrier than they had ever seen him. "A common trollop denying me, denying me my rights?" With a roar, he pushed the gun into her waist. "Start taking them off. Now!" N..o..w......n..o. .w.....n..o..w, the echoes rolled around the cavern.

Joyce shook her head. She would sooner die than let her father rape her.

Liz pulled at his arm. He shrugged her off. "Please, Jake, please take me," she begged and then had an idea. "That girl isn't worthy of you. She has the pox."

"What? The pox you say?" His face showed revulsion and he backed away. "Get away from me, trollop, I don't want no pox. Yach!" he spat onto the ground as if the thought made him puke.

"Take me, Jake," Liz begged, glad that she had saved one of her daughters.

He waggled his penis at her. "Is this what you want? Why would I want an old cow like you? All sagging udders and fat hips? Well, show me what you can do, you've doubtless had lots of practice. Come on now, wake him up," Pulling her toward him, he laughed at her shocked face.

Liz did as he told her. She took him in her mouth and tried to bring him to erection, but he continued laughing maniacally. She did little things with her mouth that she had used on him when they were first wed, but nothing worked.

"Get away from me, you old bag," he shoved her away with his foot and she fell onto the rocks. "You, young one, you do it. You can't have pox in your mouth. You come here and do it now." He pointed the gun at her again and she wept.

"Shoot me then, for I won't do that, father. It's wrong and you're a devil. Go on, shoot me."

He raised the gun and aimed it, grinning malevolently.

Liz threw herself at him. "No. Jake, don't, don't shoot her. It's murder and they'll hang you." She grabbed at his arm and spoiled his aim. Furious, he turned around and struck her over the head with the gun barrel. She fell senseless.

"That's better. Less aggravation. Where was I? Oh yes, disposing of the diseased trollop that refused to service me." Again, he took aim.

Betty was now conscious and heard this exchange. She had planned to lie as if dead, hoping he would leave her alone, but it was terribly cold and her teeth began chattering. Every bone in her body felt bruised, places where the skin had been broken were bleeding and blood poured down her arm from where he had banged it against a sharp rock. However, she thought only of her sister.

Joyce was such a baby about things, she always had been, mard she was, just plain mard, a tiny splinter assumed such huge proportions to her that she whined and complained as if she'd lost a hand. Struggling to sit, Betty looked at them. Her father's back was to her and Joyce was cowering against the rocky wall, sobbing as if her heart would break. She picked up a rock.

Her father was obviously intent on shooting Joyce, she had heard what he said and a terrible rage overcame her. With one movement she brought the rock down on his head and the gun went off, deafening her. The flash of the discharge was blinding in the dark cave.

A sudden rush of disturbed bats flew around them, their squeaks loud in the sudden silence.

"Oh my God," she gasped when she could see again. The lanterns showed Joyce still cowering in the crevice, while her mother lay as if dead at Jake's feet as he lay across a rock. He did not move.

"Joyce, are you all right?" she asked, her voice sounding far away and muffled as if someone had stuffed her ears with cotton.

Joyce nodded, moving her head so she could see her sister. "Ooh, is he dead?" she gasped as she saw him lying on the ground.

"I sincerely hope so," Betty said, moving to her mother's side. Liz moaned and opened her eyes.

"What happened? Is it over? Is he all right now?" she asked blinking to focus her eyes.

Betty looked up at Joyce. "Look after her, get her clothes." Her voice sounded peculiar and spots from the blast still danced before her eyes. "I have to get my clothes on."

Moving away, she picked up her things. Her teeth chattered with cold and shock, her hands were all thumbs and she found it difficult to catch her breath. Suffering from the shock of what had happened to her, she could not cry. She felt nothing, was empty of all emotion other than anger.

Given her state of mind, Joyce's weeping and whining was getting on Betty's nerves, amplified as it was by the cave.

"Ooh, Mam," Joyce sobbed, "What are we going to do? Betty has killed father and they'll hang us all. Ooh, Mam."

Betty turned on her, shoving her back against the wall with her arm. "Stop that stupid noise, Joyce. Nobody's going to hang. That man was a mad man, he wasn't our father. Not our father as he used to be, and he was bad enough back then."

Moving to her father, she felt for a pulse and found it, fainter than normal and racing. He was still alive and she knew what she must do.

Liz put on her clothes, and blood from the head wound dripped onto her collar.

"Joyce, take mother out of here," she ordered, "Leave me a lantern. Go on now, get out of here."

"We have to get father out," Joyce whimpered, "You can't manage him on your own."

Liz pulled at her daughter. "Leave the old bastard where he is. Betty's right. After what he's done today, let him lie."

Joyce did not accept that as she looked on the negative side of things as usual. "What are we going to tell Clifford? If father is dead, he has to know and we have to have a funeral. We have to . . .,"

"We have to do nowt," Liz said angrily, shaking Joyce, feeling groggy as her headed pounded and her eyes refused to focus. "That man was going to rape you, or maybe shoot you, and you feel he deserves the last rights? What's the matter with you, girl? If anyone is mad now, it's you. Come on, let's get out of here. Betty will see to him."

Slowly and painfully, Liz moved in the direction from which they had entered the cave. How she wanted to be outside in the fresh air. Her legs were like jelly and she clung to Joyce's arm to remain upright.

Betty waited until they turned a corner, and, picking up his gun and holding it by the barrel, she beat her father about the head until she heard bone cracking. Scared in case he regained consciousness, she did the deed as quickly as possible.

As she pounded, she muttered, "That's for what you did to me, you miserable old bastard. That's for what you tried to do to my sister, and that's for my Mam. That's for all the years of misery, all the times you beat us. You bloody old goat, you devil spawn, you unfeeling old swine."

She was breathless by the time she tossed the gun aside. Taking his legs, she pulled and tugged until she moved him farther along the stony path where a deep water filled gully lay to one side. After filling his pockets with rocks, she pushed him over, tossing the gun after him.

As the body fell, she laughed hysterically, the echoes magnifying every sound until the bats started to squeak. "Let's see you get out of that, you miserable old sod."

Picking up the lantern, she slowly made her way out of the cave. All the time she was thinking she had murdered her father in cold blood, all the time she wondered how they could explain where they had been, wondered how to explain Jake's disappearance. Yet for all that she felt no guilt, knowing he got what he deserved, though he was not responsible for his moods, had no control over himself.

As she came into the blinding sunlight, she saw her mother lying on the grass with Joyce uselessly rubbing at her hands.

Joyce was weeping again. "Mam, Mam, come on now, we can go home. Come on, Mam."

She saw Betty and looked behind her. "Where is he, our Dad? Did you not fetch him out of there? Shall I run for the men? Can't he walk?"

Betty shrugged and kept her face expressionless. The act she had committed came home to her again. She had murdered her father. Yet life had to go on and life would be better without him. Putting back her shoulders and lifting her head, she said, "No, he can't walk, he'll never walk again. Now we'll sit here until Mam feels better, and we'll talk about this."

Joyce stared at her. Her expression said it all. What had happened to father and why was Betty looking so peculiar? She sat waiting as Betty tended to their mother, her mind trying to sort out her feelings.

When Liz came revived and felt better, they sat talking. Joyce was all for going back in to fetch father out, or fetching the men to carry him.

Betty and her mother exchanged glances. Liz realized what Betty had done and was glad. She shook her head as she listened to Joyce rambling on about father and how they'd look after him once they got him home. Joyce was obtuse at the best of times, slow to catch on. When she put her hand on Betty's arm and raised her eyebrows in question, Betty told her the truth.

"Joyce, he's dead!" Betty shouted with exasperation, annoyed that spelling it out was necessary. "All right? He's dead and bloody good riddance to the old bugger. That's the end of the curse for sure. He's dead!

Joyce squealed with panic. "Oh, our Betty, what are we going to do?" She rocked back and forth in misery, her face wet with tears. "They'll hang us all: you for hurting him and us for letting you. How could you do it, how *could* you? Did you shoot him? How did you do it?" She was off and wailing again.

"You stupid child," Liz snapped, "It doesn't matter how he died. Suffice it to say, he won't be troubling us in the future. That wasn't your father, girl, he was a stranger both to me and to you. He was going to shoot you, Joyce. Did you want that to happen? Did you want him to rape you like he did Betty? He was never going to get better, and you know that. We've spent the last three months keeping out of his reach, hardly daring to breath, yet now you want to confer sainthood on him. He was my husband long afore he was your father, and I'm glad I'll never set my eyes on him again."

Betty sat, stone faced, thinking about the murder. She sighed and said. ""Mam's right, our Joyce. Forget fetching him out, forget what

I did. Still, we all have to tell the same tale. We'll say that he took us in the cave, then wandered off on his own. Let them, search for him. They'll never find him now."

Joyce stopped crying long enough to look at Betty. "Where is he?"

Betty shrugged. She would never tell.

"Aaw, lass," Liz put her arm around Betty's shoulders. "I hate him for what he did to you, hate him with a passion. The man we speak about wasn't my husband and he wasn't your father: he was a maniac. Come on now, let's get away home."

As they straggled along the moor path, they convinced Joyce to keep quiet, telling her she needn't say anything to anyone if she were scared of lying; though why she was acting so religious neither of them could fathom. If she kept her mouth shut, they could say she was suffering from shock.

CHAPTER NINE

Clifford was running through the woods calling for his mother when he looked through the thinning trees and saw the three as they trudged sluggishly along the path from the moor.

"Cooee! Cooee!" he yelled to any other who could hear. "They're back. Coming from the moor."

He raced through the woods and out onto the fell, stumbling through the bracken.

"Thank God, thank God," he cried as he enfolded his mother in his arms. She was trembling with exhaustion and more, blood ran from a wound in her hair and she looked ashen. Betty stood statue-like, while a pale faced Joyce broke into huge racking sobs and threw herself at him, hanging on as if she would never let go.

Two of the men came racing from the direction of the woods.

Clifford asked, "Are you all right? Where were you?"

Liz told them Jake had forced them at gun point into the caves and held them captive. How long they had been there she could not tell. When he wandered off down a passage, they crept out and made for home.

"Right, let's get the women to the farm, then we'll go and fetch him out. Possibly he's fallen asleep and won't know where he is," Clifford said as they each held a female by the waist and walked them to the lane. Joyce could not stop crying, Betty was mute, and Liz sighed often but did not say a word.

When they got inside, Liz made Clifford take Joyce upstairs to lie down. Betty washed her mother's head wound, then made a meal for them and the men who would return after the search.

Clifford knew there must more to the story, but was content to wait until they recovered from the ordeal. It must have been terrifying for them, his father pointing his gun at them in those bat ridden caves for God knew how long.

Michael arrived within two days of receiving his wife's letter. While annoyed at her request, he knew the time had come to fetch them home. Enough was enough of Christian charity, he wanted his family around him.

What of this lout, this farm hand Jenny was chasing? The girl had little sense in her pretty head. He had always known that, but for a child of her age to start pursuing a totally unsuitable youth meant Eliza was not doing her job properly. He planned to speak to her, to make her lack of diligence patently clear

As he rode into the farm yard, Eliza saw him from the bedroom window. Joyfully, she raced down the stairs.

"Michael, you came." She put up her arms as if to hug him, but he walked past her and into the farm house as if he hadn't seen her.

"Get that animal rubbed down and stabled," he said over his shoulder. "Where is my daughter?"

Eliza called the stable boy who led the horse away, then ran into the house. What on earth was the matter? Why was Michael treating her this way?

"Michael?" She found him in the parlour looking at the few books in the bookcase. "How are you?"

In his black broadcloth suit and snowy cravat, he looked every inch the gentleman. He turned to face her, but before he spoke, took out his handkerchief and wiped his fingers.

"Well may you ask, Eliza, well may you ask. The note you sent disturbs me since I had to take time away from the office. I resent that. I cannot make a living if you are unable to handle a young child."

"Oh Michael, you own the company. You can take as much time off as you need," Eliza said quietly. He was angry and upset, she saw that, but why couldn't he have greeted her, his wife?

"Time off is time wasted, and I think this is wasted time. Where is she?"

Eliza sat on the couch. She did not know where Jenny was as she had risen early and sneaked out.

"She's out somewhere," she murmured.

"Out somewhere? Where? Where is the girl?" Michael started beating his riding crop against his boot.

"I don't know. She left before the household was awake. She probably went for a walk. Maybe she couldn't sleep." Nervously she twisted her handkerchief.

Michael narrowed his eyes. "This is too much. You were the one who told me a country holiday would do her good. You said she would be a great help to you with Adele."

"She is, Michael, a great help."

He snorted. "Jennifer a help? We both know she is bone idle. She does nothing for herself or anyone else, and you tell me she is a great help? What's going on here, Eliza? Where is she and why did you send that urgent note? Exactly who is this farmer she is seeing? Why was this allowed to happen? Did you not watch her?" He glared at her. "That you let a genteel young lady, my daughter, out un-chaperoned is unforgivable."

Eliza listened, letting him get it out of his system. Whatever happened, he would lay the blame on her: he always did.

"Yes, Michael, I did watch her, but I couldn't watch her twenty-four hours a day. I was nursing my sister, and cooking the meals. Ask Adele, she'll tell you."

His eyebrows shot up as he grimaced. "Ask your sister? I doubt I would get much satisfaction from that quarter because she'll be on your side. I want to know why you let Jennifer wander the countryside alone."

"Father!" Jenny exploded into the room and flung herself at him. "You're here! I have such wonderful news."

"Sit down, Jennifer." His voice seemed ominously calm and she looked up at him uncertainly. She glanced at her mother whose face was closed and expressionless, and wondered what had happened. A death in the family maybe? "Control yourself, Jennifer," he said, "and try to act like the young lady you purport to be."

Peevishly she plopped down onto the couch by her mother's side.

"Don't slouch, child, sit up straight," he snapped. Then she sat erectly and smiled at him, hoping to change his mood.

"Your mother tells me you have been consorting with a country yokel."

Jenny felt incensed that her mother would have told him about Clifford.

"Mother?" She snapped, turning to Eliza, her face angry. "Why did you not wait until I could tell father?"

Eliza lowered her eyes and did not answer.

Michael slapped his crop against his boot. "Now, young lady, tell me all about it. I'm all ears."

Jenny smiled sweetly and turned to him. She knew her daddy always sided with her. "Oh, Father, he is wonderful. His name is Clifford Wright and he is to be a veterinarian. His father owns the next farm and he will inherit as he only has sisters. He is tall, handsome and he has . .,"

Michael made a short pretense of listening to her babble. "Stop this at once, Jennifer," he snapped, "How dare you consort with a young man without my consent? You have been deceitful with me and your mother, and have run wild without permission. You will go upstairs and pack your things immediately. We will return to town at once."

Jenny put out her hand. "But Father, let me tell you . . .,"

"You will not speak again until I give permission," he thundered. "I will not allow you to refer to this lout again."

Jenny jumped to her feet, hands on her hips. "He isn't a lout," she shrieked. "He's wonderful, and we are going to be married."

Michael laughed mirthlessly. "Married? Married? Have you taken leave of your senses, child? I will hear no talk of marriage."

Jenny's face looked ugly as she said, "I will not marry that fat old Richard Waithe." Childishly she stamped her foot, her hands clenched into fists. "I won't, I won't, I won't!"

"Jennifer." His voice was low and threatening. "You will sit and listen." Fearfully she sat. "You will marry the man we choose for you. You have no choice as you are still a minor, an unintelligent one at that. I will not allow you to run wild, nor will you see this rustic clodhopper again." He pointed to the door with his crop. "Now go to your room and pack your things. Eliza, go with her, make sure she does so. Try to do one thing right for a change, woman."

Eliza stood and, taking Jennifer's arm, pulled her to her feet.

"Let go of me, Mother." Jenny angrily shook herself free. "This is all your fault. You betrayed me. You're the most hateful person I know, and I'll never speak to you again." She flounced out, Eliza following.

Michael looked around the parlour. It was a long narrow room with four tiny windows of distorted glass that looked as if they had never seen water. The wooden floorboards looked in need of scrubbing and the few bits of furniture were handmade. Hanging from the picture rail was a painting so blackened with age that it was indecipherable, the long cord suspending it festooned with dusty cobwebs. To think that Adele lived here, or that Eliza would stoop to enter such a slovenly house.

Adele and Eliza, the offspring of the minister of a small parish, had lived in genteel poverty until their respective marriages. Eliza, he thought, had come out the winner.

Eliza, ah yes, Eliza. She had let him down. After the birth of Jennifer she never again conceived and he often considered adopting a son. Now she had practically ruined his daughter by letting her run wild with unsuitable people. His mind seethed with the inequity of the situation and he became anxious to take them back home where he could let Eliza know exactly what he thought of her laxity. He paced around the room, poking at things with his crop: the small crudely made picture frames on the table, the artificial flowers under a dusty glass dome standing on the fireplace mantelpiece. This was a hovel, and to think his precious daughter had been forced to stay here. No wonder the girl had taken to the outdoors, and in that regard he didn't blame her.

Leaving the room, he went down the short hall and entered the kitchen. What a mess greeted his eyes. Unwashed pots and dishes, the fire smouldering in an ash filled grate, washing hanging from a rope over the fireplace, smoked hams suspended from the beams. To his standards it looked filthy, and the only furniture was a long oak table with two benches.

Snorting with disgust, he stepped into the farm yard setting a flock of hens running. Six geese flapped away, honking loudly, resenting the intrusion. Their din brought Albert out of the barn.

"Oh, it's only you," he said grinning, wiping his hands on a piece of sacking. "Come to see Eliza, have you?"

Michael raised his chin and looked down his nose. "I came to take my wife and daughter home. Surely Adele must be better by this time."

Albert eyed him with distaste. Michael was too toffee-nosed for him, all airs and graces and sartorial splendour. He wore a stiff white cravat and cuffs, a black broadcloth suit with a matching waistcoat across which hung a thick gold watch chain. Aye, a proper toff, he was an'all, down to the highly polished riding boots. Imagine coming to a farm dressed like that! He shook his head in disbelief.

"Aye, Adele is a lot better, thanks to Eliza. She should be fit to get back to work in a couple of days. I want to thank you, Michael. Eliza has been a godsend. I don't know what I would have done without her help."

"Thank you, Albert," he said with disdain, "But my wife's place is at home. Can you direct me to the nearest livery where I may hire a coach to transport us to town? I want to take Jennifer away from here as quickly as possible."

Albert scratched his head under his cloth cap. "Jennifer? What's to do?"

"Don't tell me you don't know. I find that astonishingly hard to believe. My daughter has been seeing a young man from the next farm. Clifford something."

Albert grinned. "Aye, that'll be Clifford Wright, I 'spect. A reeght nice young fella."

"Nice he may be to a milk maid, but his like is not for my daughter. I have already arranged her marriage, yet she tells me she plans to marry this farm hand."

Albert couldn't help smiling and his grin grew wider. What a come down for the snobby Michael. "Now, now. Clifford is a handsome young chap, well educated and has good prospects. She could do far worse. That's what I told Eliza, she could do far worse."

"So you *did* know," Michael's face burned redly, "And you condoned this affair? You knew my pure unsullied child was seeing this, this, this hayseed and you allowed it? How dare you presume to know what is best for my child? How dare you?"

Albert spat on the ground by the shining boots as if to say nobody was going to talk to him like this, not even his brother-in-law, the stuck up townie.

"I'll thank you to keep a civil tongue in your head, Mickey, me boy." Annoyed, Michael took one step back. "What your daughter does or does not do, is no concern of mine, and since your wife knew about it, why should you come down on me? When Eliza found out, she wrote to you right away. Sent my stable boy to take the letter she did, never bothered consulting me."

"It's just as well she did," Michael said, turning on his heel. "I will take them both home with me at once. Now where is the nearest livery stable?"

Albert gave him directions to the market town and Michael whistled for his horse. Vaulting into the saddle, he took off like the wind, flailing his crop.

Albert watched him go. A good riddance to him and his offspring, he thought, though Adele might want to keep them here. Still, it could be Mickey was right, she had been bedridden for long enough, and what she needed now was fresh air and exercise.

CHAPTER TEN

Upstairs Eliza watched as Jenny tossed clothes onto the bed, then began shoving them into hampers and bags. Jenny's temper, now escalated to rage, blinded her and she shoved a gown into the basket any old which way.

"Stop that, Jenny, pack things properly. You'll ruin that gown if you're not careful." Eliza took the sprigged muslin gown out of the hamper and shook it.

"You pack the stuff if you want to be fussy," she snapped, "I'm going out." She moved toward the door, but Eliza moved faster and locked it, putting the key down her bodice.

"Mother?"

"You will stay here. I'm already in trouble with your father for allowing you to wander abroad. He'll not allow you outside again, and neither will I." She packed the other dresses.

Jenny flung herself onto the bed and started pummelling the pillow with her fists. "You hateful old woman, you don't want me to be happy. My father will soon find out he can't make me marry that fat old man. I'll run away from home," she threatened, "I'll come back to Clifford and I *will* marry him, with or without your permission."

Eliza smiled grimly. Up to now, in Michael's eyes Jennifer could do no wrong, but he would never allow her to marry beneath her station. Richard Waithe, as Jenny had so rightly pointed out, was a fat old man, but he was a fat, *rich,* old man and owned considerable properties around Lancashire. A marriage to Richard would ensure Jenny wealth and a standing in society that neither she nor Michael could achieve. If only the girl were not so childish, so selfcentred.

The packing finished, she stood watching Jenny pick at her nails. "Come along, Jenny, we will go down and make the tea."

"No."

Eliza shrugged, as if to say she did not care whether she came or not.

Whining, she said, "I'd rather stay here in this prison. I don't want tea. You go. I don't want you tying me to the table in case I run outside."

Eliza nodded and, retrieving the key from her bodice, locked the door from the outside.

As she heard the key turn in the lock, Jenny screamed. "No, no. Don't lock me in. Don't!" She had not reckoned with this. Her plan had been to sneak down the stairs and out the front door when her mother reached the kitchen. She planned to go to Clifford.

"Jenny? Eliza? What's happening?" Adele's voice came from the next room.

Eliza went into her sister's room and helped her into a chair by the window. "I've locked Jenny in her room until Michael takes us home. She's been running wild with that farmer's son, Clifford Wright. Oh Adele, you know Michael has already arranged her marriage, but now she has some silly idea her father will allow her to marry this farmer. Ignore her noise as best you can, Adele. I dare not let her out or Michael will be angry."

Adele smiled at the screeching and foot stomping. "She is angry, isn't she? Kind of puts me in mind of myself when I announced I wanted to marry Albert."

Eliza had to smile at the memory. "Yes, we had to do a lot of talking before Papa allowed your marriage. Still, Albert is a good man, a good provider and you have two grand sons."

"I wish they had stayed home, though. I'd not have been forced to carry another if they'd stayed home. I missed them so much and we always talk of them." She sighed. "The doctor told Albert not to get me pregnant. However, he wanted another child so much, so how could I refuse?"

"Indeed. I know that about men well enough. Michael has never forgiven me for my inability to bear more children as he dearly wants a son. Sometimes he even talks of adoption."

"I never knew, 'Liza. How awful for you."

Eliza smiled as she patted her shoulder. "Yes, it is. We all have our cross to bear and mine is Michael."

Adele caught at her hand. "You still love him, don't you?"

Eliza shook her head sadly. "I don't know anymore. Once he was my whole life. I adored him because he loved me so much. Now he treats me like a servant, and, I don't mean to shock you, Adele, but at times he treats me like a whore. I don't think your marriage is comparable to mine. Albert loves you with every fibre of his being, and it shows."

"Yes, I admit that. He's a lovely man and I'd do anything for him, even live here. I know it's horrible and not what we were used to. However, I've become accustomed to it and wouldn't think of leaving."

"Listen, is that a carriage?" Hooves and iron rimmed wheels crunched on the gravel outside and Eliza opened the window to see Michael alighting from a small carriage as the driver tipped his hat and applied the brake.

"Wait here, my man," he ordered and entered the house.

"It's Michael with a carriage," Eliza gasped, turning to Adele, "Oh my, he must mean to take us back immediately."

"Oh dear, Jenny will not go willingly, Eliza, not at all willingly."

"Eliza?" Michael's feet pounded up the stairs. "Fetch down the bags and we will leave. You have five minutes to pack your own things."

He came into the bedroom, his face red with anger and haste. "Start packing, Eliza, we're going home immediately. Sorry, Adele, you've had her for long enough. I must say you look well now, but you know we have problems with Jennifer. Hurry up, Eliza, I'm paying the carriage by the hour. I have tethered my horse to the rear of the carriage. I can't it leave it here or Albert will have it pulling a plough."

Adele glared at him, then smiled tearfully at Eliza. She would miss her sister, but realized they must resolve the problem with Jenny. She did not want to exacerbate matters.

Weary now, she held out her hand. "Thank you for letting Eliza stay for so long, Michael, I appreciate it, as does Albert." Michael nodded and shook her hand for one second. "I'm sorry about Jenny, but she is very much her own person, as you know," Adele said, hoping to cool his temper. "We couldn't be watching her every minute."

Michael snorted and slapped his boot with the crop. "I know we cannot lay the responsibility for her disobedience at your feet, Adele, as you were bedridden. I blame Eliza for what happened. The girl should have been indoors helping her mother, not gallivanting over the countryside with some idiot yokel."

"Now, now, Michael," Adele said, trying to placate him. "Clifford Wright is such a nice young man. Maybe you should meet him."

He raised his eyebrows almost to his hairline. "Meet him? Have you completely lost your senses, Adele? I'd no sooner meet that bumpkin than fly to the moon. Good health to you, sister-in-law. We leave as quickly as possible."

Eliza locked herself in the bedroom with Jennifer who sat miserably staring into space. Quickly she packed her few things, and then called to Michael.

Michael held onto Jenny with one hand as they went down the stairs, Eliza following in their wake with her baggage.

"Goodbye, Adele," she called up the stairs, reluctant to leave her softly sobbing sister. "I'll write when I get home. Goodbye and look after yourself."

Michael, who did not like sentimentality, hurried them to the carriage.

"Come along, woman, let's make haste. Jennifer, sit facing me please."

"I don't like riding with my back to the horse," she pouted. "You know that, father."

"I said *sit facing me.* I need to keep my eye on you and will not rest easy until we are home."

On the way back Jenny scanned the fields, hoping to see Clifford. As they topped the last hill, she stood looking back as her eyes filled with hot tears, then collapsing on the seat, she sobbed pitifully.

"Do stop that caterwauling, Jennifer. What will the driver think?" Michael said, pushing his handkerchief into her hand.

She cried all the way home, giving him glances that could have melted glass. How cruel he was, taking her way from her love. In her mind she formulated a plan to run away as quickly as possible, back to her dear, darling Clifford.

CHAPTER ELEVEN

"It looks like you're the new master, Cliff," Liz said to her son. "On your father's death everything comes to you."

The men had searched the caves for hours, finding no trace of Jake. For two days they ventured ever deeper into the vast caverns, even bringing men in from neighbouring farms. They found nothing, other than Jake's staff.

Clifford wondered about her comment. "Without a body we don't know that he is dead, do we, Mam?"

She faced him, white faced and adamant. "Those men searched everywhere. He must have wandered into the deep places, maybe fell down a shaft, or drowned in a bottomless pool," she said, wondering what Betty had done with the body.

Liz never asked Betty about the time she was alone with her father. She didn't want to know, and it was better that way. Clifford noticed neither of his sisters or mother seemed much concerned about his father's disappearance, and wondered why. None were grieving for him, that much was certain.

Betty was a silent wraith these days. She worked hard, but never spoke unless asked a direct question so Liz knew how terrible it must have been for her. They all knew she often woke in the night screaming and Joyce had to quieten her. Both he and his mother realized she would never be the same and noticed how she shied away from men, even himself, her own brother.

"Until they find his remains, the farm will never be mine," he said firmly. "I'll work it and help you, Mam, but it can't be mine until we have a funeral."

She nodded. "Aye, that's as it should be, but maybe we'll never have a funeral. What then?"

"When we find him we will have a funeral," he said stonily, "I intend to spend my spare time searching for him. It's only right. I don't understand why you're so cold toward him, Mam. You didn't talk about him this way even when he was alive and treating you like you were a stranger. Exactly what happened that day?"

Liz refused to say; neither could he get anything from Joyce nor Betty. It was as if a veil had been drawn over that time. The girls left the room if ever he mentioned it, and his mother quickly changed the subject. It was strange, their attitude. He felt suspicious, though he didn't know why.

Still, they had recovered from their ordeal well as far as he could see, and knowing what a bastard his father was when in one of his 'turns,' he shuddered to think what they had gone through.

As Liz set the table for supper, she glanced through the open door to where Betty and Joyce were sitting on the pigsty wall. Thank God, she thought, the sow had given them fifteen piglets this time and they had put up the feeding frame. Time would come when they could sell some and still have enough to slaughter come winter. Their pigs were famous, when they lived, that was. Last year's brood, squashed by their mother, who rolled over on them, had not survived.

"Call the girls in for their meal, Clifford. Time they washed up."

Clifford called, but they did not move. They were talking seriously as he walked toward them. Sitting with their feet inside the sty, they faced away and did not see his approach.

"What happened? You have to tell me, Betty, you have to." He noticed how serious Joyce sounded. What on earth had Betty been up to now, Clifford wondered? She never left the farm as far as he knew. Not since his father had scared off her beau with a gun.

Betty shut her eyes. What she had been through would stay behind her eyelids for the rest of her life. "No. You don't want to know. Be glad you got out of there."

"You have to tell me, Betty, or I'll have to tell Clifford what . .,"

"Tell Clifford what?" he said, making them both jump.

"Nothing, Clifford, only girl stuff. You wouldn't be interested. Honest," Joyce said as she jumped down from her perch. She grinned up at him, but he could see she felt uncomfortable. Betty said nothing, refusing to look him in the eye. He would be extra watchful, keep his ears open, and sooner or later find out what they were discussing.

"You're not talking about that curse nonsense again are you?" Both shook their heads, but he thought they looked shamefaced. "Your tea is ready. Mam says to wash up and get inside."

Both went to the pump and washed their hands, drying them on the old sack tied to its handle. Clifford watched for a second or two, then went back into the house.

"See, you and your big gob," Betty hissed. "You're going to get us all in trouble if you don't watch your tongue, our Joyce. Stop going on about it. I vowed to carry the secret to my grave, so don't bother me any more."

"Yet I need to know. I do, I do."

Betty took her sister by the shoulders and shook her roughly. "Never will you find out what went on back there, never. Do you hear me?" she muttered.

Clifford watched them at tea time, noticing how subdued Joyce seemed as Liz chattered to cover the silence.

Meal times were difficult for the women when he was present as all were scared that one of the others might let something drop. Betty never spoke, while Joyce usually babbled continuously. Liz was fearful she would suddenly say something to raise questions.

Betty put back her head and looked at each of them. Suddenly she spoke loudly. "I have something to tell you. I'm pregnant."

"Pregnant?" they chorused, then their mouths dropped open.

Clifford slapped his hand on the table, aghast. "Pregnant, how could you get pregnant when you've never been near a chap?" Clifford laughed then thinking it a joke, but the look on his sister's face made him stop. "Is this a virgin birth? What have you been up to? Did you sneak out at night, or what?" The news flabbergasted Clifford. His sister Betty having a child out of wedlock, her, who was so prudish that it hardly seemed likely. "What makes you think you're expecting? You're surely joking or mistaken, maybe confused."

When she said nothing, he appealed to his mother. "Mam?" but she sat with both hands clamped to her mouth, her face ashen.

"What the hell is going on around here? Why has everybody suddenly lost their tongues?" He looked at the three of them, noticing they did not lift their eyes. Joyce suddenly burst into tears, then ran up the stairs sobbing. His mother sat like a statue, her eyes fixed on Betty, who looked as white as a corpse.

He sat for a few minutes, asking questions that none answered and, exasperated beyond belief, slammed out of the house. Saddling his horse, he rode off across the hills.

"What are we going to do?" Liz asked nobody in particular, "Oh my God, what *are* we going to do?"

Betty sagged onto her chair and put her face down onto her arms on the table top. Not only was she no longer a virgin, she was pregnant with her own father's child.

"We've got to get rid of it," Liz said suddenly, "I'll go to see old Martha, she'll know what to do."

"No, Mam," Betty said, her voice muffled. "Don't do that. I couldn't stand it. She's killed two girls already. I don't want to be the third."

"We must find a way, we must find a way," Liz muttered as she started pacing the kitchen.

Betty looked up, her face set. "I'm going to have this child, Mam. Nobody will ever marry me now, so I might as well have something to love."

"Yet it might be a monster. You know what they say about incest," Liz said, her voice shaking.

"Yet it might be lovely, Mam. Look at those Mulligan kids, every last one of them sired by the father on his daughters they say, and they're fine, lovely kids, faces like angels. No, I've decided, I'll have this child. It's another punishment against me, but I'll serve my penance."

"Penance for what?" Liz asked astounded, Betty had always been such a good girl.

"Penance for my sins, my sins of pride, my sins of vanity. I almost let Jeth have me once. I didn't, but I nearly did, so God knew what I was thinking."

Liz wrung her hands, feeling useless in this situation. "Oh, child, this is silly talk. Every lass feels like that when she's with a lad she likes. You didn't do anything and God would have been pleased."

"Aye, maybe, but I must pay penance for what I did to father, too. I *am* going to have this child."

Liz felt broken hearted about the baby, a bastard, from her own husband. Could she bear to see it knowing how Betty had conceived it? She looked at the distant hills and brooded. Maybe God was punishing her because she had wished Jake dead . . . but they all had.

Life became unpleasant for Jenny, who figured things would revert to normal once she returned home. Now her father refused to let her out of the house without a chaperone, the servants and her mother closely watched her every move. Miserable and dying of love for Clifford, she refused to eat.

Nothing she tried affected her father: not her silences, tantrums, fasting, destruction of books or possessions, all were for naught. Her father observed her actions with barely concealed amusement. How horrible he was. To think her own father who she loved dearly, could be so cruel. When she sobbed and cursed him to his face, all he did was laugh, saying she would soon get over her schoolgirl crush, soon realize he was right. Surely she knew he had her best interests at heart?

She would never accept his edicts, she decided. What did he know of love. He had been married to her mother through an arrangement? Surely no love existed between them.

How she yearned for Clifford, for the touch of his hands, his kiss, his caress. She pined so much that she became pale and unhealthy looking. Each morning when she woke and before she had taken two steps, she felt like vomiting. This illness, she knew, was a result of her father's orders, he was killing her for love of Clifford. Surely father would have to let her see him.

"Mother, I am sick," she announced with a great deal of satisfaction. "If you won't allow me to visit Clifford, I don't know what will happen to me. I'll probably die."

Eliza looked up from her sewing. "Don't talk such rubbish, Jennifer. You will not die and are in the best of health. In fact your father was only mentioning that your fasting has given your figure a svelte look as the puppy fat melts away and the bones of your face are more pronounced." Eliza felt unwilling to cater to Jenny since Michael vented the worst of his anger on her.

"Mamma, I was sick this morning. Ask Susan." Susan was the maid they shared.

"Did I hear you right? You were physically sick?"

"Yes, mother, Susan held my head."

"My God." Eliza sank onto a chair, her hands to her mouth. It couldn't be, surely it could not be. "I'll send for Doctor Matthews right away." She pulled on the bell rope and summoned Jane the parlour maid.

Jenny watched delightedly. Now they would have to let her see her love because the doctor could confirm she was dying of a broken heart.

"Yes, madam?"

"Jane, send someone to fetch Dr. Matthews immediately. Miss Jennifer is ill."

Jane eyed the smirking Jenny, who was enjoying being the centre of attention. Pregnant by the look of it, Jane thought, her royal highness was pregnant. Jane knew from experience, having four sisters, all of whom had fallen for smooth talking chaps.

She bustled out of the room, heading for the kitchen, her cloak, and Mrs. Higgins, the cook who loved to gossip about the family.

Jenny sat on the window seat, glad to have someone listen to her for once, glad her body had revolted against this cruel confinement to town, even if it were for something as silly as an upset stomach. For such a long time everyone had ignored her, apart from Father's orders about sitting up straight, walking properly, using her manners, that and mother's repetition of his words, ad infinitum. They never spoke to her other than to give orders. Turning to glance into the room, she noticed her mother regarding her strangely. Well, at least mother was paying her attention at long last.

Eliza needed to know if her suspicions were correct. "Tell me, how long have you felt like this, Jenny? Did it just start?"

"I thought I was sickening for something last week, Mamma, and I felt so tired. Anyway, I didn't get the cold I was expecting. Now the nausea comes and goes, although today it was horrible. I felt like my stomach was going to come up."

It sounded like pregnancy but she must wait for the doctor's verdict. "We'll see what Dr. Matthews has to say, Jenny. It could well be a touch of food poisoning."

Due to lack of proper hygiene, food poisoning was commonplace. Shops did not store foodstuffs in cold cellars, but left them displayed on store shelves during the hottest weather. Butter, milk and meats often were on the turn when purchased and if left in a pantry, quickly spoiled. The average family, even of the higher classes, often came down with some kind of stomach trouble. Pots and pans, of steel or untreated iron contributed to stomach upsets, not to mention casserole dishes and basins made from clay painted with lead based paints. So food poisoning was a way of life for many. Eliza often thanked the inconvenience of it since diarrhea kept her slim.

She prayed it was the case with Jenny, but had a terrible feeling Jenny had lain more than once with the farmer. She clasped her hands tightly, imagining the trouble ahead. What would Michael say? She was tired of listening to his diatribe about her being the cause of his pure young daughter's downfall. Though then, they had thought she was only seeing the young man. How was Richard Waithe going to like damaged goods, he had asked her? That was when Michael thought Jenny's only sin was in kissing the youth. Now he would be murderous.

"Jenny, maybe you should go to your room and change into a house robe. The Doctor will want to examine you."

Jenny shook her head. "He can do it while I wear my clothes. You know Father wouldn't want a man touching me."

"This is a professional man, a doctor, and your father didn't mean the doctor," Eliza said sharply. Jenny had obviously shown no such reticence with the farmer's boy.

Jenny tossed her head. "A tonic will cure what ails me. I'll wait here for him."

"Very well." Eliza felt apprehensive. If it were only so, if a tonic could fix it, she would cheer aloud.

Eliza realized Jenny's innocence was her own fault since she had never spoken to her about sex. Eliza, because she found it embarrassing, and her husband because he said it was a woman's job. Now she was reaping the consequences of her oversight. It had never occurred to her how fast Jenny was maturing. She always treated her like a child, with her resulting ingenuousness. Eliza had thought when Richard Waithe married her innocent young daughter, he would explain sex to her, like Michael had to her on her own honeymoon. Her father, the vicar, would have no mention of sex whatever.

She stared at the window seeing nothing, her mind running in ever decreasing circles, seeking a solution to an, as yet, unconfirmed problem. Michael would be livid and it was all her fault, her fault for not talking to the girl, her fault for not being vigilant. Her stomach cramped with nerves and her hands shook.

Where was the doctor? What was taking him so long? The longer it took, the longer it took to hear the bad news, and she wanted it over quickly.

"Jenny, why don't you go upstairs and change into something loose?" she asked again, "I'm sure the doctor will want to examine you properly, without your corset." Her voice was cold, as cold as the finger of fear touching her heart.

"Oh, Mother, do stop fussing. It's only a cold or something. He will only listen to my chest, take my temperature and give me a tonic like he always does." She poked among the chocolates in the crystal dish and bit into a caramel cream.

Eliza shook her head, when Jenny had decided something she stuck to it. "All right, but I still think you should be resting."

Jenny swung from the window, her mouth filled with chocolate, and glared at her mother. "Please, mother, don't treat me as if I were only four years old. I feel well now and am hungry. I'll go to the kitchen and get myself a piece of pie or cake. I didn't eat anything at breakfast."

Eliza's heart sank even further at this revelation.

CHAPTER TWELVE

"What?" Michael roared. "What did you say?"

Eliza trembled with fear. His rage was all consuming and exactly what she had expected, but one never could prepare for Michael's rages.

With lowered eyes and white face, she said quietly, "Dr. Matthews said she is pregnant. He is positive. Jennifer has no idea, of course."

"That blasted farmer is responsible." He stood in front of the fire and glared at her through the overmantel mirror. "She will not stay under this roof for longer than it takes her to pack." He whipped around, and she cringed. "Send her to a home until the birth, have the child adopted. The slut is no longer my daughter." He swung away from her again and faced the window, hands clenched behind his back.

Michael felt like hitting Eliza, stupid woman that she was, for if it was not for her laxity, his daughter would still be pure and undefiled. Retribution could wait, for now he must get the girl away from the house, send her to a place where her shame could not reflect on the family, where nobody knew her.

Richard Waithe, what would *he* say? Michael decided to tell Richard that he had sent Jennifer to a finishing school. Surely Richard would be delighted to hear they were schooling his future wife in the niceties of society.

He swung back to face his wife. Eliza cowered in the chair, as if waiting his fist. So should she be wary of him, he thought, she deserved everything that was coming to her. His method of teaching her a lesson was to use force. To his way of thinking, she was the type who never learned anything unless he pounded it into her. Once he had dealt with Jennifer, time enough remained to show Eliza his displeasure.

"What else did Dr. Matthews say? He is aware that this is confidential, I hope?" He stood in front of her now, glaring down.

"All doctors are sworn to secrecy, you know that," Eliza said quietly, "Anyway, who among our friends would even suspect such a thing? She has never been alone with any young man in town."

"Exactly, and neither should she have been left alone when at your sister's house. You will pay for this, Eliza." Her blood ran cold and she shuddered. "No, not now, but you will pay. Go and pack her things. I will seek advice from an associate of mine who knows a man whose daughter fell to the same fate."

As she was leaving, she turned back. "Isn't that dangerous, Michael? Asking such questions might lead to suspicions when it is discovered Jennifer is no longer at home. Why don't you consult Dr. Matthews?"

"Good point." He nodded. For once she spoke sense. "Yes, I will see the doctor. You get her packed, and pack an overnight bag for yourself, for I doubt that dropping her on the doorstep will be easy. You may have to stay until they have her settled and you arrange for the payment."

"Will you not accompany us?" Eliza asked, hoping against hope.

"No, I will not. I have business meetings tomorrow and a board meeting the next day. I will, of course, tell Jennifer what is happening."

Eliza slowly went up the stairs. How was she going to explain the packing to Jenny? Well, she wouldn't. Michael could tell her.

"Are we going on holiday, Mamma? Where are we going?" Jenny, filled with excitement, clapped her hands with delight.

"Ask your father when we go downstairs. Right now he wants your things packed. Call Susan in to help, would you please?"

Susan bustled in and took charge of everything. As she worked, a happy Jenny helping, Eliza went to her room to pack an overnight bag.

Michael spoke to his daughter in the parlour. He pulled no punches, explained nothing of her condition, or how she got that way, but bluntly told her she was a disgrace to the family name.

"You have sunk so low in my opinion that I want nothing more to do with you. You will go to the home until the child is born, when it will be set out for adoption."

Jenny stood white and shaken. She did not want a baby. How had this happened? Was it from kissing or the other thing? From the books Phoebe loaned her she knew a few details, although she had not known that pregnancy could happen from one encounter. Still, they had done it several times.

Her heart thumped against her ribs, she must tell Clifford. She did not know how she could get word to him. Nevertheless, she must tell him so they could marry, and the sooner the better.

"Father, you must tell Clifford," she said through her tears. "He will marry me immediately, then everything will be all right."

"I will never tell that lout. Do you understand me, Jennifer? I'll not allow that illiterate farmer to come within a mile of you. I promised you to Richard Waithe, as well you know."

"I'll never marry that old man, never ever," she spat, showering him with hate for his choice.

Michael drew himself up, arms behind his back, his head raised, showing his position of power. "You'll marry whomever I choose, Jennifer. Put this uncouth idiot out of your mind forever. You have shamed our name, and yet you have the gall to tell me what you will and will not do? I think not, my dear, not while I am head of this household. Your mother will take you to the home I have chosen, where you will stay until the child is born. Maybe you'll have learned a lesson by the time I allow you to return. That you would bring shame onto our good name in this fashion is beyond comprehension."

Eliza stood to one side as this exchange took place, aware Michael would deal her with far more severely. Moving forward, she took Jenny's hand. "Come along, Jennifer, we must be going. Sara and Susan have brought down your things and the coach will be here shortly. Go to the kitchen and say your goodbyes."

Jennifer broke into a fresh spate of tears. "I don't want to go, I don't want to go." She sprang forward and clung to her father. "Please, father, don't send me away. I beg you to let me stay. Please, please!"

Michael firmly put her way from him. Since he was angry beyond belief, her usual methods of getting her own way would not help her this time. Her hysteria did not move him.

"Say goodbye to Martha and the others and tell them you are going on a short holiday," he said sternly. "You must be on your way if you are to arrive before midnight."

Jenny stood stock still, shocked into silence, and gazed at her father, her white face awash with tears. That he could do this to her hardened her heart against him. This was worse than knowing that he planned to marry her off to a fat old man.

With a lowered voice, a voice filled with hate, she hissed. "You send me away, father, and I'll never speak to you again. I will never marry Richard Waithe, and I'll hate you for the rest of my life." She swung around to face her mother. "As for you, Mamma, why do you not defend me? Why do you let him do whatever he pleases with my life? I hate the both of you!" Blundering out of the room, she ran down the hall to the kitchen.

While the home in Southport looked reasonable from the outside, the interior was most unsatisfactory. Even Eliza found it hard to believe anyone could relax in such a place.

The large house, once the home of an industrialist, though once luxurious, now looked austere. Mismatched furniture stood around looking lost in the huge rooms, as though the owners had never quite finished moving into them. Several young women, in various stages of pregnancy, sat in the lounge. All stared rudely at the newcomers.

Eliza immediately noticed from their clothing that they were not upper class young ladies and sounded barely educated. She had thought Jenny would be among her own peers, young ladies of good homes.

The matron, a fat woman of dubious training, showed them around. On the lower floor were the lounge, a dining room, the kitchen, a scullery and a wash house. Over all hung the stench of disinfectant that burned the inside her nostrils and made her eyes water.

On the second floor were furnished bedrooms with single beds: each room had a least two or more. The third floor housed the matron's living quarters and bedrooms available for visiting parents. These were more acceptable, although not to Eliza's usual standards.

"We find that having a room mate helps the youngsters," the matron confided as she showed her the room Jenny would share. "They like to know someone is at hand if anything should go wrong. Young girls have strange fancies, as you know, and company eases the little spots of bother that are basically nothing to worry about."

Eliza looked at the room where her daughter would live for another seven and a half months. It held two single beds, two chests of drawers and a dressing table with a cracked mirror. The floor was of bare boards, though a small hooked rug lay between the beds. The view from the barred windows was of the river estuary - presently mud flats as the tide was out. A strong odour of rotting sewage drifted from the partially opened window. It was comfortless. She knew Jenny would hate it.

Jenny looked at the sparsely furnished room. "I'm not staying here, mother." She shuddered theatrically. "Take me home at once."

"Now, now, Miss Bradley," The matron said, having heard it all before. "You'll be comfortable here. You'll like your room mate. She's from an affluent family, so you won't lack for treats. The other girls call her 'the princess,' and she's exceptionally classy."

"I don't care who she is. I'll not stay in this dump." Jenny grabbed her mother's arm and started pulling at her. "Take me home!"

Matron smiled knowingly. "Would you like to stay here tonight, Mrs. Bradley, until we get her settled? A good night's sleep and she'll see things differently."

Jenny snorted. "Who could sleep in this place? It's horrible and it stinks. To think my father is paying for this . . . this prison." Jenny flounced out of the room and they could hear her feet pounding down the staircase.

"Jenny?" Eliza moved to the door, alarmed that Jenny might run out of the house.

The matron had witnessed the same scene a thousand times. "Now, Mrs. Bradley, don't you worry, she can't get out. We have special locks on every ground floor door and window. This place is always a shock to a well-raised young lady. We find a lot of our little mothers try to run back home. It'll be a week or two before she settles down, but rest assured until then we'll keep a careful watch on her."

Eliza sighed. This place was not as she expected, but what *had* she expected? A palace? A home away from home? This was probably better than most such homes for the price, for although it was Spartan, at least it was clean. She suspected Michael had asked for the address of the cheapest place. Why, he would have argued, why should he spend money on the mistakes of a stupid girl, a girl who had dishonoured his name?

As she rode home on the train the next day, Eliza sat in a third class carriage and tried to reconcile herself to Jenny's future life. It was incarceration, as though they had locked her in a prison, no matter what they called it. To her dismay, the home had no servants, only the matron and four warders they called nurses. To keep the house running, they employed the girls during daytime hours. They did the cleaning, cooking and washing. El;iza left for home before Jenny found out about that.

Eliza mused on the injustice of it, knowing if it had been left to her, she would have kept Jenny at home, secluded, confined to the house, but at least at home. She would be hidden from visitors, remain isolated until the birth, when the midwife would take the child. That surely was the more humane way, not committing her to some Borstal as if she were a criminal.

The fact they expect her to work her stay will shock her terribly, Adele thought, because all her life she's been pampered by servants. She has no idea about laundry, or cooking, knows nothing of cleaning other than to watch and criticize. Poor Jenny is going to find her stay at The Lilacs a shattering experience: and yet it well could be that the discipline and surroundings may be the making of her.

How she dreaded the upcoming confrontation with Michael. Everything would be her fault, while he would be blameless. All she could do was pray he did not use his fists again.

CHAPTER THIRTEEN

As her pregnancy advanced, Clifford noticed his sister Betty's face growing rounder. He thought she looked prettier.

Betty remained silent as ever on the subject of her lover. Although Clifford asked around between his neighbours and acquaintances, it did not appear the father of the child was anyone they knew. No matter how often he asked her, she walked away, saying she would never tell, that it was none of his business.

"Anyway it was my fault as much as his, you know. Don't keep on asking me, Clifford, I won't tell you."

Neither Mam nor Joyce would discuss it. He figured they knew who the father was, but were reluctant to tell him in case they shamed Betty.

The house had changed a great deal since that terrible day when his father became lost in the caves. To Clifford it was a tangible feeling, something nasty imbued in the atmosphere of the house. Joyce had developed a habit of continually looking over her shoulder as she worked, as if she were scared of something or somebody, and no longer did she sing as she laboured. Her song mangling had always been a cause of laughter in the house as Joyce couldn't carry a tune in a bucket, but she sang her heart out as she did her chores. Now she was quiet and sullen.

The sisters discussed the curse, blaming it for all their misfortunes. He overheard them and no matter how he explained a curse was a figment of their imagination and nothing bad could possibly happen, they would not have it. Everything that went wrong, from soured milk to a sluggish fire, they blamed on the gypsy.

Clifford noticed how both girls had changed since the episode of the cave, how it had affected their minds. On the other hand, his mother sang as she worked, and he often wondered why she had never cried for his father. Not one tear had Liz shed, yet when the man had been sick in his head, she still loved and cared for him. Nevertheless, she didn't seem to care about his loss.

Though Clifford had regarded his father with much animosity, thinking him unreliable in character and quick to find fault, he was, after all, his father. He did worry about him and often dreamed about his father wandering around the labyrinth caves, scared and alone. At weekends he searched the caves, going further and further into the interior, using two or three lanterns before he came into the light of day. Spelunkers were often there and they searched with him. They found nothing of his father, no clue which way he had gone, not even a footprint.

Clifford became convinced the caves must have more than one exit. One weekend he spent five hours working his way though the caverns toward a draft of fresh air, thinking to find another exit, but when he reached the place where the wind howled, it was a narrow fissure that ran up through the cave ceiling, no way for a human to move.

Meanwhile he had the farm to run and hired on another helper, a man named Arthur Coulter. Arthur and he made a good team, working the far uncultivated fields while the other men concentrated on the ones already under hay or grain. A young lad from the workhouse worked the farmyard area, tending the pigs, hens and geese, the orchard and the farm garden. Betty and Joyce looked after the dairy and the eggs while his mother did the canning, pickling and the girls helped her with the housework.

Aye, if things continued as they were he stood to make a tidy profit this year. He worked sometimes eighteen hours a day. Time enough for resting when the weather turned inclement.

Twice he rode over to Mayhurst Farm on errands that were nothing more than excuses to discover Jenny's whereabouts. He still pictured her lovely face, and often relived the times when he made love to her, and her a virgin.

Albert's fortunes, Cliff saw, were on the rise, his new men had tidied the place and cultivated more fields. It appeared Albert could also make a profit in the next year, and both thanked God for the good weather.

Jenny's departure was so sudden, he hadn't even said goodbye. Often during his long days he thought about her and, while not prepared to marry anyone, not even Jenny, he thought he probably loved her. It became important for him to get her town address so he could write.

The last time he called, he asked Mrs. Stockton where the Bradleys lived.

"Sorry, I don't know Clifford." She looked guilty and he knew she lied, for hadn't Adele written and asked her sister to her aid?

"Why did they leave so suddenly?"

"I have no idea why their departure was so abrupt. Mr. Bradley came with a hired coach to take them back."

He felt a flare of anger. So Jenny had used him and cast him off, had she? Well, that was the last time she could make a monkey of him. His rage helped heal the wounds and he no longer hankered after her, firmly pushed her out of his mind and set his eye on the young daughter of a neighbouring farmer.

Mary Baxter was a lovely young woman. Silly and headstrong at eighteen, but farm born and bred, she would make a good wife. Giving up the futile search for his Dad and forgetting Jenny, he began courting Mary.

"I see our Clifford has big eyes for Mary Baxter," Liz said one afternoon.

Betty and Joyce remained quiet on the subject, well aware that if he married her, Mary would become the new mistress of the house, and her younger than them both They worried in case she wanted to move them out of their home.

Betty, now ungainly, her huge stomach getting in the way of many of her chores, relegated herself to kitchen work while Liz and Joyce made the butter and cheese, collected eggs and took their produce to market each Friday. Betty never left the farm for any reason.

On the Sunday when Clifford brought Mary over to the farm for tea, they all felt anxious. Betty, reluctant for anyone to see her, said she preferred to stay in the bedroom, but they wouldn't allow it, saying she was part of the family and soon the child would be another family member. Better that Mary saw what faced her if she married Clifford.

"This is my mother," Clifford said proudly as Mary giggled shyly at meeting the family. "This is my sister Joyce."

Mary shook hands with both, "How do?" she said broadly.

"My sister Betty, she's a widow," he said by way of explanation, for Betty looked like she might pop at any second. As she put out her hand, the baby kicked and she gasped.

"Oh, you poor thing. When's it due?" Mary asked, looking sympathetic.

"Soon," Betty said, glaring at Clifford.

Liz glanced at Clifford with delight, that was a good reason for the pregnancy and she wondered why they had not thought of it earlier. Yes, they could say Betty had been married in Manchester or somewhere like that, and her husband, a sailor, was lost at sea. The idea perked her up and she smiled at Mary, taking her hands and welcoming her to their home.

She's nice, is Cliff's Mam, Mary thought. His sisters are a nuisance. Neither of them like me. I can tell by the way they look at me. That Joyce is uppity, looks at me as though I'm something the cat dragged in, and the pregnant one, she's miserable with it. Never smiles or speaks from what I can see.

She turned to look at her intended, thinking Clifford very much the master in the house, seeing how they all bowed to his wishes. Aye, I could like it here and them girls will soon wed and leave. His mother is nice and would be a help to me when we marry.

Clifford showed her around the farm, pointing out with pride the wellpopulated pigsties, the new boar in his own pen, the reconstructed barn, the flocks of sheep and cows dotting the hillside. He had assumed ownership, he told her, since they lost his father.

"You've got guinea hens," she said, shooing them with her skirt so they ran startled in all directions. "I like guinea hens but my Da won't 'ave 'um. Sez they're useless for eating' and no good at laying, only pecking and making a din."

Clifford squeezed her hand. "Mam likes them, she was the one that bought them. I think they're special myself. Lovely plumage."

He listened to Mary chattering about her Da's farm and realized she was practically uneducated. He wondered if she could read or write, but decided not to ask since it would not take long to discover. It would not matter to his way of thinking but left her with little in the way of intelligence. She was a grand lass, though, he knew and he thought he loved her as much as he could love any woman.

Not like he loved Jenny, though, he thought ruefully. Jenny was special, she had made his blood sing. His love for Mary was more of familiarity, of comfort and ease: he could kiss her and touch her body and still walk away from her. With Jenny the longing for closeness had been a madness in him. Maybe with time he would feel the same about Mary, though he doubted it.

At tea, Mary was all nervous giggles. Betty and Joyce stared openly. They looked at each other with raised eyebrows, especially when Clifford was acting silly, and him a grown man.

"Black pudding on toast, that's my favourite," she was saying, smacking her lips. "My Da luvs black puddings. We make um, mi Mam and me whenever he slaughters. We've got'um hanging up like Chrissmus decorations in our howse."

Liz smiled. At least from what she had said Mary knew all about cooking. While black, or blood, pudding was not one of Liz's favourites, she was glad to know the girl was well schooled in catering for a family.

"I like muck and duffins too," Mary gabbled. She was jittery, Liz knew.

"Do you mean savoury duck and muffins?" Clifford had to smile, knowing she was striving to make them like her. Mary had no edge to her, none at all, being down to earth in all things.

"Aye, savoury duck. My new Mam, my Da remarried tha knows, makes a grand job of that. Mind you, it takes a lot of bones to get the gelatine, but she's good at boiling out marra. Never a slaughter goes by that she doesn't put up a big dish of savoury duck."

Farm wives made savoury duck from odd bits of meat, chicken, lamb, pork, beef cooked and set in gelatin. Not they ever wasted one scrap of edible meat on a farm. Why they called it savoury duck was anybody's guess, but it tasted delicious on hot toast or muffins.

"My Da loves tripe, an all. My new Mam pickles a lot of it. He'll even eat it for his breakfast, he will. Oh aye, my Da is a right one, he is. He's a hard worker, mind, and our farm makes a good living for us."

Clifford picked up the slack whenever she stopped talking long enough to eat. His sisters sat silent and their speculative eyeing of Mary didn't exactly warm his heart. His Mam didn't speak much either, though she smiled and patted Mary's hand from time to time. He could see his mother approved of Mary.

"Well, we'd better be off for our walk. Time to head you home, Mary," Clifford said as he stood, rubbing his full stomach. It was a long time since the Wright's had entertained and today his mother had outdone herself.

They'd had bacon and egg pie, slices of home cured ham, salad from their own garden, homemade Cheddar and a gooseberry and blackberry pie with cream. Aye, it had been a grand feast and Mary had eaten far more than a young lady should.

"She eats like a pig!" Betty said as she helped clear the table. "Did you see the way she was cramming it in? When she stopped to take a breath, she practically cleared her plate. Seconds and thirds she had, too. What's the matter with our Cliff?"

Liz smiled. Mary was still growing. By the looks of her reddened and rough hands, she worked hard on the farm and she hadn't an ounce of fat on her.

"Mary's still a growing girl. Think back to when you were her age, our Betty, eh? We thought you were hollow inside, we did."

"Yes, but she's so uncouth," Joyce had to get her licks in as well. "Did you hear the way she speaks? Didn't she ever go to school?"

Liz threw up her hands. "Now girls, let's stop this, shall we? She's a nice girl and if she talks like that, it's because she was brought up in a house full of men and they all talk that way. Her real Mam died when she was ten, so what do you expect? Her dad never remarried until two years past."

"I don't care. I don't like her," Betty snorted. "Our Cliff could do better than her."

"I think Clifford loves Mary and he'll marry her soon," Liz said, wondering what would happen when Mary moved into the farm house.

"She's not living here, that's for sure. I'll see to that," Joyce said, tossing down the dish towel and walking out the back door.

"Oh my, *she's* going to get a shock, then," Betty said, watching through the window as her sister climbed on the pigsty wall. "If Mary does come here, and I expect she will, would she want us here? Me and Joyce, I mean, and what about the baby?"

"Now Betty, it's early days yet. Mary might not want to marry him after seeing her future in-laws. Neither of you was nice to her, were you? I saw you both sniggering at her, rolling your eyes and nudging each other, and don't think she didn't notice that."

"I don't care, Mam, I've got other things on my mind than our Cliff's love life. In fact I think my time has come." She plopped down onto the settle and put her hands under her huge stomach. "It hurts like a cramp now. My back doesn't half ache. Is that it?"

"Oh, Betty, come on we'd better get you upstairs. That's how it always started with me."

Liz put her hands under Betty's armpits and hauled her to her feet.

As they walked slowly across the kitchen Betty's water broke and she gasped, "Ooh, hey, I've peed my pants."

"That's the water breaking. Come on now, upstairs with you. I'll send Joyce for Mrs. Moore. You never know with a first child, it could be hours or days, or then again, a short while."

CHAPTER FOURTEEN

Betty's child was a boy, a well formed, sturdy, black haired boy. If his lungs were anything to go by, the entire county would know of his arrival, because from taking his first breath he never stopped screaming.

Betty loved him for all his caterwauling. He clung to her from the start and didn't want to leave her breast. She held him as long as she could because once she put him down, he set up such a wailing that drove the cat outdoors to seek peace.

Joyce was overjoyed with the baby. "He's lovely, Betty, absolutely lovely, and I was worried that he'd look like the devil, have horns and a tail. I mean, who knows what that curse on us will do?"

"Stop that, Joyce," Liz said, taking the child from her. "I'll have no more talk of the curse. That finished when your father died."

Joyce looked as if she were going to say something, but when Betty shook her head slightly, she said nothing. Now was not the time for an argument.

As Betty and Liz admired the baby, they talked about a name. Liz contended it was bad luck to choose names before the birth, for giving an unborn a name meant that if you lost the child it made it that much harder. Nor had they bought much in the way of baby clothes.

Mrs. Moore, the midwife, brought them a bag of used baby things. The local women shared baby clothes because babies grew out of them so quickly. Once the child outgrew this assortment, they would return them to Mrs. Moore who put them in the bag for her next lying in.

"He needs a strong name, 'cos he's going to be a strong lad," Joyce said, admiring the way he hung onto her little finger. "He's already got some strength in him, by gosh."

"Samuel maybe," Betty suggested. "Like Samson but more acceptable. Sam is a strong name. Samuel Wright, Sam Wright," she tested it. "How does that sound?"

"What about Henry as a second name?" Liz suggested, "The name of kings, that is, and the way he carries on he thinks he's a bloody king. Scryking for nothing all the time." She smiled as he goggled toothlessly up at her.

Clifford did not think much of the baby. It was always crying, always sicking up, always smelly, and took too much of everybody's time. He looked at him, his new nephew, and knew this child would rule the roost if given the slightest leeway. What would Mary think of the baby, he wondered?

This Sunday she was to come over for the afternoon, and already he and Betty had quarrelled over the child. Clifford wanted her to take the baby out for a walk so that it wouldn't be constantly crying while Mary visited, but Betty essentially told him to go boil his head. They were not speaking to each other.

CHAPTER FIFTEEN

While Jenny felt miserable, wretched and disconsolate, her room mate was exactly the opposite. This did little to raise Jenny's mood, it made her more miserable.

While Matilda eagerly awaited the arrival of her child, though her parents had requested immediate adoption, she constantly chattered about her lover, Philip. She rhapsodized on her feelings of love for him: how he was waiting for her: how, when she got out of this horrid place, they would discover where they had sent the baby. Then they planned to elope to Gretna Green, get married and take back their child. She bubbled over with joy, and miserable Jenny could have killed her.

Even when it came to the community chores, Matilda worked hard, saying she needed to learn because once they married, they could not afford to hire servants. She must learn how to do everything, simply everything and she sang merrily while doing the most menial of tasks.

Jenny hated every second of the day. At seven they were forced out of bed to wash and dress for breakfast. The matron personally made the breakfast porridge, and watched from the top of the table while they ate. The 'nurses', Jenny noticed, ate bacon or ham and eggs, sometimes kippers, while the inmates ate the tasteless, salt and sugar free porridge with plain milk and no cream.

Breakfast finished, those whose names were on the kitchen duty roster started work: washing breakfast dishes and preparing luncheon.

Two girls were the day's bakers and made bread and rolls, pies and cakes. Two worked on vegetable preparation, one on meat. A 'nurse,' who never lifted a hand to help, supervised this activity. The others were set to clean the rooms, dust, wash windows and floors.

Both Monday and Tuesday were days for washing. The laundry in the low ceilinged windowless basement was always hot and humid. They washed sheets, pillow cases, towels and other household items first, after which they washed the inmate's clothing and also the staff uniforms. Ironing they did every day of the week, and it was never completely finished before the next week came around.

After lunch, the young women lay on their beds for an hour's rest. Then they went out for a walk along the front for exercise, rain or shine. Jenny often wondered what regular people thought when the crocodile of expectant girls, clad in all enveloping capes, walked two by two down the front. Surely no one could mistake them for a school outing as Matron and the 'nurses' accompanied them, guarding and watching. All liked their daily walk as it was the only time they got any fresh air.

After walking, it was time for knitting and sewing where they all helped make baby things, tiny vests, jackets, bonnets and mittens. After afternoon tea, they wrote letters which they passed to Matron who censored them before sealing the envelopes. They could not mention their chores or living conditions, so it was all personal trivia. How soul destroying Jenny found it because she longed to write to Clifford, care of Mayhurst Farm, wanted to tell him she was having their child, beg him to come and take her away.

As they sewed, they listened as either Matron or a nurse read from an uplifting volume, usually boring. All sighed constantly, wishing the reader would shut up and allow them to talk amongst themselves. They didn't get much chance to talk to each other. Jenny surmised this was because a group of girls, combining ideas, could make good an escape. She could only talk to Matilda, and Matilda's only topics of conversation were Philip and their future.

Four more months to go, how could she stand it? How could she go through the long miserable days with only Matilda's inane chatter for company? Each day when out walking, she searched for some way to escape, some way of creating a diversion to draw attention away from herself. Her heart still yearned for Clifford, the handsome man who had attained even more qualities since their separation.

With Matron at the back and the nurses, one to each side and one at the front as they walked, escape seemed impossible as their warders were so vigilant. Her fellow inmates she personally thought brainless as none ever tried to escape. No one heard whispered stories of girls who had fled. She could tell by the other's common accents that they had little education, and when listening to their rough dialects, thanked God for Matilda. Never could she have shared room with a'moron' as she privately called them.

Once a week Matilda's wealthy family brought her a hamper and this she unselfishly shared with Jenny. They ate cakes and biscuits, sometimes had fortified wine, though more often lemonade and soft drinks, toffees and chocolates. Matilda shared only with Jenny, and the others, jealous and cowed at Matilda's obvious wealth, looked down their noses at the two. This suited Jenny down to the ground. "Riff-raff," she said to Matilda, "All so plebeian, so ill bred."

One afternoon Matron came into the lounge where they sat sewing and clapped her hands for attention.

"Young ladies, attention please! Today His Worship the Mayor and his lady wife are inspecting us. I expect you to be o n your best behaviour. Do not speak to His Worship unless he speaks to you first. You must not bow or curtsy. You will remain seated at all times."

"Yes, Matron," they chorused looking at each other in wonder. The home never allowed people other than parents inside the horrible place. The chimney sweep came, as did painters when Matron decided a room needed refurbishment, but on those occasions they were either shut away in their rooms, or taken to walk along the front.

Jenny recognized this as an opportunity for escape. It meant all manner of disturbances, and if she knew anything about Matron and the nurses they would be dancing attendance on His Worship. It would create the diversion for which she had hoped.

"Matilda, could you come upstairs for a moment?" she said quietly.

"Why?"

"Don't ask, just come."

They went quickly upstairs before Matron saw them, and went quickly into their room.

"What is it, Jenny?"

Jenny took her savings from the handkerchief tidy at the back of the drawer and put the money in her pocket, feeling a surge of excitement.

"This, Matilda, is our chance to escape," she said smiling widely.

"What is?"

"This visit by the Mayor. You can bet there'll be his aide and her lady in waiting, or whatever they call the hangers on, and a score of others milling about. We can escape while His Honour is doing the honours!"

"Yet how? The doors have special locks." Matilda did not want to escape. She shook her head. "Count me out, Jenny. My Philip knows I'm here, I've seen him watching as we took our walk, and he waved to me. I told you that."

Jenny screwed up her face with disgust. "Look, Matilda, I *can't* stay here any longer. If you want to stay, all right, but you have to help me get away."

"Where will you go? Have you any money?"

"I have the twenty pounds I took from my money box before my mother brought me here. I will go to Clifford. He will look after me."

"What do you want me to do?" Matilda asked uncertainly, as the door opened and a nurse stood looking in like an avenging angel.

"What are you two doing in the room at this time of day? Is one of you not feeling well?"

Both shook their heads. "No, nurse," Matilda said, "We wanted to fetch a hanky from my drawer. I think I am getting a cold," She shook a tiny lace edged scrap and held it to her nose.

"That doesn't take two. Come along, I'll have to report this to Matron. You know the rules."

Standing to one side, she saw them out and down the stairs, then went back into the room and looked around. Everything was in order. Even the drawers looked neat and tidy.

At two o'clock His Worship, Mayor Brackman, and his lady wife arrived in a large carriage drawn by four grey horses. Attending them were other carriages of assorted councillors and wives, along with minor officials. Local businessmen tagged along in their own conveyances.

By this time Matron, wearing her best navy blue uniform with a starched white hat trimmed with lace like a coronet, had the girls about their business. Under the watchful eye of the nurses, who now wore best white with real nurse caps, the group in the lounge worked on their needlework. In the dining room, the less noticeably pregnant kitchen workers set out a buffet meal for those of the party who felt need of sustenance. They set a sideboard with glasses and bottles of sherry.

Jenny felt a prickle of excitement. If they all came into the lounge, she could possibly make her way into the hall and be out the front door before anyone noticed. Surely the stragglers would ensure the door remained open. She felt in her pocket for the money, thinking it fortuitous that she'd had the foresight to fetch her savings. The money could pay her fare as far as Weatherly and there she could go to see Clifford. How delighted he was going to be, how happy she had come to him.

Clifford watched Mary as she fed the chickens, seeing the graceful the swing of her arm, the smallness of her waist. He had ridden over on a whim, ostensibly headed to the farrier to have the horse shod. While the family expected him back in two hours, the shoeing had only taken an hour.

"My mother is looking forward to your visit on Sunday, Mary," he said, as she scattered the last of the feed.

"Me too. I like your Mam. Not that I think too much of them sisters of yourn. They'd sour milk, they two."

"Aaw Mary, they're not always like that. Betty's pregnancy was getting them both down because Joyce had to do her work. It didn't half make Joyce mad, I can tell you."

"Aye, well, that's as maybe, but they din't have to look at *me* like that."

"Like what?" Clifford only saw what he wanted to see, knew nothing of body language or tone of voice.

"Bloody hell, Cliff, you're like most men. You never see anything unless it bothers you. Them sisters of yourn don't like me and make that plain."

"Hey, don't let that upset you, they don't count for much in the scheme of things."

Somewhat mollified, she asked, "How's the baby? Is he nice?"

"I suppose." He laughed. "He's a loud little bugger, if nothing else. Built like a navvy, he is. All muscle."

"His father must have been a big man, then. Din't she lose him early, though? Her husband, I mean," she said as she saw Clifford's puzzled expression. "A shame, her losing a new husband and her already in the family way. Did they have to get married?"

Clifford cursed himself for telling the lie. A lie always seemed to grow on itself, becoming more convoluted at each telling.

"Not that I know of, she was unlucky."

"What's her name now?" Mary asked as she stood swinging the feed basket in one hand.

"Betty, of course, what else would her name be?"

"Her *married* name, silly, what's her married name?"

A surge of fury ran through him. Damn and blast it, why had he felt it necessary to embroider his original lie? His mind rapidly searched through surnames. He did not dare pick a name that they knew hereabouts or that might start more talk. He knew Mary would tell everyone.

"Langford, that's her married name, Langford."

"Is his family from hereabouts?" Mary looked up at him, wondering why he was acting so strangely.

"No, from Liverpool."

"Liverpool? How did she meet him?"

"Look, Mary, let's drop the subject. Talk to my Mam about it. I want to ask you something. Shall we walk in the orchard?" if only they hadn't lied. When he got home, he must tell Mam what he had said. Knowing Mary, she would go on and on about Betty, and the baby, and the dead husband until she had gotten to the truth. Well, let his Mam sort it out. He wanted no more of it.

Half an hour later all thoughts of Betty Wright vanished from Mary's mind. She was to marry Clifford.

In the cluttered cosy kitchen of the farmhouse, the family gathered to offer their congratulations.

"Congratulations, lad, she'll mak thi a fine wife, even if I do say so mi'sen." Ernie, Mary's oldest brother shook Cliff's hand so hard that he thought it would drop off.

"Thanks, Ernie."

"Same from me, lad, mind you, we're going to miss her some'at rotten," Harold, her father, said. "She's a regular wonder around this house. Good job we've got Ernie's lass to look after us and I 'spect he'll wed right soon now that Mary's looked after."

"You'll wait until Ethel and me are wed afore you walk down the aisle, though, won't you?" Ernie said, sounding alarmed.

"Don't worry about that, Ernie," Clifford assured him. "Mary and I can wait until then. We only now got engaged. No point in rushing too fast, is there?"

"Not unless there's cause to, no," Harold said looking his daughter up and down.

"Aaw you, Dad! How could you!" Mary flung her apron over her face to hide her blushes.

Clifford laughed at her discomfort. "I've got to get back soon, before milking time. Cows don't understand if you're late."

Harold shook his hand. "Aye, well come over often now and we can have a crack and a smoke. Talk about the arrangements, what with her not having her real mother like, and her stepmother not being up on owt like this."

The stepmother, from what Clifford could see, was short on grey matter and spent her time dusting an already spotless fireplace. Old Harold must have married her for her company, not her wit.

Clifford rode home wondering if he had done the right thing. The fact that he was wondering made him think he had made a mistake. What about his plans to become a vet? What about his dreams? All gone for nothing now he had promised to wed Mary. She would want him at home, on the farm where she was happy.

Mary sang as she scoured the milk churns. Soon I'll be Mrs. Clifford Wright of Hillshead Farm. By, but that sounded grand, it did an' all. Mrs. Mary Wright, Mrs. Clifford Wright, Mrs. Wright of Hillshead Farm. Wait until my other brothers hear. They'll be dead jealous of me, going to my own farm, and that's more than any of them will have. This farm will go to Ernie once Da dies. Still, the other two could come to work for Clifford or stay with Da. My marriage will broaden their horizons.

She idly wondered about her other brothers, Mike and Jeff, as she worked. Both were in their twenties now, yet neither showed any signs of getting married, and if they were courting, they were keeping it a secret. She never knew them to go further afield than the closest market town, and that only once a week. Mind you, being younger sons did not leave them much to aim for, nothing in the way of land or property would come to them. Strange her Da didn't seem to think about things like that.

When Ernie inherited, what would Mike and Jeff do? Would they stay here for the rest of their lives working on someone else's land, staying for their keep and clothes? Da never paid them a penny that she knew of, and the farm was profitable now he had paid off the land taxes. She knew her Da had a bank account in Addisford as she had once gone with him.

As a woman she had the better chance because she could marry and move away, and she was going to move. Oh, not far, only as far as Hillshead Farm, but it was not this place.

The only dark cloud on her future that bothered her was a conversation she overheard at the market where she heard Joyce tell a woman that a Romany woman had put a curse on the family, that her father's mysterious disappearance was a result of the curse, how neither she nor Betty had felt comfortable since. A curse, she had thought? Surely no such things existed, but then hadn't Mr. Wright wandered off into the caves and disappeared? Clifford didn't contradict the story when she asked, although he said it was all poppycock. Nevertheless, the farm was prosperous and Clifford was handsome, so what else did she need?

If only her mother were still alive. How she missed having her mother to talk to, to tell of her uncertainty. She knew most engaged females felt this way, unsure of their promise, afraid they had made a mistake. How delighted Mam would be to hear she was to marry a farmer, and a well thought of one at that. Hillshead was one of the better run, profitable farms of the county and Clifford was talking about buying more land.

She clattered the clean churns into the cold room and went to fetch the first pails of warm milk.

CHAPTER SIXTEEN

Eliza gasped as she rose from the chair. Since Michael viciously beat her with a broom handle, her back throbbed with pain. He laid into her so badly that she'd bled internally and while the pain inside was terrible, she dared not see the doctor or Michael would have become even more furious.

From the day she came home without Jennifer, her life had not been worth living. Not a day went by without him hitting out at her for real and imagined sins. Now under her clothes, she felt bruised from head to foot. He always managed to inflict the worst damage when the servants were away or employed outside.

The Michael Bradley she married was not the same person she lived with today. When she first met and married him, he seemed such a gentleman in every sense of the word, Their honeymoon was wonderful and she fell even more in love with him. Yet from the minute they returned to his house from their month of bliss, she lived in fear.

Michael had set ideas concerning his wife's deportment. In the bedroom he expected her to be wanton, a thing Eliza could never be, yet in public she must be a perfect lady with impeccable manners. No matter what she did or did not do, it was never enough or correct. Eliza read every book she could lay her hands on concerning etiquette, but to no avail. The author's point of view usually diametrically opposed

Michael's ideas; even one whose name included a title and who obviously knew everything.

Now she dreaded each public outing, knowing he expected her to be gracious and charming, reflect the good taste of Michael Bradley. These occasions were usually business dinners at lodges and clubs and she detested them. The women were all of the 'nasty smell under the nose type', the men a 'how soon can I get her into bed without her husband knowing' lot.

Each time they arrived home after one of these affairs, Michael battered her with his fists. She had ignored Alfred Smith or Robert Brown, or she had failed to acknowledge Mrs. So and So, a person she would not have known even if she tripped over her.

Lately she came to realize that Michael's business associates were a bunch of dirty old men, who either played around with the full knowledge of their spouses, or dumped their wives on a country estate while they lived openly in town with a comely young mistress.

Was Michael also supporting a mistress, she wondered? Was he like the others? She did not know, as his many business dinners at the club were closed to her. For all she knew, he might have more than one mistress and she prayed he had. Sex had become distasteful to her. She might have felt differently if he had remained a lover, not even a good lover, but Michael was no lover in any stretch of the imagination. His only aim was to satisfy himself and satisfy himself he did on her body far too often.

How she had loved him when they first married and on their honeymoon. Michael showed her the delights of sexual pleasure, showed her how to please him. It had never occurred to her that she was also supposed to feel pleasure. After the birth of Jennifer he was most caring, until he discovered she could never bear another child. It was then his temper had shown itself, from then on the short sharp slaps had become hard blows, blows that bruised and caused deep pain.

Why was he this way? What had she ever done to bring out the cruelty in him? What lady would ever reveal that their husband was a brute? Her friends considered her fortunate to have such a charming husband, one whose business was on an upswing.

Currently she knew many mill owners were having a hard time with strikes, walkouts and machinery smashing. Luddites were rampant now. Gone were the good old days when an employee did his or her job without complaint. Today they organized combinations and societies, talked back to their bosses, and wrecked machinery in a futile effort to get their own way.

Michael blamed it on education. "Allow a servant or worker to read and write and they get ideas above their station, want to be like the bosses," he raved. "The leaders of these groups play on this vision. The rabble, these leaders say, should fight for their rights. They point out how the bosses live in huge houses with servants, while they the workers live in dirt floored cottages with no running water or toilet facilities."

Eliza said nothing. This was an old rant. "Still, surely they do live in poverty, Michael," she said.

He ignored her comments. "Even the servants are getting uppity and want to share the luxury of their masters. Again agitators are constantly infiltrating their ranks so when they are outside, they usually fall into conversation with some provocateur who points out how the master takes advantage of them. I've heard that some servants use the master's bed when he is away, or the parlour or dining room while the family is on holiday."

Eliza said nothing. Now she brooded on the state of the English north-west, the mills in particular. Things looked exceedingly bad on the labour front, and every publicized set back caused Michael to take it out on her. The servants were well aware of Michael's proclivity for violence as many had felt the back of his hand or his walking stick. They pitied Eliza, though they never would have voiced this.

Eliza and Adele, taught well by their upper class mother, did not converse with the lower stations, thinking themselves a cut above. Eliza never knew Sara was only too eager to sympathize with her, for Sara, her personal maid, had often seen the terrible bruises her mistress wore.

Eliza's cook, Mrs. Sterne, a fat old biddy, had worked for various titled persons until they fired her, usually for stealing or drinking. After hearing her hard luck story, Eliza took pity on her and gave her a job. Mrs. Sterne, grateful to have a roof over her head and enough to eat, did not steal as many perks as she had previously done. She considered Eliza more of a lady than those titled personages for whom she worked, because Eliza treated her like a person, a person with feelings. Every day when Eliza came to discuss menus, Mrs. Sterne looked at her carefully. She could always tell when the master had been at her for Eliza's eyes would be red rimmed, her hands shaky.

After they sent Miss Jennifer away in disgrace, Mrs. Sterne, who noticed the pain in Eliza's eyes, spoke out against the master and Eliza found a friend in her cook. She now had someone to whom she could unburden herself. While it went against the grain to talk about private matters with a servant, Mrs. Sterne was so sympathetic that she cried when she saw the bruises on Eliza's arms and legs. It was through Mrs. Sterne that Eliza got an ointment to treat many open wounds and for that she was extremely grateful.

Today Michael sent a messenger with a terse note saying tonight he would bring home his bank manager and his aide. They would dine at seven, he said, and ordered roast lamb: she should have champagne chilled and the wine and port decanted.

Eliza and Mrs. Sterne planned the menu and set the table with newly polished silver and the best china. Susan they dispatched to fetch fresh flowers for the table arrangement and side tables while Mrs. Sterne baked a torte and an apple pie. Susan then ran to the fishmongers and brought back the sole for poaching in white wine as first course.

"That's the lot, Mrs. Sterne," Eliza said, even in view of their new relationship she was still Mrs. Sterne and Eliza was the madam.

"It is indeed, madam. Why don't you go and rest? I can manage nicely with Sara and Susan. You'd better rest up while you're able."

Yes, she nodded, knowing she had better, for after the guests left Michael would beat her for something. She knew she would not get much sleep tonight.

Jenny, enveloped in a cape and a hat she grabbed from the front hall, walked as fast as she was able down the front steps and along the street. As she reached an intersection, she turned right and slowed her pace, taking off her cape and carrying it over her arm. Now she looked like a young woman out shopping or taking a walk. An unaccompanied female running, she knew, would draw attention.

Making her way to the train station, she bought a ticket for Weatherly and sat on a bench to wait the half hour. This was exhilarating, for apart from the time spent with Clifford she had never been alone, really alone. To think she was going to see *him*, her love, her promised husband.

Sitting in a first class compartment, she thought how worldly she had become. Here she was travelling solo, and she had not seen one other unaccompanied female. Travelling alone was unusual for young women of good family, yet somehow instead of making her nervous, it made her feel proud that she could look after herself.

When the train arrived at Weatherly, she sought out a carriage and asked the price for a journey to Hillshead Farm. The driver didn't know, as he normally did short runs, and asking around, came back to tell her it would cost her a pound.

"Then we will go," she said, stepping up into the carriage.

"Did they forget to meet you, your family?" he asked her, noting her neat dress, leather shoes and gloves. Her attire classed her as a young lady of good family.

"Yes, they did," she said, thinking it a good excuse.

"Tt..tt..tt. I bet it was your dad, not your mother. Your mother would never have let you travel alone."

"Mm, yes," What could she say? She did not want to carry on a conversation with a driver, a country rube at that.

Each time he made a comment, she looked away, showing her unwillingness to talk. Eventually he shrugged and kept quiet, wondering why such a welldressed, pregnant young woman would be going to a farm.

As Clifford kissed Mary on the lips in front of his mother, Liz smiled and looked away. At that precise moment Jenny arrived at the farm.

"Goodbye, Mrs. Wright, goodbye, Joyce, goodbye, Betty and Sammykins," Mary said, smiling around, "Si'thi all next week at our 'owse."

The next Sunday they were to go over to talk to her family about the wedding. The wedding day was set for two months from now, in October. Ernie had married only last week. Now he and his bride lived at the farm.

Clifford was putting his hands on Mary's shoulders as he saw her to the door when he spotted the carriage and Jenny alighting.

"What the . . .?" he gasped.

"Who is it?" Mary whipped around and followed his eyes. "Who's that, Clifford?" Mary noticed the young woman was a real lady, from the tip of her leather shoes to the posh bonnet on her head.

"Go home now, Mary. Go home before she starts on me," Clifford said, giving her a push. He felt angry, flabbergasted, and embarrassed.

"I'll do no such thing," she said hotly. "Who is this woman?"

Jenny wobbled across the cobblestone farm yard and came face to face with Clifford. The girl she did not look at, thinking her a servant by her attire.

"Clifford, darling, I came as soon as I could. My father locked me up in a home, and I had to escape," she gabbled, putting her hand on his arm and looking up into his eyes.

Mary gasped and went pale. Who was this young woman? What connection had she with Clifford?

"In a home? Why?" he asked. He looked grim and his lips were a flat line.

Mary put a hand to her mouth. Was this a crazy woman? Was that the reason she had been shut away?

Jenny continued to babble. "When he found out about you, he took me home and when they discovered I was having your baby, they were furious."

"Having your baby?" Mary shouted. "This woman is having your baby? Who is she? How? Why?" Running out of steam, she burst into tears.

Liz, and Betty with Sammy in her arms, came to the door to see what was causing the commotion.

"Who is this? Introduce the lady, Clifford," Liz said coldly, her eyes narrowed. Whatever the trouble, it did not augur well.

Clifford took Jenny's arm. "You have to leave right now. Look at the trouble you're causing."

Jenny shook him off and shouted angrily. "I ran away to be with you. You have to marry me now. I'm having your child," she yelled, tears running down her face. How could he do this to her? How could he turn her away?

Mary pulled at his arm. "What's going on, Clifford? Who is this, and what does she mean about a baby?"

Clifford pulled his face. "Aaw Mary, I dallied with her ages ago, long before I met you. I only saw her a few times. It was a lark, that's all."

"A lark?" Jenny gasped, her face whitening. What she had taken for love was no such thing. "You took advantage of me, Clifford Wright, and the best thing you can do now is make me an honest woman by marrying me."

Clifford shook his head. "I'm to marry Mary and I will. I care nothing for you. It's just that you threw yourself at me. What man could refuse?"

The carriage driver sat on his box leaning forward as he drank in every word, thinking it as well he had not left.

"How dare you!" Jenny slapped Clifford's face with her gloved hand. "How dare you say that! I was a virgin, you know that, and would never throw myself at any man. My father will shoot you when I tell him where you live. I refused to tell him your name, as I thought you'd marry me once you knew. I even lived in a horrible home for unwed mothers until I escaped. Now I have nothing and nobody. You are a bastard, Clifford Wright and God will punish you for this, That's if my father does not find you first."

Clifford stood dumbstruck. Mary, astounded, stood open mouthed like an idiot. It was the curse and she had been right to worry about it. She looked to Joyce who stood with her hands at her mouth, scared.

Betty stared until her eyes felt like they would drop out, as Liz stood with her hands clasped as if in prayer, trying to make some sense of it.

The driver sat back grinning hugely. What a tale he could tell at the pub later. "Miss? Miss?" he called, "Will you be wanting to go now? You'll make the train back if we leave right away."

Clifford put his hand on her arm to lead her back to the carriage, but she struck his hand away as if it burned her. How ashamed she felt. She had acted like a ten-year-old, not an adult. How stupid she was to think he even remembered her, and he was marrying someone who looked and talked like a servant. How mortifying.

"Take your filthy hands off me. When the child is born, you can be assured I will send it for adoption. I would not want any child of yours."

Turning, she almost ran to the coach, her face awash with tears of shame. The driver helped her up, giving her a sympathetic smile.

"Don't take it so hard, Miss," he murmured, "He's not worth it, even I can see that."

On the way back to the station she wondered what she was going to do. Then it came to her.

"Driver," she called, "Take me to Mayhurst Farm, please. It's the next turning to the left."

"Yes, miss." This was strange, he thought, wondering if she was going to do the same thing again at another farm.

When they reached the farm yard, Jenny jumped down from the carriage before he could help her and beat a rat-tat-tat on the door.

Adele gasped when she saw Jenny.

"Oh, Auntie Adele, please help me," she cried throwing herself into her aunt's arms.

Adele hugged her for a moment. "How long are you staying?"

Jenny squealed with annoyance. "Oh, I only got here and now you don't want me. What am I to do?"

"Jenny, all I am doing is finding out if we need the driver to stay."

"Send him away, I already paid him," she said, wiping her eyes and moving to go inside the house.

The driver said, "Hey, she paid me to take her to Hillshead, not this place. She owes me money. I can't be driving her around the county for what she's paid."

"Ooh, you stupid man," Jenny said, digging in her pocket. "Take this guinea. Go away at once."

The sooner he left the better she would feel, for he had witnessed her shame at Hillshead. She had no doubt that he would tell the tale, suitably embellished, at the Weatherly station where the carriages waited for fares. Well, what did she care?

Adele and Jenny sat in the kitchen drinking tea while she related her adventures. Adele knew about Jenny's disgrace, as her sister had written and knew Jenny dare not return to Wigan or her father would send her back to the home.

"So what are you planning to do, Jennifer?"

"Can't I stay here until the baby is born?" she begged. "I can't go home. I can't marry Clifford, now I don't know what else to do. If you gave me some money, I could rent a room somewhere until it is over."

Adele, tempted to agree immediately, had her husband to consider, and what could Eliza say? "It is not up to me, you must realize that. Your Uncle Albert must decide."

"Oh, Uncle Albert will let me stay," Jenny said emphatically. "Uncle Albert likes me. He's my favourite uncle."

Yes, he would be, Adele thought, he's also the only uncle you have. Albert thought Jenny a spoiled brat and had said so several times, the last time being when her father took her home. Still, maybe Albert would not turn the girl out, not in her condition.

"You'd better let me do the talking, Jenny. When he comes in, you go upstairs to the room you had when you stayed here. Even if you hear shouting, you must not come down. Your Uncle Albert is excitable, as you know, but I know how to handle him. Do not attempt to talk to him yourself until we have decided. Do you understand?"

"Oh yes, Aunt Adele, I will do as you say," Jenny nodded her head eagerly. Uncle Albert would let her stay. He had to.

CHAPTER SEVENTEEN

Eliza knew it meant trouble as she answered the door to a messenger. Who could be sending a telegram and what could be so urgent?

"I'll wait in case there's a reply," the boy said, sitting on the low wall of the stairs, staring at her curiously. He liked his job delivering telegrams. By, the things he'd seen when they read them. Some fainted dead away, others started screaming with anger, some said nothing but their faces got white. A few smiled widely and gave him a big tip.

Eliza put her finger under the flap and opened the envelope. As she did, she wondered if she were doing the right thing since they had addressed it to Mr. Michael Bradley. He would be angry if she opened his mail, but she must read it and today he was in Huddersfield on business.

"Mr. Michael Bradley. Sir: Jennifer has left Lilacs. If she has returned home inform us immediately. Do you wish a search? Advise your wishes. Matron Wallace"

"No answer," she said to the staring boy, unwilling to let him know of their troubles. Jenny had run away, was missing, but she had not come home. That would satisfy Michael. She knew he wouldn't want a search. That would require policemen and might get into the newspapers. For over an hour she sat in the parlour, staring into space.

Had the father of her child come to take her away? From where had she got the money to escape? After all the precautions the home took, Jenny had used her brains to make her break.

In one way Eliza felt glad Jenny had run, even as she shuddered to think what Michael might do when he found out. Should she even tell him? She contemplated that scenario. He knew nothing about the telegram so if she did not tell him, he would never know. Then again, suppose Jenny showed up here? What then?

After wrestling with the problem until her head ached, she decided it better to tell Michael. Somehow she knew even then that he would find some way to blame Jenny's flight on her. Picking up the telegram, she wandered into the kitchen to talk to Mrs. Sterne.

"She what? Give that to me immediately," he demanded, as if looking at the words would make a difference. Did he think she couldn't read? Eliza passed him the small yellow envelope. He took out the telegram and read it for himself.

His face reddened with anger. "This wire is addressed to me. Why would you open anything addressed to me? How dare you!"

Eliza kept her voice low and even. "Michael, it was a telegram. Surely that is different? It could have been a death in your family, or something about which I needed to contact you immediately."

"God damn it, woman, how often must I tell you? Mail of any kind is private. You should not have opened this."

Not daring to look at him, she stood with her eyes meekly cast down, even as her mind was hating him. "Yet the boy was waiting for an answer, Michael," she said quietly. "What was I to do?"

"Tell him no, and put this by my plate so I could open it when I arrived home. Eliza, if I have said this once I have said it a million times, you are semi-illiterate and unmannered. You know nothing of polite society, nor do you make any effort to learn. Your sainted father has a lot to answer for since you read trashy books written by ignoramuses, then try to tell me about good manners. I cannot fathom why I ever married you, and your daughter is a direct product of your background. No daughter of mine would bring disgrace onto her family in such a way. I wonder whose child Jenny is . . . she's not mine."

Eliza stood, shocked. "Michael! How could you accuse me of such a thing? I have never been alone with another man since our wedding night. This is too much for me to bear, too much." She burst into tears.

He detested any show of emotion. "Control yourself immediately, Elizabeth. This is another example of your bad upbringing. You don't see the upper classes resorting to common emotions. Parents carefully train them never to let their feelings show in public. I myself, am master of my emotions, or I would not be so successful in business. Look at you, you look like a fishwife, bawling like that. It's easy to see why Jennifer is so uncontrollable."

Eliza wiped her eyes, attempting to stop the sobs. How cruel he was, how insensitive

"What are we going to do about that?" she gestured to the yellow slip he still held.

"What I would have done if you had not opened it, my dear. Treat it with the respect it deserves." He crumpled it and tossed it onto the fire. "That is what we are going to do."

"S. s. s .suppose she comes home, Michael?" She had to ask.

"If she dares to come here, you will send her away. That girl is not to enter this house. You will instruct the servants accordingly."

"Yes, Michael," Eliza whispered. How could she turn away her own child? A child in trouble, a child who needed her parents more than ever at this traumatic time.

As they ate dinner, she listened to his talk of deals and business until she could have screamed. He expected her to ask questions, intelligent questions, so he knew she understood. An informed wife was a happy wife, he always said.

As he talked, she wondered again if he had a mistress. His frequent trips to Huddersfield might be the reason, for she knew of no other business that he would be involved with in that industrial town. Every time he came back from Huddersfield, she listened to his conversation, trying to figure out what he did there on these visits. He spoke of banks and stock brokers, printers and tool makers, parts manufacturers and supply houses, but never the prime reason for his visit.

Yes, she decided, Michael had a mistress. Good luck to her, she thought, thinking her husband probably gave the best to her, even as he beat her, his wife.

One afternoon as Eliza worked on her embroidery, she contemplated things as they were. In the two months since Jenny's departure from the home, Michael had found little to complain about and life had been comparatively quiet. In a way, she felt this amnesty was his way of proving it was her daughter who caused much of the mayhem. Jenny's running away from the home was yet another example of how dimwitted the girl was, and these days Jenny was her child, not his.

Eliza did not care. It was enough that he beat her less and talked to her more. They even entertained, large dinners at which a string quartet played popular classics. At long last she felt content in her marriage, and yet it had taken the digressions of her child to fetch this anxious tranquillity. When the telegram's arrival displayed Michael's subsequent lack of feeling for the girl, Eliza tried to put his intolerance out of her mind. After all, what could she do?

Then a letter came from Adele. Jenny was living with them, she wrote, and did Eliza think she could find time to come visit as Jenny dearly wanted to see her mother?

What to do? For a start she could not, dare not, tell Michael of Jenny's whereabouts so she burned the letter immediately after reading it. How could she find some excuse to visit Adele?

Could she formulate a plan to get Michael to allow Jennifer back home after the birth? It was her dearest wish to have her daughter back, no matter that Michael had washed his hands of her. Surely the girl must have learned something from her terrible experience? It might take a while, but if Jenny was careful in her speech and actions, her father might yet make a good marriage for her.

Two days passed before she dared mention it. She chose a moment when Michael, replete from a good meal, was sipping port and smoking a cigar.

"Michael, do you think I might pay a visit to Adele? She has written several times and asked me to visit. I would dearly like to see her."

"What?" His eyebrows shot up. "Why waste your time in that place? It's a working farm, and a badly maintained one at that. What your father was thinking of in allowing Adele to marry that yokel, I do not know."

If she could have answered him, she could have said Albert was twice the man he would ever be, was hard working and loved his wife. Her father had seen the love Albert held for Adele and, being a good Christian, held no prejudice against him. If Adele loved the man and he loved her, that was good enough for father.

In fact, she mused, her father had warned her against Michael. Yes, her astute father sensed that Michael was not an honourable man, but she, eighteen and foolish, was so blinded with love that he did not have the heart to forbid the marriage. Twice before the wedding he pointed out that if she changed her mind, he saw no shame in it. Not seeing his point, she recalled laughing and saying she would never change her mind, that she loved Michael Bradley. If she had only listened to father. Now he and her mother were dead and she could not tell him that he was right, that her life was usually a misery.

"Albert is a nice man, Michael, he cares deeply for Adele."

"I presume that is to point out to me that I do not care for you?" he said sarcastically.

"If . . ."

"'If the cap fits, wear it,' is that what you were going to say?"

She ignored his jibe because she longed to see Jenny. In a small voice she said, "I was going to say that if I went on Friday, I could come home Monday afternoon."

"Pray what will I do with my weekend while you are running barefoot through the mud and mire? Have you even considered that?"

"Now, Michael dear, the servants can look after you as they always do. You will not exactly be alone here."

"Pah! You expect me to talk to servants?" His voice rose and she knew he was becoming irritated.

She kept her face pleasant, covering her anger, kept her voice even. "Please, Michael, I never ask for anything, do I? I would like to visit my sister, who is, after all, my only living relative. You could stay at your club."

He exhaled a plume of smoke. "Huh, too bad Adele didn't expire the last time." Eliza gasped, what a horrible person to say such a terrible thing. He did not notice, but continued, "I suppose you'll want the carriage to take you to the station and money for train fare? I'll be better pleased when you're attending a funeral out there in the wilds. Then maybe we can have some stability in this house." He waved his cigar in her face. "My wife gallivanting around the county on her own does not look good, and I'll be damned if I ever again set a foot in that hovel."

Her heart leapt in her chest and she wanted to smile. He was going to let her go, but she dare not show any joy in his decision or he might retract it.

She suddenly recalled the time when she wanted a new coat and hat and had seen the one she liked in a smart shop, pointing it out to him as they rode past in the carriage. She felt amazed when he agreed, even more when he ordered the driver to stop so they could go inside.

Eliza, blushing with happiness, tried on the maroon coat and hat which suited her admirably. The saleslady exclaimed how good it looked and Michael nodded, smiling fondly, every inch the doting husband.

"Please may I have them, Michael?" She admired her reflection in the long mirror and stood with her hands at her small waist, a waist sharply defined by the skilfully cut waistband. "I love this outfit." Her face was flushed with joy, her eyes shining. She looked beautiful. He noticed that, of course.

"Hmph," was all he said as he stood. "I do not like it, it is not suitable. Come along, Eliza, we will be late."

Eliza took off the hat and coat, her eyes full of tears. She sensed it was his innate cruelty coming to the fore. He stood at the door, impatiently tapping his cane against the marble floor and she was all fingers and thumbs as she tried to fasten her own coat.

"It looked beautiful on you, madam. They could have made it for you," The sales lady said, making worse her anguish.

Michael heard. "That outfit makes my wife look like a cheap trollop, madam, and I will thank you not to put ideas in her head."

"Sorry," Eliza whispered to the woman as she passed her handbag.

As they rode away, Eliza tried to staunch her tears. She felt so disappointed. The outfit had suited her, the colour perfect. The seamstress, she thought, was a wonder as the coat was so beautifully cut. From that point on she never showed any enthusiasm for anything she coveted, knowing it was bound to make him refuse her.

Now she sat quietly, ostensibly reading a book while her mind went a mile a minute, planning for her trip. What would Jenny like her to take? All her possessions still remained in her bedroom. Maybe some of her beloved books? Clothes? Money?

Money. The silver piggy bank still stood on the chest of drawers and Michael had always been generous with Jenny, refusing her nothing. Yes, she must take the bank with her.

For four hours they sat in the parlour, Michael reading his paper and smoking, Eliza sitting motionless so as not to draw attention to herself. She didn't want him to change his mind.

CHAPTER EIGHTEEN

"Mother!" Jenny said as she waddled toward Eliza with open arms, delighted to see her.

Eliza looked at her daughter. She was huge, her stomach preceding her by nearly a foot, the loose linen farm smock making her appear even larger.

She hugged Jenny and kissed her on both cheeks. "Jennifer. You look good, an absolute picture of health. Adele, my dear sister, how are you?"

After the greetings were over, the three women sat in the parlour drinking tea and talking.

Albert agreed to Jenny staying until the baby was born. Eliza, aware Albert did not like Michael, was allowing Jenny's stay out of spite, but that did not matter to the sisters. If Jenny had a roof over her head, they could live with Albert's dislike of his brother-in-law.

The baby was due in a week and Jenny seemed both scared and excited. She learned something about childbirth from Adele, who pointed out that woman had children every day and it did not seem to cause them much trouble. She was young and strong, and probably her labour should be short. In Adele's case she had been much older and in bad health, even so she had survived and look at her now.

"Do you think you can stay, mother?" Jenny asked worriedly. "I'd dearly love to have you with me when the time comes."

"I must return home on Monday afternoon. I shudder to think what your would do if he knew you were here. He was reluctant to allow me this journey, and if I want to come again we must not anger him."

"Yes, my sainted father, mean bastard that he is, we must never anger him," Jenny said scathingly. "He put me in that terrible place. It was a prison, a real prison. I will never forgive him. Never."

Eliza knew that if Jenny wanted to return home later, she must not think of her father in such a manner.

"Jenny dear, you must not think about your father like that. He was doing what he thought was best, and doing it for your own good. Remember you were the one who practically broke his heart, taking up with a farmer. I know, I know," she said as she saw Jenny opening her mouth to argue the point, "Clifford is not an ordinary farmer. In your eyes he is wonderful, but since you told me he refused to marry you, I consider your father right in this instance."

Jenny pouted, knowing her mother was right. Everyone was right about Clifford. "Father thinks he can play God, Mamma, but he can't, you know. Just because you go along with his every word, does not mean that *I* have to. Once the baby is born, I want Daddy to see his grandchild."

"Jenny!" Eliza gasped. "He must never see this child. He already hates me for allowing you to get into this condition. According to him it is my fault, so imagine what he might do if he ever saw the child in your arms?"

Adele cleared her throat. "Eliza, dear, I have something to tell you," she said. The tone of her voice made Eliza turn.

"The child will stay with Albert and me, and we will adopt him or her. Jenny has agreed. As you know, I cannot have another baby, and we do so want another child. It will be one of our family, and how could we see the baby go to strangers? Jenny can visit and so will you. I think we made a good decision."

"Oh, Adele, how wonderful," Eliza said, hugging her sister. "It's a perfect solution to a knotty problem. If you say you adopted the baby, Michael will never guess it is his own grandchild. Not if we tell him about the adoption before the child is born. I'll tell him when I get home, say that was the reason you wanted to see me." Eliza kissed her sister. "This has made all the difference in the world to me, my dear, thank you."

"Yes, thank you Aunt Adele," Jenny said, "I, too, think it is wonderful."

"What have we here? The ladies sewing circle, is it?" Albert said fetching a strong smell of manure into the room.

"Albert, it's good to see you," Eliza said smiling and giving him a short hug. The good honest stench of the farm yard did not much appeal to her and she pulled away.

"Nice to see you. 'Liza. Michael isn't here, I hope? He didn't bring you, did he?"

Eliza chuckled. "No, Albert, we can all relax. I came by train."

Albert looked around as if Michael might suddenly pop out of the woodwork. "No chance of him, showing up, is there? We have to think about Jenny."

"I doubt it. He said he'd never again set a foot in this house. I don't think he likes you, Albert," Eliza said, laughing up at him.

"Well, so there's two of us hating each other. I think you'd be better off living here as well. That man is a nasty bit of goods. I've always said so."

Eliza nodded, but said, "I don't think it's as bad as that, Albert, but it's nice to know you'd take me in if ever I had to leave him."

"You'd be more than welcome, love, you know that. Isn't it nice that soon me and Addy will have a new little babbie? We have Jenny to thank for that. It's the ideal solution, I think."

"Yes, it is. Now Jenny, we have to talk about you. I think once you are over the birth, you should return home. Your father will find you a suitable husband, and I can assure you it won't be a fat old man like Richard Waithe, who, by the way, is now married to a widow woman of his own age, who happens to be wealthier than himself."

They talked about Jenny's return home over the next two days, and decided that once Jenny regained her figure she would arrive as if from abroad. Nobody of their acquaintance had thought anything other than she was at a finishing school.

Late Monday morning a tearful Eliza bid farewell to her family and caught the train to Wigan.

"What news is there from Weatherly?" Michael asked at dinner that evening.

"Such wonderful news, Michael." Eliza tried to look as happy as possible. "Albert and Adele are adopting a child. They are so happy about it."

"Is it a boy?" Eliza had dreaded that question for how did they know what sex the baby would be? After much discussion they had decided that she would say a girl. If it were a boy, they could come up with some reason why they had given it back and taken a girl.

"No, a girl."

"A girl?" Michael looked astonished. "Surely Albert wants an heir. Why a girl, I wonder?"

"Adele has always wanted a girl," she assured him. "They will see how this goes and maybe then adopt a boy. Then they will both be content."

Michael snorted derisively. "A lot of trouble if you ask me. Too bad that your family has such unsatisfactory breeding capabilities. First you and then Adele. Adele had two sons, but they couldn't stand that tumbledown farm, and left as soon as they could, and I don't blame them. At least you got one child out, whereas the birth of the last one nearly killed Adele from what you say."

She looked suitably chastened. "I'm sorry, Michael, I do try, but each time I fail."

"Yes, you do fail," he sighed, "I need a son to carry on my name and yet you give me a girl who has the morals of a whore. Better keep trying, Eliza, for I intend to have a son. Adele is no better, she bred ingrates who reached a certain age, then walked away from their heritage, such as it is."

How was he going, she wondered, to have a son? Knowing she could never bear another child would he divorce her? No, that was not Michael's way. A divorce would blacken his name, no matter what the reason, point him out to the world as a man who could not keep a wife. No, he would have a son by his mistress, she was sure of it and wished him well. If he had another woman to occupy him, he would stay away from her.

They dropped the subject of Adele and Albert's new child and she breathed a sigh of relief.

The baby, born at six in the morning after eighteen hours labour, was a girl.

Jenny, totally unprepared for the rigours of childbirth and horrified at the pain, became weak from loss of blood. They feared for her life. She seemed to pass into a coma shortly after giving birth and the midwife called a doctor to attend her. At four that afternoon Jenny died. The baby, although orphaned on its first day of life, already had a new set of parents.

While he was distraught over Jenny's death, Albert realized that going through a formal adoption was now unnecessary. They would keep the child, he told Adele, register her as their own.

A telegram addressed to Eliza arrived at the Bradley home bearing the news. Eliza almost fainted when she read the sad words. How was she going to tell Michael? Or should she? He would know Jenny had been at the farm, that the baby Adele adopted was his grandchild.

All their planning had come to naught. She dared not ask if she could attend the funeral. She dared not suggest that she again visit Adele and Albert. What *was* she going to do?

After an hour of deep thought she decided. With Sara's help she packed her bags and sent the outside man to fetch her a cab. She would go to Weatherly, and to hell with Michael. When she was last there Albert had offered her a home, and now she intended to accept.

The last thing she did was leave a note for her husband, thinking it the least she could do. In it she told him she had left him, although she did not give her destination. Eliza knew he would assume she had run off with another man. Michael would always think the worst of her.

On the train journey, she sat in a first class carriage and counted the money taken from the bureau. It amounted to nearly four hundred pounds, and because it was Michael's money, he might set the police onto her. Well, she didn't care anymore. He was responsible for the death of her only child, for if Michael had allowed Jenny to remain at home, she would have received the best medical treatment instead of a country midwife. After Adele's own experience of home delivery, she wondered why her sister had gone that route.

The Stockton house felt dismal. Mourning bands hung from the bannisters and they all spoke in low voices. They buried Jenny in the village graveyard under a spreading elm tree. Jenny would like this, Eliza thought, as she looked at the lacy branches overhead. A gawping sprinkling of villagers stood at the graveyard wall, those to whom a funeral was an occasion, no matter that it was a stranger. Apart from Albert, Adele and herself, the vicar was the only other person at the internment.

The tiny baby in Adele's arms squalled constantly, poor little mite, and Eliza wished the ceremony were ended. Never had she thought she would bury her daughter. Jennifer who was so full of life, whose voice could wake the dead when she put her mind to it, whose vitality impressed everyone she met. She had been young and healthy, even while pregnant, and that she died because of childbirth was hard to fathom.

The local vicar had never known Jenny apart from speaking to her once and so mouthed platitudes. Soon the first shovel of dirt hit the coffin lid.

Back at the house, they tended to the baby, then sat drinking tea and eating sandwiches made by the dairy maid. It was so uncomfortable an interlude that Albert left to see to the cows.

"Adele," Eliza asked, "Do you think Albert will let me stay? He did offer."

"Oh, Eliza, when he saw that mound of luggage, he knew immediately what was in your mind. He won't blame you one bit, and you'll be such a help now we have the baby."

The sisters hugged and cried for both sorrow for Jenny and joy for the new baby.

Adele idly wondered aloud if the Romany curse put on the Wright family might have anything to do with this latest situation. While not given to fanciful thinking, she knew the village gossip said the curse had passed to Clifford. It resurrected talk of the curse when his fiancé walked out on him, although they had already arranged the wedding.

Adele became convinced after Jenny told her she had gone to see Clifford, and that he spurned her, this had caused the breakup of his engagement. Jenny had been Clifford's lover, was carrying his child, so did this mean that the child also carried the curse? She shivered and decided to talk to the vicar, even as she pushed the idea aside as being ridiculous.

CHAPTER NINETEEN

1881

Betty watched Sammy pull himself up and cling to the table leg. A big boy for his age, nearly eighteen months, already attempting to talk, she smiled at his attempts. He called Joyce, Jo-Jo and his grandmother, Ganna, Betty was Mama. The farm hands who he saw regularly he greeted with various sounds that apparently made perfect sense in his small mind as they were identical whenever he saw that person.

Anyone seeing him for the first time took him to be much older. When they took him to the market, Betty often had to explain that he was not a slow two or three, but an advanced year and a half. He had all his teeth and ate solid food, and how he could eat.

"If he goes on at this rate, he'll eat us out of house and home by the time he's six," Liz said, laughing. "I never saw a child eat so much."

Yet he had not an ounce of fat on him, despite his chubby red cheeks. Samuel was active to the extent that he never stopped, and quickly tired the adults. When the sun rose, so did Sammy. He clambered out of his cot and woke everyone by screaming and laughing with the joy of a new day.

Betty always hurried to feed him, for once she fed and dressed him, he would sit outside the back door on the bench to watch for sometimes as long as ten minutes as the hens and geese pecked around the barn yard. From time to time he would try to catch them. His greatest joy was when a farm hand took him for a ride on the cart. Then he'd laugh joyfully and say 'hossy'.

Yes, Betty was proud of her son. She loved him more than life itself and Sammy was such a cuddler. He liked her holding him in her arms and rocking him as he planted sloppy kisses all over her face.

What did life have to offer him? They had no idea if he would remain as he was and this worried Betty. Her mother said his rapid growth might result in a lack somewhere else, like his mind. Sammy was so happy all the time and wasn't that peculiar? Surely he should have bad moods or throw tantrums, what child didn't? Yet not Sammy, he was sweet and lovable every day God sent.

Worried, Betty took him to a doctor in Wigan who pronounced him supremely healthy. When she voiced her concerns about Sammy's mental abilities, he showed her, through a few simple tests, that her son was intelligent and would probably become more so as he matured.

Clifford, still upset at Mary calling off the marriage, said she and her son were always sure of a home under his roof. That stilled her fears, but Sammy could never inherit the farm, would simply be a farm hand. In view of this, Betty decided her son needed an education, maybe move away when he was old enough to work, and must be more than a farm worker.

How she would accomplish this, she did not know. She did not receive any pay for working: none of the family did. They purchased basic needs on market days when Clifford paid for everything. So unless Sammy became a genius and won scholarships, she had no idea how to get him an education.

"Mik, mama, mik," he demanded.

"Mama will get you some milk in a minute, Sammy, wait until I have done this." Betty poured the boiling milk onto the rice and set the pan on the stove.

Sammy watched her. He was incredibly curious about everything and it did not surprise her when he gurgled, "Wice puddy, wice puddy."

"That's right, Sammy, rice pudding. Your favourite." She picked him up with a groan, he was so heavy. "Now, let's get Sammy some milk, shall we?"

One market day, with some left over money, she bought some canned goods and these stood proudly along the shelf. Commercial canning was something relatively new and the upper classes bought them by the case. They were expensive, so expensive that Clifford almost had a fit.

Some cans were of condensed or evaporated milk and Sammy got the benefit of it as the others watched to see what ill effect it might have on him. Now Joyce contended it was the canned milk that made him grow like a weed. Maybe it was, Betty thought now seeing how tall he had grown, how well formed.

Clifford started work on a dormant tract of land. The twentyacre strip had lain fallow for so many years that the bracken and gorse had overgrown and spread. For two weeks he slashed, hacked down the young trees and brambles. For two weeks he hauled out rocks and laid them at the end for a wall. Soon it would be ready for the plough.

His entire body was a mass of pain for he had done all of it on his own, and while he never shirked hard work, this was rough going. The men were working on the hay harvest, the year's first cutting, and since both cart horses were working elsewhere, he was forced to use sheer muscle power to shift both brush and rocks.

As he worked, he thought about his life, what lay ahead for him. Mary had slapped his face, calling him a bastard, saying she would never marry him, not even if he were the last man on earth. That she had spurned him was a blow to his ego. Whereas Jenny showing up pregnant with demands that he marry her, achieved the opposite. That made him feel proud. Not that he ever dare say it aloud.

Now, whenever he could find a spare minute, he was courting Agatha Brown from Weatherly End. Born on a farm, she worked at the local inn as a waitress. Although plain, she was warm and friendly and had an outgoing personality. Aye, Agatha would make a good wife and she was all for it, too. He had bedded her twice already and she was 'hot to trot' as the locals said.

Yet would she marry him? Neither had mentioned a commitment, nor talked of love. Everybody gossiped about his breakup with Mary, gossiping about the Wright curse. The curse quickly became part of local lore, was a topic of conversation every time he met one of his neighbours. Yet he knew it was all talk, It had not affected the farm in any way and he personally felt better than he had in years.

Still and all, he wanted to marry, wanted someone to share his bed, to bear his children. So far he had impregnated one childish female, had engaged himself to another who would no longer look at him, and lately bedded Agatha who was willing enough, but hard to figure out. Aye, he decided, he'd pop the question this market day when he stopped in for his noontime dinner at the inn. Time he was settled: a man had needs.

As for the household chores of the farm, Betty and Joyce were hard working, not forgetting his Mam, who had the best touch with cheese and butter. No, he was blessed with a good family, though he dreaded to think that one day his father's traits might come out in himself. God forbid that he ever turn into a tyrant like his father.

Yes, a wife could help him solve such problems. With a good wife by his side, he could work harder at making the farm bigger and better. A wife would give him the moral support and sympathy he never might get from any other person. He offered up a fervent prayer that Agatha would say yes, hoping she would not realize he did not love her.

1882

Liz Wright felt dog tired. Not a one for kidding herself, she recognized her sickness and, through various means, made sure the family saw nothing of her pain. She worked the same long hours and through great fortitude managed to fool them all. Inside she knew she was dying; a vicious disease ate at her and the flesh dropped off her slight frame.

It was the curse, it was. That being so, she said nothing to her children. The curse would surely die with her, for she was the same generation as Jake. They must give the children a chance for life without stress.

To compensate for her weight loss, she ate heartily though later she vomited. She began to wear bulky knitted clothing, claiming the cold got to her bones these days. Not one of them noticed, or they might have said something. Keeping her secret, she wasted away under their noses.

Today she had to stop while churning the butter as a dreadful pain in her side struck fear into her heart. Cold sweat poured from every pore. She was cold too, so cold that her teeth started chattering. Putting out her hands, she touched the wall, and moving to it, slid down it onto her backside. For almost an hour she rested unable to move, her haunches cold with the chill from the flagstone floor, her heart pounding as if it might burst.

By chance Joyce came to the dairy, and saw her mother sitting white as a sheet, her arms around her knees.

"Mam! What's on earth has happened to you?" Dropping the basket of eggs onto the stone shelf, she went to her mother's side.

"Aaw Mam, you're so cold," she said, looking at the tears running down Liz's frightened face. "Wait here, I'm going to fetch one of the men. We have to get you up to bed."

Dashing into the farmyard, she started yelling for help. Reg White ran out of the cow barn and headed toward her.

"What's to do? Is the house on fire?"

"It's my Mam, Reg. You must help me. She's collapsed."

Reg carried Liz up the stairs wondering why she weighed 0so little. He had always thought of her as the stocky type, big boned and with a lot of padding on her frame. Now she was light as a feather, as though the heaviest thing about her were the knitted cardigans and jumpers she wore.

When he placed her on the bed, he saw how gaunt she had become, how her eyes seemed sunk into their sockets, how her teeth looked too large for her mouth. The missus, he saw, was sick to the point of death.

"Reg, run and fetch Clifford, quickly now," Joyce said, "Take one of the horses. He's working on the new acres."

"Aye, I'll send Betty inside to you. Maybe she could help. Do you want the lad to run for the doctor? The missus looks as though she needs him."

She flapped her hands at him. "Yes, yes, but hurry up and fetch Clifford."

When Betty came upstairs carrying Sammy, her mother was unconscious.

"Oh my God, look at her," she gasped, realizing how thin her mother was now Joyce had undressed her and put on her cotton nightdress. "She's as thin as a rake."

"Gran, Gran, me down," Sammy said struggling to reach his grandmother.

"No baby, stay with me. Your Gran is sick."

"She's dying, Betty, Mam is dying," Joyce sobbed. "Look at her, there's nothing to her. Reg said as much when he held her, light as a feather, he said, light enough to float away. Why didn't we see? Why didn't we know?"

Clifford pounded up the stairs.

"Where is she?" he asked even as he saw her lying in the bed as white as the sheets. He thought she was dead.

"Aaw, Mam, wake up Mam. It's me Clifford," he said quietly close to her ear, holding her hand in both of his. She was cold, cold as death, but she wasn't dead for her eyelids twitched.

With a supreme effort, she opened her eyes enough to see him. Things seemed hazy but she knew him from his size.

"Clifford," she forced the words out of her mouth, "The farm is yours now."

"Mam, Mam!" he became practically hysterical, tears streaming down his face. Neither Betty nor Joyce had ever seen him so upset. "Come back, Mam, don't leave us. Mam?"

Liz sighed once, then she was gone. The doctor arrived five minutes later and signed a death certificate. What else could he do? Died of cancer, he told them, worked through it to the end. "A brave woman, Mrs. Wright," he said, "Very brave."

Clifford cried like a baby. He cried so loudly that it affected Sammy, who cried with him. The sight of their strong brother in tears brought the grief to Betty and Joyce and it was a room filled with lamentation.

The farm belonged to him, she had said, Clifford knew that already. Yet why had his mother made such a point of it?

Now the heart went out of him and he sat around the farmhouse staring into space for days after the funeral, as if someone had switched out the light in his eyes. Betty and Joyce carried on with the daily chores - someone had to - while the men worked hard on the harvest. All were wondering if things were likely to change, although why they should they did not know. It seemed like a death in a family brought all kinds of nasty surprises, brought home the dreaded gypsy words. It was months before they felt comfortable again.

For two months Clifford did little and then suddenly snapped out of his depression. One market day Betty insisted he drive them into the market and, near the town square, Agatha stopped the cart to offer her condolences.

After he dropped the girls off at the marketplace, Clifford went to the inn and sought out Agatha. He proposed, she accepted, and it was a changed man who waited to take the sisters home.

CHAPTER TWENTY

1886

"Angela, come inside at once. Time for tea," Adele called through the window as she saw Angela run across the yard and into the orchard where a farm hand was picking pears.

At the age of six, Angela the name was Albert's choice as he considered Jenny's baby an angel was bright as a new penny, full of life and love and as angelic as her name.

Eliza and Adele brought her up between them, although she called Adele Mamma and Eliza, Aunty. Both were proud of her. While she was wilful, she could be compliant, and though she was beautiful and knew it, she had no 'side.' Eliza saw Jenny in her rare stubbornness and selfishness, whereas Adele, who vaguely knew Clifford, saw his sweet nature and abundant dark curly hair.

Angela and her brother Freddy would soon attend a Dame school in the village run by a retired governess. Both Eliza and Adele realized an education was the means to erudition and wanted their charge to be intelligent in her conversation and knowledgeable about the world. Albert simply wanted her to be happy.

The Stockton's adopted a boy, Frederick, when Angela was two. A robust lad, a year older than Angela, with red hair and bright blue eyes. Three years old when they got him, he remembered little of his past life.

"Now our family is complete," Adele said.

"We were once a complete family before, remember?" Albert said in answer to her comment. "That both our sons deserted us caused us both a great deal of anguish."

"Yes, I still miss the boys. Still, they were your sons and you trained them to be independent."

"I think I did too good a job there, love."

"Never mind, we'll teach our new family to read and enjoy the printed word. Encourage them in every way. We owe them that. I hope our lads are grateful for what we did for them. I do wish they'd write more than once a year."

Albert snorted. "Aye, and that saying nowt."

Eliza envied Adele and Albert's life, their love for each other and the children. Adele had everything Eliza had missed in life, and to think she once considered her sister had made a huge mistake when she married Albert.

Michael, much to her delight, had not come looking for her after all. Eliza often wondered what happened at the house when she ran away. She imagined he would have set himself up with his mistress and carried on as usual. The fact she had stolen his money, yet he had not set the police on her, spoke volumes. Maybe he thought it a small price to pay for his freedom.

She found her new life agreeable, and after a year or so rarely thought about her husband. Her brother-in-law was good to her and gave her money to purchase new gowns and shoes, even as he did for Adele. The four hundred pounds she stole from Michael was soon spent as she insisted on buying things for the house, luxuries Adele or Albert would never have considered. Now they had hot water running from taps, a water closet and a bathroom with a bathtub built into a mahogany frame.

To have the time to watch Angela grow into a personable young lady was a dream come true. To come and go whenever she pleased without having to report her every move or word to Michael, was heaven.

As she again called Angela for tea, Young Freddy raced across the farm yard with a sheep dog barking at his heels. When not on duty, the dog was his constant companion. Now Angela raced to the kitchen door, wiped her feet, stepped inside, took off her outdoor shoes and stepped into her slippers.

"Here I am, Mamma, what's for tea today? I'm starving." This despite the fact that she had eaten at least three apples.

Adele smiled fondly at her. "Starving? I should think you are, running wild all over the county. Well, enjoy it, child, for when you start school next month you'll have to sit behind a desk for six hours at a time."

"Oh, Mamma, don't say that," she laughed, "But I will do it, you know. Freddy can't sit still, not like me. You know how quietly I sit in church."

"Yes, for an entire ten minutes of the sermon," Eliza said fondly, "You count the angels on the windows. I watch you do it."

"Oh, Aunty Eliza, I never do," she said seriously, winking at her aunt, who laughed aloud.

Albert's habit of winking when imparting a confidence found its way into Angela's bag of tricks and was amusing at times.

Freddy shucked off his outdoor shoes and entered in stockinged feet, leaving a trail of wet footprints.

"Aye-aye? What's all this, then?" Albert said, as Freddy put on his slippers. "Who's been paddling in the brook again?"

Angela and Freddy looked up at their father and grinned. He grinned back, thinking little imps they were, the pair of them. If he told them once about messing near that brook, he'd told them a hundred times.

Freddy was the worst offender, as he considered the brook his private property and spent hours fishing for tiddlers with a bent pin on a piece of string tied to a long branch of elder. He built little boats from pieces of wood, added a sail of paper on a stick and raced them down the faster section. The part that raced downhill and under the cattle bridge.

On hot days he took off his clothes and lay in the shallow water to cool himself. One hot day Albert caught the pair of them lying stark naked in the water under the bridge. Acting outraged, he forced himself to hold his laughter, took them home and handed them over to Adele.

Aye, a right pair of scamps, but they shouldn't play near the water. He kept telling them, yet it was like a magnet to Freddy. Then again all little boys like water, though not for washing themselves. He had loved it himself when he was Fred's age.

"He fell in, Daddy," Angela said, grinning. "I bet he fell out of a tree."

"I landed on my feet, though," Freddy bragged, shoving out his chest.

Albert shook his head. "You could have landed on your head and it wouldn't have made no difference, my lad, you'd still have been in trouble. Stay away from that water. This is the last time I'll warn you, Freddy. The only time you can be near that brook is when an adult is with you. Do you understand?"

"Yes, father, but I did want to go fishing tomorrow. Will you come with me?"

Albert rubbed his chin. "Maybe I will at that. The top field is finished. That's why I'm back so early. Aye, I'll go fishing with you, son."

"Me too, me too," Angela shouted.

"Aye, you as well, lassie. You hate being left out, don't you?" He turned to his son. "She could put the worms on the hooks, eh Freddy? How would that suit you?" He laughed as she squealed with revulsion. "Fishing ain't exactly a ladylike pursuit, so why don't you ask your Mam if you can come?"

"Please, Mamma, can I go too?"

"If you learn to ask properly, Angela," Adele said, "It's 'may I go'"

"Please, Mamma, may I go with them?" she asked obediently, making her face serious. "Daddy won't let me fall in the water."

"Very well, but I think we should make it a family day out. Your Aunt Eliza and I will join you. We'll have a picnic."

"Hooray, Hooray!" both children raced around waving their arms and dancing jigs. "A picnic, a picnic."

Yes, Adele's family life was pleasant and Eliza envied her even more, glad she shared their life.

Betty watched as Sammy shinnied up the huge oak that stood at the front of the house, forbidden to do so he was unaware she was watching. Now almost six, he was tall for his age and well formed. His youthful arms already had muscles and his long legs and muscular torso made him look older.

This year he would start junior school. Maybe that might knock some cockiness out of him, she thought, as he had become impossible to control. She wondered what the other children his age would make of him. Surely he would rule the roost in the classroom as he did at home?

She blamed Clifford for his wildness. As she often told him, he could at least pay some attention to the boy, take him under his wing, guide him. As for the women of the house, they made little impression on the wilful boy. He agreed to everything they told him, and then did exactly as he liked the minute they turned their backs.

Clifford had married Agatha, who had taken charge of the house. Now Betty and Joyce were little more than resentful servants. Betty took so much exception to Agatha's treatment that she set her cap at a single man who worked for Clifford, Harry Horton.

Harry was mad about her. Shorter than she by two inches, he was gorilla-like in that his arms were longer than normal and he was extremely hirsute. Still, a man was a man and if she married, Betty knew Clifford would grant them a tied cottage.

Joyce was courting again, for at least the hundredth time. Very choosy, was Joyce. Then again, at once Betty had been the same, though now it was a case of any port in a storm. She couldn't live with Agatha for much longer, and neither could Joyce. They talked in the orchard, well out of Agatha's sight, about their options.

If they left to travel to a town to look for work, what could they do apart from cleaning? They could marry a farm hand and stay on the land in a tied cottage. Of course, Joyce said laughing, they could be swept off their feet by a tall, dark handsome duke who, riding past, fell madly in love with one of them at first sight.

Both girls loved the farm, loved their life but both longed for a man of their own, children to cuddle, a house to look after. Since Liz's death they grew closer, and Sammy added a spark of life to what could have been a dreary house.

When Agatha married Clifford and moved in, a new element of unrest came over the girls. They felt Agatha resented their presence.

"That bloody curse is still working, our Betty," Joyce said one day, "It's sent Agatha to break up our family and she aims to push us out of our own home."

Betty, more down to earth, said, "You'd better stop seeing trouble where none exists, Joyce. Don't talk daft."

As they worked making the cheese, Betty talked about Harry. "I think I'll wed him. It might be the last chance I'll ever get to marry and I don't want to live on charity for the rest of my life. Because that's what it is, all right, the charity of our Clifford. I've thought about it for a long time, and decided love or no love, my only recourse is to marry to get away from Clifford and Agatha."

"Yet if you don't love him, how can you be happy?" Joyce asked as she sprinkled the salt.

"Is anyone ever really happy? Somehow I doubt I'll be content with Harry, but one never knows."

The only people she considered happily married were the vicar and his wife. They deferred to each other constantly, helped and encouraged each other, unlike the rest of the congregation of farm families. In many farm marriages, the man was taciturn and usually brutal. He lived with a worn out, downtrodden female who gave birth to too many children. These couples barely abided each other after some twenty years or so, although they must have loved each other when they were younger. Not that farm life was exactly idyllic. Farming was arduous and demanding. They took no holidays because cows needed feeding, milking and mucking out every day of the year. Still, like herself and Joyce, they knew no other life.

Two days later Joyce suddenly announced she was leaving. Agatha had set her to scrubbing the flagstone kitchen floor and purposely, or so Joyce thought, dropped a full bucket of cinders and ash from the fireplace across the part she had finished. Joyce exploded.

"Right! You did that on purpose, Agatha. I saw you drop that bucket." She slammed the scrubbing brush into the pail of water and stood. "You made the bloody mess, you clean it up. I'm off to the hen house." She marched out, leaving Agatha staring after her with mouth agape.

Maybe Agatha had not done it on purpose, maybe it was an accident, but Joyce didn't see it that way. Joyce looked at the mess and realized this was the thin edge of the wedge, knowing Agatha had been spoiling for a fight since she came to live at the farm.

They had not taken to each other, the sisters and Agatha, although Clifford thought things were going well. They did not like her any more than she liked them. Nobody made her welcome, nor did they speak to her unless she asked a question. Cliff never noticed because Joyce and Betty chattered between themselves much as usual, and the child constantly demanded attention.

The child, oh yes, the child. Clifford did his best to get Agatha pregnant and Agatha hated that the sisters' bedroom was right next to theirs and they heard everything. In the throes of passion Clifford was vocal, although Agatha tried not to utter a sound. Not that Agatha objected to sex, oh no, she liked it. Thee more she got,the better she felt, but to have an audience was not right to her way of thinking.

She picked up the bucket, emptied the dirty water onto the cobbles outside the back door, then went to the pump to get fresh. With Joyce gone, and not knowing when she would return, she would have to do the floor herself, and she still had the weekly baking.

At supper time, a still sulking Joyce came out with it.

"Well, I'm away tomorrow," she announced loudly, her eyes fixed on Agatha. "I'm going to Wigan to get work at a mill. You won't have Muggins here to push around any longer, missus."

Smirking at the others, she filled her mouth with food.

Clifford coughed as some food went down the wrong way. "What do you mean? You? Leaving? Why?"

"Because I'm not a servant and I won't work for her!" She pointed at Agatha with her fork. "If you paid me to do the heavy work and scrub floors that's one thing, but for her to treat me as a menial in my own home, the house where I was born, and have to kowtow to her, well, it's just not on."

Betty listened and watched as she fed Sammy. Earlier she and Joyce had talked this out, and she thought Joyce was doing the right thing.

Clifford looked amazed. Who'd have thought Joyce had enough spunk to leave home? "Nobody thinks of you as a servant, Joyce," he said, "This is your home. Why do you think you have to leave?"

Joyce, angry that he was blind to what was happening, let him have it. She felt incensed when he spent each night shoving it to Agatha and they had to listen to his grunts and moans through the thin wall.

"Because of your missus. I don't know what kind of home she came from, but she thinks she's Lady Muck now she's here. She treats Betty and me like idiots, she does. Betty'll tell you, she told her snooty friends what come over here for tea Thursday afternoons that we were the hired help. I heard her and so did Bet, said Sammy was 'the son of one of the hired help'." Her bitter tone and expression spoke volumes.

Agatha sat mute. Betty admired her for that. Joyce, she knew, was turning it into a personal vendetta, and that wouldn't work with Clifford, who was narrow minded when it came to family. He loved Agatha, at least physically, both knew that much.

"Another thing, she had me on my hands and knees scrubbing this floor, she did, then dropped a full bucket of ashes and cinders all over it. She did that on purpose, our Cliff, and nothing will persuade me otherwise."

Clifford stood up, resting his fists on the table top. "Now I know you're lying. Agatha would never do such a thing."

Agatha smiled up at him gratefully and Joyce noticed.

"Oh aye, you'll always take her part, won't you? A nice warm hole to stick it in, you've got now. We all know what you like these days. It sounds like a pig rutting through that wall at night."

Clifford's face reddened and he stood taller. With a shaking hand he pointed at her. "Better pack up right now, Joyce. Better get out of here before I knock your block off, give you a backhander. To think my own sister could turn on me like this." Suddenly speechless, he strode out of the room and they heard the parlour door slam.

Joyce looked at Betty and Sammy then turned to Agatha. "So you got what you wanted, Missus, me out of here, and if I know anything, our Betty will be next. That means you'll have to *pay* someone to do your dirty work. Aye, you will. Then we'll see how much Clifford thinks of you. Mark my words, our Clifford will see through you soon enough."

Agatha still did not speak. Betty grudgingly felt respect for her because her face was expressionless throughout the altercation.

Standing, Agatha shoved her chair under the table and turned to leave.

Joyce watched, her eyes slitted. "Can't find owt to say, can you? I'm right and you know it, you miserable cow. Worst thing our Clifford ever did was wed you. That gipsy was right, this family invites bad luck, and we'll always have it. You being the biggest bit of bad luck that I ever saw. We all know the kind of family you came from. They tossed you out from what I hear, and that got you working in a pub, 1 serving drinks and anything else the chaps wanted. Oh aye, we know all about you, we do, made more money on your back than anything else, din't you? Everybody knows what a whore you are. Clifford'll soon find out when you start giving free samples to the farm hands, for you can't get enough of it, can you?"

Agatha's face whitened and she held onto the dresser as if to prevent herself from fainting. With a noticeable effort, she drew herself up and tilted back her head.

"Please feel free to start packing," she said evenly. "You don't have to stay tonight. There's enough light for you to reach the station to catch a train."

Joyce scoffed. "Aye, that's what you'd like all right. Me going now, but I won't go on your say so. I've changed me mind. I'll go when I'm good and ready, and that's when I get wages for the work I've done in this place for the last ten years."

Clifford stood in the doorway leading to the hall. They had not seen him come back.

"You'll go upstairs and pack now, Joyce," he said, controlling his voice. "I want you off this farm tonight. The sooner the better. I can't allow you to upset Agatha, not in her condition. There'll be no talk of wages owing. I run this place, and don't get wages, yet I do most of the hard work. I'll give you a pound to pay for your fare. That's all I have in the house."

Her eyebrows shot up, so her ladyship was with child, was she? No bloody wonder, with him at her every night God sent. Betty and Joyce glanced at each other. Betty still had said nothing, thinking her sister had said enough.

Joyce pushed past them and ran upstairs. Right, if that's the way he wanted it, that's the way it would be. Her mind raced around her problem. She'd get one of the men to take her to Weatherly station on one of the horses. Surely Clifford couldn't object to that if he wanted her gone. She would catch the first train that came in, no matter where it was going. With the money her mother had left in the old tea caddy, money she stole at the time of Mam's death, she had enough to get herself a room for a week or so and find a job.

Suddenly she felt like singing, felt like Clifford had lifted a weight from her. At long last she was out of this place, going somewhere exciting, with eligible men and jobs. She sang as she packed her few things into a wicker basket.

CHAPTER TWENTY-ONE

Angela and Freddy walked slowly along Oak Avenue. School had been over for almost an hour and yet neither Aunty Eliza, nor their mother had come to fetch them.

"It's been an awful long time, Freddy, something must be wrong," Angela said, twisting her hands.

"Walk on the inside, near the hedge," he said, pulling at her arm.

"Why? I won't be able to see if Mamma is coming."

"The teacher told us about being a gentleman and said a lady always walks on the inside, in case a horse takes fright and mounts the path, or a cart's passage leaves clouds of dust that might make her sneeze."

"Oh yes, all right." Angela wanted to become a real lady so she walked prissily, as should an eight year old lady.

The Dame School taught them well. They were well-mannered and knowledgeable because Miss Grosvenor offered a wellrounded comprehensive education. Freddy was intelligent and normally top of his class, whereas Angela was the type who forgot what the teacher had said the minute the subject changed. For all that she was a pleasant, lovely girl and extremely popular with her class mates.

They attended school at a large home belonging to Miss Grosvenor, a retired governess, whose father left her the estate. Not that it was much of an inheritance, since the large old house needed repairs so she was forced to sell the surrounding acres to provide enough money to make it habitable and provide her a subsistence.

Through hard work and astute advertising, she now had two other teachers working full time with four part-time tutors. Everyone recommended the school. Her pupils were the children of middle class citizens who considered education necessary for females. Parents sent the local boys to her until they reached preparatory school admittance age because her academic standards were high, and her graduates always accepted by other institutions.

Albert thought Miss Grosvenor had done a superlative job with the children. They could talk about things about which he had no knowledge, spent hours chatting about geology or biology or some such, patiently explaining things to him. Aye, he told Adele, the best money he had ever spent was on their education.

As they reached the intersection of Oak and Marlborough Streets, they spotted their father hurrying toward them. He was dressed in his best suit and Angela knew he would not want to shame them in front of their schoolmates.

They ran toward him. "Daddy? What is the matter? Where is Aunty Eliza? Where is Mother?"

"Come along now, children. Your aunt had a nasty accident and the doctor took her to the infirmary. Your Mam went with her."

Angela stopped, tears filling her eyes. "Is she all right, Daddy?"

"Oh aye, lass, she'll be right as rain in a couple of days. Hurt her leg, that's all. Come along now, we'll have our tea at the tea rooms. How will that suit you?"

"Oh, yes, please, Father. That will be excellent," Freddy said slipping an arm through his father's arm. Angela held his hand and skipped along, pleased at the unexpected treat.

As they sat in the recently opened tea shop, Albert listened to the children talking. It dawned on him that Freddy cared nothing for his aunt, nor did he ask about his mother, whereas Angela seemed most upset about Eliza and wondered when she would return home. He noticed the difference between the youngsters: Angela apparently cared about people, while Freddy only cared about what effect a person would have on his personal life. Once Freddy heard Aunt Liza would soon be home, he felt content.

Angela sat swinging her legs under her chair, chattering about having a party when Aunty Eliza came home. "Maybe we could fetch her here, Daddy. She'd like this, wouldn't she? Such nice table cloths and lovely waitresses, and their uniforms are so neat."

"Aye, maybe we'll do that," Albert said, his heart swelling with pride at his young daughter's empathy. The fact she cared so much for her aunt, for all of them, made him misty eyed.

"I could take some money out of my money box, Daddy, so you won't have to pay so much. I don't mind spending it on a party at all."

"Nay, lass, there's nobbut any need for that. I can manage a few bob for such a do, eh."

"You do speak most peculiarly, Father," Freddy said, his own speech patterns more of Miss Grosvenor's than any of the family, even Angela.

Albert laughed. Out of the mouths of babes, he thought. "Aye, that I do, an'all. Don't worry none, son, you seem to understand me well enough."

"Yes, but you still talk in a most peculiar fashion."

"I suggest you teach me to talk proper. How about that? That's what I pay Miss Grosvenor for, so you'll talk better than me."

"Properly, Father, it's 'properly,' not 'proper,'" Freddy said, with an air of superiority.

Albert glanced around. "Aye, well, I don't want a public lesson now, son. Let's leave that for when we're at home, eh?"

"Very well, Father, but don't say 'eh?' all the time. That word does not exist unless you are referring to the hay that horses eat."

"Yes, sir," Albert said pulling at his forelock and laughing. "They'll make a school teacher out of you yet, young Frederick, they will an' all."

"I'm going to be a ballerina," Angela announced. "Miss Leadbetter says I'm graceful."

Freddy chuckled as he said, "I saw them all dancing out on the lawn, Father, like a lot of fairy elephants. The chaps and I couldn't stop laughing."

"Ooh, you are so horrible, Freddy." She pushed at him which made him laugh louder. "Isn't he, Daddy? Anyway, we laugh at you too, Freddy, when you're out doing your gymnastics. A lot of bony, little stick boys wearing shorts and vests. Estelle said that you looked like something that crawled out from under a rock, and you did, too."

Albert laughed at their chatter. They loved each other, did these kids, and to think they were from different families, an' all. A good education had been the making of the pair of them, because they stood out from the village children like a prince and princess with their nice manners and way of talking. Aye, a good education, that was it.

He planned to save enough to send Freddy to a Grammar school at the age of eleven. What Angela wanted was another thing entirely, of course, as girls had peculiar ideas at that age. This latest ambition of hers to be a ballerina only surfaced last week after she read a book about Pavlova. Next week she might want to be a nurse or a teacher. Whatever she decided would be good enough for him, if it didn't involve marrying a farmer or miner.

No, Angela must marry well, marry a young man who had prospects. To achieve this Adele said, they must save enough money to dress her properly, take her to the best places where she would meet the right people. Albert and Adele had already picked out a girl's school in Southport where she would mix with upper class girls and, through them, make friends in the right social circle.

At least that was Albert's plan. Eliza and Adele realized he was only dreaming for once these girls made friends with Angela and discovered her father was a lowly farmer, they would terminate the friendship. For now they said nothing further to each other, knowing things could change economically.

The three walked home after their tea and the children chattered about the treat. Angela became quiet as they neared the house and, when her mother came to the door, ran as fast as she could.

"Mamma, did Aunt Eliza come home with you?"

Adele picked her up, big as she was and kissed her cheek. "No, my pet, Aunty is in the hospital."

"Is she very sick, Mamma? May I go to see her?"

Freddy pulled at her arm. "May I also go with you?"

Adele put Angela down and ruffled Freddy's hair lovingly. "Sorry, but you'll both have to wait until she comes home next week."

"Father took us for tea to the new café, Mother," Freddy announced. "It was nice. I liked the waitress. She had dimples," He put both his forefingers in his cheeks. "Like this, and she called me 'sunshine.'"

"Did she now? How nice of her," Adele said, looking strongly at Albert over their heads.

"She said he was a real carrot top, Mamma," Angela added laughing at his flushed face.

"Time to wash up and change. You may have another cup of tea while you do your homework."

"So," she said, to Albert as the children scampered up the stairs, "Tea in a café, and with waitresses in uniforms yet."

"Aye, it's lovely there, Addy. We must take Eliza when she gets out. Angela's idea. Says she'll help toward the cost from her money box."

"That child is so kind hearted she'd give away her most treasured possessions to anyone who asked. Well, may she always be that way. While she's young it doesn't make much difference because we can protect her, but once she's out in the world she's going to be at the mercy of any unscrupulous person who senses that in her."

"Then it's up to us to learn her."

"Yes, it is up to us to *teach* her."

Adele worried about Angela. She was so trusting and open, so ingenuous, so naive: yet changing her would be wrong. Since they lived on a farm and did not mix much with the villagers, this protected her. However, Albert was right because once she went away to school, the ignorant, cruel or thoughtless actions of others could hurt her.

Agatha watched as Betty set up Sammy's supper. Now in her sixth month, her stomach was huge, and she was eager to learn everything about child rearing.

A lot of it, she knew, was common sense and, raised in a large family, she had learned a lot by osmosis, though never had paid much attention to her younger siblings as her mother always tended to them. Still, she watched as Betty fed the youngster, saw how she chopped the meat, watched as she warmed the cereal and milk.

Since Sammy was a big boy for his age, she often forgot he was only six. Clifford said laughing that Betty fed him too much, that was the reason.

"Keep on stuffing him like that and he'll be towering over me before too long, Bet. How soon can you teach him to plough?"

"Oh you, our Cliff, don't talk silly," Betty chuckled, knowing soon she would be away from here. When she and Harry married they would move into Lower End Cottage, a mile distant. Harry was all for them living together until the big day, but Betty would not hear of it. Presently Harry lived there alone, renovating the place.

In a way she dreaded getting married because going to bed with Harry had her petrified. Since the rape, she shrank from any physical contact with a man. Would she be able to do it now? Somehow she had conned herself into believing it would be all right at the time. She'd keep her eyes wide open and see that it was not her father hurting her. Harry was a nice man and surely understand her fears, and to ensure his sympathy she told him a cock and bull story about her dead husband being brutal and treating her badly. Still, in two weeks she'd be Mrs. Harry Horton, with all the problems that fetched, and Agatha could get on with it as best she could with the housework. She would still come over every day to look after the dairy and eggs.

For her part, Agatha looked forward to having Clifford to herself. She talked to him about hiring another dairy maid and Clifford was going to the pillars at the town hall on market day to see who was on offer.

Hiring took place once a month at the market. The grand pillared

City Hall stood to one side of the open market square and it was here, in front of the pillars, that people seeking work gathered. Prospective employers could survey them from a distance before talking to them.

Agatha said she wanted someone young, someone she could train to her own way of doing things. It would be a blessing, she said, to have someone who waited for orders and did not go ahead and do things the wrong way 'because that's the way we've always done it at Hillshead.'

Eliza lay in her hospital bed wondering why she felt peculiar. After the nurse gave her the medication, she began to feel woozy. She called for the nurse, but her voice was so weak that nobody heard her. Lying on her back, her pulse racing and her heart pounding, she felt like she might explode.

Before the doctor came on his rounds, Matron came through to check the ward. She paused at Eliza's bed.

"Why is this woman lying so untidily?" she asked the nurse who followed her with a note pad. "This will never do."

The nurse went over to the head of the bed and moved the counterpane from Eliza's face. How had she become so entangled with the bedding?

"Matron!" she gasped. "Come quickly." As the matron moved closer she hissed, "Mrs. Bradley is dead!"

The matron pulled screens around the bed and checked Eliza's pulse. Dead.

"What is going on here?" she hissed at the terrified nurse. "How can a woman die from a broken leg?"

The nurse shook her head. Thank God it was not one of her patients. "Whose patient is she?" Matron asked.

"Nurse Benton, Matron."

"Send for the gurney and keep these screens closed. Send Benton to my office at once."

The nurse shut the curtains as Matron hurriedly summoned the men from the morgue. The eyes of every patient followed the nurse's progress down the ward. Strange how the others always seemed to sense a death, she thought. How terrible that on her ward a healthy woman could die when she was due for discharge in four hours. How could it have happened? Well, it was not her problem, she thought relieved, as she hurried down the stairs.

When they set foot on the ward, the nurse told Adele and Albert to go to the Matron's office.

"I wonder why?" Adele wondered aloud as they followed the nurse along endless corridors with closed doors.

CHAPTER TWENTY-TWO

Adele and Albert, upset and grieving, decided not to tell the children right away, but tell them instead that Eliza was taking a holiday to regain her strength.

"We must contact Michael, though," Adele said as they made their way home. "He should know of her death. It's up to him to pay for the funeral as he's still her husband."

"Aye, but we don't know that, do we? For all we know he got hisself a divorce and married again."

"I somehow doubt it. He'd have had to inform Eliza and we know he never did. Nevertheless we must tell him of her passing. It's only proper."

"Aye, we'll send a telegram. I won't be writing any letters to that bastard."

When Michael got the telegram, he stared at it incredulously. "Stupid woman, and after I spent a small fortune on a solicitor to sue for divorce. Then again, Eliza never did anything right." He looked over to his mistress who sat reading a book. "All our troubles are over, my love," he said as he tossed the telegram into her lap. "She's dead. For once she did something right."

Vera read the yellow slip and smiled. Soon they'd be married and she would be a respectable lady for the first time in her life. Who'd have thought Michael would marry her? Oh, he had promised to do so for years now, but she had always thought, being a typical male, he would find some reason not to go through with the plans. Well, this time the stars had shone on her and she was to be married.

"What happened to her, I wonder?" she asked a trifle sadly, even as Michael stood rubbing his hands with glee, his grin a mile wide.

How horrible, she mused, that a man who once loved you could act as though your death was a reason for celebration. In some ways she did not much like Michael. He was a cruel man, although she accepted that because he was generous with her to a fault. However, she promised herself, once the ring was on her finger, he'd not treat her in such a fashion.

"Who cares, my darling Vera, who cares? Nothing now stands in the way of our immediate marriage."

"I mean, isn't it strange that a young woman should die so suddenly. Aren't you the least bit curious?"

He shrugged. "I must attend the funeral, of course. A man in my position has to be cautious in his social manners. My absence would be imprudent. Albert will post the obituary in the county papers so everyone will know of her death."

Vera screwed up her nose. She was curious about the death. "Do you think it was an accident? Or did she die of some disease?"

He heaved an aggravated sigh. "I don't wish to talk about this any further. If she fell into a well, it would have been an accident . . .,"

"Oh, how terrible, to fall into a well," Vera interrupted, shuddering. She could imagine it: falling, falling and then landing in the cold water in pitch blackness, no chance of climbing out, no chance of rescue, particularly if you could not swim.

"Don't be so stupid, Vera. She didn't fall into a well. That was only a remark pointing out that an accident is an accident. I will ask my brother-in-law, at least we'll have one thing to talk about. He is obtuse and ignorant so any conversation is heavy going. Now, are we going to have supper?"

Vera jumped up from the sofa, "Of course, my dear. Won't you be seated? I'll call Martha to serve."

As they ate, Vera wondered about Michael. He had moved her into the house a week after Eliza left and expected to her pick up the household supervision immediately. The servants, Sara, Susan and the cook Martha treated her with disdain, though she understood their attitude.

Her first weeks were a misery, nobody to talk to, nothing to do. She was not exactly a prisoner, but Michael told her she must not tell any of the shop keepers where she lived. It could jeopardize his position in the social strata if anyone knew he had moved his mistress into the family home. If anyone asked, she was to say she worked at the house. Her pride took a severe blow right then. Imagine having to say she 'worked at the house.'

For a few days she became cool toward him, but then he brought her flowers and chocolates, was so loving that she forgave him. She could, of course, have walked out on him anytime, but she appreciated the comfort, loved the luxury of the large house. She enjoyed having servants do the work, liked hearing Michael promise they would marry when he got a divorce. Yet a divorce took years and she didn't know if she could stand it that long. However, he showed her the solicitor's letters, so she knew he did want to marry her.

Imagine her married. Little Veronica Sully from Ince, mistress to many and wife to none. What a turn up for the books, eh? To think his missus had popped her clogs, just like that. Soon, very soon, she would be a married lady and in complete charge of this house. First thing, she decided was to tackle those miserable maids and the cook, tell them point blank they were on sufferance. They'd have to change their attitudes, and if they didn't, then out they would go.

"You look smug, my dear," Michael's voice broke into her reverie. "What were you thinking?"

She smoothed her hair and smiled. "Oh, oh, I was thinking we'd soon be man and wife, dear."

"True enough, now let us talk of the stock market."

She hid a sigh. Michael expected her to discuss business with him, to offer ideas or suggestions about the latest stock fluctuations. It was like sailing in treacherous waters because if she said something foolish, he would lash out with his tongue. On the other hand, if she said something brilliant, he would use the idea, and when it succeeded, as it sometimes did, it became his own idea.

Michael, she discovered, was a stupid man. With an inheritance from his uncle and brashness covering his ignorance, he'd managed to amass a small fortune on the stock market. He listened or eavesdropped on conversations at his clubs and on the market floor; watched trends and cultivated the friendship of those in the know. At home he had expected Eliza to listen and suggest, as now he did with Vera. He was canny enough to know women had an intuition missing in men, that they perceived things men never brought to mind. Eliza had been the cause of his first major win. Known now as a sharp dealer, other investors sought his advice. Michael liked people thinking him a shrewd and knowledgeable trader, while all the time it was the females in his life that made him.

Albert narrowed his eyes as he saw the smart carriage and two matched blacks arrive.

"He's here, all fur collar and top hat," he called to Adele who was fixing Angela's pinafore tie in a butterfly bow.

Freddy rushed to the window. "Look, Father, look at the beautiful horses. I'm going outside to look at them." He made to go, then stopped to ask. "May I?"

"Aye, don't mess with them, mind," Albert said, "They look skittish, they do an' all."

Michael climbed down from the carriage and walked to the farmhouse door. His face a mask of distaste at the mud and rough stones of the path, he knocked loudly with his stick.

Freddy opened the door and ran past him, his eyes on the horses. Albert ambled forward.

"Albert. A sad occasion." He stuck out his hand, but Albert ignored it, his eyes on his son.

"Aye, sad."

"Where is the internment?"

"At the village church, of course, but aren't you going to come in to pay your respects to Adele?" Albert looked shocked.

Adele came along the hall. "Michael, please come in. Shame on you, Albert."

Michael entered, though he fastidiously kept away from the walls. What a dump, he thought, looking at the shabbiness of it, the threadbare hall runner and stair carpet, the lime washed walls.

"This is our Angela," Adele said, drawing the girl forward.

"Ah yes, the child you adopted. Eliza told me of her," The tone of his voice changed to one of anger. ". . . before she left me without warning."

Michael stared at the sombrely clad pinafore clad child who reminded him of someone. Yes, she had a look of Jennifer, around the eyes and mouth and that hair, and yes, the blonde hair, like his daughter. He often wondered where Jenny was now and if she were married. He eyed her again. No, it couldn't be, for hadn't Eliza told him about the adoption before Jenny had her child? Still, the look of her

"Come into the parlour." Adele noted the direction of his gaze and felt a sense of unease. She opened the parlour door as Angela flitted out the front door to see the horses and talk to the driver.

The drapes were drawn and the fire smouldered, banked down with slack as they would be out for at least an hour. The drapes were drawn shut as a mark of respect and two oil lamps provided the only light. Not that opening the drapes would have made much difference, Michael thought, for as he remembered this room the windows were small and dirty.

"You met our son, Freddy? He's the one looking at your horses. His ambition is to become a horse trainer. Thoroughbreds, you know," Adele said, by way of conversation.

"Indeed. Well, it is a great profession although one which requires a great deal of capital." He eyed the shabby room meaningfully. "I suggest you talk him out of it at once. Don't put ideas into his head above his station."

Adele glared at him. This was the same old Michael, stouter and greyer, but the same bombastic, pretentious man she had known for years. How Eliza had stayed with him so long was a mystery, but then again love was strange.

Adele closed the parlour door firmly so the children could not hear their conversation. Now cocking her head, she could hear Angela outside with Freddy and Albert exclaiming over the horses.

"Well? How did she go? Was it an accident?" Michael asked, his voice harsh.

Adele told him. "Eliza died suddenly. She broke her leg when someone jostled her on the stairs of the library. It was a nasty fracture so they kept her in the hospital. We were shocked when she died so unexpectedly. It was on the day she was to come home. When we went to pick her up, they told us."

"She died of a broken leg? How ridiculous, impossible, incredible, ludicrous," Michael said, trying to keep the smile off his face. Trust Eliza to be involved in a silly accident, but to die of a broken leg? That was hardly feasible. "This is the first time I've ever heard of anything of this nature. Are you sure they learned the proper cause of death? Did they perform an autopsy?"

Adele looked blank. She had never thought of such a thing, and surely hospitals knew their business?

"No. Yes. I don't know, maybe they did. I don't know." This turn in the conversation upset her and made her nervous. Was he suggesting somebody had killed her sister? Suddenly, she also felt a twinge of suspicion. "You think something bad happened to her in the hospital? Is that what you mean?"

"Honestly, Adele, I have always found your education and that of your sister sadly lacking in many ways. Were you not sceptical when they gave you the news? What did Albert have to say about it?"

Right then Albert opened the parlour door and ushered the children inside. Adele touched Michael's knee and leaned toward him, whispering. "Do not mention her name. They do not know of her death."

He stared at her incredulously. "What on earth is going on here?"

"Please, Michael, I will explain later. Now children, go to the kitchen and help Mrs. King." Obediently they went, saying, "Goodbye, sir," to Michael.

Michael rubbed his chin. "Hmm, they have manners, I see. They sound educated."

Vera smiled. "Both attend Miss Grosvenor's school. We have registered Freddy with the Grammar school in Wigan and Angela is to attend a girl's boarding school in Southport."

"Surely this education does not comes cheaply," Michael said with a great deal of sarcasm. "Your farm must be profitable, Albert."

"Aye, it is now. I've had to take on four more men, what with buying another forty acres. My neighbour to the west left no sons and his wife and daughter couldn't handle the place on their own. They sold forty to me and the rest to Clifford Wright at Hillshead." Too late Albert realized what he had said.

"Clifford Wright? The man who ruined my daughter?" Michael's face infused with rage.

"Now, Michael, that's all in the past. Let it go," Adele said, giving Albert a look that would remove paint. "A lot of water has flowed under the bridge since that day. He's married now and has a child of his own. His mother and father died, and his sisters left home."

"I care not for his troubles or his family history," Michael said acidly. "I'd like to talk to him face to face about the grief he caused in my house. My daughter ruined and now God knows where, my wife fleeing our home because she could not stand it without our child, and now her sudden death. He is answerable for all that."

"That's not why Eliza left you, Michael," Adele snapped, her patience at an end. "And well you know it. She came to me troubled and upset because of your cruelty, because you used to beat her."

Michael jumped to his feet. "I beg your pardon! This is not a discussion of my way of life, it is about the bastard who ruined an innocent young girl."

Albert faced him down, standing hands on hips, legs straddled. "No. Today is about the burial of your wife," Albert said in a steady voice. "Keep your voice down. We don't want the children upset."

"What is the reason I am here? Why do you think I came? To attend the funeral, of course."

Albert smirked nastily. "We all know why, Mr. Bradley. It's only so you won't lose face among your high mucky-muck friends. That's why I put the obituary in the county paper, so you'd have to attend. Adele didn't want you here, and neither do I. You never loved Eliza, we all know that. This is all for show, this turning up to show respect. I suppose you've already got her replacement to hand. Aye, Eliza knew about your doxy all right."

Michael put on his gloves. "I'm going to the church. I will not stay here to listen to insults. Good day to you, Albert. I doubt we will ever meet again, but if we do meet by chance, please do me the honour of ignoring me, for I will ignore you. Adele, nice to see you. Your children are well behaved. See to their education and you'll not be sorry."

He stood, turned on his heel and left. They heard him direct the driver, heard carriage wheels turning and then silence.

"What a man. How did she ever stand him?" Albert said, rubbing his eyes wearily.

"It was her choice, Albert. She was the one who decided to stay all those years. Now my poor sister is dead before her time, and he thinks only of the possible damage to his reputation by his child getting herself pregnant by Clifford. You know, Albert, he stared so long at Angela that I think he knows."

"Let's pray not. Not that he would want the child. He'd sooner take our Freddy, bring him up to be like himself."

"Well, I hope the children do not suspect the purpose of his visit." She sighed. "I worry about that, Albert. Do you think we should tell them about Eliza?"

"Aye, when this do is over. We'll tell them at tea time. They're good little kids and they'll be upset, right enough, but they'll accept it."

"Well, Freddy will because he only thinks of himself. Angela now, well, she's so thoughtful and kind. She worshipped her aunt, and Eliza loved her. You know, Albert, I envied Eliza her blood relationship to the child though she bears our name. Eliza loved Angela so dearly."

CHAPTER TWENTY-THREE

After the funeral Michael went directly to the hospital in Weatherly and talked to the Administrator.

"What are you suggesting, sir?" Aloysius McCann gasped as he heard the accusation. "Are you trying to imply foul play?"

"A person does not die of a broken leg, not even here in this sorry excuse for a town. Certain things are indisputable, and one is that nobody dies of a broken leg. Something else caused her death. I intend to find out what went wrong."

Aloysius blustered, "The attending physician assures me he saw no other reason than her heart stopped. She died of a heart attack."

"Ridiculous, preposterous, my wife was as healthy as a horse. Where is this doctor? I would speak with him." Michael stood and glowered at Aloysius threateningly.

"Dr. Holdsworth is probably doing his afternoon rounds. Please wait here and I'll bring him."

He dashed down the stairs and into the general ward. John Holdsworth was at least seventy and Aloysius often seriously doubted some of the death certificates he filed. Still, since nobody ever made anything of them, he was willing to let such things go unchallenged. He recognized that Holdsworth's accepted competence could not last forever. Now this man was questioning the death of a woman, a young woman, from a broken leg and a heart attack. How was the Board of

Directors going to react to this situation? It could cost him, a mere paper pusher, his job.

Michael looked around the untidy office. He poked into various ledgers, read letters, opened drawers. Not a tidy man, Mr. McCann, not at all tidy. To him an untidy office denoted an untidy mind. This latest revelation that Eliza died of a heart attack seemed proof enough that it was not the real cause.

Of course, out here in the backwoods they would never question a sudden hospital death. The local people were ignorant, thinking a hospital visit automatically meant you came out in a wooden box. Yet why hadn't Albert and Adele questioned it? Why had they not made a fuss with the authorities?

He was going to set this place afire with his questions, was going to sue the lot of them. Grimly he smiled. Eliza could be worth a lot of money to him now. Good old Eliza, she was good for something after all.

1882

Agatha smiled down at the young boy. At two he was a whirlwind. The 'terrible twos' they called them, and they were in his case.

Edward, Eddy as they called him, was the spitting image of his dad and followed Cliff everywhere. A farm was a dangerous place for a youngster who could not appreciate the perils lying in wait. Agatha tried to ensure he always stayed in sight; especially when he played in the farmyard with its broken down machinery, rubbish heaps and duck pond.

After Joyce left and Betty married Harry, Agatha took on two young girls to help run the dairy and egg operations and look after the heavy housework. Betty supervised them. Even as a farmer's wife Agatha had it easy, and now that she was again pregnant, she relied on the girls more than ever.

"Eddy, come away from the water, please. Come on, I'll give you a biscuit." Eddy stood at the edge of the farmyard duck pond throwing small pebbles at the ducks, but came running willingly enough at the prospect of a treat.

"That's a good boy." She took his hand and led him indoors. "Don't go near the ducks again, lovey. They don't like you throwing things at them."

Marian, one of the new hands, a plump girl of seventeen, stood kneading bread dough at the table and smiled as they entered.

"What's he been up to this time, missus?"

Agatha told her as she wiped Eddy's face at the sink.

"Would you like somebody throwing stones at you, Eddy?" Marian asked.

"No, no throw things at Eddy, no, no." He stood shaking his head, looking at her from under his brows.

Agatha smiled. "Marian's right, Eddy, unless you want stones thrown at you, you must not ill treat the ducks or any other animals. They might hurt you as you hurt them."

"All right, Mam. Where's my biccy?"

"He's a right handful, missus, isn't he?" Marian said chuckling, "Two years is a bad age for little boys, always into mischief, always got to watch them. They'd kill themselves and think nothing of it. I recall how my younger brother climbed onto the roof and was aiming to fly down, or so he thought. He was as brave as anything and the height didn't bother him one bit. We had to talk him out of it, but my Dad had to go up and get him 'cos he couldn't get down again."

Agatha nodded. "Yes, we have to watch Eddy, all right. He's forever racing after his Dad, and he's too fast for me these days."

"Aye, well Edith and me, we keep an eye on him as well." She looked hard at her mistress, noticing the dark rings under her eyes and her air of listlessness. "Why don't you lie down? I'll watch the young'un."

"I think I will, Marian. I don't know why I feel so badly this time. With Eddy it was like I had more energy, felt more alive, now I feel dragged down, lifeless."

Marian smiled. "Then this time it's a girl. They take more out of you, they do. My Mam says so anyway. It's 'cos they have to make their eyelashes and dimples and curly hair, she says."

"I hope you're right, another boy and I'll be run ragged. Thank you, I will lie down. Keep your eyes on his nibs."

"We're going to play a game, aren't we, Eddy, my chuck? A nice game. Come on, let's stand you on this chair." Marian picked him up and stood him on a kitchen chair, pushing it close to the table. She gave him a small lump of dough to work.

"Now Eddy is going to make a nice little loaf for his Dad, eh? Watch how I do it and you do the same."

Eddy played around with the bit of dough until it grew grey and horrible. His hands were grubby to start with, but it kept him amused for at least half an hour. She gave him some currants to put in it and he rolled and patted it for ages.

When the dough went back into the pans to rise again, she set his little loaf on a plate and put it in the fender near the fire, covering everything with a clean cloth.

"Now we wait until it rises again and then the loaves go into the oven. Won't your Dad be proud of you, eh? Making a loaf for him all on your owny-oh?"

Eddy nodded his head, up and down, up and down, grinning. "My Dad likes butties," he said, "I made him a loaf, din't I?"

"You did an'all. Now wash your hands at the sink and we'll have a sup of tea. Bread making makes you thirsty, eh?"

Marian watched as he stood on a chair to reach the sink. He wet his hands and rubbed them down his overall pants. Eh, but he was a nice little lad, not too clean, but a real boy for all of that. Thinking that a dip was a wash, what next?

When Clifford entered, they were sitting at the table drinking tea.

"Dadda," Eddy said, lifting up his arms for a hug.

"Hello, young man. Where's Agatha?" he asked Marian as he picked him up.

"Lying down in the parlour. She was fair wore out."

"Aye, she didn't sleep much." He ruffled Eddy's hair. "What has the young master been doing today?"

Eddy wanted down and then grabbed his father's hand. "Come and look, Dad." He lifted the cloth to show his handiwork which by this time had risen slightly. Dark grey and studded with raisins, it looked horrible. "I made a loaf for your tea." He was so proud, Clifford could see that. "Marian showed me. It makes you thirsty, does bread making, and we was having a sup."

Clifford laughed and put his arm around his son's shoulders. "Well done, son, I'll be proud to eat your baking. As long she doesn't show you how to make cream cakes and do the ironing, I won't worry much."

Marian laughed, "He's unable to stay still for more than a second, so there's no danger of him learning much about housework."

"I'd better talk to Agatha," Clifford said as he moved into the hall.

"Dad, Dad, wait for me," Eddy said, rushing after him.

Agatha was awake and relaxing when Eddy burst through the door. "Mam, Mam, I made Dad a loaf, and he's to have it for his supper, haven't you, Dad?"

Clifford chuckled. "Sush now, keep your voice down. They can hear you over at Mayhurst. Sounds like you're calling the cows home. Pretty soon the yard will be full of them, milling around and wondering what's to do."

Eddy sank onto the floor and looked up at his mother apologetically.

"Is something wrong, Cliff?" she asked.

"Your friend Ellen from Rockburn sent you this. Her husband was passing and gave it to me." He gave her an envelope.

Eddy jumped to his feet. "Is it for me, Mam? A buffday card for me?" The only envelopes Eddy had ever seen were his birthday cards. He leaned on her as she put her finger under the flap.

"It isn't your birthday again for about ten months, son," Clifford said. "That's a letter for your mother. Now outside and play and stay away from that duck pond. Marian?" he called down the hall, "Look after Eddy would you?"

"Yes, master," Came the reply and Marian hurried to the parlour to take Eddy outside.

"Oh my, Ellen is pregnant," Agatha announced. "She's due four months after me. It's her first as you know and she wants me to go visit Thursday. Could you take me over in the carriage or on the cart, Clifford?"

"Of course. It'll be a break for you. You need company and a change of scenery."

"Thanks, love. Whew, that little boy is wearing me out something rotten, bless his little curly head."

"He's a right tomboy all right, takes after his dad I would say."

She chuckled. "Aye, and as much trouble, too. Look Clifford, can't you stay closer these days instead of working the far fields? I don't feel at all well lately, and I'm sure something bad is going to happen."

"Don't talk like that, Agatha, every child is different. My Mam used to tell me about when she had us. One time she was well, the next sick. Everything will be all right, you'll see."

Then someone rapped at the kitchen door and Clifford went to answer it. A gypsy woman and her child stood on the doorstep. Both were filthy and dressed in rags. The woman offered him a handful of poorly fashioned clothes pegs.

"Only a shilling, mister, a bargain," she said, showing yellowed teeth. The little boy smirked and put out his hand. "Please, mister," he pleaded.

Clifford was on the point of ordering them away. The farm didn't need beggars, no farm did. Old Wilfred at the next farm had given succour to a woman and her daughter and the next thing to happen was he had a barn full of nomad Romanies, eating his stored winter vegetables and apples. One should never encourage gypsies, they possessed no conscience.

Agatha came to the door. She pushed Clifford aside. "Are you hungry" she asked.

"Yes, missus," the boy said quickly glancing up at his mother.

"Now, Agatha," Clifford warned.

"Wait here," she said as she turned and went back into the kitchen.

She hacked off half a loaf, a pound or so of home made cheese and four apples. Wrapping them in an old clean cloth she passed them to the woman who grinned her thanks. The boy grabbed one of the apples and devoured it hungrily.

Clifford grunted, shrugged and went back into the kitchen. "Mind yourself, Agatha, take care."

The woman smiled and put out her hand. "Read your fortune, lady?"

"We don't want any of that rubbish, thank you," Clifford shouted. He had been listening as he drank his tea.

"Cross my palm with silver and I'll tell you what the future holds for you, lady."

"I'm sorry, we don't have any coins. I gave you food."

The woman looked at her, looked at Agatha's stomach and patted it with a dirty hand. "Due soon?"

"Yes. Tell me, can you lift a curse?" Agatha asked.

"What kind of curse? A Romany curse?" The woman screwed up her face so she looked like a hag.

"Yes, I think so," Agatha said, waiting for Clifford to say something, but he was silent.

"I don't know that I can unless I knows the words and the signs."

"Agatha! Come away from that door. Leave things be," Clifford shouted, his voice angry.

"I'm sorry," Agatha said, her hand on the door catch, "I must go inside."

The woman sniffed her annoyance and turned on her heel. "It won't ever come off, you know. Romany curses are potent to the hundredth generation, but if you pay me, I can remove the worst of it. Too bad that your husband won't let me, but then again he carries the curse. He's the next in line."

Agatha shivered as she closed the door. How could this gypsy know about the curse on the Wrights? Since she did, did it mean the story about the gypsy's curse on the family had credence? Cliff's sisters always talked about it in hushed voices, talked about the bad luck that had befallen both parents. It made her feel uneasy, but then she had never felt at peace at this farm, not even with a good husband like Clifford.

CHAPTER TWENTY-FOUR

Michael sued the hospital for the astronomical sum of fifty thousand pounds for the untimely death of his wife. The barrister handling the case thought they might settle out of court because the hospital records showed many such deaths, none easily explainable. Coincidentally, Dr. John Holdsworth suddenly retired and went to live with his sister in Surrey.

He allowed Vera, content with her new life as Michael's wife, to attend certain functions with him, venture out in public and give her name as Mrs. Michael Bradley. The honeymoon they spent in Brighton.

When they returned home, Michael turned his thoughts to the acquisition of more money and, while she felt ignored, she was not rash enough to voice it. He had once beaten her black and blue when she spoke to a business associate of his before the man spoke to her. Now she was reading the many books on etiquette the last Mrs. Bradley had purchased.

As for Michael, he was flying high on a wave of success, his latest acquisition being a cotton mill in Manchester. His usual way of handling such take-overs was to fire the current executives and replace them with men of his own choosing. These men would work to his methods, pare expenses to the bone, get more work out of the staff for lower pay and make use of landed immigrant Irish women who worked for less than half the current rate.

The local people resented the Irish that arrived in droves at the industrial cities. In an Ireland famished after the potato famine, they lived in such indigence that the poverty in northwest England seemed comparative luxury to them. Taking jobs at the lowest wages, they put hard working Englishmen on the street.

It seemed to the Lancastrians that the Irish equated owning a pig as the height of sophistication. Even those who lived on upper floors would share their cramped quarters with one. It was tiny when they first got it but one could only imagine what living conditions were like when it reached maturity. Michael heard of one Irish family who bred their pig to a neighbour's boar and now had fifteen piglets running around the second floor of a two up, two down house. Apparently the absentee landlord didn't care if they paid their rent.

While Michael was making money, he lavished things on Vera and this she relished, paying him with love and kisses as his generosity more than made up for his fists. He bought her a fur stole, evening gowns and jewellery, took her to dine at the finest restaurants.

Vera was beautiful in a hard as nails way, tall and straight with a terrific figure. From a distance you might have thought her upper class by her deportment, though when you drew closer and heard her speak, you knew better.

To redress this problem, Michael hired a speech teacher and each afternoon she took elocution lessons, lessons hilarious to both her and the teacher. The teacher, Harold Oldham, a handsome young man, had a flirtatious way about him. Vera quickly learned not to finish a sentence with 'eh?' and not to swear in public. Her progress must have been evident for Michael mentioned that she had much improved her manners and speech.

Vera wanted people to think of her as upper class and worked hard, though not as hard as she worked on getting Harold to kiss her.

When Caunce Mill changed hands, Michael spoke to the office

staff and, while the office clerks had hoped things would continue in much the same way, all were shocked to hear him announce they were sacked. Some almost fainted, one had a heart attack, others muttered oaths, and all swore to get even.

As the office staff departed, Michael stood in the window of his large second floor office and spoke to his new manager.

"Have you read the manual, Hawkins?"

"Yes, sir, Mr. Bradley, I have, and I understand everything."

"I will not tolerate wastage of any fashion, Hawkins, either in labour or purchasing. We will pare down wages. Sack a worker who is not willing to take the cut and hire as many Irish as are available. I want to see a profit within one month. Is that perfectly clear?"

"Yes, sir," Alf Hawkins said, as he wondered how these things were possible. Caunce Mill, he knew, had always been profitable, but to ask for more out of it seemed preposterous, and to sack people and hire Irish workers who worked for less seemed deplorable. Michael Bradley, he quickly learned, felt no concern for his workers, did not care that he was sentencing them to the workhouse. Too, the people hated the Irish in this district and Bradley was ordering him to take on more. No matter, it was not his decision but he needed this job, him with six children and one on the way.

Vera snuggled closer to Harold. This afternoon she wore a diaphanous tea gown trimmed with marabou. Her perfume clouded his senses and he swallowed nervously. Slowly he edged away, and, as slowly, she leaned toward him.

"What did you say this word was?" she leaned over further showing the tops of her breasts and he could not help but look.

"Reciprocation," he said, swallowing nervously.

"Reciprocation. What does it mean? I know you told me, but I've forgotten."

Harold stood, he was not safe next to her. He knew full well what she was doing and finding it hard to resist, but resist he must. She was a married woman and Michael Bradley was a hard man.

"It means that if someone invites you to supper or gives you a gift, then you should reciprocate by doing the same for them. Tit for tat, as they say amongst the peasants." They laughed. It was not funny, though, he thought as she stood, wound her arms around his neck and leaned against him.

"Does that mean that if I kiss you, you must reciprocate and kiss me? I like the sound of that, Harold."

He groaned as she kissed him passionately, her lips open and her tongue forcing its way into his mouth.

Grim faced, the solicitor handling Michael Bradley's suit against Weatherly Hospital, left a meeting of the hospital Board of Directors, furious.

They, having done their own investigation, informed him that Bradley had not lived with the woman for years and had remarried. They further stated that the writ was fictitious enough to sound as though he and his dead wife were madly in love and his lifestyle suffered from her absence. The man had lied.

The investigation revealed that a trainee nurse administered the wrong medication, and while they could not publicly admit it, an inside informant whispered it to his aide. A nurse also told him Eliza Bradley had lived with her sister for years, and had left Michael because of his cruelty. He also now knew about the daughter and Michael's subsequent action of putting her into a home from where she had escaped. The tabloids had featured the home, after being closed down by the authorities, when an astute reporter discovered that they induced and sold babies for profit.

Businessman or no, Mr. Bradley was not a respectable person. Well, he had squashed the suit when he withdrew it from the court roster today. If Mr. Big-Shot-Liar-Bradley wanted to pursue it any further, he was welcome to hire another solicitor and start from scratch. He was unwilling to help him any farther; mentally he added another ten percent to his fee.

Michael sat at the breakfast table and smiled as Joan poured his second cup of coffee. Vera's choice of servants suited him, they were all young and shapely. Even the cook, a young widow, was slim and attractive.

"Your mail, sir," the maid said as she passed the silver salver.

"Thank you." He picked up the small pile of envelopes and flipped through them. "Bill, bill, invitation. You open that, my dear," He passed it to Vera who rarely received mail. "Letter from my bank manager. That can wait until I get to the office." He tossed it on the table, paused and smiled, "Ah, this is a letter from my solicitor. The suit must be finished. I hope they settled out of court." He slitted open the envelope with the silver letter opener and removed the letter.

"What? God damn it!" He slapped the table so hard that the china rattled. "The man is mad, completely mad. He has withdrawn my suit!"

Vera looked startled. What was making him so angry?

"Why?" she asked.

"Why? Because the man is a moron, that is why. I must go over to his office immediately. Send for my carriage."

"Yes, dear," she said, hurrying from the room.

Harold and Vera spent the lesson time in her bedroom. She sent the servants out on errands and even gave the cook the afternoon off to visit her sister because tonight the Bradley's were dining with friends.

"Oh Vera, you are wonderful," he murmured into her hair.

"So are you, my love, so are you. I wish I was married to you, you know? Instead I got stuck with that cold as ice bastard. He often hits me, did I tell you?"

"Yes, you did. Why do you stay with him? Why don't you leave?"

Vera often wondered, but she knew well enough. She liked living in a nice house with servants, liked the clothes and jewellery, and the respect she got from shop keepers. Her married name opened many doors previously forbidden to her. No, she must stay with Michael if she could, for she knew that sooner or later he would tire of her. Then she could take up with someone like Harold, someone young with ambition, but with money, of course.

They stayed in bed for two hours, two of the most fantastic hours of Harold's life. Where had she learned all those things? He always thought of sex as a one position exercise, but she showed him things he would have thought impossible. He could not get enough of her.

Michael went to the mill when he left the law chambers. So he and Eliza had been separated, he fumed, but that didn't mean anything. He was entitled to compensation from the hospital, he argued. They had killed his wife. No one, he argued, knew about their imminent reconciliation.

"I see, and what was to happen to your current wife?"

Michael's face flamed redly as the solicitor quietly told him to find himself another legal man and politely showed him out.

Irate, Michael walked to the mill executive offices to find the Manager's office filled with a deputation from the mill floor. He smelled them before he saw them.

"Stand back at once," he ordered, poking two men in the back with his silver headed cane. They moved aside to let him through. "What's going on here?"

"Mr. Bradley," the spokesman said, "We can't go on like this. We've had our pay cut until it's not enough to keep a sparrow alive. You've increased the hours and taken away our noon break. You've got young children working ten and twelve hours a shift and that's against the law. You sacked fifteen women who were the sole support of their families because they were pregnant. You have to change the rules, Mr. Bradley or . . .,"

"Aye!" "Yes." "That's right." The others raised their voices.

"Or what? Who are you, and by what authority are you slacking? Who is running your looms? You know that time off means I will dock your pay."

"Aye, you'd do that too, wouldn't you? We can't work under these conditions, Mr. Bradley. You have to do some'at."

Michael raised his chin arrogantly, regarding them with superiority. Someone had to show them they were dispensable.

"If you don't like the conditions of employment, far be it from me to keep you here, my man. You may leave immediately. Hundreds of others stand in line for your job. I suggest you all leave now, before I call a constable."

He took out his handkerchief and held it to his nose. The office stank of stale perspiration and dirty bodies. "Well, what are you waiting for?"

"We want to talk sense, Mr. Bradley." The man was sweating heavily, he had not expected this ultimatum, but something must be done for the workers. The other men shuffled their feet, glancing at each other with shifty eyes. They were scared, Michael noticed. Good.

"Can't we talk this out?" the spokesman pleaded. "Surely we have some common ground . . .,"

"Common ground?" Michael sneered. "I am the owner and you are a worker, that is all the ground I see. You heard my decision and it is up to you whether you like it or not." He stood with his handkerchief to his face, smiling behind its cover.

"Surely the workers are entitled to a living wage?" The spokesman argued, "We're not yet slaves, but we soon will be if you have your way."

Michael thumped his cane on the floor. "Don't talk stupid man! The Irish don't have any trouble living on what I pay. They line up for a job here."

The shuffling men snorted derisively and cursed. Everyone hated the Irish.

"Mr. Bradley, can we talk this out or not? If not, then I must tell you that we'll walk out, not just us few, but the lot of us."

"What? Are you people organizing a worker's group? I'll have none of that in my mill. Are you Luddites? What's going on here?"

Mr. Hawkins, the manager pushed to the front. He didn't want to face his boss down, but maybe his words would carry more weight. "Mr. Bradley, the men are right. A living wage is all they ask. They've had their pay cut twice this last two months, and food does not go down in price. I'm sure you realize . . ."

"I'm sure you realize that I have sacked you, Hawkins." He poked him with the cane, pushing him backwards. "Get out of here. You men get either back to work, or leave with him."

Hawkins stood slack jawed. "Sacked? What on earth am I going to do now?"

"I don't know, and I don't care," Michael snapped.

The spokesman looked around at the assembled men and nodded. "We'll leave all right, but we'll take everyone out, Mr. Bradley. Don't ever say we didn't warn you."

They left, clomping loudly down the stairs and grumbling about the unfairness of it, swearing and spitting. Hawkins cleaned out his desk as Michael stood watching.

"Don't worry, sir, I am only taking what is mine," he said caustically.

"What is in that bag?" Michael put out his hand.

Hawkins opened the bag and took out a linen wrapped package. "My meals, sir. I can't afford to dine out on what you pay me. I eat at my desk at noon and almost every evening. Would you like to see what I eat?" He flipped open the cloth. "Here you are, four slices of home baked bread with a scraping of lard. That's all it is and that's all I can afford. I've six children relying on me to feed them. I have to go without so they can survive."

Michael sneered. "Don't talk to me of your martyrdom. I didn't ask you to have six children. I would have thought you'd have the intelligence to know why you have them, instead of impregnating your wife once a year."

"No wonder you are childless, sir," Hawkins was sarcastic now. What did it matter? "No woman could put up with you in that way. You must be a right pig in bed."

"How dare you! Leave the premises at once and don't ever set foot on my property again."

"Gladly, but I think you're in more trouble than you think from the sounds of it." Moving to the window, he looked down and laughed. A solid stream of workers moved out through the gates. They had all walked out, every last one of them.

"Hurray!" he shouted, "They've got you on the bloody ropes now, Mr. Bradley! Finished you they have, and bloody good luck to them." Tossing all the paperwork on his desk into the air, he left, whistling loudly.

Michael stood watching as the workers left. Hawkins was right about one thing, they had him on the ropes because even the Irish had walked out, and that was saying something.

To think the men at his club had slapped him on the back when they heard about his wage cuts. All of them followed suit in the following weeks, leaving him with the impression he had done something good for the industry. They mentioned his name in all the right places and the company's stock had risen considerably. Now look what that had achieved. What was he going to do without workers?

Vera kissed Harold goodbye in her bedroom and hurried him down the front stairs. The servants would soon be back and she could hear someone clattering around in the kitchen. Now to have a hot bath and get ready for their evening out. She felt relaxed after her wonderful afternoon.

Before she called the maid to run her bath, she opened the windows and sprayed the room with perfume to cover the strong salty smell of sex. It would never do for Michael to catch a whiff of another man in her room.

Joan took the freshly laundered bath towels up to Vera's bedroom. The mistress liked to bathe, she grumbled, to Mrs. King, and she bathed an awful lot these days.

"Thank you, Joan. Take out my pale green gown, the new one and press it, will you?"

Joan scurried down the stairs. Such news to tell Mrs. King. The mistress had a love bite on her breast, she had seen it, and it hadn't been there this morning when she handed madam her clothes.

CHAPTER TWENTY-FIVE

1889

Betty felt disgusted with Harry. He was such a pig, always dirty, always pawing at her, always getting drunk. He shied away from water, too, so he smelled bad. Why had she ever married him? They lived a life filled with hostility, for both now hated the other, and yet they stayed together. What choice did they have?

As for sex, it was an altogether nauseating experience because he was an animal, a rutting animal who gave no thought to her feelings. While she despised him during daylight hours, at night she detested him. Sammy was attending the village school during the day, so if she stayed home to do her housework, she was alone at the cottage. Harry always watched for her.

Each day she thanked God that she had not fallen with child. That would have been the last straw. Because of her failure to conceive, Harry took it as a slight against his manhood and pounced on her continually. Once he had pushed her into a bed of nettles and had his way with her.

He had already forced himself on her before breakfast while Sammy was still asleep, nothing stopped Harry if the urge came over him. Once he had taken her in the hen house, once in a field, and if he came at her again today she vowed to run away, go back to live at Hillshead where Clifford would protect her.

Harry walked across the lower field as she watched from the kitchen window. As he neared the house he took out his penis and started rubbing at it.

"Oh no!" she gasped and raced out the front door, running as fast as she could down the lane and through the woods. She ran back to Hillshead and started work in the dairy.

Vera, dressed to the nines when Michael arrived home, waited impatiently in her finery. As he opened the door, she said, "Tah-dah!" posing for him on the staircase. Joan had arranged her hair on top of her head in curls and she wore a crystal brooch at the front like a small tiara. She looked ravishing.

"Take that off. We're not going anywhere tonight," he snapped.

Her face fell into a pout and, as she moved toward him, he put up his hands as if to ward her off, his face cold and closed.

"I'll eat supper in my study and do not wish anyone, and I mean *anyone*, to disturb me."

Slamming the study door, he walked to his desk where he sat and put his head in his hands.

Vera stood in the hall. She looked beautiful, she knew she did, and yet he had not noticed. How mean he was. Still, this mood of his must mean something terrible had happened.

As she slowly went up the stairs to change, she thought about it, unable to imagine what it could be as he rarely shared any of his business affairs. Suppose he had lost all his money? Vera stopped short, a hand at her mouth. If that was true she must make arrangements. She might be married to him but she wasn't going to live in penury, not for Michael Bradley or anyone else.

Joyce left the mill with everyone else. She didn't want to leave as she desperately needed the money, but she had no choice when everyone walked out.

The new owner, Michael Bradley, she knew, was a tyrant, a definite skinflint when it came to paying out for work. The charge hands told the spinners and weavers that a lantern could only be lit when they gave the order and not before because Mr. Bradley decreed they were wasting too much oil. Since some looms had a million threads running and the windows were dirty and small, it was practically impossible to see in the gloom.

Some workers brought in small candle stubs and lit them, but this resulted in the levy of fines. Open flames were forbidden in mills because of the volatile cotton lint floating in the air. The women on night shift had to turn off the lanterns when given the order, for by that time the sun was coming up. Aye, it was not a good way to make a living. Even the Irish grumbled about it and they would take on anything.

A large group of working men formed a committee that met at a local pub once a week. When Bradley cut wages and managed to keep his mill operational, other mill owners followed suit. Now the unemployed did not race to find a job at Horsall's, or Ridley's because the pay was the same throughout the area, rock bottom.

Then came word that a mother and two small children had starved to death on Clover Court after Bradley fired her. The father came home after searching for work to find them dead in their bed. While the deaths warranted but two cryptic lines in the local newspaper, the entire neighbourhood was up in arms. After the walkout, in desperation, the workers agreed they would starve together to force the government to do something about the unfair business practices of Michael Bradley and his ilk. Sadly, the local churches urged them to go back to work, reluctant to offer assistance. This resulted in almost empty churches, apart from the upper class who sat in their private, paid for pews as if nothing were amiss.

When the local MP came north to hold an open air meeting, they booed him back to London. How dare he come here dressed in a fur collared coat, they said to each other, telling them they were in the wrong? Him, whose hands were lily white, who had never worked a day in his life. The workers knew the bigwigs of the town, the landowners, had elected him; he was one of them and didn't give a damn about the working man.

The chap that organized the revolt had the gift of the gab. He explained to them their rights as he stood on the steps of the corn hall and shouted his message.

"We have rights, and the bosses are contravening them. In the early eighteen hundreds, thousands of men and women banded together against the tyranny of their upper class bosses. All they wanted was enough money to buy food, clothing and shelter. The Combination Acts of 1799 and 1800 prohibited combinations, and this stripped the workers of any recourse as a group to action. Employers held us workers in their power and cut wages and hours any time they felt like it, meanwhile living in luxury in large country houses built many miles from the industry they owned.

"This, as you know, caused the formation of the Luddites in Lancashire. King Lud, we know is a fictional person though the bosses don't know. Our troubles started when wealthy men bought new machinery to spin and weave the cloth. The spinners and weavers became incensed that the wealthy had killed their cottage industry. They now had to work for those men, the men who controlled everything, even their lives. Those that tried to carry on at home soon found themselves jobless and destitute. This is what started the Luddites. Well-organized, they smashed machinery, set fire to factories, and burned down mills, but unfortunately none of this helped the ordinary working man who now had nowhere to work. Mills are the only source of cotton and wool employment in this area, that and the coal mines. We must stand firm this time against this tyranny and let the government see that we mean to fight to the end.

"We must not resort to violence. Violence is never the answer. It didn't change anything during the last uprising. I know that watching your family starve isn't easy. I know you want to lash out with your fists. I know you want justice. I face the same uncertain future but I do know that resorting to violence will not help us."

Men shouted him down, bolstering each other's wish to use their fists, or start setting fires, anything to hurt the bosses who stayed home on their estates, caring nothing for those who had worked to put them there.

. The unrest redoubled when Bradley lowered wages and hired the Irish who worked for pennies. That the other mills had followed suit antagonized the entire population of mill workers and now everyone publicly castigated Bradley for his part in the stoppage.

When news of the first walkout spread, the workers held secret meetings at other mills, so that, one by one, they too walked out. If they stood united, they agreed, the bosses must change the pay rates. Meanwhile the unhappy workers relied on meagre savings and the parish to help them survive.

Groups of unemployed hung around outside the mills, talking, always talking. Unsure of their motives and finding the situation grave, the government posted soldiers outside mill gates and factories. Seeing this, the working man became convinced his government had failed him and his employers were exploiting him again. At this point, the old Luddite movement went underground.

The rebellion of the Luddites could well happen again, Michael knew, destroying both mills and machines. Because now combinations were illegal, the bosses had thought the working class content. What the employers did not know was that the workers had sworn a secret oath and machine breaking regularly took place. Machines mysteriously shut down even in a crowded factory, yet no employee questioned had seen anything.

It was this underworld that Michael feared, thinking he had started another war between boss and worker.

In Joyce's case the walkout became a blessing. Down to her last copper, she walked the street looking for a shop job without much success. She went into a laundry to ask for work just as a girl was leaving in tears.

"Is there any work?" she asked for what seemed like the hundredth time that day.

"Talk about dead lucky," the small fat woman said looking her up and down. "See that girl that left? Well, she got sacked for scorching two linen sheets. Can you start right away?"

Joyce went to work in the laundry. It was not hard work to one who had been used to the constant heaving and carrying of milk churns and hay bales. No, she didn't find it hard, in fact sometimes it was positively dead easy.

Agatha lost her baby and was in labour only two hours. After the still birth, she lost her zest for life and Eddy couldn't understand why she didn't cuddle him or fuss over him.

Clifford felt unable to cope. No matter what he said or did made any difference to Agatha, who could not seem to shake off her depression. He tried to talk to her, tried to show her how much life still had to offer, told her they would have another child soon, but she refused to listen.

"The gypsy was right," she shouted, the tears streaming down her face. "This house is cursed, this family is cursed. Why didn't you let the gypsy remove the curse from us, Clifford? She said it was on you, that you were the next in line. This death is to punish you, to make you unhappy, but it's killing me."

Clifford could not make her see sense and the doctor could not prescribe anything for her malady. Two months later when she jumped down an abandoned mine shaft to her death, Clifford became inconsolable. Eddy took to whining and bed wetting and the entire farm functioned under a blanket of gloom.

One day when he was driving the farm cart back to the farm, he saw a young girl run down the hillside waving at him.

"Stop, please stop." The words came thin and high. He reined in the horses and waited until she clambered over the dry stone wall.

"Please, please come, sir. My brother has fallen and I think he has broken his leg. Please come, sir." She climbed back over the wall and Clifford followed her.

"Come on then, lass," He picked her up, thinking this might get them there faster. She clung to his neck, still sobbing. "Stop crying and tell me which way to go."

"Up near the old pit head. He fell off the old wheel gear," she gasped, struggling to get down. She ran ahead of him and he struggled over the hummocky grass and boulders.

"Now, laddy, what's to do here?" he gasped as they reached the boy.

Freddy lifted his head, raised his tear stained face. "I appear to have hurt my leg, sir. I can't walk. I'm so sorry."

Clifford saw the neat clothes, the hair cut and heard the upper crust accent and knew this was Albert Stockton's boy. Attending a snobby school, he was, a posh Grammar school at that. Albert was getting above himself, the locals all said, sending his children to classy schools so they could lord it over the other kids. The boy he knew, was ten and the girl a year younger.

"Just lie still, lad. I'll get you home before you can say 'pickled owls' eggs.'" Clifford smiled and picked up two lengths of wood. Digging in his pocket, he found a jumble of twine and picked out the knots. "Right, lad, lie still and we'll fix this."

"Could I help, sir?" the girl asked and he looked up at her. God! His heart skipped a beat. She was the spitting image of Jenny, the first girl he had ever loved. Maybe this child was his daughter!

He moved to his task, his mind racing. His daughter, his own child was standing watching as he helped her brother. It had to be she, who else would have such a likeness?

Clifford looked up at her and smiled. She was calmer now. "Hold him steady while I put on this splint. We can carry him on our arms down to the cart and then it's an easy stretch home."

As they slowly walked the horses to Mayhurst, he talked to her. "What's your name, lass?"

"Angela Stockton," she said, "You know my parents, Albert and Adele."

So that was it, he reckoned, Angela was the adopted daughter. That made a lot of sense for if she was who he thought she was, she was both his and their blood relation.

"Aye, you must have been away at school, eh? I haven't seen either of you two for years. Has he?" he nodded with his head to the back where Freddy was lying on a pile of old sacks, "been away, too?"

"Yes, he's a boarder now at Alderley Grammar School. This is our summer holidays."

Freddy groaned as the cart hit a rut and joggled him roughly.

Clifford looked back at him, saw the perspiration on his pale face. "Soon be there, lad, and here comes your Dad if I'm not mistaken."

Albert walked toward the approaching cart. A visitor was rare at Mayhurst, especially an unexpected one.

"I've got your lad in the back, Albert," Cliff shouted, "Fell and hurt his leg. I'd send for the doctor if I were you."

Albert and Clifford got Freddy up to his bed and Adele and Angela fussed over him.

"Thank you, lad, you've been a lifesaver, an' all," Albert said, patting Clifford on the back. "Come on now, we'll have a drink to celebrate his safe return. I've sent a man for the doctor."

They sat drinking home brewed ale and talked of crops and the weather until the doctor arrived.

"Well, me for off, Albert. Thank you for the dram."

"Thank you for looking after my boy. By the way, how's your young lad these days?"

Clifford shook his head. "Not good, he still misses his mother. Maybe you could send your two over to play with him when Freddy can walk. Eddy is a terrible trial to me, and I don't mind admitting it. Withdrawn and moody, miserable as sin and I can't get through to him. Neither can Marian, and he likes *her*."

The doctor came down the stairs before they had finished speaking.

"Nothing to worry about, Mr. Stockton, a pulled muscle and a few bruises. More hurt dignity than anything else, I would say. That splint was a good idea, though his leg is not broken. At least when he thought it was, he wasn't moving around too much. Unfortunately now he knows it isn't, he's raring to go outside. Keep him in bed for the rest of the day. Tomorrow he'll be top notch."

Albert and Clifford laughed. "Aye, boys will be boys."

"Keep him way from that old mine," the doctor warned. "It's dangerous and I understand your girl was with him. Nasty place that, nasty."

Angela and Adele came down the stairs. Angela smiled up at Clifford and he felt his heart thump painfully. She was so like her mother, down to the dimple.

"Thank you, Mr. Wright," she said sweetly, "Freddy also says thank you. You saved his life."

"Aye, that I did." Clifford chuckled. "He couldn't have walked far on that leg, and he might have missed his tea. Well, tell him the next time he goes near that place I'll tan his backside, and that applies to you as well. Don't you go anywhere near the top. There's mine shafts and God knows what up there."

"No, sir, I won't and I won't let Freddy go, either," she said as she smiled and bobbed a curtsy.

Clifford watched her as she went into the kitchen. "A nice lass that," he said, "Well mannered and pretty."

"Aye, that she is, that she is," Albert said, nodding. "We were dead lucky when we got her, all right. She's the light of my life. Young Freddy now, not taking anything anyway from him mind, is a right boyyo and lad after my own heart, but Angela is my angel. She's what I live for."

"I can well understand why, Albert. Why don't you fetch them both over to Hillshead sometime? Try and get my young'un out of the doldrums. Maybe that's what's missing, someone who can talk with him, kids nearer his own age."

"Happen you're right, Clifford. I'll do that when Freddy gets up, and if the what the doc says is right, it might be any second."

Laughing, both clattered down the passage and went out onto the forecourt.

Within twenty-four hours, Freddy was rushing around much as usual with a light bandage on his leg. Albert and Adele talked about young Eddy and arranged that Albert should take them over to Hillshead for the afternoon.

"If it works out, maybe Clifford could fetch Eddy over here for the day," Adele said, "A change of scene may well be the thing." She could not see young Eddy taking to Freddy as he talked 'with a plum in his mouth' as the locals called it.

"Aye, that's an idea," Albert said, "I'll put it to Clifford. Anyroad, we have to wait and see how this afternoon goes. Don't forget our two speak different, and since young Eddy's too young for school, he'll be miles behind our children." Albert also realized his children were a cut above the locals.

"Children are children, and they'll soon find their own way of communicating." Adele looked over to where her two were petting a farm cat. "Poor little Eddy, he must miss his mother."

"Aye, well I'd better be off." He raised his voice. "Angela, Freddy, come on, let's go."

"Wait a minute, father," Freddy said as both he and Angela rushed upstairs to come clattering down the stairs carrying various objects.

"What on earth have you got there?" Adele asked, curious.

"Well, Mamma, Miss Grosvenor said we should never visit someone empty handed, and since you told us that little Eddy is upset that his mother died, well . . well . . we thought we should take him some toys. Didn't we, Freddy?"

Freddy looked put out. "You decided that, not me. Now I have to give him my toys because you only have silly girl things," Freddy said, annoyed.

"What have you chosen to give him?" Albert looked at the small stock of toys, all well used, pleased the children would think of such a thing. It went to show what a good education did for the soul.

The children spent their afternoon with Eddy, and both thought him a cry baby, but by the time they left with their father, he was starting to come out of his shell and chattering to them without prodding.

Albert smiled as he saw Angela give Eddy a hug.

"Well now, young Eddy," he said, "Your dad says he'll fetch you over to Mayhurst tomorrow if you'd like to come."

"Aaw, yes please," he said, nodding furiously. Angela and Freddy laughed at that, but he took it in good part and joined them.

Thank God for that, Albert thought, realizing his children had gotten Eddy to smile. He nodded to Clifford who stood atop the hay wain he had driven into the farm yard for unloading.

"Fetch him over when you get the chance, Clifford," he called, "He'll be fed and watered, I promise you that."

"Get away with you, man," Clifford laughed. "You'd better make sure I get him back in one piece."

"Father!" Freddy said.

Simultaneously Angela said, "Daddy!" embarrassed at their exchange.

CHAPTER TWENTY-SIX

Vera felt down in the dumps. These days Harold was her only joy in life and his lack of imagination was beginning to pall.

Michael had become difficult to live with, but she understood it after the Luddites burned his mill to the ground. Keen to get his own back, he evicted any workers unable to afford the rent, and squatters, mostly Irish, almost instantaneously moved into the empty houses. The constabulary futilely tried to evict them. However, this was useless as the squatters simply boarded up doors and windows, and moved in and out of the houses through the attic space of the terraced houses. Inside the terraces were over a hundred people they couldn't get out. All the time the houses were thus occupied, Michael could not lease to paying tenants, or collect rents.

The destruction of his mill and his subsequent stock market losses, resulted in his bank account being whittled down to a last twelve thousand. While a meagre thousand would have supported a family of four for a couple of years or more, Michael lived well, so well that ten thousand to him was almost poverty. It was all relative.

Vera, miserable because he did not take her out to dine, or to the theatre, sulked because they did not entertain and invitations were few. She seriously considered leaving him. One way out was to move in with Harold and, although he was not exactly what she wanted, he would suffice until the right man came along.

"Harold?" she breathed into his ear one afternoon, "Harold would you let me live with you?"

"What? Live with me?" He pulled back on the pillow to look at her incredulously. "What about your husband, or had you forgotten him in your passion for my body?"

"I *want* to leave him, Harold. He's too old for me and too much of a penny pincher."

She lay amid the tumbled pillows and bed sheets, naked and desirable and he felt a great passion for her. Yet to want to live with him?

"Now, Vera, you know he has business problems, what with the mill burning down, then his stock market losses. You should stand by him. Isn't that what your wedding vows said? For richer, for poorer?"

She pulled a face, stroked his arm. "I don't want to be poor. He says we are poor now, and I like money. I mean, that's why I married him, not for his good looks or his body. Now *your* body, that's a different matter. You're young and good looking, and you make a decent living. I know what Michael pays you and you also have other pupils."

"I also have a wife and a child," he said quietly.

Vera gasped. It had never entered her mind that he could be married. "I thought you were single."

Harold chuckled. "Did you think your husband would allow a carefree bachelor to be alone with you every afternoon?"

The revelation took her aback. Harold was such a sexual neophyte that she had never thought of him as married. "No, I don't suppose so. I never thought about that."

Damn the man, and to think she thought him single, had spent hours teaching him how to make love to a woman. Putting back her head, she laughed aloud. She pitied the poor woman married to him because if you didn't tell him what to do he had no idea. She wondered if he practised his new found prowess on his wife these days.

"What's so funny?"

"You being married. Your poor wife. Did you make love to her properly after I showed you how?"

Harold sat up and put on his shirt. His stony expression told her he felt insulted.

"Don't talk silly," he said tersely, "What *we* two do is not making love, it is common unadulterated, or should I say *adulterated*, lust, and you know it. I love my wife, Vera. It's only because you insist on doing this that I do it. Why should I refuse a free gift? What man would?"

She jumped from the bed and stood blazing at him. "How dare you! Get out, get out and never come back. I'll tell Michael I've saved him some money. He'll be delighted, I can assure you."

Throwing back his head, he laughed loudly. "Sorry, my dear, but your husband paid me a lump sum for your lessons. He paid me for a year. So he saved nothing, and you, well . . . you gave it away."

"Get out, you bastard, get out." She threw a slipper at him, but he dodged it skilfully, shut the door and ran down the stairs.

Vera sulked for ages, until she glanced at the clock and realized Michael would soon be home, if he hadn't gone to his club, that is.

These past months he had not come to her room for any reason and she wondered why. He couldn't possibly know about Harold because if he had, he would have beaten her. She knew he was struggling to regain his fortune and had formed a consortium with four others to rebuild the mill.

She sighed as she fixed her hair. Would they ever be rich again? The reconstruction process was taking a long time, what with cash flow problems and labour stoppages, and Michael was still not sure he could ever again get the workers to work for him. He had told her that to bypass that possibility, the mill would have a new name, the name of the other partners, Mills, Gormley and Hardcastle. The name Bradley would never appear on anything the work force was ever likely to see. Further, to ensure his anonymity, they had moved the mill offices to the town instead of on the mill premises.

Vera, unsettled for all his promises that things would soon return to normal, was not at all sure she could stay with him.

"When," she asked that evening, "are you going to take me to purchase my new wardrobe? The winter season is approaching so I require gowns and furs."

Michael, while annoyed at her inability to comprehend she had no reason for the purchase since they were not to entertain or accepting invitations, opted for peace. "Next week we will travel to London where you can shop to your heart's content."

This was a stop gap measure to gain breathing space. He had no intention of spending money on Vera for she bored him now, always asking questions, demanding that he buy this or that, questioning his whereabouts. In Huddersfield he had a young mistress, a pleasant young person, of only seventeen and in comparison with her fresh young beauty, Vera looked like an old hag. No, he'd continue to make promises he had no intentions of keeping and hope she got the message.

He could, of course, beat her once or twice so she would learn faster. That he had considered more than once, but he got no pleasure from beating her as she usually managed to turn it into something sexual. The act of beating was a ceremony she had learned to please certain men, and she knew how to turn it to her advantage.

For once in his life he was at a loss, how to rid himself of the woman he now considered a blood sucker. When he thought about it, he realized he had never had a normal relationship with any female.

His mother died when he was small. He never knew her and his aunts raised him. The two old maids, man-hating spinsters, were not exactly competent to raise a small boy and took their antagonism out on him in one way or another, so over the years he developed a hatred for women. As he matured and developed physical longings, he tried homosexuality but found it displeasing. The only relationship that seemed to afford him any pleasure was an abusive one.

Not that he could ever have harmed a hair of his daughter Jennifer's head. She had been his only joy in life. He had harboured great ambition for her, yet she had turned out to be one of 'them', no better than the filthiest whore on Market Street. Her defection hurt him so deeply that he completely turned against the entire female tribe.

Vera was merely the means to an end. A man in his position needed a wife, a hostess. While she then suited his purpose, now his fortunes had changed she was under the impression it should not affect her life of ease. Because of his financial reversal, she reverted to her real self, a selfcentred bitch who wanted everything handed to her on a gold plate.

Michael was good at dissembling so Vera suspected nothing. He planned to get rid of her, and wasn't she going to be shocked when he did the deed?

The letter he opened at breakfast brought him to his feet.

"You bitch! You slut!" he yelled.

She stared at him, open mouthed. Was he talking to her?

Dropping his napkin, he strode around the table, hauled her to her feet and held her against the wall. Joan heard the chair fall to the floor and dashed into the dining room through the swinging door. Michael did not hear her.

"What's the matter, Michael?" Vera gasped, terrified. His hands were around her throat, his face purple with rage.

"What's the matter?" he roared, "What's the matter? I get a letter from someone who wishes to remain anonymous informing me that you spend the better part of your afternoons in bed with your tutor, and you ask me what's the matter? You sicken me, you slut, make me want to puke."

Vera struggled to free herself, but he was too strong. He had pinned her against the wall like a butterfly on a pin. "Please let go of me, Michael. That is a poison pen letter. How could you think such a thing of me?"

"Master?" Joan said loudly.

He heard her, but did not turn. "Get out of here, you whore. You're as bad as she is, since you let the man go upstairs with my wife. You're sacked and take that stupid cook with you."

Turning around suddenly and releasing Vera, he went for Joan who ran screaming into the kitchen. Vera slid down the wall, her legs like jelly.

Oh my God, who could have sent such a letter? She scrabbled across the floor, grabbed and looked at it. It was a woman's hand, she could see that. What woman, though? It bore no signature, but then there never was on such missives. She looked at the postmark and saw it was local, the Market Street Post Office. Whoever had sent it wanted Michael to attack her, obviously aware of his rages, maybe wanted Michael for herself. She was welcome to him, stupid old bastard that he was.

Dragging herself to her feet, she hauled herself up the stairs, hand over hand on the bannister and locked herself in her room, where she started throwing clothes onto the bed. Time to leave, time to leave.

Michael chased the women out of the kitchen, slammed and locked the doors on them, then started upstairs.

"Vera! Vera!" he roared. Turning the door handle, he cursed and kicked at the lower panels. "Open this door. There's no need for this. This is my house and I demand that you open this door immediately. Do you hear me, Vera?"

She stood by the bed, her arms full of dresses and heard his ragged breathing. He sounded terribly angry, so angry that she dared not open the door.

For five minutes he pounded and then seemed to run out of steam. Then came comparative silence, although he was still there, she could still hear him gasping. Maybe he was having a heart attack, she thought, or maybe he was near collapse. She prayed that was the case, anything that would help her escape from the house. Moving quietly closer to the door, she put her ear against it.

On the other side, Michael stood catching his breath and making plans. Suddenly turning and running to his room, he started opening and shutting drawers. She could hear him.

"Vera?" His voice was kind and gentle. "Open the door, dear, come on now. Let's make up. You know I don't like it when we quarrel. You're right. I've thought about it and I don't believe that letter. Some mischief maker sent it, probably an old employee from the mill."

Oh yes? she thought, did he think she would believe that? She knew damned well that the paper was expensive, the penmanship educated. No, a worker had not sent the letter.

"I was jealous and it made me angry." His voice sounded soft and pleading. "Please forgive me, my darling, and let's be friends."

"Go away, Michael. I don't want to talk to you," she said quietly. "You can't play with my feelings this way. That you could even think for one moment that I'd cheat on you is incredible. I have been true to you from the moment we met."

Oh sure, he said mentally, you whore. "Please, sweetheart, open the door. I want to hold you and kiss you and make it all up to you. I'll never do it again, I promise you, please, please open the door."

"Go away, Michael. We'll sleep on it, but for today I don't want to see you," Vera insisted, wondering whether talking to him this way was wise. If he stayed calm, she would be all right. When he was asleep she could flee the house.

"Come closer to the door, Vera. Let me talk to you," he wheedled.

"No, Michael, I'm going to sleep now. You have upset me too much."

His ear to the panel, he sensed she was close to the door. Yet which side was she? He had to keep her talking.

"Remember when we first met, my darling? Remember?"

She leaned against the door wearily. How long was he going to keep this up? "Yes, I remember."

"I can't hear you, say it again," he murmured, listening intently, hearing the silk of her gown against the door.

"I said yes, I remember."

Putting the barrel of the gun against the door, he shot through the right panel, heard her intake of breath and a yelp, then quickly moved it to shoot through the left. She screamed, then fell solidly to the floor.

It was done, she was suffering now, like she had made him suffer. Laughing maniacally, he staggered down the stairs.

Someone hammered again and still laughing with tears streaming down his face, he opened the door. Joan and a Constable stood there.

CHAPTER TWENTY-SEVEN

1891

Betty ran away from home on a Friday morning. Harry had gone to the market with a load of potatoes and she was alone with Sammy.

Sammy thought it great fun as they climbed the hill at the back of the house. When he got to the top, he hollered with joy. Who would have thought the world was so vast?

"Come on now, Sammy, we have to keep moving," she urged. Earlier she told the eleven-year-old they were going to the seaside and he was eager to know what it was like. For ages she described the waves, how they came in and went out, how ships of all sizes floated on it and how they would sail on one. He was so excited, bless him, and how could he know they might never reach the sea? They were miles from it and the hills ahead of them would hide it from view until they reached the top of the last of the Pennines.

Once Liz and Eddy had taken her, Joyce and Clifford to the seaside. Betty never forgot it though she was only a toddler. The grand vastness of it, the screaming gulls, the steady offshore winds that blew her clothes about and took the bonnet right off her head.

That day her father had gone to Bispham to pick up a bull from a stock farm and while he conducted his business, they were left in the fishing village to wait. It was a poor place, the people were shabby, most were bare footed. A couple of older men wore wooden clogs. The sound of the irons on them made her laugh as they clattered over the cobbles causing sparks. The clatter sounded like horses' hooves, not people.

A fisherman took Clifford on board his small craft to look around, Clifford, always curious about things, came back stinking of rotten fish. How they had laughed about it later because the smell of him was so bad that Dad eventually made him walk home behind the cart. She smiled now thinking back.

"Could we catch some fish for us tea, Mam?" Sammy gasped as he struggled to keep up with her.

"Maybe we will, my boy, maybe we will." She hoisted the large bundle of their clothes higher on her back and thanked God she had brought enough food to last them for a couple of days. The lad's legs were long for his age, but not long enough to keep up a fast pace. They were still in sight of the cottages, she noticed nervously glancing over her shoulder as they crested another ridge. It seemed like they had been walking for hours.

It was a pleasant day for walking. The sun shone and a breeze moved the puffy clouds around. Ahead she could see a patchwork of fields in all colours, yellow and green, brown and orange, depending on what crops were growing or were newly harvested. A hedgerow on the higher hill side of the field marked the boundary. Along the lanes she saw cottages, white in the sun, with gardens around them. Woods and copses abounded near the peaks. Strangely she saw not one sign of human life, apart from smoke rising from chimneys. Yet being away from Hillshead farm made her feel better and it was like she had shaken free from her worries.

By the time they had crossed the rocky bracken-covered hills and started down to a cultivated valley, Sammy started to complain of being tired.

"I can't go no further," he announced sitting on a fallen tree. "I want to go home and I want my tea."

"Oh, lovey, we can't go home now. Don't you want to see the sea?"

His head popped up and he stared around. "Where is it? I can't see it."

"We have a fair piece to go yet. Tomorrow we'll be there. Today we'll rest while you get your breath and then I'll make us some tea? All right, son?"

Sammy sulked as she made a small fire and boiled water from a nearby brook in the small saucepan she had brought. When it was near boiling, she tossed in tea leaves and stirred it with a twig.

"Here we go, a nice drink. You'll feel better after this."

Digging in the bundle, she found the two tin mugs and stoneware bottle of milk. Topping up his mug with milk, she handed it to him.

"This is nice, Mam. Sitting here, drinking our tea." He tilted his back his head and looked at the tree overhead. A small red squirrel sat on a branch, chattering and twitching its tail.

"Where'd it go, Mam?" he asked, eyes searching the tree.

"It jumped across to that other tree. Come on now, finish your tea and then we'll walk a while."

"My feet is too sore, Mam." he whined, "Can't we stay here?"

"No, we must find shelter for the night. We can't sleep in the open. Suppose it rains? You wouldn't want to get wet now, would you?"

Sammy grudgingly followed as she walked down the hillside. He could see cows and sheep on the lower slopes. That meant a farm nearby, he knew.

"Maybe the farmer will let us sleep in a bed," he said, "maybe we can eat a nice supper with the farmer. Maybe the farmer . . .,"

Betty sighed, poor lad and it was all her fault for fetching him. "All right, Sammy, that's enough. We won't be eating with any farmer. We can't. I'll ask if we can sleep in a barn or outhouse."

Sammy stopped dead and sat on a rock, put his face on his hands, his elbows on his now dirty knees. "I want to go home. I want to sleep in my own bed and see Dad. I want my supper. I hate you, Mam. You said we were going to the sea, you promised. I don't want to walk no more, my feet hurt." He started sobbing.

Betty stopped and put down the bundle. Walking was a mistake, she realised, and if she'd had found a way of cadging a lift from someone going to market, they might have fared better. On market day, the town filled with such crowds that Harry would not have seen them and they could have taken the train to the coast. No, maybe not, since it cost so much.

"All right, son, we'll stay here, but you're going to be cold when the sun goes down. We can't go home now. It's too far to walk back," she said, her voice expressionless. She felt weary, tired to the bone.

Sammy was young, but he was not stupid and he carefully thought about what she said. "All right, Mam, we'll walk some more, but not far, mind. You could piggyback me and I'd carry your bundle."

She had to laugh, the size of him. She couldn't even pick him up with ease because he was big and stocky with it. Carry him *and* her bundle?

"You daft ha'porth, I can't carry you. You're too big for me."

Half an hour's slow walk later, they reached a large decrepit barn. Once it had probably held hay or crops, but now the doors sagged outwards. It looked abandoned.

"We'll stop here tonight, my lad," she said as she looked inside. "This'll do us perfectly."

She put down the bundle inside the doors and looked around. Lots of old timbers had fallen. Enough for a roaring fire, she thought, and the wood was dry.

"Come on, let's make a fire and have our supper," she said, making her voice light and carefree. Sammy picked up on her tone of voice and started whistling tunelessly as he carried bits of wood to a central point outside the old doors.

Betty managed to light the fire and was boiling water for tea when a man appeared.

"Oy! What you up to down there?"

Shading her eyes, she looked up at the road. "Who wants to know?" she called. The man could be a tramp.

"That barn is my property and I don't want you burning it down. What're you doing?" As he asked, Sammy ran from behind the building, a can of water in his hand. "How many are you?"

"Me and my son. We needed to rest and need somewhere to sleep. We've been walking all day."

He came to stand in front of where she sat on a rock. Betty saw before her an upright man, about forty with all his own teeth, smiling right at her. He looked friendly enough.

"Hello, mister," Sammy said, putting out his hand.

The man shook it and said, "Hello, lad, and what's your name, eh?"

"Sammy, it's Samuel, but that's my Sunday-go-to-church name."

"Aye, a right mouthful, it is an'all, and you?" He smiled down at Betty who was trying to push bits of her hair under her bonnet to tidy herself.

"Betty," she said, wondering whether she should add her surname. Better not, least said the better.

"Where are you heading?" He seemed to want to talk and she idly wondered who he was.

"The coast or as close as we can get. I've got a relative at Blackpool."

"Married or widowed?" he asked, eyeing her up and down in a way that made her feel uncomfortable. She wasn't going to answer questions, that might mean trouble.

"Look, all I want is permission to stop here for the night. My lad is tuckered out and needs to rest. Can we stop or not?"

"If you want," he said slowly, "but you'll find much better accommodation at my farm down the road. I hate to think of the lad sleeping in this old place. It's full of rats, you know." Noting her horrified glance around, he added, "And snakes."

Immediately she stood and started stamping on the flames. "I'll take you up on that offer, mister. Sammy get some more water and douse this fire."

He smiled. "Good, you'll have a warm bed and a hot meal before you know it." He helped stamp out any remaining embers and waited until Sammy poured the water on the ashes.

"Right, let's be off."

They walked up the bank and onto the lane. After about five minutes they rounded a curve and a farm came into view.

"That's my place," he said proudly, "Oakapple Acres."

Betty looked up at him. Strange name that. "Acorn you mean? That's what an oakapple is."

"Aye, my dad inherited from his dad. There's been a Longstaffe farming here for many hundreds of years. That barn, the one you left, that's been standing for almost four hundred years and it's past fixing now. My granddad abandoned it, but it's so well built that it don't seem to want to fall down."

They walked down the short worn path to the farm yard. It was not well kept, she noticed, not like Hillshead. The usual abandoned rusty equipment stood around, making the space look like a rubbish tip. Piles of manure stood near the outbuildings and the pond looked stagnant, covered as it was in green slime. If the outside was this bad, she shuddered to think what the inside was like.

"Will your wife mind?"

"About you? I don't think so, I haven't seen her for over six years. Aye, she skipped out with a tinker. She allus was a randy sod," he laughed mirthlessly, "That's why I married her. I guess I should have known better."

When they went inside the dark kitchen, she almost heaved. It smelled putrid.

"Do you mean to tell me you can live in this pigsty and not notice it?" she gasped.

"Mam, it smells nasty," Sammy whined. "I want to go home. Let go my hand, mister, I want to go home."

He released Sammy's hand and shrugged. "It's up to you, Betty. You're welcome to stay, but I won't force you. Don't sleep in that barn, not with those rats and snakes."

She trembled at the thought. Looking around as her nose became accustomed to the stench and her eyes to the dim light from the dirty window, she figured she could clean it some, move out the rubbish and clear the table.

"If I stay, will you help us clean up this mess?"

"Aye, and gladly. I don't know where to start. I'm not much for house work."

For an hour he helped move out the heavy stuff so she could wash the floor. She found an old mop and a couple of scrubbing brushes, but she was not going to bottom it, simply tidy it. Once she washed the floor and removed the spoiled food and rubbish, the place looked decent, not clean but decent.

"What's your name, seeing you're being free with mine?" she asked as she scrubbed the table with sand.

"Harry, Harry Longstaffe."

"Harry?" Well if that didn't take the cake, his name was Harry, too. She felt like laughing.

Two hours later they sat at the table and ate a hot meal. Harry brought in a large smoked ham from an outhouse and she sliced and heated it. Mashed potatoes and Brussels sprouts made up the rest of the meal.

"Bah gum, Betty, that was smashing. You can cook, there's no getting away from it." He rubbed at his full stomach.

They were chatty now, so she said, "Get away with you, Harry, you ate that so fast it didn't touch your teeth or tongue. Is that the first meal you've had since she left you?"

"No, of course not. I can fry things and I have a hot meal every day, but I can't cook like that. Anyroad, my spuds are always like bullets and my Brussels tough as tree trunks. I didn't know you took any leaves off them and cut the stems. Deary me."

Betty and Harry laughed as Sammy sat fast asleep in his chair.

"Oh, I'd better put him to bed," Betty said as she looked at her son. "You wouldn't think he was only eleven, would you? He's almost the size of a man when he stands up straight."

"Bah gum, I thought he was older than that and backwards." Betty reared back when he said that, but she had heard it too often to take offence. "No wonder the young'un is off his feet with sleep. Look, leave him here while I show you where he can sleep."

They went up the four broad uneven stairs and around a bend from where rose another seven narrower stairs. "It's not much, but it's better than that barn," Harry said as he struck a match and lit a candle. "In here."

He moved into a small room that held a truckle bed, holding the candle high so she could see. "You'll find some blankets in that chest and a pillow."

"This is fine. I hope the bed isn't too damp. How long is it since anyone slept in it?"

"Must be ten years. I use to sleep there when I was a lad. It's cosy enough when you've got a blanket."

"Right." She opened the cedar lined chest and took out two blankets that she spread and then got a pillow. "He'll be cosy here, Harry. Thank you. Now let's fetch him."

"No, you stay here and I'll carry him."

While he was going down, she looked around. No window in this room but that didn't matter for one night, although she knew Sammy would yell if he realized it. He had always been afraid of small confined spaces and liked to see outside. She recalled the afternoon he had got himself locked in the dairy at Hillshead. That day he almost screamed the place down in panic.

She popped into the short hall and looked in the other two doors. Both held beds. Good, that meant she could also relax tonight. Harry's bed was messy, the sheets filthy, but the other narrow bed in the other room looked clean enough.

"Here he is," Harry said as he rounded the bend, "I'll put him down so you can get the boots off him."

As they went back down the stairs, Betty wondered why he was still unattached and living like this. It must get on his nerves, all that mess and still he didn't try to clean it up. What made him tick? Somehow she felt vaguely uneasy.

When Vera died of her wounds, they charged Michael Bradley with murder and incarcerated him to await his execution.

"Look at that, Albert!" Adele exclaimed as she passed him the Manchester Guardian.

"My God, he shot his wife and got charged with it," he said disgustedly as he tossed down the paper. "Says he went out of his head and is as mad as a hatter."

"I always thought something was strange about Michael, something not right. Thank God Eliza got away from him when she did, or he might have killed her like she said." Her face grew sad. "Poor Eliza and to think I used to envy her, all those clothes and that posh house. My poor dear sister."

Albert put his hands on her shoulders and shook her gently. "All right now, don't start bubbling. The bastard got what he deserved by the sounds of it."

"What bastard, Daddy?" Angela said, making him start. They had not seen her standing near the china cabinet.

"Angela!" Adele said, hands over her heart. "Don't ever do that again. I could have had a heart attack. Please make your presence known. We were talking about something in the paper. Now start your homework like a good girl."

Adele flashed Albert a look and picked up the paper which she folded and put under her arm. She would cut out the article and use the rest to make tomorrow's fire.

The paper was still full of ongoing news about the world wide influenza epidemic which had already killed so many. They had heard about some county cases and were lucky that it had not decimated the village. Today the news was of the Factory Act newly enacted to stop child labour. Parliament had ruled that no child under eleven could work in a factory or mill.

She sighed as she later set the table for tea. To think that Angela was Michael's granddaughter, that his blood ran in her veins. The girl must never know. Still, no reason why she ever should know because her name from christening had been Stockton.

In one way, she supposed Jennifer's death had solved a lot of problems. If an adoption agency were involved (although they swore nobody would ever know because they sealed the records), it could well have been that Jennifer could have discovered her predecessors in the future.

Never must she know about her parentage, Adele thought. She and Albert often talked about it. Freddy was the kind who wouldn't care about his adoption. Everything rolled off him as water off a duck's back. Fed, housed and loved, he wouldn't take it to heart. However, Angela was such a caring sort, so soft hearted, always feeling so badly for anyone or anything that suffered. She was also charitable in that she was willing to give away everything she owned to make another person happy. If she ever discovered Adele and Albert were not her parents, God only knew how she would take it.

That night after Angela was in bed they reread the clipping. "Throw it in the fire now, Adele. We don't want it lying around for her to find. She'll be asking questions about hanging and such."

"Oh, she doesn't go poking into things. Freddy does, I'll give you that. He wants to know everything about everything. Yes, best place for it, I guess." She tossed it into the flames.

"That's the end of the chapter there, Adele. The very end. We'll never mention it again."

"No, we never will," she agreed, "I promise you that."

CHAPTER TWENTY-EIGHT

etty and Sammy stayed on at the farm for two days. Harry was hospitable although Betty felt more than a little apprehensive. Sammy had taken to the man right away and followed Harry around much as he had followed his 'dad' Clifford. Sammy, she realized, needed a male role model.

She spent her days cleaning the farm house. It was like it was hers now for Harry and Sammy were outside during the day. Sammy went with Harry when he went to harvest and mucked in with the rest of the workers, as he had at home.

Already the small house began to sparkle. If he had paid her for doing it, she thought, she would be rolling in it. Stupid her, she had done it for nothing. She was thick, she was. Harry Longstaffe, aye, he was quids in, getting a free cleaner, she thought as she hung out sheets to dry.

Mould and mildew spotted every item of laundry, a huge pile that he had shoved into the scullery. Why was she doing it? Why hadn't she left as she had said after staying the one night? Maybe for Sammy's sake? Sammy seemed content for the moment, but it could not last. Betty sensed something peculiar about a man who could live in a midden and not even look for someone to clean for him.

That night as she lay in bed a sound woke her. Holding her breath, she listened. The short curtains were not drawn and she saw clearly by the light of the nearly full moon that the door latch lifted. Thinking it was Sammy, scared of the dark or something, she sat up and saw Harry standing in the doorway stark naked, his penis standing up like a rod.

"Oh my God," she gasped, grasping the bed clothes around her. "Harry, don't do this. Go back to bed at once."

"Now Betty, love, you want it as much as me. I saw the way you looked at me when I was washing my chest. Come on now, move over, make room for me."

"Go away." She struggled to get out of bed and keep the coverlet around her body. "Go away, Harry." As she stood on the other side against the wall, she knew she had made the wrong move for now he had her trapped.

"Aaw, you don't mean that, love. You like men, I can tell. I watched the way you walked, the way you put up your arms and pushed at your hair, it was all to show me your tits, wasn't it?"

"No, no, it wasn't," she cried. When had she done that? She couldn't recall and if she had done so she'd been unaware of his watching her. "Don't think that. It was never that."

He moved closer and put his hands on the bed, leaning toward her. Betty's eyes flickered around like a trapped rat and suddenly he was on the bed, pulling at her arms, tugging at the coverlet.

"Come on now, come on sweetheart, come here and love me. You want it, you know you want it."

Betty looked around for a weapon but nothing came to hand. Even as she pulled away, he pulled her forward until her knees were up against the bed and with a sudden tug, he had her and was pulling her under him.

"Don't Harry, don't do this," she begged, wanting him to stop. "I was raped once and I don't want that to happen again. Stop it, Stop it!" As her voice rose Harry chuckled and put his hand over her mouth, stopping her cries, not wanting to wake the boy.

"I know you want it, bitch," he hissed, "Come on now, let's have this thing off you. Show me your titties."

He ripped her nightgown down and she was bared. "That's more like it," he said as he mouthed her breasts, biting at them painfully.

She tore at him and tried to bring her knee up, but Harry was a big man and stronger than she.

As she lay torn and bleeding, he towered over her smiling. "That was good, eh? We'll do it again in a minute. You're tight for a mother, real tight. I like that, I like it a lot."

With all her strength she pushed at him, and managed to bring up her knee. Harry gasped with pain and rolled onto his side, his hands cradling himself.

"You bastard," she hissed. "You raped me, and after me thinking you were a gentleman. You won't do it again, not if I have anything to do with it. I'll wake Sammy and we'll leave right this minute. Night or no, I won't stay here another second."

He looked suitably chastened. "Aaw, Betty, I thought you liked me, I did an' all. You stayed here for two days and you cleaned the place. It looks beautiful and I thought you wanted to stay. I thought you'd stay with me. You wanted loving and I was good, wasn't I? I loved you properly."

"No, you bloody well raped me, you nogood bastard and I wouldn't stay here if you paid me double. I'm taking Sammy and leaving. I'll stay in the kitchen until daylight. Now get out of this room."

Harry felt confused. He was not the brightest person in the world, but had thought her staying on meant she wanted to stay for good, that she liked him. The house had never been as clean, and she had cooked good food. She had been wonderful to love, tight and squirmy, like she was enjoying it. The fact he was cutting off her air supply had not occurred to him, or that she was tight because he was raping her. Then Harry only had experience of his wife who had been a right whore, always ready for it.

Harry was not bright, far from it. His looks belied it, but he was an idiot. They had not talked enough for Betty to realize this fact, because if she had, she'd have left sooner. Now she thought about it they only talked of farm things. How stupid could she have been, thinking they had landed on their feet here? She had thought it would continue the way it was until Sammy as rested enough to continue walking: her being the housekeeper and he doing his farming. Now she could have kicked herself.

Quickly she dressed and went down to the kitchen. Earlier she had banked up the fire with slack and as she stirred it into life and put on more wood and coal, she could hear Harry moving about upstairs. Damn his hide. She wrapped a loaf in a clean towel along with a heel of cheese, thinking that and a bottle of water or milk should suffice until they reached the coast. Going to the cold house, she picked out four large apples. Right, she would wait until dawn and then wake Sammy.

As she sat waiting, she thought about Harry Longstaffe. What a shame he had acted like an animal, for she liked him well enough. Aye, that was the reason she had been in no hurry to leave. Yet, now she thought about it, he had always talked about tomorrow, or next month, or next year, as if he expected her to stay.

She shivered with revulsion, the touch of his hands and mouth had been horrible. Here she was nearly twenty-five, and the only men who had ever touched her had raped her. What was it in her makeup that brought this onto herself? Her father was mad, her husband Harry was little more than an animal, and as for Harry Longstaffe, well Harry had taken advantage and was not intelligent enough to know that 'no' meant 'no'.

As day dawned, she woke Sammy and he dressed quickly, eager for another day on the farm. She gave him porridge for his breakfast and after drinking mugs of tea, they left without looking back. Sammy became agitated when she said they were leaving, especially when Harry shouted from the door. "Come back Betty, come back. I promise I won't do it again. Come back, please?"

Now Sammy pulled back and tried to get back to the farmhouse. "Aaw, Mam, let's go back. Harry and me were going to go over the hills to a lake and he was going to show me how to catch big fish. I don't want to go to the seaside now. I want to stay with Harry."

Betty kept a strangle hold on his arm and pulled him along. Drag his feet he may, but she kept heading forward.

Maybe she should let him go back to Harry, she thought at one point but knew that Harry wouldn't want the responsibility of a young lad. No, Sammy, mythering sod that he was, had to come with her. How far the old curse had travelled, how far it had come to set this man on her when she was beginning to feel safe. Would it follow her all her life, she wondered?

The journey took most of the morning and the day was warm. Both felt exhausted as they came over a rise of land and saw the sea filling the horizon in both directions. A stiff wind blew the ozone into their faces and Betty, shading her eyes to take it all in, laughed aloud.

"There it is, son, the seaside. Isn't it grand?"

"Eeh, our Mam, it's so big," Sammy said sniffing the air, "It smells like fishes."

"Aye, it smells like the sea. You'll remember that first sniff for the rest of your life. I always remember my first sight of it. Come on now, not far to go."

An aunt on her mother's side lived in Blackpool. She had racked her brain trying to think of somewhere to go where she would not be alone in the world, and this was it. Yet how could she find her aunt? Betty knew she lived at the south end of Blackpool, that her name was Shaw, Ethel Shaw. Yet was that scant information be enough to find her?

Blackpool was a growing city. People came from all over the country to walk the piers and ride the electric tram cars. In 1885 it was the first place in England to have such transportation and they were a grand invention from what she had heard. The town had plenty of places to work, she knew, and no doubt she could find a job. She was young and strong and willing. However, Sammy posed a problem because she'd have to find somewhere for him to stay while she worked, find him a school.

By the time they reached the outskirts, she became filled with hope, for everywhere throngs of people walked along the sea front, rode horses or donkeys on the sands, or rolled in horse-drawn carriages along the front. She assumed they were too far out for the electric trams as the road here was unpaved.

Briskly she strode out and even Sammy became excited enough to keep dashing ahead pointing out things he had never seen before. He was not tired now, not one bit. As they walked, she looked for somewhere where they could stop to eat. Both were hungry. They had eaten the apples as they walked.

"Here, Sammy, we'll stop here and look at the sea while we eat.."

She looked down at the beach. Along the way they had smelled excretion from the open drains. The seaside houses emptied their effluence into a drain, which in turn drained to the beach to huge sewage scars that ran down the cliffs, the arrangement presumably made so the sea would clear it out at high tide. It was extremely smelly, almost nauseating. How people could walk along the beach, stepping over open drains was beyond her. A farm never smelled so bad for they had always emptied their slops into a cess pit far from the house. Like her dad had once said, man was the only animal whose excrement stank.

The spot she chose was far from any house and appeared to be cultivated farm land. The hedges stopped about twenty feet from the sea front, marked by a low cliff, and here they ate the bread and cheese.

Down below, two lovers strolled arm in arm, children ran screaming and Sammy stood, eager to join them.

"No son, you can't go down there. We have to be on our way now."

Sammy whined pitifully, he wanted to play, to run along the sands. "You said I could go paddling, you said, Mam, you did."

Betty looked up at the angle of the sun, it was long past midday. "Aye, well I was wrong because we've got a fair piece to go yet. We still have to find my aunt before it gets dark."

"Aaw, Mam, why can't we walk on the sands, and why can't I paddle like them others?" he whined sullenly.

"Because we can't. Come on now, buck up. We want to get there in time for tea, don't we?" She sighed and took his hand, pulling him along as he tried to slow down by digging in his heels.

They walked along cliffs that slowly grew higher. The houses grew to be huge mansions surrounded by low walls to give the owners a glimpse of the sea while keeping out interlopers. When they wandered too close to one estate, a man came out with a shotgun and warned them away.

Bigwigs must live in this area, she thought, seeing primly uniformed nannies with babies, noticed welldressed mob capped maids hanging out washing. By, it should only take things a minute to dry in this strong breeze, she thought, what with the bright sunshine.

They walked and walked, yet it did not seem so far while they had so much to see. Soon they reached a built-up area and along the seafront, in front of hardly visible houses, stood stalls, so many of them that she couldn't count. Sammy wanted to stop and stare at each.

The stalls sold everything from kitchenware and china, to clothes and jewellery. Many sold cheap shoes and boots and she put that in the back of her mind, for if they continued to do much more walking they would both need new boots. Souvenir stalls, prawns and oyster sellers, ice cream and rock candy, fortune tellers, phrenologists, quack doctors, toe corn cutters, photographers, jugglers and acrobats, men singing and playing accordions, concertinas or string instruments.

Throngs of people walked along the front, stopping at the stalls and blocking the roadway. It was like a carnival, noisy, colourful and brash. Betty felt a great deal of excitement at being here, as did Sammy who looked around in wonder. Gone were his aches and pains, now he wanted to see, taste and touch everything.

Two hours later they came into sight of the South Shore area. Never in her life had she seen so many people and they were all smiling, all happy. Sammy started whining for something to eat and she spent part of her money on a meat and potato pie. They sat on the front and ate, watching the passing parade of holiday makers.

"Can we stay here, Mam? I like it here," Sammy said around a mouthful of pie which was more potato than meat.

"If we can find my aunt we will, and maybe we'll stay permanently if I can find a job."

"Lots of work here, Mam," he said seriously and that made her laugh. What did he know about work?

"Aye, if I can find it, son. Come on now, we'd better make tracks and no stopping to gawp all the time."

Taking his hand so they wouldn't get separated, she walked along the outer perimeter of the gaily adorned stalls and headed for the pleasure park at the south end.

Even as they walked, she could see a huge wheel towering above the amusement area and, in the little cars suspended from the wheel, she could make out people waving. Nobody would ever get her in a thing like that, she thought. She had seen signs advertising the Gigantic Wheel along the front and had wondered what it was. Well, now she knew.

"Look at that," he said, his eyes like saucers. "Isn't it fantastic? Can I ride on it?"

"No lad, sorry. We have to keep what money I have in case of emergency." His face fell. How horrible it was to deny him a ride, she thought, as he burst into tears of frustration, but if she didn't find her aunt tonight, they would have to pay for food and shelter.

The area surrounding the back of the pleasure park was of terraced houses, hundreds of them, maybe thousands as the streets seeming to stretch for miles. How could she find her aunt? Who could she ask?

Then she spotted a constable and asked him.

"I don't know anybody of that name, but I don't come from Blackpool." He shook his head as he listened to her questions. "How would you go about it lass? Well, you've got me there. Don't you have any idea at all of her address?"

"No, I must have lost it when we were walking here."

"Well, let me have a think on it." Rubbing at his forehead, he thought. "Why don't you ask at the shops down there? The local shop people know all sorts, a talkative lot they are. Surely somebody will know the name."

"Aye, that's good idea." This man had gumption, knew how to go about it.

"Then you could try the churches, if you know her faith, that is. There's a church for everybody here. Call in and ask the Reverends. Then there's the town hall, maybe you could ask there. If she's a householder, they'd have the records."

"Oh thank you, constable, you've been a big help. Stop it, Sammy," she said, as she tugged him back. Sammy wanted to be off, wanted to ride the giant wheel.

The constable looked down at the boy, wondering how on earth they would manage if she couldn't find her relations. She was probably penniless and he had seen enough incomers trying to sleep rough, live on their wits. Most ended up in the poor house.

"Seeing as you have the lad, if you can't find her, I think you should go to a church for help. They could find you a place to stay that wouldn't cost you much. They're good, are the churches, especially when there's a youngster involved."

"Aye," she said wryly, "He's becoming a problem with so much going on here."

"Always keep his hand in yours as there's many a youngster gone missing. They've got men out looking for likely lads for the sweat shops and he's a good age. Oh, not here in Blackpool, but inland. Even more reason to keep him on your hand. Now you take care and run to a constable if you find any trouble."

"Aye, I will and thanks for your help." She turned to head down the street to the shops and Sammy balked.

"I want to stay here near the wheel. You go and I'll wait for you."

She noticed his eyes fixed on the giant wheel and did not dare leave him. "No, you have to come with me."

They went into the first shop, and the second and the third. They worked their way along the row, shops of all kinds, shops that were full of patrons and she talked to them, too.

After an hour, she felt exhausted and no wiser. Nobody knew of Ethel Shaw. She would have to go to the town hall and have them check their records. Still, when she did so, they had no knowledge of Ethel Shaw and pointed out her aunt might have married, or even died.

Two days later they were sleeping in a church run boarding house where she did odd jobs for their keep. The house she thought primitive because it had no running water. It amazed her that in this thriving bustling metropolis many thousands of houses had no water, but bought it by the barrel each day. Many homes had pumps in their back yards and these were kept locked because unscrupulous people stole the water.

Sanitary facilities were also primitive. Ash pits and cess pools abounded. This backwards system of drainage and water supply she found shocking because thousands of people were packed into the area, and all lived in worse conditions than she ever experienced on the farm.

She learned from the Reverend that so many visitors complained about the constant drainage of sewage into the sea, that the city fathers had formed a committee to study this health hazard. Each summer many hundreds of people contracted cholera. So many, in fact, that the council became afraid the bad publicity would result in loss of the lucrative day tripper business that had arrived with the completion of the railway.

Betty was tired. Tired of spending her off time walking the streets asking for Ethel Shaw, tired of Sammy who sulked and protested when she wouldn't stop to rest.

She must get a job, but though the place was positively tumultuous with people, finding work proved difficult. The church deacon sent her to two places who were seeking maids, but at both places the mistresses who heard her thick provincial accent, decided they had already filled the job.

After another futile week, miserable with the constant rejections, knowing that when she opened her mouth they sloughed her off, she had reached bottom. Spending money she could ill afford, she travelled as far afield as Raikes Hall Park.

In 1871, a group of businessmen had developed 51 acres into a pleasure park with gardens, an aquarium, a roller skating rink, a miniature railway, and other attractions. It offered lavish shows, pageants, bicycle tracks and firework displays. Applying for one of the many positions posted that required little ability, she was disappointed yet again for they rejected her application.

Betty tried getting work on all three piers and got turned away, same at the many stalls and shops where she asked. Eventually she set her mind on leaving and heading for Manchester where she had a cousin. Surely there she could get work in a mill or factory.

As she lay sleepless and worried, she decided the curse had followed them. That had to be it, for why else could she not find a job? Why else was she feeling so miserable? It was always there at the back of her mind, the guilt of murdering her father, the way the family had changed since the murder. Even now it was possible someone would find his body and realize someone had killed him. She sighed miserably, knowing the future looked bleak and her son's future unsure. Now he would never work the land, never work at his uncle's side. What was to become of them?

CHAPTER TWENTY-NINE

Sammy became fractious when Betty told him they were leaving. He thought Blackpool exciting and animated, a place he would like to stay forever. He was gone from his bed when she woke the next morning. The other house residents had not seen him, but they were a lazy lot and stayed in bed most of the morning.

Frantic, she went to find a constable. Blackpool had a large constabulary because of the problems caused by drunken day trippers. The constable she found completely unsympathetic. He said Sammy would probably come home, not to worry. Yet she did worry because he was guileless, so she headed to the south shore pleasure park and the rides, the home of the great wheel that drew him.

Nowhere, he was nowhere to be found, and she wandered around heartbroken, sobbing bitterly. She was alone in a strange place and nobody would help her. Sitting on a bench as she sobbed into her hands and prayed. 'Please God, lift the curse, save my son, bring him back to me.' Then she felt a hand touch her shoulder.

"Are you in trouble, my dear?" a soft voice asked.

"No . . . yes," she stuttered seeing the well-dressed man who stood in front of her. Taking off his hat, he made a small bow.

"My name is Samuel Welland and I cannot see such a lovely young lady sobbing this way. How can I be of assistance to you?"

"Oh sir, it's my little boy. He's only eleven and he's run away and nobody will help me find him." Pleased to have somebody listen to her tale of woe, she stopped crying. This man was a gentleman, surely he could help? "What's going to become of him?" She twisted the piece of rag she used as a handkerchief.

He looked around as she gazed up at him, thinking how well dressed and urban he seemed. "Come with me." He offered his arm. "I think I can help you as I have resources that will find him."

He sounded so congenial with his warm voice and seemed so considerate that she went willingly. They walked through the crowds and passed onto a street heading east.

"Where are we going, mister?" she asked, wondering why he was heading inland.

"My name is Samuel Welland. Why don't you call me Sammy? I have a large house where you can stay while my men seek your lad. A good meal and a warm fire will soon put the heart back in you."

Samuel was not his real name but he had heard her sobbing, "Oh, Sammy, Sammy." Gerry Banks knew that using the same name might persuade her he was harmless. He was far from harmless because he ran the largest prostitution ring in Blackpool. Twenty five of his girls worked Raikes Hall Park and another forty worked the seafront pubs and stalls.

Many of his girls he picked up when he spotted them working the streets. They liked his protection because another gang of rival and unscrupulous pimps worked the area. Some girls were like this one, lost and alone in the city, and she was a country bumpkin if ever he saw one. That accent alone turned his stomach, but the customers liked someone they could relate to, especially those who needed urging. She would fill the bill.

Although it cost him money to get a girl on the job, he was willing to invest in the more stupid ones for they worked for years, or until they died of disease. With careful attention they made him a lot of money. The smart ones moved on quickly, aware they could make more money on their own. Many found a rich man and became his mistress. Many more headed back home and started in business for themselves, and more than a few found a proper job and got off the game. Too, many committed suicide, and he had sometimes found it necessary to remove others.

Sam and Betty left the terraced houses behind and the streets changed subtly. Large detached homes stood in gardens bordered by iron railings with fancy gates. This was obviously an affluent district and, worried as she was, Betty admired the large homes and gardens.

"Here we are, home sweet home," he said as he swung open a wrought iron gate onto a red gravel path. They walked up the path to a shiny red painted door of a fourstorey house. A maid opened the door before they reached it.

"Good afternoon, sir," she said bobbing a curtsey.

"Good afternoon, Sheila," he said, handing her his hat, glove and cane. "This is Betty. She's to stay with us. Fetch us some tea and food."

"Yes, sir." She scurried down a long passage and disappeared behind a white door.

"Come along now, Betty." He shepherded her into another room. "This is better, isn't it?" She nodded as she glanced around the large comfortable room with its couches and chairs, grand piano and roaring fire in a marble fireplace. Long windows overlooked a garden at the rear and velvet drapes hung on each side to match those on the front bay window with its window seat. It was wonderful and the nicest place she had ever seen in her entire life.

"Sit by the fire and relax," he said, "You stay here and have your tea while I talk to my men."

Bonelessly, she sank into a cosy chair by the fire and extended her hands to the blaze. It was marvellous this room, rich and tasteful and yet cosy with it. She almost forgot the reason she was here . . . Sammy.

She must have dozed because the maid Sheila woke her when she brought in a large tray and, moving a small table near the fire, set it down.

"Here we are, Betty," Sheila chatted. "You'll like it here. The master is nice, we all get lots to eat well and are well housed."

"How long have you worked here?" Betty asked seeing that, at close range, the girl looked fifteen or sixteen.

"About a year now. He found me wandering along the front. I came on a day trip and decided to stay. When I couldn't get a job, he found me. You'll like it here, they all do."

"All?"

Sheila liked to chatter. "Oh yes, we have all kinds here. We've got about fourteen right now. He'll find you a nice place when you start work for him, you wait and see."

"Sheila!" the voice said loudly and she jumped. "Sorry, sir." Putting down her head, she left hurriedly, her face red.

"Don't listen to Sheila. I've told her not to stand around talking nonsense, but she's only a child and it's hard to teach her."

Betty's stomach cramped with nerves. This place was not what it seemed. "She said you had fourteen here now, what did she mean by that? Have you sent someone to look for my son?"

"Forget Sheila, she talks nonsense. Yes, my men are out searching. Don't you worry, he'll turn up. Now, here we are, how do you take your tea?"

Betty glared at him, knowing he thought her stupid. How could he search for Sammy when he didn't know what he looked like, or what he was wearing? She took the proffered cup, her mind racing. Something peculiar was going on here and she didn't like it.

"I've arranged for a room for you," he said, smiling. "The housekeeper is making it up as we speak."

They drank tea and ate sandwiches. On a large stand was a cream cake with chocolate icing. She accepted a slice, greedy for a cake that she had only ever dreamed about.

"I want to go back to the church house," she said as she put down her empty plate. "They'll worry about me and Sammy. Thank you for the tea and the lovely cake, but I can't stay."

When she saw the way his eyes narrowed, she felt a trickle of fear.

He tapped the ends of his fingers together and regarded her over the steeple of them. "My dear, it's best if you stay here tonight. Let my men find your boy and then we will take you both back."

He was lying and she knew it. "I don't believe you. How can you look for him when you don't even know what he looks like? I don't like it here and I want to leave."

Not as stupid as she looked or sounded this one, he thought, glad she had taken the second cup of tea.

When Betty stood her legs felt shaky. As her head seemed to spin, her eyes began to blur and she knew he had drugged her.

Sammy darted around the pleasure park and gazed with wideeyed delight at the various stalls and rides. After a while, bored because he had no money to pay for anything, he walked along the front where he jealously watched the children riding donkeys. He asked the man if he could have a ride but he refused him for lack of the halfpenny required.

When he was hungry, he stole bits from stalls, some shrimps, an oyster, a mussel, an apple. Watching as an iced milk man made wafer sandwiches for eager customers, he told the man he didn't have any money, but could he please have some? The man aimed a boot at his backside. Sammy swore and ran into a crowd where he stood watching a Punch and Judy show.

About two hours later he realized he was lost. If the sea was on that side he could not get too lost, he had told himself, but now he didn't know what side it had been on when he set out. Starting to feel scared, he sat on a low wall.

A constable found him and took him to the station house.

"Where do you live, son?" the man asked but Sammy didn't know, only knowing it was a farm.

"What's your name?"

Sammy thought about that as he burst into tears as his Mam had told him not to give his real name but he couldn't remember what she had told him. "Sammy. My name is Sammy."

"Sammy what?"

"Just Sammy." His mind wouldn't tell him what his mother had said.

"Just Sammy?"

"Aye, Sammy, Samuel it is. I feel sick, mister, real sick."

The man scratched his head and went to talk to another man. "He's either retarded or big for his age. He doesn't know his surname, doesn't know how old he is. He doesn't know where he comes from, only that it's a farm. What are we going to do with him? He keeps saying he feels sick."

The sergeant, a family man, laughed. "Oh, he's only sick because he's lost. We'll hold onto him for a few hours in case his mother comes looking for him, and if she doesn't we'll send for the authorities. They'll probably put him into a home until his parents can be found. Get him a drink and a biscuit and put him in the back room."

Sammy was content enough for an hour and then he began to whine. "I want my Mam, get my Mam. My stomach hurts."

The constable on duty said, "Look, sonny, we're looking for your mother, but if you don't know where you're staying we're going to have to wait until she comes looking for you."

That shut his mouth, though he pouted. After a while the place bored him and felt nauseous, and when his stomach went into cramps, he shouted. A man took him outside to the toilets and brought him back, white faced and limp.

"He's sick, that kid," he reported to his superior.

"Kids are always getting sick, don't worry about it. He'll be right as rain once he finds his mother."

"Who's he?" a constable asked as he walked into the office and saw Sammy sulking on a bench.

"Lost child, name of Sammy."

"Oh aye? Sammy, eh? Aye, that was the name. His mother were looking for him this morning, down on the south shore, it was. I didn't get where she was staying, but she'll show up here sooner or later I should imagine."

The sergeant glared at him. "How often do you need telling? Get more details when someone reports a lost child. You know we've got that gang operating in the core. Mr. Cowther will probably sack you this time. That lad is pining for his mother, sick with it he is, and we could have taken him back to her but for your stupidity. Now he's going to have to go to the council orphanage."

Chief Constable Joe Pennington shook his head. The corporation was hiring a low class of man these days. With crime and corruption following hot on the heels of trippers and holiday makers, Blackpool had more crime per square inch than any inland town. Taking on people like Herbert White went to prove that the city fathers had little brains themselves.

At six that evening, they handed Sammy over to a woman from the orphanage who took him away kicking and yelling for his mother.

"He's contracted cholera," the doctor announced. "Isolate him immediately."

The nurse rushed to fetch a gurney to get Sammy out of the dormitory. Last night he arrived feverish, had not wanted to eat but they put that down to his fright at being lost. When this morning, they could not get him out of bed, the matron sent for the doctor.

Blackpool Municipal Orphanage, run by a consortium of local churches, took in abandoned children, lost children and those taken from their parents for one reason or another. It was a grim red brick building with bars on the windows, looking to those unaware of its purpose, like a prison.

As the child's mother had not shown up at the constabulary to report him missing, the police did what the law dictated, sent him to the home. Sammy would be kept for two weeks, after which, if she had not come to claim him, they would move him to the workhouse. The city fathers, who had no time for coddling lost children at the best of times, insisted their charges subsist on work and education until the age where they could apprentice them to a manufacturer or shop keeper.

The workhouse did not pamper its inmates. Many did not reach the age of sixteen but died of disease, hard work or neglect.

Betty woke in a room on the second floor, her head woozy, her eyesight peculiar, as if she saw things through fine gauze. On finding the door locked, and aware he had drugged her, she knew she must escape. Quickly she made her way to the window, managed to raise it, and saw the room underneath had a bay. She could lower herself onto the top and jump down to the lawn. It was almost dark although still light enough to see what she was doing.

Landing on the soft grass, she quickly dived into the massed rhododendrons to check out the lie of the land. Apparently nobody had seen or heard her escape and she blew out a relieved breath. Working her way through the bushes and undergrowth, she moved into a small wood separating two homes and made her way to the street. After climbing over the wrought iron fence, she ran as fast as she could on rubbery legs toward the sea front.

In ten minutes or so she reached the south shore where she mingled with the crowds. The entire area sparkled with lights, all of them electric, something she had never seen before. It looked like fairyland. People walked around as if it were daytime, went on rides, stood watching the giant wheel rotating.

It must be at least ten, she thought, wondering how she could get to the constabulary building or where it was. Then she saw a constable.

"We can't keep children here, you must realize that, we can't cope with them," The sergeant said officiously after her furious criticism.

Betty, furious they had sent her boy to an orphanage, explained a man had taken her to a large house and drugged her. They were so interested in this misadventure that it was almost two hours before they allowed her to leave, giving her the address of the orphanage on the outskirts of the city.

"Thank you for your help, Mrs. Bradley," the Chief Constable said, shaking her hand. She used her maiden name, in case Harry started searching for her.

"And thank *you* for nothing," she said angrily as she stormed out of the station office.

It was late by this time and she had to get back to the church house to secure their room. The police did not offer her tram fare and it took another hour's walk before she reached the house, exhausted. All the way she dodged from shadow to shadow, scared Mr. Samuel would see her. Yes, she and Sammy had to leave this place and quickly.

Next morning she walked the five miles to the orphanage, getting lost three times. Now she stood looking at the building. It looked grim and forbidding. Poor Sammy, stuck in this horrible place. He was going to be so happy to see her and would never run away again. She could take a bet on that.

"Sammy you say? Brought in last night?" the woman at the counter muttered. Taking out a large ledger she turned the pages. "Yes, here it is. Wait over there and I'll get someone to help you."

Betty sat on a hard bench and looked around the area, seeing bare green walls and a grey floor. Four utilitarian gas lights hung from twenty-foot ceilings and the smell of carbolic almost made her gag. It was institutional and cold with its unadorned dark walls.

What seemed like hours later, a plump uniformed woman bustled along the corridor and headed in her direction.

"You are Sammy's mother?" she asked, her voice echoing around the empty space

"Yes, I am, where is he?"

"I'm afraid Sammy is ill. We have him isolated in our sick bay." The woman was businesslike. No time for emotion with her. "Unfortunately he has cholera, and the doctor does not hold much hope for his recovery. What has he been eating and where was he?"

Betty panicked. "How the heck would I know? I lost him. He ran away and I've been looking for him ever since. Maybe it was something you fed him here."

The woman stared at her angrily as if it were Betty's fault.

"Your son is ill and extremely contagious. You can see him through the window, but we cannot allow you to be in the same room. We must guard against transmission of the disease to the other children. Now come along with me."

They walked down endless carbolic scented, bare and echoing corridors with doors spaced along them and somewhere she could hear the sound of children reciting the times tables. Then they passed outside into what should have been a garden but was only a patch of weeds, through a door into a small building.

Inside, they stepped into a corridor where on her left was a wall of glass behind which were the isolation rooms. Each narrow room held a single hospital bed, a few of which were unoccupied.

"What's the matter with them?" she asked as they walked along the passage. "Do they have the same thing as Sammy?" She felt inquisitive as they all looked terribly ill.

"We have six cases of scarlet fever and one of diphtheria. Your son, because of cholera, is at the end away from the others."

Sammy lay in the bed, his face white, his eyes sunk into his head. He bore no resemblance to the rosy lad who had run around so excitedly a few days ago.

"Oh, Sammy," Betty stood with the tears running down her face, both hands pressed flat against the glass. "Can't I go inside to talk to him, please? I want to hold him and comfort him."

"No, it is forbidden," the woman snapped. "We allow only nurses inside to see to him. He is under the best of care, you can see that. We are doing everything possible to help him."

Betty doubted that. All that stood in the glass walled room were a medicine cabinet and the bed. If he opened his eyes he'd be frightened for no matter which way he looked he could not see one other human being, unless they were standing where she was now.

"How often do they see him, the nurses?"

"Every half hour. Don't worry. See, here comes the nurse now."

Betty watched as the nurse lifted the covers and checked that he had not fouled the bed. It shocked her to realize they had tied him down; no wonder he was lying on his back. Sammy never did like that, preferring to roll up into a fetal position when he slept.

"Why is he tied down?" she asked worriedly. "It's cruel, isn't it?"

"We must be sure he doesn't fall out of the bed when he starts to move around, and I can assure you he does move a lot when he convulses." The woman sounded glad to be telling her all the horrible facts.

"I want to be with my son," Betty cried. "He's my son and I want to hold him. Don't you understand?"

"Yes, of course I do." They might as well have been talking about the weather for all the feeling the woman had in her voice. "Nevertheless, it's against the rules. Contagious diseases must be isolated and you cannot go inside."

"I want to see my boy," Betty became hysterical. She had found him and yet she could not get at him. "Let me see my son, right now!"

The nurse looked around as Betty's voice rose, but said nothing. Soon Betty was screaming at the top of her lungs, but Sammy did not move. His eyes did not even twitch, and she began beating on the glass wall in frustration.

The woman took her arm to pull her away. "Come along now, you're disturbing the other patients. Come along at once."

"Let go of me, you old bitch! I'll stay here until he is better. Do you hear me? I mean to stay here and nobody is going to move me." She slumped down onto the floor and, putting her back against one wall and her feet against the other, wedged herself firmly.

The woman sighed with annoyance and walked back down the passage. Betty watched her go, glad she had won the battle, at least for the time being.

They left her in the passage. Nobody came to see her or tried to move her. After an hour or so Sammy moved around in agitation. Then she could see why they had tied him in the bed. He yelled something excitedly although she couldn't understand a word. As she stood watching, the nurse ran in and attempted to calm him, another joined her and they sponged the sweat from his face, tried to get him to swallow water from a spouted jug.

A doctor arrived soon after that and gave him an injection of something that calmed him. Betty watched as the doctor shook his head as he talked to the nurse. His back to her, she saw the woman's face take on a look of anguish, then she must have mentioned Betty for she gesticulated in her direction and the Doctor turned to look at her.

"How is he?" she mouthed.

He shook his head wearily, saying nothing.

An hour later Sammy died. She stood and watched her son die, wanting to hold him in her arms. As they covered his face, she sank to the floor and sobbed as if her heart would break. He was dead, her son was dead and him such a big strong boy.

The curse had reached as far as Blackpool; she had brought it with her. Then she realized she would never know peace.

CHAPTER THIRTY

1895

Angela at fifteen was a beauty. Freddy, who now insisted his parents call him Frederick as they did at school, was tall for his age, a bean pole of a boy with bright red hair, the bane of his life.

When he finished Grammar school, he planned to go to college and Albert was all for it. The farm was doing well and they had money enough. With profits from previous years, they'd added two new wings to the old house. They knocked together the old kitchen and parlour into one huge kitchen. The ground floor of one wing held the new parlour and the other had the dining room, and a room they called the library, which was in reality the farm office.

The village consensus was that Albert Stockton was putting on the dog. Living far above his station, sending his children to posh schools, letting his wife have her own small carriage and matched horses. They were all jealous, Albert knew, and didn't let it bother him.

Adele didn't allow it to bother her either, and was still part of the Grange ladies' auxiliary and a member of the sewing circle. Nobody gossiped about Adele in the way they talked about Albert, for Albert had been born and bred on the farm and look at his fancy upstart ideas.

Adele, slowly accepted as part of their village, came from a town and had always been posh. This they could accept. How Albert had ever met her or wed her was a mystery, yet they didn't hold it against her, even as they held it against him. To them, too, their children's schooling was a bone of contention.

Why would an ordinary farmer think he could educate his son and daughters to gain them entry to a higher class of life?

They weren't even his own flesh and blood, adopted they were, both of them, they yammered, so why did he think they were better than the rest of the children? What was so bloody special about them? Probably bastards the pair of them and now look at the way they spoke, all posh and correct. They never swore, they never argued and they were always smiling and proper. A pair of the devil's own spawn, they had bewitched their dad into spending all his money on them.

The villagers were old-fashioned. All had been born and raised in the same house as their parents and had never travelled further than a neighbouring village for a wedding or funeral. Content in knowing they had a job for life on the farm or working for the squire, they were lower class and proud of it. They never envied their betters, for their betters had huge problems. No, they were happy as they were and resented any one of their kith or kin that tried to make the move into another stratum of society, like Albert Stockton.

'Aye, them childer will send him to an early grave,' they said, 'for once they've had their use of him and his money they won't want to know him any more and he'll end his days in loneliness. Hasn't his older sons walked away from the land already?' They figured that's what their own children might do if they'd got all that book learning and fancy manners. A child should stay within its own world, not aim to move into another sphere. It made no sense at all because the upper classes could see right through the likes of upstarts.

Angela, already a young lady, wore good quality clothes of a modern style and outshone the village girls. The villagers bitterly resented this and gossiped about the girl, picking her to bits, telling their daughters she was a bastard and common with it. Constant repetition of the facts gradually wore down the village girls who stopped to talking to Angela and now snubbed her. This upset the kind hearted Angela, who was ignored even as she sat in church.

When Freddy came home for his holidays, he and Angela took long rides through the countryside and visited scenic spots. As they had no friends among the local youngsters, this weighed heavily on the gregarious Angela who needed company other than her mother and brother.

"It isn't fair, Freddy. They say I'm a snob and yet I grew up here on the farm. Father should sell up and move us to a town. I hate it in Weatherly," she pouted.

"I hate it too, and say, that's a ripping idea. I'll ask father one evening. I could find a much better class of friend if we lived in town. He must have masses of money saved by now and we could live in a nice house with servants."

Angela smiled. What a good idea. "Oh yes, Mother would like that. She shouldn't be making butter and cheese like a common farm hand, although I must say she doesn't seem to mind. I'll never do such a thing." Angela admired her white hands with their rosy nails.

Freddy laughed. "True, I can't imagine you working in the dairy. Never mind, you'll marry well and have servants and everything." He sighed deeply, "I'll have to find myself a career before I could even consider marrying, unless I find a nice heiress to fall madly in love with me."

"Oh, Freddy, don't say things like that. You'll take over the farm when Father dies. He's always talking about it."

He snorted. "Father has another think coming if that's what he thinks. Why should I waste years of education to work as a farmer? Why did he send me to a good school if that were what he had in mind? I think you must have misunderstood."

"No, Freddy, he said it right out." She aped her father's thick accent, 'When ah die t'place'll be in gud 'ands wi my Fred. The lad's got an'ead on 'is showders and will expand even farther.' Freddy laughed at her impression. "That's what he said, honestly. I shuddered to think of what you would say about it, so I said, "Freddy won't want to be a farmer, Father. He wants a career."

"And?"

"Mother told me not to interrupt, that you were intelligent enough to know where your loyalties lay. So you see, she also thinks you are going to run the farm."

Freddy sat miserable and pensive. Surely his father couldn't mean it? Why would he send him to college? It was a waste of money if all he was destined for was the farm.

Right, he wouldn't do it. He must find a way to leave home and get himself a place in town. Possibly he could find a job to help support himself while he finished his schooling, and that would show his father he was never going to come home.

The reason his older brothers left home made perfect sense to him now. His father never spoke of them and had once tossed an unopened letter onto the fire. Maybe they had educated them, too.

That night he took out his hidden box of savings. Freddy was frugal and his class mates usually found themselves paying for sweets or pies as he could out fumble the lot of them. The major amount of the pocket money from his father never left the farm and remained hidden under a loose floorboard in a tin box.

Seventeen pounds he counted, seventeen pounds on which to run away and start a new life. Well, if he stayed here until it was time to go back to school, his father undoubtedly would give him more allowance and if he had twenty pounds, so much the better. Things were expensive in town.

Angela and Adele were busily assembling new clothes for her trip back to the girl's school where she would stay until she reached eighteen. She chattered about the finishing schools the other girls would be attending, and Adele was glaring at Albert, warning him not to burst her bubble. They had already decided that Angela didn't need any further education as surely she would marry young.

Young Eddy Wright, now nine, came over to Mayhurst a lot these days. The three youngsters spent hours riding around the countryside, stopping at farms to beg a drink of water which sometimes turned into a meal. Adele, glad the boys allowed her daughter to accompany them, knew Eddy had a crush on Angela.

Albert scoffed at the idea. "He's nobbut a lad. Anyway, no daughter of mine will ever marry anyone from Hillshead. Aye, Clifford has some nerve, seeing as he's not wed again, yet I hear he has a bastard son over in Padmore."

"Albert!" Adele was shocked. "How on earth could anyone know that? Are you sure it isn't another rumour? You know how they talk around here. Look at what they say about us."

"Aye, well, Ernie Wallings told me, sez her parents are real upset for they thowt he were going to wed her, and it was them as pushed them together. Now the deed's done and he wants nowt more to do with her. Poor lass, and her as plain as a pikestaff."

"Yet obviously willing enough," Adele said, "Young women of her ilk usually lie with more than one man, then name the one they want to catch."

"Go on with you!" Albert said, eyeing her admiringly. She was deep, was his Adele. She didn't half surprise him at times. "Aye, happen you're right there, for I heard say she was once going to wed young Spencer's lad."

"So why do you disparage Clifford? He's probably innocent and if he lay with her, it was because she threw herself at him. He's a catch, you know. Look at that farm of his, it's bigger and better than ever and more profitable than Mayhurst, good as the place is now, so you can imagine what profits he's coining."

Albert laughed. "Aye, and no wife spending it like watter either, nobody adding bits onto the house or buying carriages and fine horses. I ask you, what did I ever do to deserve this?"

Adele hugged his shoulders and kissed the top of his balding head. They were a good pair, they worked well together, had raised four fine children and still felt a great deal of love for each other. If she did spend his money, it was on his insistence, for he said he saw no point in making money if you weren't going to spend it. If he couldn't take it with him, they might as well enjoy it here on earth.

Albert, a caring man, had set up a trust fund for the two sons he never saw. It would come to them on his death. He also set up a trust fund for Freddy who could start collecting the interest when he was twenty-one and not before. By that time Albert figured he himself would be past working and ready to hand things over to his son. With a guaranteed income, Frederick could survive until he had learned the hands-on farm operation.

Adele overheard the children talking as they sat under the large sycamore tree outside the kitchen window. Freddy was all for having a career, while Angela planned to marry a man of title. Nowhere was there any mention of the farm.

"Albert?" she said as he drank a mug of tea before going out to check on the milking.

"Yes, love?"

"What will you do if Freddy doesn't want to take over the farm?"

"Not take over?" Albert looked shocked that she suggested such a thing. "Has he said some'at?"

Oh lord, she hadn't put it right. She shook her head. "No, it's hypothetical, but suppose he doesn't want to farm?"

"Nay! The lad knows where his loyalties lie. You've said that before and so have I, an'all. I wanted him to get an education so he knows about business because we should run this farm like a business if it's to survive. Aye, things change, things allus change and maybe I'm old-fashioned, but I'm not that old-fashioned not to know that education is the best thing a youngster can have. Look at me, hardly able to read properly. Mind you, I've always had an 'ead for farming and know what I'm about, all right, but then I took to it when I was a toddler." He stared into space, thinking back. "Maybe I should talk to him."

Adele felt alarmed. Time enough to raise the subject, not now with Freddy about ready to go back to school. "No, I wouldn't do that yet,

Albert. He's got years to go. When he's ready to leave college, we'll talk to him then. However, we sometimes forget Freddy is not our blood child, and you've got to admit he doesn't take to the land like you do."

"Now, now, he's our lad, and don't you start that, Adele. That lad has been raised here from a babbie and don't know no different. He's a farmer's son, all right."

Adele wondered. From the way Freddy spoke more than once, and from what Angela let slip, Freddy thought nothing of the farm or the countryside.

She sighed and picked up her sewing.

"I'm going to become a barrister." Frederick announced one afternoon.

The three youngsters were sitting by a small lake watching the pair of swans that called it home. Near the far bank, four tiny cygnets paddled furiously as they tried to keep up with their mother. Bees bumbled through the clover bobs and overhead a lark sang.

"A barrister? That takes years and years of working as a solicitor," Eddy said, impressed.

Angela lifted her head and smiled up at Freddy, who sat on a rock while she lay on the grass face down, her head on her hands. "Does Father know?" she asked.

"Of course not. I'll tell him when I come home for the Christmas hols. Bet I get a good score this term."

She laughed up at him. "You get a good report every term, Freddy. You're too intelligent for your own good, I think."

He was pompous, was Freddy. Look at him sitting proudly, his head held high as though he were already a high court judge.

"I study hard and I learn quickly. The other chaps pay me for answers so I earn a good bit during term."

"How much?" Eddy worshipped Frederick, thinking him the smartest person he ever knew.

"Four pounds last term. I spent it on tuck and cigarettes."

"Oh! You smoke?" Angela sat up. She had always wanted to try smoking. It looked so sophisticated, and she had seen her pal Evelyn's mother smoking at the school field day. The way she let the smoke trickle out of her nostrils was most charming, but then Evelyn's mother was *very* modern.

"Do you have any cigarettes with you?" Eddy asked, his face alight.

"No, worse luck. I smoked my last one on the train coming home. Anyway, what if Mother had found cigarettes in my luggage? She'd be angry."

"If I give you some money, will you buy some when we go riding tomorrow? I am dying to try it, Freddy," Angela said, pulling on his tweed pants leg. "Oh, do say you will."

"Yes, will you, Freddy?' Eddy asked, his face shining.

"I might," he said magnanimously, looking down on his devoted slaves.

The next day Angela gave him a pound from her savings and, when they reached the village of Foxhead, he went into the general store and bought a package of Gold Flake. They rode short distance and then stopped by a river where he produced the packet.

"Tad-dah! I hope I have some matches with me. I usually do." He started patting his pockets as Eddy and Angela watched excitedly.

After her first puff, Angela decided smoking was disgusting. "Ugh, I don't like it at all. Why do people do it?"

"Don't inhale at first. It makes your head swim until you get used to it." Freddy laughed and blew a perfect smoke ring.

Eddy tossed his cigarette in the water. "I don't like it, either."

Angela was not so easily deterred. "I didn't say I wasn't going to learn. It's the latest thing to do," she said as she took another puff. Weren't the girls at school going to be jealous when she told them she smoked?

Freddy lay back smoking leisurely, watching Angela turn a delicate shade of green as she inhaled.

"Ooh, I feel woozy, Freddy. I do hope it stops soon or I shall have to be sick," she gasped, glad to see little remained of the cigarette.

Freddy smiled. "Then you must have another one at once so you acquire the taste. After you have smoked one or two, your head won't spin. Look at me, I can hold the smoke for ages now, and I never get sick." He inhaled deeply and held it, smiling as he did so. Then he let it out in a long stream.

Angela was not so sure, but Evelyn's mother had not looked sick and, in fact, had smoked two cigarettes while they sat watching the field hockey match. She had a long cigarette holder with gold stripes. Yes, she must learn to smoke. It would be worth it to wave a cigarette holder around with such aplomb.

"All right. Give me another, please. I *will* learn to smoke and I'm sure I'll enjoy it eventually."

"It makes you look grown up, Angie," Eddy said loyally.

"It does?" she beamed at him, her nausea forgotten for a second.

After the second cigarette, she felt even worse and they decided to ride back, Freddy saying the exercise would make her feel better. She was sick twice and they stopped to wet a handkerchief with cold water and lay it on her brow. They walked the horses slowly as any rapid movement made her feel terrible.

It was when they were at the top of Bonfire Hill that she insisted on stopping. Standing at the top of the rocks, she looked down on the valley, hanging onto a lone fir tree to keep her balance. "The wind makes me feel much better," she said.

"Come on, Angela, we'll be late for tea and you know Mother is a stickler for punctuality," Freddy shouted from the path.

"Then we will be late, I can't . .," as she spoke she let go of the tree, turning to them, and her movement caused her foot to hit a large stone. She disappeared over the edge in a flash.

"Oh my God!" Eddy cried as he climbed the rocks, Freddy jumped off his mount and raced over to help.

She screamed as she fell, a high shrill sound that echoed off the rocky cliffs. Then silence as they looked over the top. They could not see her, only the tops of bushes and trees lower down.

"Angela? Are you all right?" Eddy shouted, panic stricken.

All they heard was the wind soughing in the trees and a crow croaking an alarm. Both called her name but heard no reply.

"Come on, we'll have to climb down. She must be hurt," Eddy shrieked hysterically, his face white.

'Of course she's hurt, you idiot,' Freddy felt like saying, but simply nodded and moved to the edge seeking a foothold. They gingerly made their way down the rocks, hanging for dear life onto roots and branches of stunted trees. Soon they came to a deep gully in which stood taller trees, beeches and sycamores. Reaching the bottom was not easy, but by working their way around, they managed to climb down a tree close to the edge.

They found Angela lying half in and half out of a brook. Her face looked white like marble and her eyes seemed the only thing that had colour for the small veins in her eyelids looked bright blue.

Eddy was in tears. "She's badly hurt, Freddy. One of us will have to fetch help."

"I'll go. I can ride faster and my horse is better than yours. Here, take my coat and cover her. We should try to keep her warm against the shock."

They moved her out of the water and laid her on a grassy mound under a huge oak.

"I know we aren't supposed to move her, but we can't leave her in the water," Freddy said, "I hope we haven't caused any internal damage. We did joggle her though we were careful."

Freddy ran through the trees and out onto a grassy meadow. He looked around and whistled his horse. He kept whistling until the horse came down from the hill and approached him.

"Good boy, Trojan, good boy," he said as he vaulted into the saddle and took off like the wind was at his heels.

When Freddy arrived home to tell his parents about the accident, he was practically incoherent. Albert called in the hands to help and they put Angela onto an old door, tied her down, then took her in the back of the carriage to Weatherly Hospital over the rutted and rocky roads. As the journey on the hard packed ruts shook and jolted her considerably, she moaned.

When they took Angela to the hospital in Weatherly, Albert and Adele sat all night waiting for news. Freddy became so agitated that they insisted he stay at the farm. At Hillshead, Eddy Wright became prostrate with grief, as if the accident were his fault.

If only he had not abetted her in smoking, Freddy thought miserably. Nice ladies didn't smoke, he should have told her that. Oh, why had he done condoned her foolishness? What about Eddy? Suppose he told Clifford what they had done?

All night Albert and Adele sat in the comfortless high ceilinged anteroom waiting for someone to fetch them news. Neither were allowed to see her. Various people told them the doctors were operating. Operating on what? they asked but nobody would tell them. Adele, full of despair, thought they might never again see her alive, whereas Albert stoically attempted to be optimistic.

It was nearly six in the morning when a matron came to announce the operation was over and their daughter was in good hands. More than that she did not say, nor did she know when they could see Angela.

For another four hours they sat, asking each hospital worker, nurse or cleaner - it didn't matter to them - what was happening with their child. Freddy and Eddy showed up at ten to find them still waiting.

Freddy took charge. It was not good enough, he told the matron in his upper class accent, and he put it on, that his parents sat all night in a cold tiled room. No one had given them any sustenance or support. Who was in charge? he demanded. Bowing to his superior tone of voice, she scurried away to find a doctor.

Adele and Albert mortified at the way he carried on, squirmed in their seats. He was drawing attention to himself, and to them. How the other waiting visitors stared at him, gasped at his gall. Nevertheless, it worked and a doctor called Frederick aside.

Adele and Albert looked at each other. "Goes to show what education can do for you, love," he said quietly, "He's got their attention now."

She nodded, wondering at her boy, how adult he seemed standing there with his head raised proudly, looking down his nose at a doctor who was at least twenty years his senior, but did not possess the upper crust accent. They had done the right thing in educating him, yes indeed.

"She's still unconscious," he said as he came back to where they sat. "The operation to patch her stomach and lungs was successful, but they cannot operate on her head until the specialist arrives from Manchester. Anyway, she shows signs of stabilizing. They think she has a good chance. She has broken ribs, broken legs and a broken collar bone."

"Oh, my dear God," Adele said, her hands to her mouth, the tears streaming down her face.

"Now, love, come on, think positive," Albert said as he put his arm around her. He was terribly worried, and sighed with annoyance. To think the staff had stuck them out here in this cold horrible waiting room while his lovely daughter was God knew where having terrible things done to her. "When can we see her, lad?"

"In about an hour. They're moving her into a private room. She's been in the operating theatre since shortly after you arrived. They've set the broken bones, but apart from the internal damage, she has severe head injuries."

Adele sobbed uncontrollably and Albert didn't know how to comfort her. "Come on, love, come on, buck up now," was all he could say.

"Don't worry, Mother, they're fetching the finest brain surgeon from Manchester and soon she will be sitting up, chattering," Freddy said with an optimism he did not feel.

He could have shot himself for his foolishness in buying the cigarettes. When it came down to it, this was all his fault. He dreaded Eddy telling Clifford about it, dreaded the day when his parents discovered what caused the accident. Better that he go away to school and simply disappear rather than face them when they heard the truth.

"She's what?" Clifford said, shocked. "What on earth were you three doing up there, anyway? We have told you enough times, lad, not to go climbing around those rocks. They don't call it lover's leap for nothing."

"Angela felt sick and said she wanted to feel the wind on her face. She was, she was sick, Dad, all white and sweaty when she went up there."

"Sick? How sick?"

Eddy, though shame faced, felt he had to confess. "Sick because we were smoking. She insisted, honestly, she did, Dad, so it was her own fault. She wanted to try smoking and made Freddy buy them with her money at Johnstone's 'cos she said her school chums mother did it. Said it looked so grown up and sophisticated."

"And you?" Clifford glared at his son. He'd always seemed slow, had Eddy, was always doing things because someone else did them.

He recalled the day when Eddy was home late and one of his school chums that he spotted climbing the oaks in Hares Wood told him they had all been swimming in the manor lake. "Eddy drownded," he said loudly, grinning.

"What did you say?" Clifford had felt his blood run cold.

"He drownded. Eddy went under and din't come back up, mister."

Clifford rode fast to the lake and found seven or eight boys swimming, Eddy among them, splashing and yelling as they dived and took each other's legs out from under them. In a red rage, he ordered Eddy home, making him walk all the way behind his horse.

t transpired this was the story they were to tell if anyone, their parents in particular, asked their whereabouts. It had been Eddy's idea in the first place, Cliff later discovered. His reasoning being that if their mother or father thought they'd drowned, when they showed up they would welcome them with open arms and not beatings.

The lake was out of bounds and they were risking both their parent's jobs and the roofs over their heads because the squire did not hold with children having fun on his property. Since then a boy drowned, caught in the weeds, and now the Squire had signs posted. Even so these did not worry the small boys who were drawn to the lake, as a nail to a magnet.

Now the young idiot was telling him they had been smoking. Of all the stupid things to do, and it had led to Angela lying in a hospital bed, broken and torn.

"I threw mine in the water. It was horrible, Dad. I didn't like it at all."

"How about the others?"

"Freddy smokes at school and Angela, well you know how Angela is, she thought it sophisticated and wanted to learn. Then she got sick."

"You young fools. You could have killed her. Why didn't one of you stay with her? Letting her scramble around those rocks on her own. Didn't it occur to you that she might slip?"

Eddy looked ashamed. The thought had occurred to him, but he stayed on his horse because Freddy had done so. He could have kicked himself for his stupidity, and now his beautiful Angela was lying in a bed of pain because of it.

"Do the Stocktons know about this smoking?"

"I don't know, Dad. I expect Freddy will tell them."

"Aye, and if he doesn't, I will. I don't imagine they could ever accept the fact the girl was wandering around those rocks while two able-bodied boys sat and watched, knowing the danger."

Later Clifford sat smoking his pipe and staring into the embers of a dying fire. When would this family know any rest? Angela, daughter of his first love, now lay maimed and probably crippled. She carried his blood in her veins, was part of his family.

It occurred to him that the curse had struck again and he felt afraid for the future.

CHAPTER THIRTY-ONE

Two months later Angela still remained hospitalized although her broken bones had knit well. This week they planned to remove the last plaster cast.

Angela had changed beyond recognition. When they shaved her head to operate to relieve the pressure on her brain, she had lost her long hair, her pride and joy. Thin to the point of emaciation, her once rosy cheeks looked white and sunken. Even her once bright eyes were dull and her expression one of hopelessness.

She had grown into adulthood without having a chance to savour her teen years for it was uncertain if she could ever run or dance again. From being garrulous and a live wire, she was now apathetic and uncommunicative. Albert and Adele watched their daughter sink further into a deep depression that no amount of cajoling could move, and feared for her sanity.

Freddy returned to school seemingly unaffected by his sister's near death experience. They had not heard from him for a month now, although Adele had written him a long letter to bring him up to date with things at home. It was after she had mailed her letter that a missive arrived from the headmaster addressed to Albert and she waited in a state of extreme nervousness for him to return for his midday meal.

"The lad has done a runner. Vanished," Albert said, his face angry as he read. "Left a bloody note saying he'd finished wi school and gone to work in Leeds." Albert tossed the letter to Adele. "At least he left a letter addressed to us." Opening the small note, he quickly scanned it.

"The bloody young fool," Albert seemed near tears, she could hear it in his voice. "He sez he's going to work for a solicitor, wants to be a barrister or some such rubbish. Can't stand the farm."

Albert put his head in his hands, crushed. His adoptive son, the light of his life, the one who was to take over the farm, his heir, had turned his back on him. All these years he had proudly watched him grow, secure in the knowledge that one day Freddy would take over, run the place better than he ever had himself. How ungrateful, how unappreciative of the life they had given him, how mindless of the money they had spent.

Was this how it was going to end? His two first born walked away from the farm, not liking the land or the work after reading the library books he pressed on them. Now his adoptive son had done the same thing. He felt like crying. What *have* I worked for? What did I save for? What have I done to deserve this treatment from my sons?

He raised his head. "That's the last we see of him, like the other two." His voice was harsh and she could hear the threatening tears. "I don't care if he's starving to death, I wouldn't give him a crust." Tears started trickling down his face and he dashed them away with the back of his hand. "I don't care what happens to him. I no longer have a son, and neither do you," His voice rose as he stood and started pacing. "The mindless stupid fool, it was him that bought cigarettes and ruined Angela, and I'll never forgive him for that."

"What?" Adele was even more shocked, revelation on revelation. "What do you mean, Albert?"

"Clifford Wright told me. Eddy said his nibs bought cigarettes and Angela was learning to smoke. That's why she got sick and giddy. If it hadn't been for that young fool, she'd still be our same little girl."

"Oh, Albert," Adele wrung her hands. Her family was breaking up, her family was no more. "We can't cut him off like this. He's been our son all these years. We can't turn our back on him."

"You listen to me, Adele, never again mention his name in this house. He is no longer my son, no more than t'other two are." Albert hacked off a hunk of bread and left muttering angrily.

Oh, Freddy, how could you do such a thing, Adele thought, reading the note sent to his father. Leeds, he said, where though? Where in Leeds could he be? How had he managed to get a job at the age of sixteen?

She told Angela when she went to visit that afternoon. Angela listened though her face showed no expression.

"Your father says we must never mention his name again. What do you think of that?"

Angela sat like a stuffed dummy, saying nothing, making no movement.

1896

As each day passed Albert became more melancholy and within six months lost all interest in the farm. Entire fields lay fallow because he could not be bothered to plant them. He sacked four men, put the others on short time and spent his days down at the village inn drinking ale and talking to the old men.

The locals nodded sagely and talked about the curse on the Wrights, convinced that because Albert had sold Clifford some land and Wright money had passed into Albert's hands, the curse had tainted Albert too. The adjoining acres allowed for the Romany curse to travel on the roots of weeds and grasses. Speculation as to the next misfortune to visit the area was the main topic of discussion after Albert staggered home.

Adele became worried about Albert for he was now fat and bloated, his girth such that he could not bend down to pull on his boots and she feared for his heart. Yet even as Albert drank himself to death, Angela lay on the parlour couch all day, making no effort to move. Outwardly, apart from her shorter hair and her thinness, she showed no signs of the accident. However, she displayed no interest in anything around her and ignored her father completely.

Adele found it hard to cope, and the nurse, hired to take care of Angela while Adele did her work, quit when Angela threw a mug of tea at her.

"Get me some tea, Mother," Angela said as Adele came to tend the fire.

"Angela, you are not a baby," Adele said as she added coal to the embers. "Stand up, go to the kitchen to get your own tea. I cannot be at your side all day."

"But Mother, my legs hurt and I have a headache," she whined, her voice petulant and childish. "I can't walk, you know that."

"I don't know that." Adele was tired of waiting on her. "I know you are perfectly capable of walking, of doing things for yourself. Are you going to lie there for the rest of your life?"

Angela's face set itself into its usual peevish expression. "It looks like it, doesn't it? This isn't my fault, you know! I'll never dance or ride again. Young men don't want a cripple for a wife, so I guess I'll die a spinster."

No matter how Adele argued, or how the doctor argued, Angela refused to try. By year's end Albert was a drunkard, the farm showed no profit and Adele had become thin and nervous. It was as though some evil spirit had descended on the farm.

Even young Eddy, who still liked Angela, stayed away. Angela lay on her couch complaining until Adele could have cheerfully murdered her. The situation could not continue. It didn't, because Albert fell off his horse when drunk and broke his neck.

Few local people attended the funeral, for the villagers thought he gotten what he deserved. Thinking he was better than them, sending his kids to posh schools, they muttered, and where had it got him, eh? The daughter a cripple lying on a couch, the son run off to God's knows where, two older lads already gone, and a farm that had been a showplace now a ruin of its former self. Two or three farmers had their eye on it, thinking the widow would surely sell, and at a good price, to be shut of it.

Angela attended the funeral at her mother's insistence, carried to the carriage by Eddy and sitting in it as they buried her father. Never did she look at the ceremony, but sat churlishly, eyes cast down, face belligerent. Nobody spoke to her. She looked pale and thin and the two village curiosity seekers that attended, reported to their cronies that the house of Stockton was fallen.

Clifford Wright offered Adele his condolences. Young Eddy had shot up in the few months since he had called on the Stocktons and was a now tall, broad framed young man with a head of thick black curly hair. As the group left the grave side, Angela suddenly noticed him as if for the first time and eyed him with a great deal of interest.

Before she left the graveyard, Adele visited Eliza's grave to placed a sheaf of flowers. What would her sister have thought of the Stocktons now? Adele wondered, recalling how often Eliza had told her she envied them.

As she stood, head bowed, Alfred Scully approached her.

"Er, Mrs. Stockton, can I come to see you this afternoon? It's important," he stuttered.

"Alfie, come away from there," Clifford said taking his arm. "This is neither the time nor the place."

Alfred pulled himself out of Clifford's grasp and hissed. "Oh aye, that's because you think you're going to get the farm, eh? Sending your Eddy over to chat up the girl? I know all the dirty tricks, Clifford Wright, so don't try to pull the wool over my eyes. I'm sure the family don't need your bad luck rubbing off on them. They've got enough of their own."

Clifford tried to sound reasonable because the vicar was watching. "Now Alfred, you know I don't want Mayhurst because I've more than enough land of my own to handle. I bought a half hundred acres to the north earlier this year and still have to clear it."

"Aye, but you'd put the boot into anyone else who wanted to take it over, wouldn't you?"

Alfie slunk away muttering. Clifford stood under a tree, leaning against the trunk, to guard Adele's privacy for a few minutes. He looked over to the path where Angela sat like a queen in the carriage, her face blank and uninterested. This was a tragic family, he thought, and that selfish young woman was his child. Poor Adele, what would she do now with Angela to care for and no income?

Adele also had the same worry and knew she had to sell the farm. She had no other choice. That afternoon she told Angela.

"What?" Angela sat up in amazement and almost jumped off the couch. "What do you mean, sell our home?"

"Exactly what I say, Angela. We have no money and no way of working this farm. With your father gone we have no other choice."

"What about his savings? Surely Father had lots of money. I mean what about all those thousands he spent on Freddy's college fees? He wouldn't have done that if he wasn't rich."

Adele shook her head sadly. "That was a long time ago and we have nothing left of our savings. The farm has not made a profit for the last two years because, as you know, your father lost interest when Freddy ran away. We had your medical expenses to pay out of what we had saved,"

"Huh! Some excuse. What man sits back and lets his livelihood disintegrate? You'll have to find Freddy and get him to come back to run the place."

Adele drew herself up, she raised her voice. "I will do no such thing. Your memory has been affected Angela. I'm sure you recall that Freddy always said he would never stay here as he has not the faintest idea of what running a farm involves. If Freddy wants to contact us, he will do so. I even put an obituary notice in the Leeds paper, but he didn't attend the funeral."

"You're a wishy-washy sort, Mother," At that, Adele gave her daughter a glance that would bend iron. "Put some backbone into your thinking. Hire a manager and get him to run the place under your direction. You know what has to be done, you've lived here long enough to know the routine."

"Well, thank you for that, at least." Maybe Angela was right, maybe they *could* manage if they had a man to supervise.

Then she saw a way to get Angela on her feet. If she acted helpless, Angela with her smarts would take over the reins. "I'm so afraid that I won't do things right. Your father did all the farming, don't forget, and while I listened to his talk about sowing and reaping and tilling and ploughing, I don't know too much."

"Oh Mother," Angela scoffed. "Obviously I know more about it than you. I've watched them work the fields and I know how to handle the men, how to make sure they do things properly. When I went with Father on his rounds, I heard how he instructed them. He told me they were all thieves and needed strict handling. Anyway, when you get a manager you won't have to worry about such things."

"What do we know about hiring a manager? What are his duties and how will we pay him? We don't have enough for ourselves, never mind a manager." Putting down her head, she covered her face with her hands.

Angela sat up, then swung her legs onto the carpet. Adele watched through her fingers, glad she had finally got the girl to move.

"Get the boy to fetch around the carriage," she ordered, her voice strong. "We must ride around the farm and see what is to be done."

Adele stood and put her arms around Angela's shoulders. "Come now, I'll take you to the kitchen. Maybe you could make us some tea while I ready the carriage. Our boy left because we couldn't pay him."

"Oh Mother," Angela sighed, thinking it was about time she took charge. Her mother was useless. "You should not be harnessing horses. A lady doesn't do such things."

Adele wanted to retort that if she didn't do such things they would never get done, but held her tongue. At least Angela was up and about at long last.

Clifford watched with some amusement and a great deal of interest as Adele and Angela ran Mayhurst Farm. They hired back their old employees, who worked willingly enough for work was short in the area. Because the Stockton's had little available money, they worked for a share of the fruit and grain harvest. The trees were heavy with fruit and they could make more than if they had worked for a weekly wage. From time to time Clifford went over to Mayhurst to give the ladies tips and advice.

It stuck in his craw, however, when young Eddy began spending more time at Mayhurst than at home and, by his addled expression, was again lusting after Angela. At the market he heard rumours circulating that Angela had set her cap at him, wanting to merge the two farms. The village gossips were at it again.

"Aye, young Eddy is allus there these days. Wants to wed Angela, spoiled as she is," the gossips said. "She'll never get over that fall, she won't. It affected her head they say. Lay on a couch all that time, waited on hand and foot, and look at her now, riding around in carriage, giving orders to men old enough to be her grandad."

"Aye, but she's looking better. Not as skinny and she's got colour in her face."

"So she should have, out there in all weathers like a peasant, and her educated within an inch of her life. Thought she was going to wed into the aristocracy, she did. Well, it all falls back on Albert's shoulders It was him that put grand ideas into her silly head. The man was mad, and look at where it landed him," he laughed, "Six feet under."

Angela felt dissatisfied with her lot in life. While she rode around the acres, she stewed on the rotten hand fate had dealt. She was at an age where she should be attending a good finishing school, planning her coming out ball and knew her ex classmates were doing so. Yet now her father was dead and they had no money.

Well, soon she would find a way out of this back water, somehow discover where Freddy lived and planned to join him. Her brother was smart and Angela pictured him already sitting in an oak panelled office wearing a wig and gown, ready to go to court to defend some rich person. Yes, when she saw the harvest in, she would hire someone to find him.

When they patrolled the lanes in the carriage, Adele and Angela found the workers hard at work. What they did not know was that always one was on look out and their approach was well broadcast. Even Angela found it hard to believe it had taken nearly a week to scythe one corn field. The stooks as they propped them against each other to dry, looked sparse and yet the field should have given a good yield.

She mentioned this to Clifford and Eddy when they came over one evening and Clifford put back his head and laughed.

"They've been having you on. They've taken that corn for themselves."

Angela was puzzled. "Yet they have gleaners' rights. I don't mind, that, but how can they take more?"

"Look, Angela, while you watch them you say they work, but imagine what happens when you're out of sight. They'll work far apart from each other so that large sections are left standing. This they'll claim as gleaning rights. They'll also cut high on the stalk so the stalks can't be bound, also more gleaning for them. I bet for every stook they stand for you, they've taken one for themselves."

"Oh, what am I going to do? I can't be out all day watching them. Why are they robbing us?"

"That's the way they are, that's the way it has always been. Every farmer knows those tricks and guards against them. You need someone watching them. Mind you, I'm lucky with my men and their wives. They show a great deal of loyalty and I treat them fairly so they don't rob me." He felt sorry for the Stockton women: they were so naive. "How about if I lend you Eddy?" Eddy stood statue-like as his father continued, "He's a sharp lad for his age and knows how to talk to the men. Could you do that for the ladies, Eddy?"

Eddy eager to be near Angela, said, "Yes, I'll do that. You say you've still got four fields to harvest?"

"Five, if you count the potatoes."

"Right," Eddy nodded, knowing it would give him valuable experience in supervising men, experience he would need when he took over Hillshead. "I'll start tomorrow. What field are they in now?"

Within a month Mayhurst was running like a well oiled machine. Eddy quickly became invaluable and Angela knew they would miss him when his father called him back to Hillshead. Maybe, though, they would make enough money to take on a manager. She offered this suggestion to her mother.

"I don't know about that, Angela. We still have the seed to buy and wages to pay. Let's wait until we find out what price we get for the grain. The seed merchant will soon be on our doorstep since the harvest's almost finished."

Oh well, it was in God's hands now, Angela thought. She had enjoyed working the farm, enjoyed bossing the men around, telling the women what to do, and missed it when she relinquished control to Eddy. Still and all, it was no job for a female and she had seen the way the men stared at her, as if she were out of her mind as they begrudgingly moved to do the work. She had heard one say scathingly: "Here she is, the boss in skirts."

Things might have been different if she had not taken the fall that changed her entire life. Since then her father had gone crazy and had killed himself while drunk. Now she had no chance of going to finishing school, of mixing with a better class of people. No, she'd languish on this godforsaken farm for the rest of her days.

Her mother didn't seem to care. She never suggested a visit to friends where she might have a chance to meet a nice young man, but then again who would want her? Her body was scarred, her hair was short and scant and her eyes rapidly failing, so much so, she thought she might have to wear spectacles.

Eddy liked Angela, though he thought now she was on her feet that his admiration had turned to love. Since his tenth birthday, he had matured a great deal and was as tall as his father and as wide in the shoulders. The hard work he had done for the past years, combined with his sudden growth spurt, transformed him into a tall, broad young man with well-defined muscles.

Each evening he stopped in at the farmhouse to report what he had accomplished for the day. Angela regarded him with ever more interest, thinking that if she could dress him in a good suit, he would draw the attention of most women. She was especially nice to him and one evening casually invited him to take tea with her in the parlour.

Eddy refused. He was dirty, sweaty and tired, having been on his feet since five-thirty in the morning and it was now sundown.

"No, thank you, Angela. I must get home and bathe. My father will have kept my meal and he'll worry if I'm too late."

"Oh, your father will know where you are. Here with me." Putting a soft white hand on his arm, she dimpled her cheeks and flirted with him from under her brows.

He noticed her manner and felt puzzled. Angela was older than he and surely was treating him maternally, but it looked like she was flirting. "No matter, I must go now. We could have tea Sunday maybe, after church?"

"Yes, that might be nice. Good night, Eddy, take care and thank you."

As Eddy wearily rode home, he wondered why she was thanking him. Was it for working for her? Was it for asking her to take tea Sunday? Why was she saying 'thank you?' Knowing her of old, he knew she had never thanked anyone for anything in her life. She had grown up saying 'I want' and she got. She demanded more than asked, and it was common knowledge her father catered to her every whim.

Freddy too, she had known how to play him to gain her own ends, and look at what that had wrought. Maybe she had changed since the accident; he sincerely hoped so. She had changed her attitude to him, that was for sure, because before he started supervising their men, she had ignored him, treated him like a peasant. Why now was she looking at him with fluttering eyelids and smiling?

He idly wondered where Freddy lived these days. If ever he got to Leeds he must go around the courts to see if Frederick had become a solicitor or barrister. Somehow he thought it could take many years to attain those careers, and it was only two years since Freddy had left. The papers or the library must have a list of legal men.

CHAPTER THIRTY-TWO

1897

Joyce, now thirty-three, was in charge of the Halliwell Laundry, a position she had gained not as much from knowledge as by attrition. Employees did not stay more than a few months, because the work was hard and the hours long.

She was content now as she supervised from her glass fronted office. Watching them toil and struggle, she often smiled to think what a lofty position she held. The only flaw was when she had to sack them for slacking or taking time off with the excuse they were sick. While she thanked her lucky stars for her own good health, many who took laundry jobs, all of them women, were sickly and underfed, and most had children or unemployed husbands.

This morning she noted they had finished the hospital sheets and were packing them into large hampers ready for shipping. When they were gone, the cart would pick up the linens from the town hall used for last night's supper given for Queen Victoria's Golden Jubilee. She checked and entered the figures into the large ledger ready for the Director, who picked them up once a week.

A consortium of invisible men operated the Halliwell Laundry. Joyce had never seen the people she worked for, though neither had anyone else. The only go-between was the old man who came in to pick up the ledgers. Money never entered the premises, everything from invoicing to collection was handled from an office in the bank building. This office also made up the payroll.

Still and all, she had a good life now and a nice young man. John Black, who worked in a haberdashery and drapery shop, was courting her.

From time to time her mind drifted back to Weatherly and she wondered how things were back home. Only a month ago John asked if she would like to go on a day's outing at Easter and Joyce asked that they journey to see her home, Hillshead.

Would it be the same? she wondered, her stomach clenching with rare excitement. Would her mother and Betty still be running the place? Aye, Clifford and his wife Agatha, she could bet they had many children now. Only one more day and she would be there, back in the bosom of her family, for although she had been away a long time, her heart still lay there. The curse entered her thoughts and she shivered. Was it over, she wondered?

Sunday morning was bright and sunny as they set out for the station. Joyce looked enviously at the fine ladies in fancy attire who were also catching the train, their husbands dressed like lords.

She compared them to herself and John. John wore his best suit. He had slicked down his hair with Macassar oil and it gleamed in the sun. Glancing at her best dress, over which she wore a cloak, she thought them neatly attired, even if they were not as classy as many other passengers. They wore better clothing than others who were obviously farmers. Farmers wore clogs and smocks, and pants, both sexes dressed alike. In the past year she had purchased one good gown from a shop but could not wear it to the farm as it was not a day dress. To think of wearing her shop bought, second best, made her proud, because when she lived at home, they bought the cloth and made their own.

When they arrived at Weatherly, they still had to travel to Hillshead and that was at least ten miles on rough roads. Nothing much had changed in Weatherly, not at first glance.

"Come on, John," She said, looking down the long, dusty lane. "Shank's pony from here. It isn't too far." What was she going to say? That it was ten miles of tough slogging, and most of it uphill?

They started well enough and John strode out manfully, talking cheerfully about the countryside and the cows in the fields. John, unused to walking any distance on gravel with shoes not exactly made for tramping, before long had developed painful blisters and worn holes in his hose. Bravely he soldiered on, loathe to reveal his pain; he was the man and if she could do it and still smile, then so could he.

Eventually he stopped, unable to take another step.

"I can't go any further, Joyce." Sitting on the bank, he removed his shoes. "My feet won't let me. Sorry, but if I'd known it was this far I wouldn't have worn these new shoes. I bought them for Sunday wear."

Joyce stood looking at his feet. Poor sod, blistered and red raw, they were. If only he'd said something. She knew it was her fault, for ten miles was a long way to someone unaccustomed to much walking and, as for herself, she had to admit she was finding it tough slogging now she had a sedentary job.

"I'm sorry, John. Why didn't you say something when we started walking?"

John blushed. "Well, Joyce, I didn't want to seem soft or a cry baby. I could have hired a carriage or horses if you'd told me how far it was."

She laughed, spoken like a city man, she thought. "On a Sunday? There's no place open for business on a Sunday around this neck of the woods, John. I thought we might meet up with someone travelling in our direction and they could have given us a lift. I blame myself for this."

Even as she spoke, a farm cart crested the top of the hill heading in their direction. As it drew near, it slowed and the farmer reined in the horse.

"Be having trouble now?"

"Oh, hello Mr. Jennings, it's me, Joyce Wright. Can you give us a lift? My friend isn't used to walking and his feet are in a bad way."

"Hop on t'back, lass. Been gone a long time now, Joycey, ain't you? Big goings on since you left Hillshead."

As they rode in the dirty cart, Joyce listened to Mr. Jennings as he rattled on about Agatha's death, of Betty's marriage and her leaving with Sammy. He seemed to get great joy from Clifford's single status, him with every eligible female for miles chasing after him, and about Eddy, now the spitting image of his dad.

"Aye, 'tis said that Romany curse is still strong around Hillshead. You did good to get away."

She shook her head. "That's a lot of old rubbish, Mr. Jennings. People bring bad luck on themselves by anticipating bad luck. You have to look on the bright side and good luck will follow." Joyce said with more confidence than she felt.

"Superstition is the plaything of the devil," John interrupted, "Like I told you when you told me about your father. Words affect only those of weak mind, no matter who says them. Look at the so called Christians who are the meekest at church and yet the biggest crooks on the street."

"Sush, John," Joyce said, looking at Mr. Jennings who was about to disagree.

"Curses are curses, young man. Romany curses are the most powerful. No one can ever lift or remove them. Donna talk about what you know nowt about."

As the cart slowly meandered along the lanes he spoke of the farm, of the village, of the county. This astonished Joyce because when she lived at home nothing happened from one year's end to the next, and yet it seemed that a regular circus had taken place since her departure.

They arrived at the long lane leading to Hillshead and Mr. Jennings let them off. "My regards to Clifford and Master Eddy," he said with a small salute and, geeing up the horse, left in a cloud of dust and a creaking of wheels.

"Whew!" John said, beating about his clothes to remove the dust. "I think I shouldn't have dressed in my best after all." She could see he was annoyed, but she didn't care. She was home and that was all that mattered.

They walked slowly up the track, at least Joyce walked as John limped painfully and as they rounded a corner, the farm buildings came into view. She could see smoke rising from the house chimney and the slop house where the pig's mash was cooking.

"What a horrible stench," John said, holding his nose. The wind was in their faces and the mash did not smell exactly palatable, though it probably did to the pigs.

"Mash," Joyce said, annoyed at his attitude. It wasn't her fault he had worn new shoes, it wasn't her fault that they'd had to walk, and for him to say her home stunk was the final straw. "For the pigs."

"Oh."

"We breed some of the finest pigs in the county. We've won prizes for them and our boar is much sought after as a fine breeder." That should tell him.

"I can't imagine you living here, Joyce." His arm swept out, encompassing the outhouses and the farm yard which was its usual muddy state and populated by ducks, geese, guinea hens and the rooster who vainly paraded himself, loudly crowing his superiority. A farm cat made its fastidious way toward the barn and a sheep dog lay on the front step, twitching as it chased imaginary rabbits.

To Joyce it looked beautiful. The mossy roof slates, the overgrown rambling roses around the door. She noticed the sheep and cows in the fields, the ducks on the pond, a new addition to the cow barn, a new piece of rust free machinery that looked like a tiller.

The farmhouse itself looked so welcoming, the garden alive with daffodils and crocus, its weedy patch of lawn green and soft looking from their vantage point. Somewhere she could hear a cuckoo and overhead a chaffinch sang joyfully. She was home.

"Come on, let's go," she said as she strode out. Joyce felt like running, like singing for joy. As the front door opened, Clifford stood on the doorstep with the dog now frantically barking, she flew as fast as she could to greet him. John limped on slowly, fuming and miserable.

"Joyce!" Clifford wrapped her in his arms and hugged her. Pushing her back, he looked her up and said: "My, oh my! You're smart these days. Is this your husband?" he asked, as John reached them.

"Oh no," she laughed. "This is a friend of mine. John Black, meet my brother, Clifford Wright."

"Nice to meet you, John." He noticed John was favouring his feet. "It looks maybe as if you've walked too much."

"That I have. I had no idea it was so far."

"Come in, come in. We'll soon get your feet fixed." He stood aside to let them enter.

Joyce entered into the house and went through the passage and into the kitchen, and her eyes filled with tears as she looked around. It was still the same. Here she had worked and eaten, here they had talked and laughed, here she had been a child, loved and happy.

The old furniture still towered against the walls, the deal table looked scrubbed to a white sheen and the fireplace looked recently black leaded and burnished. She took a deep breath, this was home.

A plump woman came into the house from the back door and Joyce looked at her with interest.

Clifford held up a hand. "Joyce, this is Nancy, she's dairy maid and cook. Nancy, this is my sister Joyce."

Joyce smiled. The woman was plain and fat but she looked friendly enough. Her brother was safe from the likes of her. "Nice to meet you, Nan."

"Likewise, I'm sure. Would you like some tea?"

"Yes, please, and one of those scones if you don't mind."

"Certainly, sit you down. You too, Clifford. I can't move with you all standing around."

Clifford was it? Joyce's eyebrows lifted in surprise. Surely that was familiar for a dairy maid, but why was she thinking this way? Her brother was the master now and if he wanted his staff to use his Christian name, then so be it.

It rankled her that someone else bustled around the kitchen, someone other than herself or Betty. It was still as clean, still as welcoming but no longer hers.

"I was sorry to hear about your wife, Cliff," she said, touching his arm.

"Aye, poor Agatha. Still, I've got Eddy, and a fine lad he is."

"Where is he?"

"Over at Mayhurst. Maybe I'd better tell you about the Stocktons."

John sat, his shoes off, feet in a bowl of warm salted water, drinking tea and eating scones with clotted cream and jam, listening to the saga. The Stocktons of Mayhurst Farm had fallen on hard times, it seemed, accidents, deaths, poor yields, bad workers, they had experienced the lot. Apparently they were on the point of bankruptcy and yet a girl who survived a bad accident was the star of the show.

"Hey up! Someone's coming," Nancy said as she looked out the window. "By, its master Eddy and that Angela. Come in her mother's carriage, too."

Clifford rose and went to the door to greet them.

They were laughing about something as they reached him. "Go on, tell Dad what you said, Angela." He turned to his father. "She's puddled, Dad, she's right puddled. Go on, tell him." He fell about laughing.

Angela giggled and shook her head."No, no. Eddy. It's silliness. I won't tell you, Mr. Wright, never."

Clifford could not help but smile. They were both acting silly. It was a joy to see Angela so happy after all she'd been through. Still, youth had a way of brushing aside worry, could smile and get on with life and work through a problem.

"Aye, well, we've got company. Your Auntie Joyce has come to call with her young man. Wipe that silly grin off your face, Eddy, and come away in."

Joyce oohed and aahed over Eddy, hugging and kissing him until he blushed beet red. "Look at the size of you!" she exclaimed. "You're as big as your Dad."

A clear, cool voice interrupted her tender ministrations. "Hello. As you know, I'm Angela Stockton." Joyce realized Angela still wanted to be the centre of attention. That much had not changed.

"Pleased to meet you again, I'm sure. I'm sorry to hear about the way things have gone at Mayhurst, but from what Clifford says, you'll soon be back to normal and profitable."

"Profitable yes, but back to normal, no. Nobody can bring my father back, and my mother is getting old."

Joyce thought about that statement. Adele was about ten years older than herself and she didn't think of herself as getting on in years. Then to a girl like Angela, she supposed thirty-three was ancient.

John sat bewitched. The girl Angela was so beautiful that he couldn't take his eyes off her, her voice was so pleasant, educated, refined. Even the way she moved was graceful and her gown was of good quality, though old-fashioned. To him she resembled a rose surrounded by common weeds. To think that such a girl lived in such sad surroundings, in a farm house, one such as this, a hovel to his eyes.

Nancy made fresh tea and served more scones with fresh baked bread and butter, and cake. It became a party with much hilarity and the young people laughed and giggled as if they were drinking wine instead of tea.

John's eyes were firmly fixed on Angela. Joyce noticed and pulled a face of annoyance. Suddenly she didn't much like him and if he thought he had any chance with her ladyship he had another think coming. She nudged him, making him joggle his mug so it spilled.

"Yes, Joyce?" he said, turning to face her.

"I'm still here, John," she said grimly in a low voice. "Do you think you could talk to me occasionally, or has the beautiful Angela stolen your heart and soul?"

"Sorry. I wasn't aware I was doing anything wrong." Even as he spoke, he could not help glancing back to Angela who was regaling them all with a story about a gamekeeper her father once employed.

Joyce sat back and simmered. This was to have been her day, her homecoming day and yet nobody talked to her, nobody deferred to her, not even her own brother. He was like the rest of them hanging on every word Angela uttered.

For an hour they talked and laughed, for an hour Angela held court. Joyce noticed Eddy was in love with the girl. It was obvious from his expression when she spoke for his eyes revealed his true feelings. She felt sorry for him because Angela was one of those who could never love anybody as much as she loved herself. Lover's eyes speak for them, she knew, their gaze is undivided and they never seem to blink as they take their fill of the countenance of those they love.

"What about your brother, what about Freddy?" Joyce asked, breaking the spell. "Do you know where he is? Clifford told me he ran away and that caused your father's death."

Angela did not like anyone to remind her of those dark days and flared at Joyce. "My father died because of many things, my accident being one of them. He loved me dearly and hated to see me struck down in my youth. No, we do not know where my brother is and I don't think it is a matter for speculation or gossip."

"Sorry, I'm sure," Joyce said, unwilling to give up the floor. She caught everyone staring at her blank faced. "I thought as how Freddy owned Mayhurst now, he'd want to come back and look after his inheritance."

"I doubt that," Angela said imperiously, "My brother had no feeling for the land. He much preferred the legal profession and I'm sure he will do well. I love Mayhurst and, as my father's daughter, I can make it profitable enough to ensure an adequate income for myself and my mother."

"Still, it's not yours, is it?" Joyce insisted. "It still belongs to Freddy and he could come back anytime and claim it, even sell it. Why you, a mere female, think you can run a farm, beats me. You'd be better off . . .,"

Angela's chin went up. "One moment, please. Who are you to come waltzing back here to talk to me like this? I don't need your permission to look after my home, and my family affairs are none of your business."

"That's right, Angela," Eddy said defending his love. "Stop it at once, Aunt Joyce, it's none of your business."

John sat admiring the beautiful, intelligent young woman who had enough business sense and acumen to run a farm profitably. Even he would have little idea of how to assume that much responsibility, and he considered himself intelligent. He forgot his sore feet as he gazed on the woman of his dreams and everyone else in the room faded to oblivion. She could hold her own against the sharp tongued Joyce, he thought. Angela went up several steps in his opinion and he ignored Joyce.

The tea party broke up when Angela wanted to go home. Eddy went with her of course, as did John's heart. He must find out where Mayhurst was and pay the young lady a call as quickly as possible.

Clifford took Joyce and John to the station in the cart and they passed Mayhurst on the way, or at least the laneway. Right, John thought, he would come back next Saturday morning and hire a horse in Weatherly. Already his heart was singing with the thought of seeing her again and he spoke not a word until they bid goodbye to Clifford.

"Come back again soon, Joyce," Cliff said as he hugged her. "Seeing you looking so well was a pleasure. You've lost a lot of puppy fat since last we spoke and it suits you." His face sobered, "You know you've always got a home at Hillshead if anything goes wrong." As he said this, he flashed a glance at John who stood gazing starry eyed into a future neither could imagine.

"Goodbye, John, come again," Clifford said, not meaning a word.

John shook himself back into the present and did not forget his manners. "Goodbye, Mr. Wright, thank you for the lovely tea and for bringing us back to the station. I don't think I could have walked another inch."

"Aye, buy some proper walking boots if you come again. Well, so long. I must be getting back."

Joyce watched him walk to the cart. A well built, muscled man whose looks caught a great deal of attention, for he walked tall and drew women's eyes. She wondered why he had not married again.

She chattered on the train, trying to get John's attention.

"It was appalling," he said as she talked about the farm house. "How you could have lived like that, I do not know."

She bristled. "That is my home and I like it, but you don't have to. All *you* liked was that little bitch, Angela Stockton. You never took your eyes off her. I was so embarrassed."

John opened his eyes wide, "So you should be, the way you laid into her about their farm. How could you? She had lost her father. You talked as if somehow she were responsible, and then to suggest her brother might come back and evict them?"

"I never said that and you know it."

"You implied it and must have seen the way everyone stared at you. You were in the wrong, Joyce. Angela was a perfect lady throughout and you lowered yourself in everyone's eyes."

"Lowered myself? I could never sink as low as Angela Stockton, not if I dug a trench and crawled on my belly." Incensed, she decided to tell John what she knew. "She's not even a Stockton, but someone's bastard. They adopted her when she was about two days old. For years they've speculated in the village about her mother, who she was. Yet old Albert spent a fortune educating them two kids, both bastards, and all he got out of it was a wooden box."

John stared at her as if he had never seen her before. He said nothing, nor would he ever speak to her again. A mouth like a fishwife, he thought. What had he ever seen in her?

Next week he planned to travel back to Weatherly to visit Angela.

CHAPTER THIRTY-THREE

Betty pushed the heavy, ember filled iron over the greyish sheet. Her incontinent mistress went through as many as five sets of sheets a day. Betty soon discovered putting down pads was futile because the old lady insisted they were uncomfortable and tossed them out of the bed. She also refused to have a rubber sheet and the bedroom stank of the urine that had soaked into the flock mattress

For six months she had worked for Mrs. Moxley. From the workhouse at Blackpool, they sent her to the grand old house in Bispham. Here she was an unpaid housekeeper for an old woman who insisted on spending her last days at home.

She shared the house with a nurse who did little other than take Mrs. Moxley's temperature and sit around reading. Outside a handyman/gardener kept the grounds groomed and immaculate. To help she had a young girl. Sally, also sent by the workhouse, who was an imbecile. She did things like scrub floors and clean out fire grates, not having the brains for anything that required thinking.

She sighed, reflecting that when this lot was ironed she would have to start tea. Mrs. Moxley, and the nurse liked to eat at four prompt, and around four was when Mrs. Moxley's friends came to call.

Putting the finished sheets in a basket, she called for Sally, who popped up like a jack-in-a-box from under the table on which she had been ironing.

"There you are, girl. Take this basket up to the linen room and put it on the floor. Come right back. Don't walk along any corridors or go any further up the stairs. Do you understand?"

Sally nodded, her fingers in her mouth, dribbling.

"Take your hands out of your mouth and get upstairs to the linen room. Hurry up, there's potatoes needing scrubbing, and you want your tea don't you?"

"Yis, yis." Lifting the basket, Sally scurried down the passage to the service stairs.

Betty shook her head. She was more trouble than she was worth, that girl. One day it had taken four hours to find her because she had gone right to the top of the house and into the attics. Once there, she became disoriented and unable to find her way out. She was fast asleep in a corner when Betty eventually found her.

She also spent one afternoon in one of the bedrooms and was discovered asleep on the bed. Betty was anxious in case she wandered one day into Mrs. Moxley's suite of rooms. She could see merry hell to play then. After her two-month stay at the workhouse, Betty would never want anyone to ever have to go back to such a place, not even stupid little Sally.

Taking yesterday's homemade bread from the pantry, she sliced it thinly. She sliced almost a loaf as she never knew how many acquaintances would visit. Catering to these daily visitors was difficult because, since her last stroke, Mrs. Moxley never left her suite of rooms. Tea time meant many trips up the stairs, taking cake and bread, tea and coffee.

Betty was happy enough in the position for she had an entire house at her disposal. Sure she had to clean the downstairs reception rooms in case anyone stuck their noses into them, and she had to do all the housework with only Sally as help, but she had nobody giving her orders.

The nurse relayed Mrs. Moxley's instructions and since Mrs. Moxley had no idea how the place looked outside her bedroom, Betty did not hear much in the way of demands. The trouble was her mistress was on her last legs, the nurse confided one day as Betty iced a particularly luscious cake she had baked.

"I wouldn't send that upstairs at tea time," she said, "Mrs. Moxley must stay away from rich foods. I'll have some of it and you, Sally and the handyman can finish the rest. You make nice cakes. I must warn you that Mrs. Moxley is ill, her last stroke left her more affected than she realizes. If she has another, it will be her last. I like this job and we must keep her going as long as we are able."

"Ooh, she's that bad?" Betty felt a flash of alarm. Already she could see her cosy billet disappearing and didn't want to go back to the workhouse.

"She's very bad, but we must soldier on, eh? The longer she lives, the longer we reside here. She's an angel compared to my last case, I can tell you."

So Betty baked plain cakes with a scrape of cream filling for upstairs, although the ones she made for downstairs and the nurse were scrumptious. She kept on the nurse's good side, knowing nurse had the means to keep Mrs. Moxley alive.

Two months later, on Friday morning while at the market, she spotted Clifford talking to a man near the animal stockade. As they talked, she moved closer. They were arguing about a bull.

"Hello, Clifford," she said, putting a hand on his arm.

"Betty, well as I live and breathe. It's me sister, look here, Mr. Scully. It's our Betty."

Clifford smiled hugely and gave her a hug. She was that glad to see him and he her.

"Well, Mr. Scully, let's leave it at that. Me and Betty have a lot to discuss, that's a fact."

They went to an inn and sat drinking ale as they caught up on each other's news. The tap room was crowded with farmers and their wives, smoke rose from pipes, chatter and laughter rose all around them. Betty breathed in the odour of old beer and roasted beef, manure from boots and sweat from clothing.

"Do you think you can come back home, Betts? I'd like you there working with me, not that Nancy I've got now. Nan can cope but it's just that she's not family. I keep waiting for our Joyce to come back, but she's all citified now, what with her fancy man and her fancy clobber."

Betty nodded. "If Mrs. Moxley dies, and she will soon, I wouldn't mind coming back, but what about Harry? Have you forgotten I ran away from my husband?"

"Aye, I'd forgotten that, but Harry's long gone."

A wave of relief washed over her. "To where?"

"He left about two months after you did. Gave no notice, either. We only found out when someone told me he'd taken a cart load of things with him. Anyroad, he's gone so there's nowt to stop you coming home. Your lad, he's welcome as well."

The tears rushed to her eyes. "Aaw, Clifford, about Sammy . . .,"

CHAPTER THIRTY-FOUR

1898

John Black spruced himself up for his visit. He bought himself a fancy waistcoat and had the haberdashery tailor refurbish and clean his best suit during the week. He had his hair cut professionally and even had the barber shave him. Not one penny did he begrudge of the time and money he had spent on the visit, not while he sought the hand of the fair Angela.

John had visited Mayhurst Farm often and since his first visit he dropped Joyce like a hot potato. Joyce was now walking out with another man.

Angela liked John, thinking him well spoken, well dressed and intelligent. Smiling, she compared him to the fatuous, love sick, juvenile Eddy, and given a choice she'd take John any day. Also he lived in town where he had a suite of rooms, he told her, part of a converted mansion. The way he described it, it sounded nice, being in a pleasant part of town with affluent neighbours. His work paid well as he was now shop manager, had prospects of an inheritance from his grandfather on his mother's side. The old man was nearly ninety.

Yes, Angela decided, John was the man for her. She could have fine clothes and live in a mansion, albeit converted. Each weekend she enjoyed his visits, while during the week, for want of something to do, she smiled and flirtingly thanked Eddy, who still supervised the men and brought much money to their coffers.

When John arrived on a hired horse, he immediately walked around to the orchard where he had seen her sitting, immaculately dressed, arranged as prettily as a picture and reading a book.

"Angela, my dear," he said as he approached, his hands offering a box of chocolates.

"Oh, how nice, John, and these are for me?" Taking them, she smiled up at him. Shaking her head, she said, "How lovely, but you don't need to bring me gifts. I'm sure you spend far too much of your hard earned money on me already."

"I'd spend every penny I possessed to make you happy, Angela. You must know that by now."

She smiled, smug. Yes, she knew all right, she knew where she held Mister John Black. If only his name was not so common, but then again that was not his fault: he had no choice in the matter. Mrs. John Black, Mrs. Jonathan Black, or even Mrs. J. Black, none appealed to her. Still, they could change it easily enough. Blake was a nice name, or Blaketon, or even Blakely. Angela had deliberated long and hard on it and, knowing he planned to propose, knew she would accept. Not at once, of course, there had to be some suspense, but she would marry him and move to town.

John sat admiring his love. Her soft white hands as they held the book, the shining oval nails, her creamy complexion, the mass of shining dark blond hair, her rosy lips. He was dying to kiss her. He had not done so yet for one should never rush a young lady, not one with sensibilities like Angela's. He cared not that her body was scarred, something she had hastened to tell him when he commented on her beauty.

Mrs. Stockton liked him, he could see that and was prepared to talk to her today to ask for her daughter's hand. He stood.

"Oh my," Angela looked up in alarm because he had only recently arrived.

"I wish to speak to your mother, Angela. I will be back shortly."

"Yes, John, I understand," she murmured. She watched him walk away, admiring his long straight back and curly hair, his polished boots. He was, she knew, going to ask for her hand in marriage.

How she wanted to know about love before it was too late and how her body yearned for him. She put up her hand and stroked her lips, the lips that begged John to kiss her, although she felt much same when she was with Eddy. She shrugged as he entered the farmhouse and smiled. Soon she would have a ring on her finger, and later live in town.

When Eddy arrived in time for tea, they were already celebrating. They had toasted in elderberry wine and all seemed tipsy. Eddy looked around in dismay, unable to understand the jubilation.

"Come and join us, Eddy," Adele said her cheeks rosy and her eyes shining. "Angela is engaged to be married to John. Isn't it wonderful?"

"Wonderful," he said dully, and, with a thump, his heart broke. How could she have done it? All those looks and smiles, all the sly innuendos. Had they only served to keep him working for a pittance? Why hadn't he spoken up before now asked, her to wait for him? He had known Angela since he was a child, they had grown up together. Surely they had a strong bond, surely she had never looked on him as a brother? No, he knew she hadn't by the way she flirted and touched him.

It was this townie, this gigolo with his flashy clothes and smart talk that had turned her head. The wine suddenly tasted like vinegar and he put down the glass and, turning on his heel, walked out before he said something he might regret.

"Eddy, come back," Angela said, running to the door, but he was already on his horse and moving away.

"Now, Angela," Adele said, "You know Eddy thought a lot of you, and not as a friend. His eyes followed you everywhere. I would have thought you realized that." Adele felt suddenly sorry for Eddy. She had known of his youthful passion for Angela, had thought Angela well aware of his feelings.

"Come on now, no long faces, not on this day of days," John cried putting his hands around Angela's trim waist. "I think we should all walk outside and take some air. This wine is heady."

They walked in the orchard and talked about the wedding. Angela decided the sooner the better now, even as Adele tried to convince her a wedding took time to arrange. John held Angela's hand and smiled. His dream was coming true.

Eddy morose and silent, slumped on the wooden settle and from time to time give a heart rending sigh. Clifford looked at him and knew the signs. Eddy always had worn his heart on his sleeve when it came to Angela, so they must have had a falling out.

Clifford was proud of his son and his work at Mayhurst. The experience gained would stand the lad in good stead, and when Angela married, or left, they could combine the farms. Aye, it would be the finest farm in the county then.

Nancy set the table for their supper, casting anxious glances at both father and son. Clifford sat reading a back copy of the paper as young Eddy sulked. It would be a difficult meal, she could tell, and she had cooked a leg of lamb.

Suddenly Eddy stood and threw out his arms. Clifford looked up, alarmed.

"It's Angela!" he said, "She's marrying that chap from Leeds, Dad," Eddy's eyes filled with scalding tears.

"What chap?"

He spat out his words. "Him as came here with our Joyce, that ponce."

"John Black, you mean? The man with the sore feet?"

"Aye, and he's been sniffing around Angela ever since. He's sweet talked her into wedding him. Aaw, Dad." He sobbed into his hands.

Clifford stood and put his arm around the young man. "Come

on now, lad, buck up. Pull yourself together. Yet if you knew he was sniffing around, what did you do about it?"

"Nothing, and I could bloody well kick myself," Eddy dashed the tears from his face and stared stonily into the fire. "I thought she liked me and you know how touchy she's always been about people being too forward. Oh, I know I'm too young for her, but she could have waited. I thought she knew I loved her. I showed her with my work, I showed her when I talked to her. Nay, I didn't come right out and say it, but she must have known."

"What women know and what women do and why they do it, is a mystery to most men, Eddy," Clifford said quietly, knowing words would not help his son right now. He was right in that he was too young, no matter how adult he looked. Women liked a man older than themselves. "Don't take it to heart. She can change her mind tomorrow and probably will, once she's had time to think about it. Come on lad, can you see her leaving Mayhurst after she fought so hard to keep it?"

Secretly Clifford was relieved a young man had taken Angela's fancy. How could he ever explain to his son that he and Angela were, in fact, half-brother and sister?

Eddy's face shone with hope. Maybe his Dad was right and she would change her mind tomorrow. Tomorrow he would go over at first light, set the men to work, then see her and talk to her, tell her of his great love for her.

Yet when he spoke to her Angela refused to listen to him. She was to marry John Black, and would never wait for him. With murder in his heart, Eddy rode to the fields plotting Mr. Black's death.

Mrs. Moxley suffered a massive heart attack in July, died almost instantly, and Betty was out of a job. Staff would be retained only until the legal men sorted out the estate.

Much to her surprise Mrs. Moxley left her five hundred pounds, a small fortune. An inheritance from a woman whom she had seen only a few times and then only to receive a tongue lashing. Sally got fifty pounds, the nurse two thousand.

Mrs. Moxley attained sainthood in the house in a matter of minutes. Suddenly she had been all sweetness and light instead of the miserable old bitch who enjoyed making them work.

Sally left quickly. She was heading to Southport to stay with an old infirm uncle.

"I haven't seen him since the family broke up when mi Dad died," she told Betty. "Not since mi Mam and me was separated at the workhouse. Mam died i'nt workhouse, tha knows."

Strange, Betty thought, now Sally had the fare and money backing her, she started talking sense. Aye, she would go to Southport where she would buy herself suitable clothes and shoes. Betty egged her on even while knowing that a fool and her money are soon parted. Anyway, she asked Sally, how did she know her uncle was still alive?

"Oh, he's still there. He's too mean and miserable to die. Mi Mam hated him, and he were her brother. He'll have to take me in, though, won't he?"

"I suppose, but don't start counting on it until you know, Sally. Spend that money wisely, don't fritter it away and don't tell anyone about it, otherwise someone will rob you."

"Yes, missis, I've sewed it in my petticoat. Well," she glanced around the kitchen one last time, "I'm away now. Ta-ra, goodbye, Betty."

Betty stayed until the solicitor brought around a man he introduced as Mrs. Moxley's nephew. The man nodded around the neat kitchen and told her she could stay and act as caretaker until he brought in his own staff. When his own staff arrived she could find a job with him in the capacity of a scullery maid or kitchen helper, he added magnanimously, adding "After all that might be preferable to the workhouse."

So he knew where she had come here from, she thought, annoyed, and what was it to him? He needn't have mentioned it. His attitude toward her made her blood boil. Toffee nosed twit, all airs and graces.

"I'll leave this Friday evening, sir. I have a home and don't need your charity. Mrs. Moxley left me five-hundred pounds. That's what madam thought of me, your lordship." She was sarcastic in tone, "Not as a scullery maid or kitchen helper, but a housekeeper."

"Please yourself," he sniffed, "I'll hire someone else immediately. You can show them the ropes."

"I won't show nobody nothing," Betty said hotly. What a moron. "I don't have to have to listen to this, either. I'll leave right away." She stalked out of the kitchen, head held high and went up the front stairs instead of the servants' stairs

As she passed Mrs. Oxley's room, she took a couple of statuettes she had always admired. Served him right, heir he might be, but he'd never boss her around.

As she walked the long sandy road to Blackpool, she knew she had done the right thing. Now she had enough money to rent a room at a boarding house and take a short holiday before she headed back to Weatherly and the farm.

Betty arrived back in Weatherly in early August. The harvest was well under way, she noticed as she sat in the hired coach looking at her home acres. The men had neatly scythed the fields of Hillshead, stooks sat plump and solid, close together and it looked like the crop had been a good one.

As she passed the orchard, she saw a gang picking the early apples. Every year these itinerant workers arrived to help with the harvest. Many were women with children of all sizes. She noticed the usual couple of men. One man, the gang leader, was in charge. He sought out the work, he collected the money and ordered the others around.

It could not be much of a life for the women, she had often thought, reluctant to get too close to any of them because they were filthy and dressed in verminous rags. They slept in the barn for the three weeks of their hire, huddling together in the old straw when the night became cold.

Her mother had always felt terribly sorry for them and prepared huge buckets of stew to feed them. Other than that, they apparently ate whatever came to hand, turnips, potatoes, apples. As a young girl she averted her eyes if she came on them without warning, detesting the matted hair, the dirty bodies and rotten teeth. How lucky she was in having a good home and a loving mother.

She had once talked to one of the younger women, asking her what life was like for them. What did they do during the long cold months of winter? How did they survive?

"Oh, we work in coal mines or cotton mills," she said. "We gets jobs where we dunt need much book learning. We never get to school, being on the road like, not that we miss it. We like to be outside in the fresh air, and we likes to move around, not stop in one place."

Betty could not understand that. "Don't you ever want to live in a house? Stay put?"

"Nah, we're wanderers, allus have been. We all do our bit for the family. When I was small I learned from my Ma to pick stones. All the little ones learn that, that and scarecrowing. Then I got to go gleaning, then to apple picking."

"It must be an extremely hard life," Betty said as she looked at the young woman's dirt engrained fingers.

"Nah, it's good. I don't like it much when we have to work in the pit. It's so black and scary. Me, I like the summer when we pick the new potatoes, when there's tomatoes and peas and soft fruit going. I love the summer and we're always busy. We travel from north to south."

"How far do you go on your journeys?"

"As far as we can and no further," she had said as she walked back to the orchard.

Now she averted her eyes as a young skinny girl darted from between two trees, her basket full of half ripe windfalls. Betty was sure they would eat them, worms and all.

Within a week it was as though she had never been away. She assumed the household duties, leaving the dairy work to Nancy. Nancy was well pleased as they got along well together and Nancy had less work.

Clifford, now thirty-nine, delighted to have her home, suggested she write to Joyce about coming back. Since he had no wife, he wanted his sisters around him, he said. What he needed was a wife, Betty realized, no doubt about it. She looked around at the shoppers on market day thinking that she could pick out a likely female and make friends with her. Clifford rarely went out, so having the odd friend visit her would bring the woman to his attention.

She cultivated Ruth Hislop and Jennifer Arnott as friends and invited both over to Sunday tea where Clifford stalwartly ignored them. Both felt attracted to him, that much was obvious, but it was as though Clifford had shut away that part of his life.

Through Ruth she met Pansy Bradford. Pansy was a live wire, always on the go, always laughing. She had buried two husbands already and was eager for a replacement. When she came to tea, she forced Clifford to pay attention to her for she boldly put her hand on his arm and shook it to make him look at her. To say she was handing it out on a silver platter was putting it mildly. Betty became red faced at her forwardness.

However, these tactics appeared to move Clifford because he sat chatting for nearly an hour. He, who had little time for anything but discussions on farm matters, said, "Come again soon, Pansy, we can talk about your allotment." He shook her hand as she stood to leave.

"Aye, and we can talk about yours, too!" Pansy laughed as if it were the biggest joke in the world, and he even joined in, much to Betty's surprise.

Betty eyed Pansy with consternation. Imagine having her as a sister-in-law. She must have been mad to invite her. Now Pansy had found Clifford, she stuck on like a limpet and soon Clifford was out walking with her in the evenings, and when he came home he seemed relaxed and verbose.

He was having it off with her. Betty knew that look, oh my God, Pansy, the slut, had hooked her brother.

However, Clifford had no intentions of marrying Pansy, no matter how much she hinted. Why would he bother when she was giving it away? Not unexpectedly, when she told him she was pregnant and that he *had* to marry her. He laughed in her face.

"Come off it, Pansy, I know you're mucking around with Arthur Stockely, he told me about it, bragged he did. When you're giving to all and sundry, you can't expect any of us to marry you."

"Well, you've not heard the last of this, Clifford Wright, not at all." She stomped off in a huff and he never saw her again. She never did have a child, was too experienced to get caught that way.

Betty ceased her match making because she didn't want another episode like the one with Pansy. From then on she and Clifford settled down as though they were old married people.

CHAPTER THIRTY-FIVE

When Angela married John Black, the entire village turned out for the wedding. A church wedding with all the trimmings was something everyone enjoyed, whether or not they knew the couple.

Angela looked like an angel. Her white satin gown and Brussels lace veil worn with a small diamante tiara transformed her from being merely beautiful to a vision of loveliness, unworldly and fantastic. Adele felt the church adrift on a sea of tears when they repeated their vows, and yet she knew the congregation could not stand the Stocktons, in particular, the precocious snob Angela. Adele had placed a wedding notice in the Leeds paper thinking Freddy might see it and attend. He didn't.

After the wedding breakfast held at the farm, the happy couple changed and left for Liverpool from where they took a ferry to Dublin to travel to their honeymoon in Antrim at the country home of one of John's Irish relatives.

Adele waved them off in a grand coach decorated with ribbons. Now for the first time in her life she was alone, completely alone. She felt abandoned.

First her two sons had left, then Freddy ran away, Albert had died and now her daughter had married. She looked around the parlour, cluttered with empty glasses and dirty plates. Knowing she must clean up, her eyes blurred with tears.

"Come on, Adele, I'll help you," Betty Wright said as she bustled in. "You sit down. You've done enough work already and it was such a lovely wedding."

"Yes, it was, wasn't it?" she admitted, dabbing at her eyes. "Well worth all the effort."

"Too bad his parents couldn't attend. Odd that, don't you think?" Betty commented as she piled plates on a tray.

Adele nodded. "I think Angela was disappointed, and I know I was. Strange, but I seem to recall that a long time ago he told me his parents were dead. Anyway, I might be wrong. Angela mentioned a death in France of one of his mother's sisters. His family is spread around a lot. France, Ireland and he talked about an uncle in Australia."

"Hmm. Well if he can keep her happy and 'in the style to which she is accustomed' as they say, that's all that matters."

"Yes, I suppose." Adele put her head back against the chair back and relaxed for the first time in weeks. "He has prospects and a good job in town."

"He'll need to have prospects with that young miss," Betty said and suddenly realized that she was talking to the young miss's mother. "Oh, I am sorry, I didn't mean . . .,"

"Oh, it's all right, Betty, I know what you mean. Since her accident she's become used to acting like a princess. Before that terrible time she was so giving and sympathetic to everyone's feelings. Now she likes ordering people around, watching them work as she sits back and smiles. The way she treated your Eddy wasn't at all nice."

"Eddy's all right now, Adele. He smiled when he saw her kiss her new husband. Anyroad, he's young and he'll get over it."

"I pray that she'll be happy. She's not had much happiness in her life these past years. If you had seen her after they brought her home from the hospital, you'd never have thought to see her walking again."

"Aye, Clifford told me. Still, you rest now and I'll make us a nice cup of tea. Them pots can wait a while longer."

Strange, she thought as she waited for the kettle, one minute people laughing and talking jammed the house, and now it was silent as the grave, only her and Adele.

Aye, Adele was going to miss Angela. A woman living on her own like this so far out from anyone would be afraid of any foreign sound. She must talk to her about it afore she left because someone had to worry about her and it might as well be her. It didn't look like anyone else cared.

CHAPTER THIRTY-SIX

Harry Horton stood in the shadow of the woods and looked down on Hillshead Farm house. Over the past two weeks he had made his way from Wigan on foot, unwashed, unshaved and unkempt. Although nobody would ever have recognized him, he stayed in the shadows, keeping out of sight.

When Betty walked out on him taking the child, he set out to search for them, at first close to home and then further afield. On his travels he worked at all kinds of things, road works, harvesting, apple picking, ditch digging, grave digging. His last job had been in Wigan where he worked as a machine cleaner in a large cotton mill. When they sacked him, he tried to find another job but far too many Irish were seeking work, and they worked for little more than a roof over their heads. He was jobless for a month, by which time he had depleted his few savings.

Depressed and stony broke, he had two choices: the workhouse or a job. Since jobs were few, he decided to move on. Wigan's workhouse was as bad as a mental asylum because they put morons and imbeciles in with regular people and the gaunt building had witnessed several murders.

It took a long time to get back to Weatherly, although he had ridden in a train cattle car for ten miles or so. When it slowed at a junction, he jumped off and lay in the long grass of the embankment his arms and legs numb, until the train moved away. Even now, he carried huge bruises from that ride.

Well, it should be worth it. For years he had stewed over the injustice Betty had done him. For years he had planned what he would say when he saw her again, her and that big kid of hers. Aye, that kid. Nobody knew who its dad was, no matter what she said about being a widow. She must have been a right slut.

The farmhouse door opened and Clifford exited with a bucket that he carried to a barn. Then he saw the youngster Eddy walk over and join his father. By, but he was a size and looked like his father. A size, hey now, maybe her brother Cliff was the father of Betty's child. Wouldn't that be a laugh? He chuckled at the thought.

As he waited in the woods, he saw a woman come out of the dairy, but it wasn't Betty. Anyway, how did he know if she had returned home? She could be anywhere, although some inner sense told him she probably had returned. He didn't know why or how, but intuitively he sensed she was around here somewhere.

That night he slept in the cow barn. It was warm in there with the heat from the cows and the comfort of the two cats that snuggled in with him. He ate apples from the store and drank a pitcher of milk from the dairy. Aye, he could hide out here and hide in the woods during the day.

Betty stayed with Adele for the night, offering to help spend the following day putting the house to rights. Adele talked a lot about her future life, trying to make it sound as if she could now do what she wanted when she wanted, but it rang hollow. Betty soon realized Adele was afraid of being alone.

They worked on the house the next morning and soon all was straight and clean. The dishes were packed for sending back to those who had loaned them, the borrowed glasses packed in sawdust for return to the inn. At noon they shared a meal, then Betty said she should be getting home.

"You know I only live a couple of miles away, Adele, and I want you to promise me you'll come to me, or send for me if things get you down."

"I will, dear, and thank you for your help. I'll find it strange, but surely will become accustomed to it. If I may, I might call on you a lot at first, although I think that'll soon wear off. Don't forget I have my carriage and pair, so we could travel to town to shop whenever you want."

"Aye, that'd be right grand. Thank you, Adele. Now take care and don't be sad."

Adele had been dreading the loneliness when Betty went home. The dairy maid had the week off and the harvest was already in, so, apart from herself, not a soul remained. The yard man came to see to the horses every morning, and the dairyman milked and processed morning and evening. However, she hardly knew these men. No, she was alone, completely alone.

She hugged Betty. "I won't, you've been a big help. I *will* call on you if I need anything, anything at all."

"Right, I must go now. Our Cliff will think I've run away again."

As Adele watched Betty walk down the lane, she leaned against the door frame. If only Betty had let her take her in the carriage, maybe Betty might have invited her to stay over at Hillshead. Angrily she shook her head and closed the door, leaned against the inside, and listened to the crashing silence that enveloped the house.

As she drank a cup of tea, she stood in the kitchen. Never had she felt so alone, never so frightened, even of familiar furniture that now seemed to loom. Every sound made her start, and she knew she must pull herself together. She shook her head, angry at her lack of fortitude.

All afternoon she worked in the garden, helping carry pails when the herdsman came to milk the cows. She then worked in the dairy until it got too dark to see and now stood in the lamp lighted kitchen, wondering what to do with herself.

It was a matter of organization, she decided, and, taking out a pad and pencil, listed necessary duties. One had to establish a routine, a roster of jobs.

An hour later she looked at her notes with pleasure and felt much better. Tomorrow she could clean Angela's room and throw away anything useless. She would clean her own bedroom and change around the furniture. Well, enough for one day, she thought, deciding to go to bed, her future neatly itemized on a piece of paper.

Clifford worked in the beech wood thinning out the trees. The many young saplings drew too much nourishment from the thin earth and none could grow to any size while they were cramped. He stopped sawing to stretch and ease his back for a moment and, looking down the vale, spotted Betty walking back from Mayhurst, swinging her bonnet over her arm.

She'd been a great help to Adele, had Betty. He knew that and his thoughts went back to the wedding. Aye, Angela had looked magnificent, so beautiful that it brought tears to his eyes. This was his daughter, he wanted to tell them, his flesh and blood. No doubt about it, he had good genes.

Look at young Eddy, a boy in a hundred he was, and unluckily enamoured of his sister. His thoughts revolved around his family members now, accepted and unaccepted.

Aye, Angela was not of this world, in that satin gown and her lace veil. He had felt so proud that he wanted to cheer. The young man she wed, John Black, looking like a shop window mannequin, seemed a nice enough chap for all that.

Betty puffed as she reached the top of the hill and paused to rest. Since her absence from Hillshead she had grown soft, unused to walking. Today she had gone over to Mayhurst again, pleased to find Adele hard at work, even singing as she churned butter. Spotting Clifford in the beeches, she waved. He waved back and then stooped again to his work.

As she moved down the track, Harry saw her from his peephole in the barn. He was up in the hay loft, hidden from sight behind a stack of bales.

"Got'cha!" he exclaimed as he moved slowly out of his hole.

Stealthily, he climbed down the ladder, watching out for the herdsman or stable boy, and moved into the farm yard, skittered behind the barn and into the shrubby, uncleared area. Briskly he moved to the track worn into the hillside and ran to the edge of the woods. The woods encircled the hill of Hillshead and wound their way down each side so that the farm sat surrounded by trees, sheltered from inclement weather, and overlooked the arable valley below.

Betty walked slowly down the path, singing softly, at peace with her world when Harry jumped out at her and dragged her to the ground.

Stunned by the attack, she made not a sound as he had knocked the breath out of her. Who was this madman? He was filthy and stunk to high heaven.

"Good afternoon, wife," he said showing a mouthful of green and rotten teeth.

She caught her breath as her lungs relaxed. "Harry."

"Aye, Harry, your husband. Who'd have thought I'd have found you like that, eh? Here was me searching as far as Preston, Morecambe and Blackpool. I was in Wigan when I gave up the search, and here you were all the time, sitting at home, eating high on the hog while I nearly starved to death."

Her mind raced around like a frantic animal in a box. What could she say?

"I only just came back home," she stammered, "I was in Blackpool in the workhouse. Sammy died of the cholera."

"Oh aye?" He sneered. "I bet you left him somewhere and the poor little bugger *would* be dead then. How could anyone trust a woman who'd walk out on her husband, eh? I've had a lot of time to think about it, Betty, and you've ruined my life and your own. You won't be walking away from me again."

She struggled to get out from under him. "Please, Harry, let me get up." The curse, the damned curse, it was alive and working. She was correct when Sammy died to think the future held no peace. Harry's return proved it.

"No, first I'm having my rights. I've waited enough years for them." He pulled her skirts over her head and pulled at her underclothes. She lay log-like as he raped her. What else could she do?

Harry worked himself into a frenzy. She might as well have been dead for all the movement or sound she made, and that drove him to distraction. He pounded into her repeatedly, hard enough to hurt her. It annoyed him when she made no sound. The useless bitch, useless at loving, useless at everything.

Angry, he tore her skirt away from her face and looked down at her. "You're useless, you sullen slattern, useless, no good for man or beast."

Betty lay with her eyes closed. It was over for her, that was certain.

Furiously he grabbed her shoulder and shook her. "Open your blasted eyes, goddamn you. Look at me, look at me."

Betty didn't, thinking that if she pretended to be dead or unconscious he would go away. She figured wrong.

CHAPTER THIRTY-SEVEN

Clifford heard a screech, like the death scream of a rabbit caught by a fox, and thought no more of it. A suddenly cut-off high scream was normal when a fox bit through the neck of a rabbit.

It was a good year for foxes, and the valley hunt was out once a month. He figured foxes did little harm if you respected their territory, though he never left his hens out on the range during the summer. At times this year the odd hen had gone missing then suddenly shown up with a following of chicks, so the foxes must be surviving on a diet of rabbit. Farmers treated rabbits as vermin.

Some hours later Eddy called to him from the farm yard.

"Dad? Dad?" The sound was thin but the hillside was such that the sound rose easily to him.

Dropping the axe, he went to the edge of the woods and looked down. He waved, Eddy waved back and came loping up the hillside.

"Dad, have you seen Auntie Betty? Adele Stockton rode over and said she left her place over two hours ago," he gasped as he sat on a tree trunk to catch his breath.

"Aye, she waved to me as she crested yon hill. She was swinging her bonnet like a child. Where's she got to, then? She should have reached home fifteen minutes later."

"Come on, Dad, maybe she fell and hurt herself," Eddy said taking off and running down to the path.

They searched along the usual route, a short cut they all used, along the rough track and the often used path but saw nothing.

"Well, that's mystery, all right." Clifford scratched his head, nonplussed. "Go and fetch the lads and we'll all have a look. I'll get Ranger and ride out as far as the top woods."

"Aye, Dad, we'd better get a move on because it looks like rain."

The stable boy found her. She lay in a shallow depression in a nettle patch. Someone had torn her clothes. Her head was a mass of blood, so much blood they could not tell that her head had been beaten to a pulp. It was obvious she was dead.

"Aaw, Betty lass, if only I had stopped work and walked you back." Clifford sobbed his heart out. Never had he felt such sorrow, not even when his Mam died.

They took the body to the farm where Adele anxiously waited with Nancy. Clifford sent for the doctor because they must report a death. Doctor Walters was long gone and Dr. McAdam had taken over the practice. Dr. McAdam stuck strictly to the letter of the law. Someone, he said, had murdered the woman so someone in the area was responsible. There would, he told them, have to be an investigation and an inquest

They buried Betty within two days and the farm went back to normal. Nancy missed Betty and was again doing both jobs. Clifford blamed himself for not walking his sister home and the more he thought about it the more he realized the scream he'd heard had not been a rabbit caught by a fox, but Betty's last call for help.

At night he woke in a cold sweat, thinking about her last moments. What had run through her mind in those final seconds? Had she thought he could save her, knowing of his close proximity? Clifford lapsed into deep depression not knowing why he felt so guilt ridden, if only he had . . . if only . . . . .

It must be the Romany woman's curse that had caused this latest catastrophe. What else could have brought such terrible occurrences down on the family? If his father had only fed the woman or given her a coin or two, they now might be living in harmony. If he, himself, had allowed Agatha permission to have the other gypsy seek a way to lift the curse they might be better off. Yet surely misery upon misery was the way of any curse.

Life at the farm returned to normal. Eddy soon shrugged off his aunt's death since he had known her only a short time. His thoughts still dwelled on his lost love, his Angela. Her marriage had cut him to the quick, her rapid acceptance of the fop she had only known for a matter of months had injured his very soul. That she married and left Weatherly also hurt, for he knew he might never again see her beautiful face.

He decided it might be better if she never came back. How could he stand to be in the same area knowing she was married to someone else? Even now, while his days were spent working the land, he daydreamed about Angela. His thoughts led him to plot John's death, plotted to kidnap Angela and run away with her. It was useless, he knew. She had made her own choice, nobody had forced her to accept John Black. What was so hard to accept was that she had willingly given herself to Black.

Each night he wept in the dark of his bedroom, each night he prayed for some solution to the problem, but none came. For months he suffered from a broken heart, but then, at a loss for an answer to anything, he decided he to put back his shoulders and start afresh, devoting himself to the land, to making the farm even more prosperous.

Clifford, still deeply depressed, watched his son with some amusement and a great deal of sympathy. The poor lad had it bad and nobody could help him work his way through it. As for himself he helped by not prying, by talking sensibly about anything other than Mayhurst. As he thought back, he recalled his own youth when he thought himself in love with this girl or that, days when he never spoke because of lovesickness, days when he never ate.

When Jenny came along, he had been swept off his feet with love of her, a love that was stronger than any he had felt thus far in his life. Yet he had not wanted marriage to her, to make love, yes, but to marry, no. It could well be that the Wright men were not meant for marriage, at least that's the way it seemed for him and his son.

The crops were stupendous this year, the corn heads heavy and plump. They had turned over the four largest fields to corn and that meant, at long last, they could realize enough to pay off all outstanding debts against the farm. Time now to clear the remaining land he had bought, time to put it to earning money.

So Clifford Wright finally reached the point where he was debt free. How many others could say that, he wondered? The farm ran smoothly, he had good workers, and his cattle had increased yearly since he bought the new bull. The Holstein herd produced some of the richest milk he had seen in a long time as Eddy brought in special feed for them. He was also experimenting with alfalfa, a new crop for these parts. This they planned to use as fodder. Yes, life was good for Clifford. The only thing lacking was a woman by his side.

It was at times like this he disbelieved curses, could see how profitable the farm had become. No curse could allow that to happen. No, it was over and finished.

CHAPTER THIRTY-EIGHT

1899

Angela preened in front of the dressmaker's mirror. The new gown emphasized her small waist and displayed her white shoulders. Of maroon silk trimmed with grey braid, it made her look slimmer while casting a warm glow to her white skin, her eyes looked larger, her breasts fuller. The woman was a genius with material, she thought, nodding her approval.

She could never have afforded this sumptuous gown if it had not been for her frugal mother. The material bought for a ball gown years ago by Adele and stored in an old sea chest in the attic, was perfect. Even the pattern she took from an illustration in a magazine that Adele had kept. Now she lived in town she had taken the material and pattern to the dressmaker.

The past few months had been unsettling. Their two year old marriage was not going well because she and John constantly argued. Angela was used to getting her own way in most things and John did not give in as often as she liked.

This Saturday they were to attend a ball at Harvester House, home of Lord Bricknell, to welcome the new century. How John had come by the invitation was a mystery, one that he refused to divulge no matter how she wheedled. However, she was content to think that at long last she was going to mix with quality, with the upper class. That, she imagined, was where she belonged.

Angela longed to be a *somebody*. Her aim was to join the set that belonged to the best clubs, attended the best functions. That John was but a lowly manager did not matter because, with her to guide him, he was destined for bigger and better things. All the social etiquette she learned at school from those who were blue blood and old money, came back to her.

She adopted an attitude of superiority, assumed an aristocratic bearing, became snootier than the most blue blooded girl she had ever known. It was attitude she told John, attitude was all that mattered. It did no good for him to argue they were lower middle class.

"We always will be, Angela, because we have not the clothing or the manners to be anything else."

"Yet I do, my dear John. My parents educated me with the best, the most upper crust girls you could imagine."

"Some good that will do you, Angela," he said scathingly. "Where do we get the money to meet these people? It does take money, you know, money to get into the restaurants, clubs, theatre boxes."

She waved his words away with a soft white hand. "We can easily overcome that. I will think about it. You bring home a decent wage and we do not spend extravagantly. Yes, I will think on it."

John knew while Angela worked hard to overcome social barriers, her grandiose plans were going nowhere.

"While you are thinking, don't forget our address. To do as you aspire we must have a good address. We simply cannot afford one, and will never own our own home as I do not earn enough to pay a mortgage."

That didn't daunt Angela. "We will give our address as Mayhurst, say this is our town house."

He stood glaring contemptuously, thinking her empty headed. Why hadn't he seen that? All she thought of was herself.

"It's all so simple to you, isn't it? You think it's easy to penetrate the layers of society? These people are all of one mind. To keep upstarts like us out of their sight."

"You are not an ambitious man, John," she said sadly, seeing her dreams vanish. "I had thought you ambitious, I had thought you were going places, I had thought you . . .,"

"What you thought and what I am are obviously two different things, Angela," he snapped. "We are never going to be anything other than what we are now. Get that into your head. I am a shop keeper, a manager, yes, but a shop keeper nevertheless. Shop keepers are not welcomed in society. We are the workers, they are the masters."

Yet she saw one bright spot on the horizon. "Remember John, we're attending the ball this weekend." She smiled and then sighed with annoyance. He was such a stick in the mud. "How many other shop keepers will be there? Did they receive invitations? I doubt it. You wait until they see us, see my new gown and realize I have the education and intelligence that makes me part of their clique."

John said nothing. She was in for a big surprise. Did she think any one would talk to her?

Angela planned imaginary conversations, conversations to keep them hanging on every word. Once they saw her gown, her stance, her new hair style they would assume she was one of them and when she opened her mouth they would know.

Her solitary life caused Adele to become disconsolate. Although she had the dairy maids during the day, she was alone at night. Afraid after Betty's murder, she took to bringing the dogs inside at dusk. Only one old bitch stayed in the yard, the one that had lived all its life outside. The other two sometimes had come inside when injured or when the winter was freezing cold. They were used to it, although they stayed in the kitchen on the cold flagstone kitchen floor. Even so, she slept badly and had taken to napping in the afternoon when the girls were still around.

She had not heard from Angela, not one word and it was already six months since Angela's last correspondence. Sitting in the parlour, she wrote another letter. Once a week she sent a long letter, a newsy letter about the farm and the local gossip, thinking to elicit a reply. Angela did not answer.

Adele had begun worry about the lack of communication. Maybe, she thought, she should travel to their home to see for herself what was happening. Her daughter might be pregnant by this time. Surely that was it, she was going to have a child and did not feel well.

She put enough money for her train fair to Wigan in her purse. That night she slept little, anticipating her reunion with her daughter.

A large dray killed Adele when she ran into its path as she dashed out of the Wigan station. They held the body in the mortuary until they traced her family. Angela and John's address was found in her purse.

The news devastated Angela. She still had the letter from her mother in her hand even as the man told of her death.

"Will you come and identify the body, madam?"

She blanched. "Oh no! I can't do that! I can't do it. My mother is dead?"

It was as though she could not understand. One's mother didn't die so suddenly without warning. She had been going to reply to the letter, she said, she was going to write, or maybe later this evening she would have written. In her own mind she had been the perfect considerate daughter, always caring for her mother, writing her regularly, when in her heart she knew she was not one bit interested in her mother or Weatherly now she was out from under her mother's thumb.

Town offered so much entertainment, she told herself. So many things to see to, the library committee, the old folks' charities, the sewing circle, the other committees she had joined to find entry to society. Her mother could never have understood how hectic her days, how she had to supervise the heavy housework work as she did the light work, then change into a good dress and look as though she had never washed a dish in her life. John wanted to eat properly so she often had to cook. No, Adele never could have understood town life.

Now, damn it, they now could not attend the ball. How frustrating. She would never mix with those people she yearned to befriend, and the next ball might not be for years and years.

Weeping copiously, she sent the messenger to the shop to see John who took charge of everything. He identified the body, arranged for its transportation back to Weatherly, went to Weatherly to make funeral arrangements, placed an obituary in the papers, and ordered a wreath. While he was busy with this, Angela sat fuming that the death made it impossible for them to attend the ball. They were in mourning. How could her mother have been so inconsiderate to have gotten herself killed at such a time?

So, feeling like Cinderella, she did not go to the ball and her new gown hung from the curtain rail in her room looking as wilted as she felt. How stupid of her mother to come to Wigan. If she had stayed home, had waited for the reply to her letter, nothing bad would have happened. Yet oh no, Adele had to come running to see what was the matter because she had forgotten to reply to the last few letters.

Then John came back for her in a hired carriage. They arrived in Weatherly and went straight to the farm. John said she must look into clearing the estate and pay any outstanding debts. The dairy maid Jane was looking after the place and burst into tears when she saw Angela.

"Aaw, Miss Angela, I mean Mrs. Black, isn't it awful? The poor dear lady. Your mother was always such a considerate person, and to be run down like that. I told her she should stay home or have someone accompany her, but she wouldn't listen. Now look."

"Yes, Jane. What are you doing in the house?" Angela asked in such a cold, snooty voice that John regarded her with surprise. "It is a liberty for an outside worker to enter the house. My mother would surely never have allowed it."

"This was my idea, Angela," John said. "Someone had to see to the house, keep the fires lit, be on the premises. It was either that, or we had to send someone from Wigan as a guard."

"I see." She glared at him, "Who told you that you had any say over my property?" she asked angrily.

Jane looked from one to the other and hastily made her way back down the passage to the kitchen.

John was angry. "Now look here, Angela, I know you're upset by everything, but I did it in your best interests. However, this house now belongs to your brother. Frederick is the heir, not you."

"Freddy? Surely you jest?" She tossed her head in dismissal. Freddy had relinquished any claim on the place with his departure. "Frederick left this house under his own volition, and has neither corresponded nor visited for years. He broke my father's heart and my mother never recovered from his defection. No, Freddy will never get his hands on this place, not if I have anything to do with it. We will see when they read the will. If I know my father, he must have written Freddy out of it."

However, to her chagrin, Albert had not changed his will, neither had Adele changed it, so Frederick Stockton remained sole heir. The two elder sons received small bequests and trust funds. Freddy had not come to the funeral though they had printed the obituary in all the Lancashire and Yorkshire papers and one national daily. Either he did not read it, or did not care.

"I wish to challenge the will, Mr. Bartlett," Angela told the solicitor. "Freddy gave up all claim to Mayhurst when he departed. The fact he did not come to either of our parents' funerals, proves he does not care."

"That is entirely up to you, Mrs. Black," Mr. Bartlett said smoothly. "It will cost a considerable amount of money to contest a legal will. The law is clear in that land or property goes to the son of the family, not the daughter, unless she is the only child. If Mr. Frederick Stockton can be found, then he will take his rightful place as master. If not, the eldest boy will inherit."

John sighed. "Leave the matter with me, Mr. Bartlett, I will talk to her." The look they exchanged made Angela's blood boil.

"How dare you two talk about me as if I were a bad child, or a moron?

You speak as if I am invisible. Freddy did not want anything to do with the farm when he was young, so what makes you think he will now?"

Mr. Bartlett said his last words on the subject. "Mrs. Black, no intelligent man could turn his back on such a property. He could put a manager in to run it for him. Mr. Frederick would be foolish to refuse his inheritance, for surely he will one day have children of his own."

"So will I, Mr. Bartlett, so will I." Angela tossed her head and left the room.

Those stupid men, she fumed. They wrote laws that benefited only their own sex. Women had no place in business or law, no place in society unless they were born with a title, or married one. Look how hard it was for John and herself to enter society in a dull as ditchwater place as Wigan. Imagine what it must be like in a large city like Manchester or Liverpool.

Still, if she inherited Mayhurst, she would be a somebody. She would be a landowner, have a say in her future, and gain access to many places whose doors were presently shut to her. If only Adele had used her ownership to mingle with the right people, then, as her daughter, she could have married into the upper class, married a man with prospects instead of plain old John Black who would never amount to anything. He did not possess the necessary ambition or drive.

On the other hand, John could be useful in her quest to contest the will. He recently heard that his grandfather was deathly ill and John would surely be left a handsome sum, being the only male child of the family. I can put that money to good use, Angela thought, and if John doesn't want to help me in my cause, then I will leave him. I will come here to live and run the farm the way I did before, make a profit and pay the lawyers with the profits. Yes, good financial management could help me out of this mess.

The entire village attended the funeral. Clifford and Eddy Wright spent the morning at Mayhurst, keeping Angela company and supervising their cook who, helped by the dairy maids, prepared a funeral meal.

It was soon over, the food eaten, and people had paid their condolences. Angela then walked around the farm house, touching things. All hers now, all hers, or soon to be hers. John, noticing her absence, found her in her mother's room going through the desk.

"What are you doing, Angela?" he asked as he leaned against the door jamb. "I'd have thought that too upsetting today of all days. Why don't you leave it for a month or so?"

She did not even look up. "Don't be silly, John. I'm no shrinking violet, no delicate young flower who might faint. I must go through Mother's papers because she might have bills to pay." She hoped to find another will, a will that left everything to her.

John sighed. This was so unnecessary. "Everyone will understand a delay under the circumstances. I don't think you'll find them lining up tomorrow to collect their money. Leave it, Angela."

She turned on him, her face white with anger. "No. Leave me alone, John. This is none of your business."

"Relax. I think you're suffering from nerves." His face was sad. He thought she was grieving. "The day has been upsetting, I understand that. Please come away from here, Angela, leave it for another day."

"You listen to me, John Black," she flared, "You will not tell me what to do, or what not to do. I will go through the desk *now*. I need to find any papers connected with Mayhurst that mother might hold. Go away and leave me alone."

John glowered, but said nothing. She was upset, and she had every right to be. If only she were not so bossy, so much in charge of everything. It hurt the way Angela constantly belittled him, and he resented the way she told him what to do. More fool him, because for the most part he was willing to go along with it, knowing that a happy Angela was a nice Angela.

Sometimes, though, her self-centred domineering attitude annoyed him so greatly, he could have hit her. Her selfishness and inconsideration irritated him - though this petty minded Angela had only come to light after their marriage. Before they married, she was willing to do anything for him, constantly cheerful and submissive.

Maybe he had made a mistake in marrying her so quickly after their meeting, but then again he had judged her on her mother as well as herself. Adele was such a lady, seemed so warm and caring that he believed Angela had inherited the same traits. It was a shock to discover her childish and selfish, although he was willing to put up with this on their honeymoon for she loved him so passionately, adored him with eyes that almost drowned him with love.

On their return to Wigan and his rented accommodations, Angela turned up her nose at the small rooms, though they were far more modern than the farmhouse. Then again they only had a tiny size bit of lawn at the front and a paved yard at the back with not a tree in sight. While her comments stung, he made allowances, thinking it must have been a wrench for her to leave the countryside.

However, Angela immediately adopted to life in town, loving the theatre, the shops and parks. Wholeheartedly she threw herself into making friends, joined clubs and societies in an attempt to become part of the social set. This was not to be, because although she was well educated and spoke with a refined accent, the locals soon saw through her. Apart from which, she was married to a shop keeper.

This ostracism annoyed Angela, because in her quest for entrée, she met women who spoke with thick Lancashire accents who married men who owned a mill or factory. It piqued her when such females lorded it over her, that the nouveau riche looked down their noses at her as if she were an upstart. It did not, however, deter her from trying even harder.

This was all too much for John who could not understand such ambitions in a young woman. Why could she not be content with being his wife? John had expectations, of course, and was soon aware that Angela had great plans for his inheritance. This inheritance played a large part in her schemes and she often spoke to him about it, asking how much he expected. John did not know if the amount were large or small because his grandfather lived a high styled life and may have spent much on his estate and fine living. Secretly he thought that if it were not much, Angela would blame him, not his grandfather.

Her one thought was to inherit Mayhurst. Mr. Bartlett assured John he would explore all avenues, and soon find Frederick. John hoped so. Once Freddy took over, maybe she would forget this mad scheme of hers.

CHAPTER THIRTY-NINE

In the bottom drawer Angela found a locked box. Searching through her mother's jewellery box, which held little of value, she found the tiny key. The box contained letters to her mother from various people, and a large package sealed with sealing wax. Full of curiosity, she settled comfortably on the bed to read the letters.

Many were from Aunt Eliza to her mother. Her aunt, she deduced, had married a bad man. Her uncle Michael apparently beat her aunt and drank to excess. Reading the letters left her with sense of horror, because her aunt had been such a lady, like her mother. To think that she had lived with such a cruel man. No wonder she had run to the farm to stay out of his reach.

Then her flesh crawled and felt cold as she read:-

"I trust my granddaughter Angela is growing to be as fine a person as yourself, Adele. I could not trust Jenny's baby to anyone else and I bless you for thinking of this solution. If Jenny had lived, I'm sure she'd be delighted in knowing her baby safe with you."

Grandchild? She? Oh my God, Eliza had written about her, Angela. She was not Adele's daughter? Suddenly it struck her that she had no claim on the farm after all, and her mind reeled from the discovery. She sat for a few moments, her blood running cold as the enormity of it washed over her. Then she tore the letter into tiny pieces and set fire to them in the fireplace. Nobody must know. *Nobody!*

She skimmed through the other letters noting short references to herself or Frederick, but nothing more of a personal nature.

When she broke open the sealed package, her heart almost leapt out of her chest. Shock upon shock. Adoption papers for Frederick. They had adopted him also? He was not entitled to the farm either. He was a bastard. How dare they give him the place? How dare they.

Angrily she stomped down the stairs. She found John sitting in the kitchen drinking tea with the dairy maid, Jane.

"I must talk to you at once, John," she said glaring at the girl who lowered her eyes and stared at her shoes. "What on earth are *you* doing in the kitchen? Get about your business, girl. Come along at once, John, we will talk in the parlour. You may fetch us fresh tea, Jane," she commanded.

John screwed his face into an expression of annoyance, raised his eyes to heaven and winked at Jane as he left.

"Look at this paper," She thrust it at him when they reached the parlour. "I found it in a locked box, and no wonder. Frederick has no claim on Mayhurst at all. It is mine, and mine it will stay. I am the rightful heir, no matter what the will said."

John read the paper. "So they adopted Frederick." He shrugged. "That changes nothing, Angela. Your father's will was explicit and this does not constitute an extenuating circumstance. He left the place to your mother, and on her death it was to go to Frederick. If Frederick is deceased, it will pass to Albert's eldest son, then to the younger one. You heard the will, and while it mentioned you, it was never in the context of inheriting the property."

"Oh yes, it mentioned me all right," she said angrily. "It said I'd probably be married by the time he died and he left me ten thousand pounds. Well, I won't see any of my inheritance unless this farm makes a decent profit in the next five years. Why should that bastard brother of mine get the place? It will be worth many more thousands if he sells it, and I know he will sell it." She paced in agitation, her hands clenched into fists. "Freddy doesn't like the land. He ran as fast as he could to Leeds to pursue a career in law."

"In law, eh?" John raised his eyebrows. "Maybe he is now a solicitor and knows far more about law than you or I ever will. He will fight you for his rights and I, for one, cannot blame him." John found a certain amount of amusement in watching the machinations of Angela's mind. Not that he agreed with her for one moment.

"He will never get Mayhurst, never," she vowed. "I promise that." She flounced out and went back upstairs to her mother's desk.

The fire went out in the parlour, but John sat in the chilly room, thinking. Tomorrow he must return to town to take up the reins, knowing that in his absence the staff would take advantage, and the owners were paying him to make a profit. John had ambitions Angela knew nothing about, his main ambition being to own the shop. He planned on using his inheritance to purchase it.

He was well aware Angela had other ideas, and prayed he had the fortitude to go against her. The normal way of things was that the man should be the dominant party in a marriage, but those who ordained it so had never met Angela. He knew he was in for a fight, and his grandfather was still alive.

"I am staying here on *my* farm," she replied when he asked her when she was going to pack.

"You must come home with me," he said, crossing his arms over his chest, looking stern. "What are people going to say?" As if that made any difference to Angela, who almost laughed at his stance.

"Go alone," she said, not bothering to hide a smile. "Have the maid to see to you. I must stay here in my home. I must not leave it now."

"Angela, I insist that you pack your things. We must leave."

"Go home on your own, John. Because you have to dance to the shop owner's tune does not mean that I must."

He raised his voice. "I order you to come home, Angela."

She put up her chin and stared at him coldly. "I will not. I belong here. This is my home now."

"Angela, this is foolishness. This is not your home!" His voice rose and he tried to control it. Loud words never made much impression on Angela, she said it showed bad manners. "Mayhurst belongs to your brother, and mark my words, he will arrive when he discovers that fact. Legal notices have been placed in all the daily papers. You must leave now."

Angela flapped her hands at him and turned to look out the window. "Oh, go away, John. Go back to Wigan. While you are there you can look for a good solicitor to fight my case. I do not trust Mr. Bartlett."

John, angry with her as he had ever been, drew himself up and said firmly, "I'm not going to seek any solicitor, nor will I spend money on stupidity. You must come home."

She refused to go and sat in the parlour, sulking. Let him rant and rave, she thought, I must stay here. She was adamant, *this* was her home now. He would soon see that the farm would pay better than the stupid shop, and he would miss her so much that he would concede to her demands. Oh yes, she knew John Black, well enough to know that her wishes were usually granted even if it did take a while..

After he left, she went back into her mother's bedroom to search the other desk drawers. She found more letters about her real mother, Aunt Eliza's daughter, Jenny. These she also burned. Now nobody knew the real truth about her parentage because she had destroyed everything. Knowing that her true mother and her Aunt Adele were private people, she was sure the family affairs had been kept secret from the villagers.

For a week she was content. She ordered the dairy maids around, walked the fields and spoke to the workers. When, in her ignorance, she issued stupid orders, they tugged their forelocks and laughed at her behind her back, and went on doing exactly what they knew was right and what they had always done.

One afternoon Eddy rode over to Mayhurst. How adult he seemed, she thought, as she admired his broad chest and wide shoulders.

"So it *is* you, Angela," he said as he dismounted. "One of our men said a strange woman ordered him to cut back a hedge. He didn't do it, of course, for you were on our land. I came over here to do battle."

Angela perked up, she still liked Eddy, he was so well built and handsome. "Well, you needn't have bothered, Eddy. I'm sorry, I had no idea I was on your land. I thought my father farmed that field."

He laughed knowing how she had made the mistake. "He did, but my father bought it from him ten years ago. I'll have to show you a map of our land and then you can sort out your boundaries. I'm afraid our men don't appreciate a woman telling them what to do."

She laughed. "Not even an owner? My men have to listen to me."

"Your men?"

"Oh, that's right," she smiled her best smile, the one she employed when flirting. "I'm taking over Mayhurst. I own it now."

Eddy looked puzzled. "Yet surely Frederick is the heir. He's the son of the family."

Angela smiled grimly. "Piffle. Freddy gave up the right years ago when he ran away. What you *don't* know is that he is only an *adopted* son, whereas I am a daughter of the family, the true heir." She stuck her nose in the air and surveyed her property.

Eddy had to smile. A typical stupid female, he thought, the male always inherited, adoptive or no. Anyway, he knew they had adopted Freddy, his father had told him years ago. Once Freddy came to Mayhurst, he would oust Angela, and Freddy would surely return as his father said.

"What will you do when Freddy comes to claim the place?"

"Huh! Freddy will never come here," she said with a great deal of conviction. "Anyway, I'm contesting the will. My father must have been mad when he drew it up, as I told the solicitor. I'm searching the house for another will, the one he made later, after Freddy ran away."

Eddy felt sorry for her, knowing she was deluding herself. She didn't stand a chance with the law as it stood.

"Come now, admit it, Angela, Freddy is the rightful heir, and, if he has made good his ambition to become a solicitor or barrister, you will be out of here very quickly. He doesn't have to farm it, you know. He could sell it. My Dad has talked about buying it."

As they talked, they walked through the yard and into the orchard where they sat on the small wooden bench Adele had set there years ago.

The beehives were alive with sound. Bees and butterflies scavenged through the wild flowers that grew under the trees. Angela looked around, taking it all in. Suddenly it was precious to her, although she much preferred the hectic life of the town.

She heaved a huge sigh. "I could never give this up, never."

"Yet you already did, Angela, when you married John."

"No, I didn't. I never said I didn't want to come back, now did I? That wasn't part of my marriage vows."

Nonplussed, Eddy shook his head; and to think he had thought Angela intelligent. Maybe the accident had damaged her brain, or it must be the swanky way she spoke because her obdurate manner pinpointed stupidity.

His voice was quiet and patient. "I assume that a wife goes where her husband goes. Your place is by John's side." He looked around the area. "By the way, where is he?"

She pulled a face of disgust. "Oh, he had to get back to his stuffy old job." Her tone of voice denigrated John Eddy looked at her sharply. Apparently things were not going smoothly in the Black household.

"Are you having problems with John?" he asked hopefully.

"Oh, Eddy, if only you knew." She turned to him, tears in her eyes. "He is not what I wanted at all, or what I expected."

He leaned toward her and opened his arms. She threw herself into them and sobbed onto his shoulder. Eddy could not believe it. This was the closest he had ever been to a woman, other than his sisters.

"There, there now," he murmured, his heart thundering in his chest as he held her closer.

Angela breathed in the smell of him: his skin, perspiration, hay and manure. The smell of a farmer, the smell her father always had worn. She pressed closer and turned her head up toward his chin.

Before he knew it, he was kissing her. Not a kiss of friendship, not a chaste kiss, but a kiss of passion, of longing for the love of his life, for the girl he had always loved. It was wrong, he knew it was wrong. She was married to another, but she wanted it as much as he. Angela clung to him and he felt his heart fill with a longing for more. He pulled her down onto the grass and lowered himself over her.

Angela felt like she was suddenly alive for the first time in her life. Edward, the Eddie of her youth, the one who had always been there, who had always admired her, the one who had trailed around after her. Eddie liked her more than that now.

His hands slowly caressed her thighs and she wanted him. She pulled at him, pushed her tongue into his mouth and moaned with pleasure. Opening her legs wide, she waited for him to enter her.

"Make love to me, Eddy, take me now," she breathed

Maybe Eddy loved her. How wonderful, she thrilled, he was handsomer than John, his farm was larger than Mayhurst and everyone knew Clifford Wright was a rich man.

Eddy went home that night a man with stars in his eyes and love in his heart for the sweetest, most beautiful woman in the entire world. He whistled as he went into the kitchen where his father sat toasting his toes at the fire and talking to their new housekeeper, Edith.

"Someone sounds happy tonight," Clifford said, winking at Edith. It was obvious from the shining eyes and merry look somewhere a lass was involved and Clifford was glad. "What's her name?"

"What do you mean?" Eddy asked as he blushed, having almost blurted out 'Angela.'

"Oh, it's like that, is it?" Cliff chuckled. "Well, some lucky girl is smiling as broadly as you, I should imagine. It won't be a secret for long, lad, not round this neck of the woods."

Eddy shrugged and tried to look nonchalant. Nobody must know about Angela, not until she left John and was free.

His face sobered as he considered the situation. Would she ever be free? Suppose John refused to let her go? Suppose he refused to divorce her? Divorce was a long drawn out messy business in Lancashire, and costly. What reason could they give for such a divorce? Adultery? He grimaced, imagining John taking out an action for adultery and naming him, Eddy Wright, as the co-respondent.

Clifford saw his son's face flush and smiled. Up to no good with one of the village lasses, eh? he thought. Well, a young fellow has to sow his wild oats and if none of them bears fruit, so be it.

As he gazed into the flames, his mind went back to the day when he impregnated Jenny. Jenny, the beautiful Jenny who had borne him a child and died from it. Over the years he often wondered why he had turned her away like that, but still who was to know she would die in childbirth? Aye, if he had wed her, things might have been different. Right now she would probably be around his neck like a millstone. He sighed.

Eddy sat quietly, thinking his own thoughts of passion and love. His flesh still tingled from her touch as he recalled the softness of her lips, saw the love light in her shining eyes. If Angela stayed at Mayhurst they could see each other often.

How she had clung to him as he made to leave. They were upstairs in the main bedroom by this time and there he had experienced physical love like he had never imagined. She showed him the scars from her accident, faded now, and he kissed each one. She was so beautiful, her body so lovely that

". . . penny for them," Clifford said, startling him.

"Oh, what?"

"What's going on in your big daft head? You should have seen the expression on your face. She must be a winner, this lass."

"Yes, she is." Rising, he went upstairs to think about her in private.

Angela, in an exceptionally good mood, let the dairy maid take off for the afternoon. Now she sat thinking about her affair. Eddy had the makings of a good lover, after she had taught him of course.

Since her marriage, Angela had developed a healthy need for

sex, often taking the initiative, so much so John told her she was too aggressive. Still, Eddy, a country man, didn't seem to mind at all. Even thinking about him made her nipples harden and her insides turn to mush. She felt like she had after John had made love to her for the first time, wanting more.

Yes, if she stayed at Mayhurst, she could see him almost every day. They could go for picnics and make love outdoors. She had always wanted to do that, not like today in the orchard, but buck naked and free, and for hours. John was dull and boring, only wanting to make love at night in the dark for a few minutes. Eddy had done it in the daylight, had not been averse to trying something new.

While John was back in town, she prayed he was consulting a new solicitor. She must launch her suit at once, before they found Freddy. It did not occur to her that he must be found before they launched any suit. Freddy did not enter into any of her plans.

CHAPTER FORTY

1901

Joyce returned home to Hillshead. The new owner sacked her when she refused to accede to his lustful wishes. When she slapped his face, he showed her the door.

Clifford was delighted to see her back. She blended into the household as though she had never been away, although her mood was one of simmering resentment that she had been forced to return. Her return was a last resort, though she kept this hidden from her brother while she stewed over the injustice of losing her position. She enjoyed living in town and being a somebody. Now she had become another invisible farm worker.

Eddy was set to ride over to Mayhurst when she went into the stable yard one morning.

"Are you going to the village, Eddy?" she asked as he led his horse out of the stable.

He let the reins dangle as he turned to look at her. "No, I had not planned to. Why?"

"I wanted some brown sugar for a recipe. Can you call in the village shop on your way?"

"All right."

He did not sound keen, she noticed. "Where are you heading anyway?"

"To Mayhurst."

"Sad that," she said, nodding, "Adele dying that way. It must be awful over there now. The place being empty. Are you keeping an eye on things?"

"Angela lives there now." He had to say it. News flashed from mouth to mouth in this area and everyone soon knew she was in residence. "She's taken over from her mother. John went back to Wigan." He'd said it, he had been dying to say it for ages. Joyce was a good sort and would keep his secret.

Joyce's face grew grim. "She is? What about her husband? Doesn't she care about him? She couldn't wait to steal him off me, yet she's there without him?"

Eddy looked pensive. "He was horrible to her. She told me all about it and I felt sorry for her, Aunt Joyce. I think you had a lucky escape."

Joyce leaned against the dairy wall. The bricks were warm in the sun and a cat circled around her ankles, purring.

"Horrible to her?" She knew John Black and he'd never be anything but a gentleman. "Then it was her fault," she said staunchly. "John Black is a perfect gentleman. It isn't like him to do anything horrible. She tells lies."

"I like Angela, Aunt Joyce, and she's such a lady. It couldn't have been her fault if he acts as she says."

Eddy leaned against the wall near her. The horse started snuffling at his pockets, looking for a treat.

In her mind, a light switched on. "Is Angela the reason you've been walking around looking like the man in the moon, all smiles?" His embarrassment confirmed it and she smiled. "She's good looking young woman, maybe too good looking. I never thought she'd steal my John."

"She's lovely," he said gleefully. Someone to talk to about it, someone to tell. "She's wonderful, Aunt Joyce, you know I've always liked her, ever since I was little. She's going to leave John, she told me that. She's . . .,"

Joyce shook her head emphatically. Men! "Come off it, lad, you not yet seventeen, chasing after the likes of her? She's a conniving little bitch, is Angela. She's only out for what she can get. She's cuckolding you, our Eddy. She's making a fool of you."

"She is not!" he protested, "How could you say that? You haven't seen her for years."

"I know how she was when she was a youngster and she hasn't changed at all, not if I know her. She wound you and her brother Freddy around her little finger, and both of you were mugs to dance to her tune. I told you then and I'll tell you now, stay away from her or you're heading for big trouble."

Eddy kicked at the cobbles. "Aaw, Aunt Joyce, she's not like that, not any more."

Joyce looked at her young nephew. He was a handsome youth, tall and broad of shoulder with long legs. Every lass in the village chased after him, Cliff told her, and yet he never went out with a girl more than once. They were mad for him, the lot of them, and some of the wives as well. Why he had taken up with that slut Angela, she could not fathom, other than Angela had the looks and the wiles.

"Don't tell Dad, Aunt Joyce, please?" he pleaded, taking one of her hands and pressing it between his.

Joyce shrugged. "I won't have to, lad. You can bet other people know what you're about, and don't blame me if he thrashes you."

"You won't tell Dad?"

"No, I won't tell him," she said, touching his cheek softly. "You think on and leave her alone. She's far too old for you. You'll be better off for it."

Eddy mounted and turned to leave the yard. "Thank you, Auntie Joyce," he said with a smile.

"Don't forget my sugar, now."

Joyce watched him go. He was in a great hurry to get to his lady love, she could see, but dallying with a married woman was wrong. She longed to talk about the situation with someone. Yet with whom could she talk? No other woman she know well enough to raise the subject. Her mother was dead, as was Agatha, and someone had murdered Betty.

How sad. She and Clifford were the last of the family of her generation. Nobody else would understand why they felt so bedevilled or why misfortune haunted them. It was as though every action, no matter how simple, caused a reaction that doubled in evil, causing heartache and misery. This affair with Eddy and Angela was fated to precipitate more grief for all concerned. Damn that old Romany!

She went into the dairy to check on the morning's yield and nodded as she counted cheese made last week and stacked on the many stone shelves. Going to the cupboard, she took out a large basket, and removing cheeses out of the presses, transferred them to the aging room.

Poor Eddy, she thought, a kid lusting after another man's wife. He'd not go far along that path for John would come back and order her home. Joyce only hoped it happened sooner than later as Eddy could be badly hurt.

Angela dispensed with corsets and gown when expecting Eddy, and wore a loose wrapper with her hair loose around her shoulders. They would spent an hour or so in her bed and Eddy always left happily befuddled. Yes, Eddy was good for her, she thought as she gazed at her reflection in the long mirror of her mother's bedroom. Her skin gleamed clean and white, her cheeks looked rosy, her eyes were clear and shining and her expression contented. She had never looked this well with John.

As Eddy rode down the lane, she heard his approach. Checking to ensure the dairy maids were out of the kitchen, she opened the front door to him.

"My love," she gasped as she pulled him to her. "It has been so long." She could feel his passion and almost dragged him to the stairs.

Eddy went willingly although he wondered why they never talked.

Why didn't she take him into the parlour or kitchen to chat like normal people? Her only thought was of sex, of things carnal and it started to annoy him. Did she only want him for the sex? Not that he could have walked away from it by any means, what red blooded male could? While her naked form was pressed to him and she offered the delights of her body he could hardly refuse, nor did he want to. He kissed her breasts and she pushed his head lower.

"Kiss me down there," she ordered, and it was a command.

After an hour, exhaustion took over. She knew how to keep him dangling so he begged for release while she found her climax many times. Angela believed her needs came first, even in sex. As he lay gasping for breath and she tried to caress him into erection yet again, he realized it was too much. She was a machine, a lovely one, yes, but a machine nevertheless and he wasn't.

"No, Angela, I'd like to talk to you," he said, taking her hands and trapping them in his own.

"What about?" She looked sulky and struggled to free her hands.

"About us. This cannot continue. I know it and you know it."

"Who has been talking to you? You were not like this yesterday." She watched his face for signs.

"Nobody has been talking. I've been thinking."

She sneered and scoffed. "You? Thinking? No, I don't think so," She narrowed her eyes, staring at him. "Someone has been talking to you. Was it your father?"

"No, it was not. I need to talk about this affair. It is an affair, Angela, after all. It's adultery and that's a sin. You're still married to John Black."

"Huh! As if I didn't know that already." Her lip curled peevishly.

"We can't go on this way while you're married to John. I realize that now. I've thought about this a lot, Angela. Please go back to him and get a divorce, or stay here and start proceedings. I can't relax if I know he's standing behind me."

"You've managed up to now." She pushed her tangled hair away from her face and touched his arm. "Don't worry about John and don't worry about the villagers. They know nothing about us. If we're careful and don't let anyone see us together, nobody will be suspicious."

"They already are, or so my sister says."

She drew back. "Your sister? I thought your sister died when that man attacked her."

"Not my sister Betty, my sister Joyce. She came home about a month ago. Anyway, she told me this morning she'd heard talk."

"Oh, don't be such a worrier. So what? We aren't doing anything they aren't doing. Love me, Eddy." She flung herself at him and started kissing his face.

Eddy gave himself up to passion. What was the use of fighting it? Since she gave herself so freely, he drowned in her. To heck with the village. She was right: it was none of their business and he was free and single.

Clifford was shocked when a neighbour, old George Cahill, told him.

"Aye, sounds like your Eddy is doing all right for himself wi' Mrs. Black, Angela Stockton that were, or so I hear," he chuckled lasciviously. "The lad rides over to Mayhurst most days. They spend time in her mother's bedroom and it ain't to whitewash the walls, I can tell thi."

"What's this?" Clifford went white with rage. "Who told you?"

"Oh, it's common knowledge. Cliff. The dairy maid as works there, Janey Cluny, she told the pedlar and he spread it around. Aye, the missus lets him in't front door and thinks nobody knows."

Keeping his voice even, so as not to show his anger, he said, "Right, I'll have a talk with young Master Eddy." Clifford tried to recall where Eddy was working.

"Well, if you can't find him, he'll be over to Mayhurst in't mistress's bed." Old George chuckled nastily.

Clifford rode home, checking the fields as he went. Joyce came out of the outhouse as he trotted his horse into the yard. "Where's Eddy?" he shouted angrily.

"Said he was thinning out the far copse on Cropper's Brew today. Why?"

"Nothing. See you at dinner time." He galloped out the yard and made to the east and the copse.

He's found out about Eddy and her, she thought, pleased Cliff was wise to their tricks. Served Miss Angela right, her with the posh talk and the lovely dresses was going to find herself up against their Clifford, who was a hard man.

Clifford rode to Cropper's Brew. The brew, a long low hill, standing in the east of his land was mainly used for grazing sheep as it had many outcrops of sandstone. Along one side stood four copses of young birch mixed with other scrubby trees and bushes, and the plan was to clear all but the good trees to allow them to come to full maturity. The last time these copses were cleared was at least forty years earlier, in his grandfather's time. Nature had reclaimed them and they were a thick mass of brambles and saplings.

These small woods provided homes for rabbits, hares, badgers, weasels and other small animals. A true landsman, Clifford always protected the habitat of these small beneficial creatures. He also gave foxes a haven on his land, for he saw no bad in them. They kept down the populations of rabbits, hares, mice and shrews and they mainly hid from sight. The local hunt used part of his bottom land, although he ensured they kept away from his woods and copses.

As he crested the next ridge, he saw Eddy. He was in the lower copse, clearing some brambles.

"Ahoy! Eddy!" he called as he spurred his horse over the boulders and stones of an outcrop.

"Have you come to help me?" He did not sound too pleased and Clifford figured it was because Eddy was his own man, capable of starting and finishing any job without help.

He dismounted and strode over to where Eddy stood. "We must

talk, Eddy," was all he said, but the set of his mouth and the look on his face warned Eddy.

"What is it, Dad? Is something wrong?"

"Aye, something is wrong, lad. You've been sniffing around Angela Black."

"So?" Eddy's face reddened.

"You must stop it at once, son. You must stay away from that woman."

"Why? Because you say so?" The heat rushed through him. He was not a child. "Look here, father, I'm a grown man, and I don't need you instructing me about what I should or should not do. If I want to see Angela, I'll do so, and you'll not stop me."

"Nay, I will lad. You have no idea why I insist on it, but take my word that you'll be sorry."

How could he tell his son that he was dallying with his half-sister? Nobody knew now Jenny, Adele, Eliza and Albert were gone. Most of the villagers were aware of their kinship to some extent because the coach man who had brought Angela to the farm that dark day had spread the word. He had thought they would all forget it and most had forgotten, until Angela decided to come back.

Eddy threw up his hands in disgust. "I won't listen to this. This is village rumour and innuendo."

"Aye, it is, an'all. Everybody is talking about you two. Anyway, what's she doing at Mayhurst? Her place is with her husband. Her brother Freddy is the heir."

"She's contesting the will, Dad. He's adopted, is Freddy, and he left Mayhurst years ago. Wanted nothing to do with it, so why should he want it now?"

"It's his birthright." Clifford noted the look on his son's face. "All right, all right," he said heatedly, "I know they adopted him. However, Albert left it to him so he can take it up or sell it. She's mad if she thinks she has a case, because she's no more Albert's child than Freddy."

"What?" Eddy stared open mouthed. "Not Albert's child? Adele slept with another man? Never!"

Clifford did not want to tell him but Angela had Eddy twisted around her little finger so it was necessary.

"No, Adele did not. She would never sleep with another man. She was a true lady, as was her sister. No, it wasn't that way, but Angela was as much adopted as was her brother."

"No! She doesn't know that, I know she doesn't know." Eddy gasped, shocked at this news. "Whose child is she?"

Clifford found it harder than he had thought. Time was when he'd have been proud to call Angela his own, but those days were long gone. She had matured into a selfish, arrogant woman who thought only of her own comfort and pleasure. Now he felt ashamed of her.

"Angela is my child," he said, his face showing his regret.

Eddy's face blanched. "What? You can't mean that, Father. Oh my God, Angela is my sister." He put his hands over his face unable to take it in. For a moment he stood, then raised his eyes, now full of tears. "How? Who was her mother?"

It flashed through Eddy's mind that maybe his mother, Agatha, had been Angela's mother, that for some reason she gave Angela to the Stocktons. It did not make him feel any better.

Clifford cleared his throat, himself close to tears when his mind flashed back to the beautiful Jenny and her infatuation for him.

"Angela's mother was Adele's sister Eliza's girl, Jennifer. They took her back to town and sent her to a home when they discovered her pregnancy. She ran away and came to live with Adele. When she died in childbirth, Adele took the baby because she could have no more of her own. Eliza, Angela's grandmother, mother of Jenny, came to live at Mayhurst when she left her husband. You know the rest. They adopted Freddy to make the Stockton family complete."

"Still, but Stockton had two other sons, didn't he? I recall you talking about them. This is so confusing."

"True, but the boys never come back since they left. Nobody knows where they are."

Eddy shook his head. Angela, his sister? It did not bear thinking about. Obviously Angela had no idea that she was not her mother's birth child. My God, what would she do when she found out? He must tell her, he thought. It was only fair. She was deluding herself by thinking she could claim Mayhurst as her own.

"Where are you going?" Clifford asked as he saw Eddy untying his horse from the tree branch.

"Over to Mayhurst to talk to Angela. She has to know about this."

"Don't be silly, lad. You'll break the woman's heart." Catching at the bridle, he held back the horse. "Leave it be, don't see her again. Leave her some small shred of pride."

Eddy's face was expressionless. "She's living a lie and thinking she can gain Mayhurst. This will go against her, and she'll be more hurt if a stranger tells her."

"Aye, that's true enough, but leave it for Freddy to raise the issue. I think he knows about her birth. He knows about his own adoption."

Eddy thought about it for a minute. "Surely that's surely even more reason I should tell her, forewarn her."

"No, it's even more reason why you should *not* be the one to break the bad news." Clifford had to stop Eddy, knowing he would bring the wrath of the Gods down on himself if he told Angela. "Let her remember you with love. Let her think that you'd never hurt her. You realize that once she's aware I'm her father, she will surely come over here. One thing I know about Angela is that she will switch her eye to Hillshead, for she's out for what she can get, always has been."

"You don't like her," Eddy cried, "I can see it in the way you talk about her, talking about her as if she were a gold digger. You say she's your daughter and yet you castigate her? She's a warm, loving woman and I hate you for this. I hate you."

"Now, lad, think on it. Come on, get down and we'll tackle this job together and talk about it while we work."

CHAPTER FORTY-ONE

nger surged through her as the carriage stopped in front of the house and John alighted. It was early morning and she glanced at the mantel clock. What did he want now? Trust him to come and spoil her pleasure, but maybe he brought news of a good solicitor.

As she opened the door, she smiled. "John, how nice of you visit."

"Good day, Angela. We must talk." He was carrying a large envelope and flourished it as he walked past her into the parlour.

She followed him into the room where she had been sitting reading in front of an apple wood fire and drinking hot chocolate.

"Could I offer you some refreshment, John? I can get Jane to make some coffee."

How civilized she was being, he thought. He glanced at the tray with its china pot of chocolate, the small cream cakes. "No, thank you. I see you're treating yourself well, as usual. I don't doubt you have the dairy maid running around after you like a personal servant."

She flapped her hands at him. "All right, John, there's no need to be nasty. What have you got there?"

"What I have here, Angela, is something that will put a stop to all this nonsense about you claiming Mayhurst. I set a detective to look for Frederick and he found him. Frederick is now a married man with two sons. He will arrive within the month with his family to take over.

Freddy is older and wiser now because his dream of entering the legal profession came to naught. He was lucky in his wife for she brought a considerable dowry and is assured of further inheritances."

Angela felt her heart sink. Freddy had sons, Freddy wanted Mayhurst. He was going to oust her from what she thought of as her home, and she would have to go back with John. Or did she? What about her lover Eddy? Maybe he could take her away from here and they could live together. Then she realized he would be penniless, and that did not suit her.

John stood with his arms clasped behind his back, his eyes cold. "Pack your bags, my dear wife. We are going home."

Angela stared, her eyes blazing with loathing. She hated him, he always spoiled everything. Why *had* she married him?

"I don't want to go with you," she spat, "I'll stay here until my brother comes. I can live with them. This is my home, it always has been, and always will be."

"Don't be stupid, Angela. Freddy does not want you here. Do you think his wife wants a lodger? You must come home with me at once. You're my wife and you will do as I say." He was angry, she saw from his clenched fists.

Angela stared. He was impressive when he was angry, very impressive. Somehow that moved her, somehow she thought more of him. She found his assertiveness magnetic.

"What is in the envelope?"

"Something that will move you from here as quickly as possible. Something someone should have told you. Here, read this and weep."

"Where did this come from?"

"Freddy. He had it from your mother, Adele, many years ago."

She withdrew the letter from the envelope. Addressed to her mother, she recognized her Aunt Eliza's handwriting. Again she read that she was not Adele's child, but Jenny's. It was irrefutable proof.

Darn it all, Freddy knew and now John knew. How many other people knew of her shame? To her further mortification, she read that she was Clifford Wright's love child.

Her father was Clifford Wright, and she had fallen in love with Eddy, his son? Which meant she was in love with her half-brother.

"Oh my God!" she said, through sudden tears of shame.

"I'm sorry, Angela. It is a sad story, is it not? Now come home with me and I will see you through this terrible shock."

"Yes, yes," she said through her tears. "Please take me home, John. This is no longer my home, no longer a place I want."

"Good," he said as he put his arms around her and kissed her hair. "You must forget this as a bad dream. Now go upstairs and pack your bags."

"Yes, yes." She ran out of the room sobbing. He heard her run up the stairs and smiled. She would settle down at home now her dreams of owning Mayhurst had evaporated.

As she threw things into her basket, Angela thought about the revelation. She felt so empty inside now they were taking away her birthright, or what she had always thought of as her birthright. Her mother, Adele, had been her aunt and her Aunt Eliza had been her grandmother. Most horrible to contemplate was the fact her father was Clifford Wright.

She paused in her packing and thought about him, a farmer. Yet not an ordinary farmer. Clifford Wright owned the most profitable and envied farm in the county and was a rich man. She could see some good coming of their relationship in the future.

Eddy was now forbidden to her. Giddy thinking of it, she felt sick to her stomach that she had lain with him, had urged him to make love to her so often. Suppose she had become pregnant? A cold shiver ran through her and she felt bitter bile rise to her mouth.

Oh God, suppose John found out about her and Eddy? They must leave as quickly as possible, before he spoke to Jane, before she let it slip that Eddy often came over to see her.

When they were well on their way, she smiled up at John, glad to be away from her shame, pleased he still wanted her. So what if he wasn't the man of her dreams? At least he had a position and prospects. She could stand it, at least she thought she could, and maybe in the future her father Clifford would bequeath her something of Hillshead.

Angela, aghast, realized she was pregnant. When she missed a period, she put it down to the upset. That's what she hoped, but the truth of the matter was she was pregnant with her half-brother's child.

She would tell John the child was his. They were man and wife and she had done her duty when they returned. An early first child was common enough, and who in Wigan could possibly know about Eddy?

When John's grandfather died, he inherited a small fortune. It transpired the old man had been an astute businessman and his stock holdings were considerable. After the probate, they transferred the money and stocks to John's account and he immediately bought the shop. He did not tell Angela until he completed the transaction.

"How could you do that?" Her voice rang through the dining room and the crystal chandelier trembled. "Why did you not tell me you were going to buy that place? We could have had a new home built, moved into a good neighbourhood . . .,"

He looked at her, eyebrows raised. "Still on that tack, Angela? Still determined to be one of the higher class? I bought the shop because it makes me my own boss. We have a child on the way and must think about that child's future. I now control my own destiny."

She tossed her head. "Bah! You control nothing, John, you are nothing but a shop clerk. You always were and will always be a shop clerk. You'll lose that shop within a year for you have no idea of how business is done."

"Of course, you do? You surprise me, my dear. I had no idea that you'd had experience in such matters." He was outwardly calm, although he felt angry.

"I have more intelligence in my little finger than you have in your entire body, John Black. I had a good education, an education that . . .,"

"And your parentage? That also adds to your intelligence, does it?"

He did not pull his punches with Angela any more, having changed his attitude toward her since the farm fiasco and after learning of her roots. He did not let her attack his feelings these days, refused to let her denigrate him. While he knew that acting so sadistically towards her in her condition smacked of cruelty, he said what he thought. "Ah yes, I see where you got your brains. A farmer for a father and a schoolgirl with not much between her ears and lacking in moral values, for a mother?"

She slapped her hands onto the table and stood. "How dare you? How could you talk to me in this manner?"

"My dear, talking to you like this will be the norm. I'm tired of being put down, talked to as though I were an imbecile. I now own my own shop. Oh, you can scoff, but I'm a man of means. I'm a businessman and I intend to act like one, both in my daily work and at home. As your husband, you will not talk me down. Do you understand me, Angela?"

"Yes, John," she said meekly, wondering how she could make him suffer. She had to nip this new attitude in the bud. He must learn his place in the scheme of things for as she ran the house, she also ran him.

Then Queen Victoria died and the country buried her with great pomp. Photographs and retrospectives of her reign filled the papers. The eldest son Edward was now king. Edward VII ascended to the throne after waiting too many years. He was 60 years old.

CHAPTER FORTY-TWO

Eddy fell in love on the rebound with a young maid from the manor. She came into his life when he was at his lowest, as he pined with love for his own sister. They literally bumped into each other at the market and her flashing green eyes and white smile soon diverted him.

Valerie Monk was a pert red head and full of life. Her position as a parlour maid at Squire Walton's manor had taught her manners and deportment. Eddy felt proud of her and courted her diligently. Clifford watched the courtship and thanked God Angela had returned to town.

Clifford was getting on in years, or so his body told him. He was now forty-two. Working hard since he was old enough, his bones ached with arthritis earned from working long hours in cold and damp weather. His eyes were rapidly failing and he needed a magnifying glass to read. Aye, he thought as he moved stiffly, his days as a young man had gone and left him a mature, wiser, and ailing, person.

Eddy told him to take it easy, tried to take charge, but Clifford found it hard to drop the reins of power. Not that Eddy did anything wrong. He had gained too much experience at Hillshead to ever do that, but Clifford was, and always would be, top dog.

Clifford had long realized Hillshead was his life, it talked to him, and he loved it too much to give it up without a struggle. Well, he sighed as he painfully climbed the road to the sheep barn, may be it was up to Eddy now. He would marry and raise children here, children who would inherit this fine farm. Aye, his land, his farm, his reason for living.

Checking on two isolated ewes, penned apart from the flock when they showed signs of illness and finding nothing amiss, he headed back down to the lower field where two men were harvesting cabbages. Lately Eddy demanded they try new crops, crops that they could sell at the Weatherly market. The lad was right. The cabbage, turnips and carrots sold fast and were now another source of profit.

Aye, Clifford told himself, Eddy would do all right, but then he'd had a good teacher. Clifford prided himself on his ability to pass the knowledge of years to a son who loved the land as much as he did. Now with Eddy courting Valerie, well, it made all the difference.

Aye, to think the young fool had lain with Angela Stockton. He shook his head, unable even now to accept the fact. Good riddance to her. He hoped she was now a mother and well settled in town.

At the back of his mind he knew that Angela, if ever apprised of her real father, might come back to see him on the off chance something was in it for her. Aye, but she was out of luck. He'd have nothing to do with her now, not after she seduced his son.

Within the month Eddy announced his engagement.

"We want to marry after harvest, Dad." His face shone with love. "She's going to tell them at the manor that she's leaving."

Clifford hugged his son close, his eyes full of sudden tears. "Aye, well we'd better had her folks over for a talk. The bride's parents have a lot of planning to do, but I'll foot the bill. We can afford it."

"Thanks, Dad. They'll appreciate that," Eddy said, shaking his Dad's hand. "Since her Dad got shot, things have not been good."

Graham Monk was coachman for the squire until the day a game keeper, aiming at a crow, accidentally shot him. The bullet struck his head, while it was a glancing shot, it affected his sense of balance, particularly at a height. No longer could he ride on the high coachman's seat. After losing his position, they relegated him to working in the stables when he felt fit enough, a menial job that took the heart right out of him.

Angela, huge with child was extremely ungainly. She spent her days ordering the housekeeper around and feeding her face.

John hired a Mrs. Higgins to look after the household after Angela insisted that in his new position as a business owner they should have a servant. From the day Mrs. Higgins arrived, Angela ceased doing anything. She ordered drinks and food at all hours as she sat in front of a fire, toasting herself.

Mrs. Higgins' patience soon wore thin. She disliked Angela and made her wait because she resented having to drop everything to wait on her. As a qualified housekeeper, she took offense at Angela's attitude, disliking the way the madam treated her like a skivvy.

John, unaware of any dissension in the household, gave Mrs. Higgins a raise when she baked him a special cake full of caraway seeds - seeds Angela detested.

Angela rang the bell, another of her affectations. She insisted that John install push bells in each room in case she needed help in her delicate condition. Eager to keep her quiet, he complied with her demands, spending much time at his new shop where he was making big changes and already expanding.

"Oh, that woman, she is worse than useless," Angela spat as she rang the bell again.

Mrs. Higgins looked up at the bell. "Lord, she even rings nowty."

When Mrs. Higgins arrived, wiping her hands on her apron, Angela screamed at her. "Where were you? Why didn't you answer the bell? I could have been lying on the floor hurt, yet you decided to take your time."

"I was kneading the bread dough, madam," Her voice was subservient but sarcastic, for she was a crafty woman. "I couldn't come here with my hands covered in flour, madam. Now what did madam want?"

"Madam wants you first to fix the fire, then a cup of hot chocolate and a couple of scones with cream and jam. I know you made some this morning," she said sharply, glaring at her servant, the ill-bred slavey who had pulled the wool over John's eyes.

"Yes, madam. It will take me about ten minutes," Mrs. Higgins said, casting her eyes to the floor. Look at her, she thought, she looks like a beached whale. Stupid, ill tempered and cruel, self-centred, egotistical sod, she's a nagger of the highest order. It's only because the master pays me so well, and I can skim a lot from the housekeeping because Angela stays out of household affairs, that I stay.

Stooping, she put coal nuggets on the fire and swept the hearth.

With narrowed eyes Angela watched her go, watched the way she closed the door so quietly the latch did not even click. She was sneaky that woman, sneaky and probably dishonest. Well, once she had rid herself of this huge stomach, she would start checking each household transaction. It was common knowledge that servants would rob you blind if left to their own devices.

The baby was born in late July. As it had been hot and humid for weeks, Angela, who was constantly out of sorts, and because she nagged at him for the slightest imagined slight, John took to staying away and working late.

When in labour, she screamed her head off for hours, cursed John, cursed Eddy, cursed the God who had made her conceive. It was nearly twenty-four hours before she gave birth and John had gone to stay with a friend because he could not stand her continual shrieking.

It was a girl, a daughter, the spitting image of Eddy Wright. Angela saw it from the first second, and prayed nobody else could. Not that John knew about her affair with Eddy, she reasoned, and anyway, all new babies looked alike. The baby had Eddy's eyes, the shape of them and the colour were identical, although the eyes of new babies were always blue. To top it all, she had the same reddish gold hair.

John saw nothing but his daughter, the lack of family resemblance did not bother him much. Babies changed as they developed.

"What are we going to name her?" he asked. They had not talked about girl's names as Angela felt convinced she was having a son.

"Josephine, the female of Joseph," Angela said firmly. John had wanted his first born named after his grandfather. "For a second name Tina, after my father, Albert. Oh I know it should be Albertina but that's far too long a name for such a tiny girl," She looked down on her child, smiling and maternal and John felt a surge of love for her. At least she was pleasant since the birth, more contented.

"Did you hire a nanny?" she asked, "I also need a nurse to look after her while I regain my strength. It was a difficult birth. The doctor said so."

"Yes, though it might have been a lot easier if you had co-operated," he said. "The doctor talked to me. He said you had not listened to any of his advice, had stuffed your face, put on too much weight and taken no exercise."

His voice was full of warning, she knew that tone.

She brushed away his words with a lazy hand. "Oh John, how could a man know what a woman feels like when pregnant, or in childbirth. Now, did you. . .?

"Yes," the exasperation showed in his tone. "I hired a young woman as nanny. She has good references. As far as a nurse goes, you don't need one. The doctor told me the sooner you got to your feet and took some exercise, the better it will be for you and the child. I can have the nanny start earlier if it will help, but I will not hire a nurse. You are not sick."

"Well! How would you know how I feel?" Her face reddened with rage. He saw it and waited for the outburst. "Have *you* ever given birth? If my mother or my aunt were alive, they'd be here looking after me until I got over the birth. You are a cruel man, John, plain cruel, and that housekeeper must go. She did not bring me my hot chocolate this morning and I was dying of hunger. Instead she brought me consomme and not warm at that."

"I advised her that the doctor's instructions were that you were to have only healthy foods, little sugar and no chocolate. He wants you to lose the extra weight and this is the only way to accomplish it."

"He put me on a diet? How dare he, and how dare you!" She turned away from him, her face angry and ugly.

John stood for a second. "Bad temper will not do the child any good, Angela, and your foul humour will affect your milk. You must put our child first."

"Go away, John," the bedclothes muffled her voice. "Do not come back until you have sacked the bitch downstairs."

John did not sack Mrs. Higgins, instead he gave her a bonus to put up with Angela's moods.

Eddy and Valerie were married when the harvest was in, so harvest home and the wedding became the same celebration. They did not go on a honeymoon as Valerie wanted to be near her father who had collapsed after the wedding. It could have been drink, or it might have been apoplexy, but she would not leave him.

Eddy went back to work instead of going to the Lake District for a week. Not that he minded too much, for to be away from his beloved Hillshead might not suit him anyway.

CHAPTER FORTY-THREE

At Mayhurst, Freddy, now twenty-four, did his best to run the farm but the men took advantage of his ignorance and he was too proud to ask for advice. When planting time came, he bought the seed for which they asked and let them get on with the ploughing, tilling and planting.

Margaret, his wife, detested farm life. She particularly despised the winter, so cold and so long, with nothing to do and all day in which to do it. She longed to return to the town where she was born.

To make over a garment for one of the boys was a hardship she had never reckoned with. They were so far from civilization, so far from stores. The village cottage shops had little in the way of clothing because people made their own this far out in the wilds. Freddy spent all his time out on the land, so she and the children remained in the house with only two peasants for company. It irked her that they did not work for her, but worked for the farm.

Margaret started each day with good intentions but the boys, two and three, were a handful. They demanded food and wanted to go out to play. She had to watch them carefully because bits of rusty machinery lay around, and the grounds were muddy when it rained. After she made the fire and prepared the family's breakfast, she spent her time watching the boys. When it rained, she kept them inside and vainly tried to get some work done.

Freddy did not care about the state of the house. He didn't see the dust or dirt and was content thinking himself a squire with a profitable farm. At least it had been profitable enough according to last year's figures, which was the reason he decided to take over instead of selling.

Unfortunately he was so ignorant of farming that he did not see the men were only playing at working when he was around. Nothing much got done and since he had no idea what they were doing, they got away with it. They pulled their forelock and "yes master-ed" him, then laughed like drains after they took their pay.

Freddy was the subject of much hilarity in the village. 'Serves him right,' they said, 'Someone else's bastard.' He was no farmer, was Master Freddy. They laughed and took his money with no conscience at all.

"Freddy will soon get tired of playing and he'll sell Mayhurst," Clifford said to Eddy as they stood on the hilltop overlooking Mayhurst Farm. "Those men have planted oats where they had oats last year, see that? He doesn't know they're having him on. By, he's as green as grass and I'm not going to tell him. Mayhurst will run at a loss this year, but we can bide our time and make him an offer after his meagre harvest. You can run it for you and Valerie. It's a nice enough farm and we could work it in concert with Hillshead"

Eddy considered it and nodded. "Yes, that's true. We could farm it as one farm, though we'll each have our own homes. You know, you should think about marrying again, Dad. It's not right to have only your sister for company."

Eddy worried about his father. Clifford's strength was failing him and he frequently felt exhausted. Joyce confided that maybe she would wed Victor Greaves if he asked her. Victor lived in the village and owned the general store. If she accepted, she would help him in his business and that meant Clifford would be alone. That was not good with his failing health. Of course, Freddy could hang onto Mayhurst, and in that case, he and Valerie would continue to live at Hillshead.

"Well, Dad, there's no harm in looking, but it's going to be a while before makes up his mind either way. Meanwhile we can only watch and wait."

"Aye, we can wait." Clifford said as he wheeled his horse around. "Come on, lad, let's see what the thatchers are doing."

John did not know the exact moment he realized Josy was not his biological child. It was nothing said, but suddenly he knew by looking at her that he had not fathered her.

In his family, the trait was to brown eyes, all his cousins and the other relatives were brown eyed. Both his parents were brown eyed and Angela was more hazel than blue eyed, as was he. It was obvious the baby was sired by another man for the child had bright blue eyes and reddish blonde curly hair.

He said nothing although he wondered who it could have been. Who of his acquaintances had eyes of that particular hue? Nobody that he could recall, therefore it must be someone back in Weatherly, and probably the reason why she wanted to stay there. How could he have been so stupid? How could he not have known that she was having an affair?

He watched Josy as she toddled around the parlour talking baby talk to her stuffed doll. Her gown was of smocked lawn with lace trimming and her tiny shoes were of white kid leather. She was a lovely child and he doted on her. However, she was not his and this knowledge festered in him. Tempted to confront Angela, he then got another idea as he picked up Josy who had tripped over the fireplace curb.

"I think we will take a weekend and visit your brother at Mayhurst. What do you think, my dear?"

Angela looked surprised. "A day out in the country will be good for all of us. Yes, that might be nice."

He watched her face. "We'll take Josy to see the animals. She'll enjoy that."

"Oh yes, she will," Angela clapped her hands with glee, obviously not picking up on his train of thought. "She's never been in the country. Come to Mamma, darling," Taking her from him, she told her about the cows and sheep and the chickens.

"I'll write to Freddy right away," John said, "We should give his wife time to make preparations."

"But of course, John. See Josy, see the sheep?" she pointed one out in the rag book she held. "We'll see lots when we go to visit your uncle Freddy."

John smiled as he listened. Angela was a child herself in many ways and if she thought the trip was for her benefit she'd be all for it. Over the past year or so he had learned how to handle her, and she never suspected. In a short time the father of his child surely would come to light.

When he found out, he'd confront them with his knowledge and he would . . . What would he do? He loved the child, he sometimes thought he loved Angela although it was more comfort he found with her than passion. As for Angela, if she had slept with another, did she still love the man? Did she still love him, her husband?

He pondered as he watched her play with Josy. Why *had* she come back so quickly? She had never cared what country people thought of her or her family, her only real interest lay in the social class of Wigan.

Since he bought the shop and made it successful, many male clubs made him welcome, many doors were opened to him. Due to this rise in his popularity among businessmen, Angela delighted in lording it over their neighbours, the little people who worked for others.

The new house they purchased was in a good part of town, although not in the swish enclave to which she aspired. John had electricity installed and a telephone. They lived a comfortable life, had a carriage and a matched pair and were content, at least to an outsider's eyes.

As he watched her play with Josy, he wondered how she would react once her secret was a secret no longer. Would she rant and rage and claim the man had raped her? He could hear her saying that already. If she did, he'd laugh in her face, yes he would. Rape was the last thing any man could do to Angela. If a victim of rape, she'd have screamed it from the highest rooftops and brought the law down on the man's head.

John's sole intent now was to discover whose child he was raising. Meanwhile he would pray for guidance for he did not want to hurt the child.

1905

Eddy was ecstatic when Valerie told him she was expecting. He and his father slapped each other on the back, congratulating themselves, and that evening drank elderberry wine and daydreamed about the coming child.

Valerie listened to their blather impatiently and said, "Now you two, let's not talk about the child like this. We don't know what it is going to be. Suppose it's a girl? Will she not be welcome?"

"Of course, Val. I don't mind a girl if she is healthy, but I'd like a son," Eddy said, hugging her tipsily.

Valerie laughed and pushed at him. "Get away with you, you drunken sot, and you, father-in-law, how about you? You also want a grandson, I'll be bound."

"If you don't mind, my dear." He raised his glass to her. "Still, as Eddy says, we won't mind if the child is healthy, and you come through it all right."

"Well, I'd better start thinking boy, boy, boy, as I'll never live it down if I give the world a girl." She laughed to see the men so befuddled with drink. It only took one glass and they were well away.

"What are we going to do with these drunkards, Joyce? What do you suggest?" she asked.

Joyce laughed. She was pleased for Valerie and Eddy. When she married, she didn't see any chance of having children. Surely she was too old for that now.

"I'd give them another tot or two and let them suffer the heads of the damned tomorrow morning, that's what I'd do. Now pass me the bottle and let me wet the baby's head as well."

Sure enough the two men held their heads and almost staggered the next morning as they rose at first light to go ploughing. Val smiled. Served them right, she thought fondly, as she made and wrapped up an extra special dinner, adding two bottles of home brewed beer, for their hangovers might need that at lunch time.

CHAPTER FORTY-FOUR

Angela hummed as she admired her reflection in the full length mirror. This new outfit, she thought, would set Freddy back on his heels. As she had never met Margaret, Freddy's heiress wife, nothing could be left to chance. Then again, she, a person who lived in town would obviously was more up to date and better dressed than any farmer's wife, no matter what her ancestry.

During and after her pregnancy, she had gained an enormous amount of weight. Now they had servants, she did nothing. Exercise was anathema to her, and while she was now obese, she did not see that in herself. She only saw a well dressed, stately woman, and thought of herself as voluptuous. Her specially made corsets were stiffly whale boned and held her trapped as in a vice, but she now measured forty around her once 18 inch waist.

The wife of a shop owner was a major step up from a woman whose life revolved around milk and eggs. As for Freddy, she wondered how he was doing with the farm. Her mother had run it efficiently and made a lot of money. Enough to leave Angela five thousand pounds, enough operating capital for Freddy, and this after he paid the death duties.

Then again, if she had stayed to run the farm, she could have made a far greater success of it. In her own mind she knew she had the brains of the family, was more intelligent than Freddy for all his higher education. Anyway, he had been stupid enough to throw away his education to pursue a dream, a dream that never became real.

John waited as Angela made her way down the curving staircase. She liked to make an entrance, even for him. The nanny stood patiently with Josephine in her arms. Angela never carried the child if she could help it . . . that's why they had servants, she said.

As she sauntered slowly down, she fastened her glove buttons. "You have checked everything with Mrs. Higgins, John, I hope? I do not want to come home to find crooks have burgled us, or burned the house to the ground."

He sighed. "Yes, Angela, of course I have. Mrs. Higgins is a professional and we're only going for two days."

Angela tossed her head and made the feathers on her hat flutter. "Two days or two hours, it is all the same. That woman could allow riff-raff into our home. I think she should go elsewhere while we are away."

John glared up at her as she paused on the second stair. "We've had this out at least four times and, I repeat, we're only going for two days. Anyway, the house should not be left empty. Get your cloak and let's leave now or we'll never get there."

"Dada, dada, dada!" Josy gurgled, and he took her from the nanny. She crowed with delight and tried to remove his hat.

"Come along now, Angela. We must go."

The nanny stood and watched her charge leaving. At last, two days peace and quiet, she thought, her taut nerves already relaxing.

"Two days without Mrs. Black nagging and carping about everything from Josy's untidy hair to the toys on the floor," she had said to Mrs. Higgins, "It's as if she thinks the child is a small adult and doesn't need toys, or to make a noise." A normal child, Josy cried or screamed with delight as it took her.

"If it hadn't been for Mr. Black, I'd have left long ago. Still, he's a good man, the master."

"True enough and without him I'd have gone the first week. Mrs. Black is a bitch of the first water."

Both hated her selfishness and nastiness and the way she continually agitated for their dismissal.

CHAPTER FORTY-FIVE

It was almost tea time when they arrived at Mayhurst. Freddy and Margaret, expecting them, stood beside the front door as they drew to a halt in front of the house.

"Come on inside. Welcome sister, welcome John," Freddy said offering John his hand, "So this is young Josephine. What a big girl! Come to your Uncle Freddy. Look, this is your Aunt Margaret."

After the introductions, they went into the parlour where Margaret had tea waiting.

"It's good to meet you, Angela. Tell me all about your new house," Margaret said, taking Freddie's advice in getting Angela to talk about herself.

The boys, Freddy junior and Neville, came in shortly after and the small room was full of noise. Josy liked the boys and they delighted in making her laugh by playing peek-a-boo from the back of an arm chair.

"Enough now, boys, she'll be sick if you get her over excited," Angela said sharply. Margaret felt like contradicting her, but wisely said nothing as she had realized from the first moment that Angela was one whose word they must instantly obey.

The boys subsided into sulks and went upstairs to play with their toy soldiers. Josy crawled onto her father's lap and went to sleep as Angela rattled on about Wigan, about her social life, her new gowns, the shop, about herself, until they were tired of listening.

As she took a breath to start again, John spoke. "That's enough, Angela. Nobody else can get a word in edgewise. We have two days for you to tell your life story." He looked to Freddy who sat in a wing chair. "Now, Freddy, what about the farm. How is it going?"

Freddy talked about the crops, how sparse they were compared to the neighbouring fields belonging to Hillshead.

Angela snorted. "That's because you're a fool, Freddy. You know nothing about farming. You hated it as a boy and, let's face it, you have no feeling for the land. Mother should have left it to me."

Freddy did not lose his temper, he was well used to his sister. "Ah, but as you know Mother never made a will. Father's will remained in effect and that named me successor." Freddy did not like his sister much now, thinking her too opinionated, too bossy and much too fat these days. She had definitely not improved with age. Where had the beautiful lithe girl gone?

He also disliked the way she talked down to everyone.. And the way she gave orders, that was something else. Talking to everyone as if they were mere servants sent to do her bidding, but he noticed John only took it for so long before he stopped her. Though, when she did stop, it was only to sulk.

"I think we will take some air before supper," Margaret said as she stood. "The orchard is pleasant for a short walk."

As they walked, they talked and this time, with John holding firmly onto Angela's arm, they spoke of many things. Josy chattered from her perch in John's arms and they laughed as a butterfly landed on John's shoulder and she sat still for fear of scaring it.

"A country lass, if ever I saw one," Freddy laughed as he watched her, her eyes fascinated. "She likes it out here. Look at the way she admires the butterfly."

Nobody noticed Angela's face blanche. It all flooded back, a country lass he said; yes, indeed she was because her father was a farmer. As for herself, she preferred people to regard her a lady of the town, an educated person of impeccable background. Since moving to Wigan she had worked hard toward this end and here was her brother, her stupid brother, saying her child was a country lass. Oh no, she wanted better than that for her daughter. How foolish they had been to come here.

"John, could we go back inside?" she asked. He looked down at her, noting her pallor and the perspiration on her brow. "I do not feel well. Maybe I ate something that disagreed with me."

Sure, you ate everything put in front of you and more, John thought, hating Angela. How dare Angela cast aspersions on Margaret's culinary abilities?

Angela went upstairs to lie down, taking Josy with her, and a companionable silence filled the kitchen where they sat drinking tea.

"I don't know much about farming, Fred, but I think your men did a terrible job." John said. "They did not sow the fields properly because I see too many arid patches and far too many weeds." He felt sorry for Freddy who was trying so hard to make it work, but simply had no affinity for the land. "Did you get the gangman with his crew to come in and pick the stones and thistles?

"No, what?" Freddy looked surprised. "Gangman? What's that?"

"Ask Clifford of Hillshead, he'll see to it."

Freddy nodded and sighed. "Wright said much the same thing, John, that I should ask him for help." He blew out an aggravated breath, "I watched those men work for months; I watched every move they made. Unfortunately I didn't recognize what they were doing was wrong. Never mind, this was my learning season. Next season they will find things changed. I've studied books, many books. I know now what has to be done, and how, and when."

The boys clattered in talking about a wild horse they had seen, and did father know about the gypsies camped in the woods?

"That's the last we'll see of the wild horse then," he said, "The gypsies will soon catch it. It might be theirs, anyway," Freddy said, fetching a plate of scones from the larder. "Here you are, you young hooligans, wrap yourself around those."

"Not all of them, mind," Margaret warned, "One each, please. Take your scone and I'll put these back. We have guests."

"Well, I hope you baked a lot because that plate full is only a snack for Angela," John laughed, and they joined him. The boys went back upstairs to play with their soldiers. They were presently fighting the Wars of the Roses.

John glanced from Margaret to Freddy. "You don't have to say anything. I know Angela is hefty now," he said. "She must have changed a great deal since you last saw her, Freddy."

"Many women put weight on when they have a child," Margaret said defensively, casting a warning glance at her husband, knowing while John may denigrate his wife, he wouldn't want anyone else to do so.

Frederick smiled. "I don't know where she gets it from. Her mother and aunt were slim in build. Albert, our father, was plump for some years, but then he came from good old peasant stock. Still, then they adopted me, so God knows who I take after."

John looked amazed, he had thought Freddy aware of their parentage after giving him the envelope. "I thought you knew all about Angela, Freddy. You had the details in that envelope you gave me."

"Oh, I only know about the legal papers, I didn't read the letters. Were the details in a letter?"

John nodded. "Angela is also an adopted child." He decided it was time to tell the entire truth. "She's not Adele's child, or Albert's. She's the child of Clifford Wright and Eliza's daughter, Jennifer."

Fred and Margaret sat mouths agape, trying to absorb this news. They knew nothing about Jennifer, but both knew Clifford.

"What?" Fred gasped. "Clifford Wright of Hillshead?"

"Yes, that's a surprise, isn't it? It was the reason Eliza came to live here with Adele because in that way she could be close to her grandchild. Albert must have gone along with it as she was his relation by marriage, and with him family came first. I don't see how they could have given the child away. They didn't bother with any legalities, they had no papers stating the adoption, and since it was all in the family, who was to argue? They registered Angela as a Stockton. Strange how things turn out."

Margaret spoke first. "Does Clifford Wright know?"

"I'm sure he does. Angela has a look of him, don't you think?"

Freddy gasped. "Good lord, I never thought about it before, but she does. Yes, she does, take away the fat."

"More importantly, does Angela know?" Jeannie asked.

"She does now. I let her read the letters."

"How did she take it?"

John shrugged. Who knew what went on in Angela's head? "Well, she didn't make a fuss. She was upset, of course, after thinking Adele her mother for all those years."

"We'll be seeing the Wrights tomorrow at church," Margaret said, "I do hope we aren't all going to stare at them, but maybe Angela won't want to go. We must not force her to come with us."

"She'll go all right," John said firmly. "I want to have Josy there. She'll love it."

"Josy's a lovely child. She must take after her grandmother, Jenny," Frederick said, "Those eyes of hers are so startling in their blueness, particularly with the dark eyelashes and brows. Real Irish eyes, as they say."

"Yes, indeed," John said, realizing he had no idea what colour Jenny's eyes had been.

Angela rose early as she had much to do. She must see to her hair style and her gown. She must appear prosperous and stylish when the villagers saw her again.

This small bedroom was cramped, almost to the point of making her claustrophobic. She struggled with her hair, aggravated that she had not brought her curling iron with her, but then how could she heat it? The room had no fireplace.

Finally she fussed with the front, knowing her bonnet would cover the back.

The day was sunny and already warm when they took the carriage to the village. The boys were boisterous as they drove along the lanes and made Josy laugh until she cried. An angry Angela told them off and it was a subdued group that alighted at the church steps. Freddy led the horse and tied it to the railing at the side under the trees and, as they waited for him, Angela primped and preened as the curious villagers stared openly.

They nudged each other. "That's Angela Stockton that was. My word, but she's fat now. Cripes, would you ever have thought that lovely girl would have bloated so much?"

"She thinks a lot of herself, don't she? What's she got that's so much better than us?"

"Look, she's all airs and graces, her born and bred on a farm. Look at her, acts like the bloody queen now, she does."

"Time was when that waist of hern was the size of her arm right now. Not many of her to the pound is there?"

They made all these remarks with smiling faces and looks of welcome. If Angela had known what they were saying she would have stormed away in anger, but, in her vanity, all she perceived were looks of envy.

When the group made their way to the family pew, curious eyes took in every detail of Angela's gown and the feathered, beribboned hat that made her look like a carnival ride. Someone sniggered, and she glared around trying to spot the culprit.

Josy had never been in a church before and crowed with delight at the stained glass windows that made colours on her white and pink flounced dress. When she started to chatter her usual nonsense, Angela shushed her.

"I don't think you need chastise the child, Angela," Jeannie said quietly, "We are a permissive church. Children are welcome. Their laughs and cries make no difference."

Angela turned on her and hissed: "She must learn discipline. No child of mine will make a fuss in public." She stared pointedly at the boys who were openly sniggering and kicking at the plump kneelers.

When the service ended, John immediately stood and looked around the pews and saw the Wrights. As he stared at them, Eddy lifted his head, his eyes blazing bright cornflower blue in his tanned face. So that was it. He might have known, his suspicions were correct, Angela and Eddy. He felt his blood boil and glared down at Angela as she pulled Josy's dress straight, looking forward to showing her off to the congregation.

The Reverend Perkins stood at the church door, shaking hands with the parishioners. People stood around the steps talking, checking out the latest gossip and eyeing each other's attire.

Angela paused at the top of the steps and looked around, letting them ogle her fashionable gown and the special bonnet purchased for the occasion. She smiled down on them, a queen bestowing her largesse, Josy at her side. Taking them in at a glance, she could see she was easily the best dressed and most fashionable person present. Slowly she moved toward the Wrights, whom Freddie had invited to share Sunday dinner.

Valerie, who was hugely pregnant, looked most uncomfortable. Angela noted with malice that her gown was old and let out. Trust Eddy to marry a frump, and after he had loved her so much. It was a triumph and she felt not one bit of shame as she walked straight to him.

"Hello, Eddy, nice to see you," she said warmly, her voice changing to a sneer when she said: "And *this* is your wife?"

John could not believe her gall. That she simply walked up to the Wrights and started talking to Eddy in front of everyone, taking Josy, the obvious result of their affair. Anyone looking at the child would immediately see the resemblance between Eddy and the child. He found it hard to believe that Angela could not see it.

Maybe he was wrong, he thought, as he glanced around, seeing many blue eyed people among the chattering crowd. So maybe Josy was a throw back to one of his own family, or a throw back to Jenny's blood line. If Angela could walk up to the man and start talking so brazenly, then Josy could not be Eddy's child. He must be mistaken.

John stood a short distance away with Freddy talking to Clifford Wright. Glancing from his wife to Clifford, he could see the resemblance, although Clifford was still slim and his bones well defined. Later, at the dining room table, he would look more closely.

It was a jolly meal. Clifford, in good shape, his aches and pains slight today, made small jokes for the children. Josy, between Freddy junior and Angela, sat on the same side of the table as Eddy and to John the resemblance was startling. He could not take his eyes off the pair of them. Surely even Clifford seemed to take a second look.

Still, was the fact they possessed the same eye colour any proof that Eddy was Josy's father? Angela gave no sign of noticing; then again that could be duplicity on her part. Angela was canny in many ways, and John thought her thoughts probably ran along the line of 'if I brazen it out, then perhaps nobody will notice.' As Angela only worked toward her own end, that was probably the case.

Then again, surely somewhere along the line of Blacks there had to be blue eyed people, and on Jenny's side of the family, as they were fair haired, some *must* have blue eyes. Maybe he was making something out of nothing after all, or maybe he didn't want to know, because he loved Josy.

After dinner, the children ran outside to play on the front lawn as the adults drank tea in the parlour. Clifford sipped and looked over the rim of his cup at Angela, wondering why on earth she had allowed herself to become so fat. When younger, she was constantly aware of her image and continually primping and preening. Today her facial features were hidden in bloat. Bulging cheeks and overlapping eyebrows hid her eyes, once so large and sparkling. They looked piggy, yes that was it, plain piggy. He flushed at his thoughts. While a teenager she was greatly proud of her tiny waist, now she was grossly obese yet seemed comfortable with it. In an area where hard work and proper nutrition were the order of the day and people were trim and sleek, she stood out like a melon in a bed of asparagus.

John didn't seem to mind, Clifford thought, thinking he still regarded her with love. She primped and posed constantly, using her soft white hands to punctuate her words, drawing attention to herself. Yes, she was his daughter all right. He could see it in her expression, the way she held her head when she listened. Jenny, her mother, was as beautiful as was Angela when she was younger, and to think that beauty now lay under a ton of blubber.

He talked about crops with Freddy, who was aware the farm expected to experience a loss this year. Clifford agreed, pointing out the fault was Freddy's because he was inexperienced in handling the men. Diplomatically, he pointed out that countrymen did not jump like the town men did when a boss gave them an order because they had been born and bred on the land and knew its whims. They felt for the crops, could forecast within a ton about how much grain a field would yield. They worked loyally for any man who loved the land as they did, a man who could perceive the hardships lying in store for both parties if things were not done right. Freddy listened with a sinking heart. Clifford was right, his men showed him no loyalty and glumly he realized they had worked against him.

The Mayhurst workers thought Fred a townie who had lots of money and were taking him for as much as they could get. Fred added to that impression, talking about his town house and his inheritance as if he had come into a fortune. His wife added to it again because she wore the finest gowns and bonnets to go to the village shops. Her town purchased gowns were far finer than anything the local women could have sewn, though she had paid little for them. Her air of what they thought was condescension, but was shyness, rubbed the local women the wrong way and nobody spoke to her much.

The children also gossiped. The two boys thought themselves too good to mix with the village children, laughed when some youngster's pants were more patches than fabric, or when a sole flapped on a shoe. Neville and Freddy Junior, being born and raised in town and schooled there, thought clothes made the man and people should know their place. In their own minds they *were* better than any of the ragged kids in the village, and their snooty attitude led to all out war on the Stockton boys. Now they were wary of venturing too near the village because of the gang of rough youths out for their blood.

Josy came toddling in with a daisy chain the boys had made her.

"Look, Mamma, daisy chain," she chortled as she passed a badly mangled chain. "Mamma wear it."

Angela took it and smiled. "Mamma will save it for another day, Josy. It does not match Mamma's dress." She set it on the table.

"Oh, put it on, Angela. Please the child for once," John said testily, picking it up and tossing over her head.

"John! It will stain the silk. Please let me be the judge of what I wear."

Josy stood watching this interface and her little face grew dark. Tears threatened.

"Come along, little one, come to your Uncle Eddy," Eddy scooped her into his arms and smiled down at her. "Let's go and make your Aunty Valerie a daisy chain. She is most jealous that she hasn't got one."

He took her outside and they could hear her yelling to the boys to pick her more daisies.

"Honestly, Angela," Freddy said hotly, "The child was trying to please you, and what harm can a daisy chain do to anything?"

"It can mark the silk of my gown, that's what it can do. Look here, a mark." She saw something no one else could and rubbed at it with her small lace trimmed handkerchief. "I do think you should allow me to know what is best for the child. She constantly gets her own way with you, so it's as well she is under my control during the day or you would completely spoil her."

John said nothing further but looked angry.

"So, John, how goes the shop these days?" Clifford asked, breaking the uncomfortable silence.

"Very well, if the receipts are anything to go by," Angela said, preening. "We've enlarged the premises and now carry many more items of a superior quality."

John cleared his throat. "Clifford was addressing me, Angela."

She darted a peevish glance at him and shrugged as if to say he didn't know the answer.

"It's hard to forecast, but we might break even this year," John said evenly, glaring at Angela. What did she know about business? He knew that when she saw the bank deposit she thought it was all profit, never taking into account bills and wages and the stock purchases. "I think the expansion was a good move, though, as we're now getting a better class of clientele and many repeat customers. However, I think it might be about five years before we show any real profit."

Angela laughed loudly as though he had told a joke. "Oh my, I have a stitch in my side. John is *so* humble. Imagine that . . . saying five years. Why, I saw over two hundred pounds a day going into the bank and that means a thousand or more a week in receipts. Any shop that takes in that much must be extremely profitable."

John felt his anger rise. Why was his wife talking this way? He felt embarrassed that she talked money in front of these people. Farmers never saw money like that. Never.

"Angela. . ." his voice held a warning and Valerie sank back against the cushions uncomfortable to be involved in a family dispute. Embarrassed, she put a hand on Clifford's arm.

John suddenly felt determined to show his wife who was boss. She was not going to humiliate him this way in front of people he hardly knew and his rage was such that he stood and faced her.

"Angela, I have asked you not to talk about money in front of people. At least these people are essentially family, but I do wish you'd desist. The money that goes to the bank is not profit, nowhere near it." He slapped one hand on the other counting. "It pays the wages, the suppliers, the gas and water bills, the rates and other items." Angela's lower lip curled and she started to push at her hair. "The money you saw doesn't cover the cost of the renovations, the new signs, or the advertising." She sulked and pouted, tossed her head peevishly. "Kindly keep your mouth closed when in company, unless you have something nice to say, something constructive. People don't want to hear you bragging, especially when you don't know what you're talking about."

Angela pouted, her hand over her heart. She had become red in the face and perspiration broke out on her forehead, however, she said nothing and Clifford realized this was not the first time John had spoken so harshly. Poor Angela, from a lovely innocent child she had grown into an ugly, fat and vituperative wife . . . and to think she was his daughter.

"Look it, look it." Josy came running in holding Eddy's hand and Clifford's heart jumped painfully in his chest. Josy looked the spitting image of Eddy at the same age. Could she be Eddy's child? Those eyes, the unusual cornflower blue that had been Agatha's. Yes, Henry and Hugh, Agatha's brothers, had such eyes, as did his son Eddy.

CHAPTER FORTY-SIX

Clifford took Eddy to one side when they got home. Valerie was in the kitchen talking to the dairy maid as she sliced cold meat for their supper.

"Eddy, I don't know how to put this so you'll not be angry. However, I have to ask. Is Josy your daughter? Did you lie with Angela?"

"What?" Eddy's face went dark red and veins stood out on his temples. "What did you say?"

"You heard me, son. That child is the spitting image of you at her age and since both John and Angela have dark hair and John's eyes are brown, John can't possibly be the child's father." He put his arm around Eddy's shoulders. "Was it you? Come on now, lad, between us two?"

"No. It was not." Eddy pulled away. "How could you think such a thing? Lots of people have blue eyes, lots of folk the around the village and imagine now many there are in town."

"Aye, true enough. Don't take me wrong,"

"Don't take you wrong?" Eddy hissed, trying not to raise his voice. "How could you think such a thing, Dad? How *could* you?"

Clifford looked shamefaced. "Well, as I recall you were up to Mayhurst a lot when she was in residence. For years you were smitten by her and she was always smiling up at you as if some'at was going on."

Eddy faced the fire and put his hands on the mantel, fuming. He had to deny it, though he had a sneaking suspicion his father was right.

"Well, that child is not mine. Why don't you ask Angela? She's the only one who knows."

He slammed out of the room and Clifford heard him stomping up the stairs. When Valerie came in, she looked around for Eddy and did not see him.

"He's gone upstairs, lass," Clifford said, "He'll be back in a second. Now talk to me about our visit. I want to know what you thought of Mrs. Black and her child."

Valerie pulled a face. "She's extremely snooty, isn't she? It's as though she were not from this area at all, the way she speaks, all lahdy-dah like."

She began to set the table for tea.

"Aye, Albert sent both his kids to a posh school, though God only knows why. I mean look at Fred now, he's nowt but a farmer like me, and who needs plums in the mouth to work the land? He soon dropped his snobby attitude when he settled here, but he can't get rid of it all. No wonder the chaps who work for him don't take to him. It's as though he were a nob and they were serfs."

Valerie paused as she laid the cutlery. "Their daughter, Josy, is lovely. I hope if our child is a girl, she'll be as good looking. She doesn't take after either of them, not from what I saw. I must say she favours my Eddy a whole lot." Clifford shot her a glance but her remark seemed innocent. "Isn't that peculiar? I could see it when he picked her up and took her outside. They're as like as two peas from a pod."

Clifford stared at her to see if she were speculating on the resemblance, but she did not appear to notice. "Aye, right peculiar, that is. Still, looks don't mean much in a child that age."

"No, they all look alike, blonde and angelic. She'll probably grow up to be like her mother."

"Hey now, don't wish that on the poor little lass," Clifford said and laughed.

"No. Angela's an awful size, isn't she? Eddy told me she used to be so delicate and slim."

"Aye, time was when my hands could span her waist and she was so fine skinned that it was like porcelain china. Poor Angela." He puffed at his clay pipe, thinking back to when he had first known Jenny was having his love child. By, but she had been a looker back then. Angela had inherited the best of her looks and his, but had gone to seed too quickly.

"The trouble with Angela started after her accident. That changed her a lot," he said, confidentially. "We all thought she'd be crippled for life."

Valerie had not been aware of that. "Oh my, tell me about it."

Clifford did and she listened with interest.

"The poor thing, how terrible for her. Well, everything turned out all right and she's a going concern these days, even if she is on the hefty side."

"Well, what am I going to get from you, do you think, a boy or a girl?" Clifford asked, deftly changing the subject.

"I don't know, dear, could be a girl, 'cause it's quiet at times," She cradled her stomach in both hands, "But then when it starts playing football in there and I think it's a boy. We'll soon know, though, only a couple more weeks."

Eddy came clattering down the stairs, whistling. He had changed into his working clothes.

"Hey! Where are you going?" she asked him, seeing him heading for the back door.

"Going to check on that cow up on the top pasture. She didn't seem too bright when we came past. Want to come along, Dad?"

Clifford shook his head. He'd had his say and since Valerie didn't think it curious that Josy had the look of her husband, he wasn't going to broach the subject again. "Can't be bothered changing, son. You go ahead."

He put his head against the high wooden back of the chair and gazed into the fire. Maybe he should not have told Eddy that Angela was his daughter, though it was surely obvious to anyone who looked closely. As for himself, he thought Angela was beginning to resemble him even more. Thank God she had put on all those pounds, or the likeness might have been startling. Anyway, the way she dressed, all frills, lace and bows, drew people's attention away from her features. It wasn't necessary for him to tell anyone, nevertheless he'd had to tell Eddy to get it off his conscience.

Yet suppose her child was Eddy's? A child begotten by a brother and sister could never be right. At some point in the future health problems might arise or, God forbid, mental problems.

That blasted Romany woman had cursed his family with a vengeance.

Josy sickened when they arrived home. Bright as a new penny one minute, she was vomiting and white the next. Angela sent for the doctor while the nanny bathed Josy in cool water in an attempt to bring down her temperature.

Later Angela turned on John, this was something she couldn't fix on her own. "This is all your fault, John. We shouldn't have stayed at that dirty place. Those boys, they had her playing in a farm yard. All those germs, all those dirty animals."

John listened as she nagged, knowing if she had owned the farm, nothing would have been dirty or germ ridden. His ears turned off her whining as he worried about his daughter. The doctor sent in a full time nurse and Angela was forbidden to enter the nursery. Hysterically she berated the world for fetching this pestilence onto her child, and her shrieking upset Josy.

Yes, the trip had been his idea but suspicion had driven him to find out who Josy resembled. Now he thought his suspicions proven correct. Eddy Wright had sired the child. Last week he had spoken to his old aunt about their family background and she could not recall one blue eyed person.

Angela was a right bitch if it were Eddy. She had lain with a farmer while he was in Wigan working night and day to make a name for himself. He recalled the way she had practically dragged him back to town. Yes, she must have known then of her pregnancy.

He was a dupe and a fool. Angela had hoodwinked him. Well, let her rant and rave, he thought, as she strode around the parlour spouting off against the doctor and the nurse. When Josy recovered, he planned to send them to the seaside for the child's convalescence, and during that time he would think about his life with Angela: whether or not he was going to divorce her.

How could he live with the knowledge of her perfidy? She had committed adultery, so how could she talk to him as if she was a wife that loved him, a steadfast, loyal wife? Since his marriage he had never looked at another woman, not even when Angela was at her worst. He felt nothing for her now, he realized, nothing that resembled love.

Suddenly he could not stand any more of her nagging. "Shut up, Angela, for heaven's sake." He snapped. "The doctor knows what he is doing. He has spent years learning his craft. Shut up about it at once."

"Well! What on earth. . .?"

"What on earth has come over me? Is that what you were going to ask? I'll tell you what has come over me. I'm tired of the sound of your voice, your constant peevish whining, your continual complaining. Sit down and read a book and for once keep your mouth shut."

She stared at him as if he had lost his mind.

"How could you talk to me this way? My daughter is ill and you don't understand."

"I am also worried about Josephine," he continued, ignoring her, "But I know the doctor is competent. If he wants you to stay out of the room, then you will stay out of her room."

"But John . .,"

"But John nothing," he snapped, towering over her. "I've heard enough from you about other people's failings. Look at yourself occasionally. Are you completely blameless in all things?"

"What do you mean?" she whispered, scared of him. It showed in her face and he smiled.

"What I mean is your constant derision of any person who enters this house, myself included. Are you so perfect? Have you ever listened to yourself? You are constantly nagging. I have to pay the servants far more than they are worth as they are always on the verge of walking out of the house. They hate you, Angela, positively hate you."

She looked at him as if he were mad. "Oh, how could you say such a thing. Mrs. Higgins has worked here for over five years. I'd say that shows a great deal of loyalty, and she only deals with me. We get along very well."

"Oh, is that so? It might surprise you to know that Mrs. Higgins has quit at least a dozen times over the years and each time I have persuaded her to stay by giving her a raise in pay. She's the best paid housekeeper in Wigan today and would be a fool to leave."

"What?" Angela jumped to her feet, her eyes blazing with anger. "Yet when I asked you for more money for the housekeeping, you said we had to cut back. You mean to say that woman has been making money while I've been scrimping and scraping?"

"It might seem that way to you, my dear, but it was a matter of survival. How could we have entertained without Mrs. Higgins? How could you have had your ladies' teas and bridge games without her? How could you have run this house on your own? You're not domestic, Angela, let's face it. You're good at giving orders and that's about it."

She stamped her foot and almost growled. "I have heard enough, John. That woman will leave this house today." As she moved to leave the room, he caught at her arm.

"Don't be stupid, Angela. What will we do without her? What about the special meals for Josy? What about the dinner party tomorrow night?"

"I don't care. I will not have a gold digger working under my roof."

"She is not a gold digger." He sighed with exasperation and dug in his fingers. "Maybe I didn't explain this properly. I pay her so much because nobody else will work for you. That's right," he spat each word out separately as if it would make her understand better. "Nobody . . . will . . . work . . . for . . . you. When I took her on, the agency told me point blank she'd be the last person they'd ever send to this house. The many women that left went back to the agency told them what a tyrant and horrible person you are. Servants are people too, they have brains and feelings, no matter what you think."

"I don't care. I want another housekeeper and I will get another housekeeper." Again she stamped her foot as if she were a child.

"If Mrs. Higgins leaves, you will do the housekeeping yourself. I don't want another person. This is my home and I'm completely satisfied with Mrs. Higgins." He released her and crossed his arms across his chest, daring her to move. "I order you to stay out of her kitchen. Do not try to countermand my orders, Angela. Mrs. Higgins stays."

Ultimatums did not sit well with Angela. "This is my house too. If you insist she stays, then I will go."

"If that is the way you want it, my dear. Please be my guest," John said, gesturing to the door, knowing she'd balk at leaving. Where could she go?

Her face white and set, she flounced to the door. "I will pack my things at once. Josy and I will go to Mayhurst."

John's face reddened and his lips thinned in anger. "That child goes nowhere. By rights she should be in a hospital. That's another thing. Dr. Wilkinson knows best but, oh no, she had to stay at home you said, and now you complain because we have a full time nurse in the house. You really take the cake, Angela. Josephine will stay here. If you wish to leave, go right ahead, be my guest. Please do not let me detain you."

Her voice rose into a shriek. "You're a cruel bastard, John Black. You want me to leave, yet you want to keep Josy. As for me, I cannot even rid myself of an incompetent housekeeper, and that nanny, well, she thinks the child belongs to her."

"Anyone else you'd like to deride? How about me, my dear? How do I measure up to your stringent standards?"

She was so angry now that she could not have stopped even if she tried. "Oh you. Mr. Know-It-All! You're only a shop keeper, no matter what you call yourself. We can't get into the right circles because of your low breeding." Her face grew dark and repulsive. "I can talk myself blue in the face to the right people, but once they find out you work in a shop . . .,"

She closed her eyes, looking back. "If we had not missed the century ball at Harvester House we might have had a chance because my gown was the finest they would ever have seen in this town, but oh no, we had to go to pretend-mother Adele's funeral and that put the kibosh on our social life."

John's face revealed his shock. "Why do you call her that? She raised you from a tiny baby, she was your *mother*, more of a mother than Jennifer Bradley. Surely you would not have missed her funeral so we could attend a ball?"

Angela's mind scampered to find a way out of her faux pas. It had been what she felt and had always felt, missing a wonderful ball to attend a stupid woman's funeral. Nevertheless she should not have said it, not to John, not to anyone. Yet this was different. Why should she not spit it out?

"Oh yes, I would," she blurted, "She was never my mother. She didn't act like a mother, more like a friend. Anyway, she'd have wanted me to attend the ball. I'm sure of it."

John regarded her with pity; she was a sad person. He blew out a sharp breath. "Look Angela, I'm tired of your attitude, tired of your nagging, complaining and carping. I have no intention of listening to a litany of my faults as you see them. If you want to go, please go, but Josephine stays. I think I'll ask the doctor to transfer her to his private hospital. She'll receive better care there."

Angela stood with hands on hips. "Oh no, you don't. That is my child, my baby, and you'll not take her out of my house."

"Your house? You surprise me. I had thought this was *my* house, that *you* were my wife and *she* was my child. I pay for the house, I pay the servants, I pay for our food. What do you contribute?"

"I could tell you a few things that could turn your hair white, but I . . .,"

John stood, his hands clenched. She was too much, she drove him to distraction. He felt like putting his hands around her throat and shutting her up for once and for all. "About Josephine's father? Was that it? Don't bother, I already know who sired her." She gasped and backed away, hand at her mouth. "I know it wasn't me, that much is obvious to everyone who sees her. Twice I have been asked if we adopted her."

Her look of shock was wonderful. She stood holding her breath. Had she thought he would never find out, he wondered? Probably, for that was Angela's way.

Her breath came out in a rush. "What, what do you mean?"

"I know Eddy Wright is Josy's father. She is the spitting image of him."

In the hall, Mrs. Higgins stood listening with bated breath to the ding-dong battle. The nanny had come down the stairs and they stood close together, ears to the door.

Angela's voice was shrill. "How dare you! Are you accusing me of adultery?"

John laughed mirthlessly. "Come now, let's not beat about the bush. You and I both know you had an affair with Eddy while you were at Mayhurst."

Angela started pacing, casting blistering glances in his direction. "I do not believe this. I cannot believe my ears. You are accusing me of sleeping with Eddy Wright?"

"Please spare me your outrage. You slept with him, yes, and Josephine is his daughter."

"I don't have to listen to this nonsense." Again she turned away and made to leave. However, he caught her arm and held her back.

"I'm sorry, Angela, but this time you'll stay and you will listen. The similarity between Eddy and Josephine is so marked that anyone can see it. It surprised me that nobody blurted it out, but I can assure you they all noticed."

"This is madness, John. How could you accuse me of such a thing?" Suddenly she paused and looked up at him. Lifting her chin, she announced, "It is impossible as Eddy is my half-brother. We have the same father."

His face set, he felt his heart thump painfully. "What?" he asked, incredulous that she could tell him such a thing so baldy.

"Oh yes, Mr. Know it all knows nothing, does he? Clifford Wright is my father. You didn't know that, did you?" She sounded smug. "How do you think I'd feel toward my own brother? A brother eight years younger than myself. Do you think I would ever sleep with him?"

John stared at her, his brain reeling. What she said shocked him, but he knew incest was not unknown in rural areas. He would like to think that maybe she had not known of their relationship to each other at the time.

He shook his head. "I doubt if that would have stopped you, Angela."

She gasped and threw her arm out in anger, as if to slap his face, and he clutched at her wrist.

"I don't much like you any more. I hate you," she said, her voice high and shrill. "I don't trust you, I don't think I ever did. You will leave this house at once and you will never come back. I am entitled to a roof over my head, both for myself and my daughter."

"Pardon me, Angela, but as I recall it, this is *my* house. If any leaving is to be done, it will be you who leaves. Josephine stays here with me. I will not allow your bad influence to affect the child."

They fought for over an hour. An hour while Mrs. Higgins and the nanny, then the nurse, listened avidly. Vases were smashed, Angela threw knickknacks, overturned small tables. None of them liked the madam, none felt any sympathy for her. To think she had slept with her brother, well, that was going too far. They nudged and winked, shook their heads sadly or gleefully. It was as good as the theatre.

Two days later Angela packed her bags and went to stay at Mayhurst, where, while Freddy and Margaret did not welcome her with open arms, they said she could stay until she found herself a place.

This was not at all what she had expected. She had thought they'd take her in and care for her for if she wished to stay. To add to her annoyance, Margaret asked her to help around the house.

CHAPTER FORTY-SEVEN

John and Josy became relaxed without Angela. The house was a happy place and the servants were cheerful. Josy soon recovered from her illness and was flitting around the house, getting into mischief.

"Lord, would you look at the child," Mrs. Higgins said as she saw Josy sitting under the kitchen table cuddling the cat. "She's been in the coal bin again."

The nanny jumped to her feet. She had been drinking tea and eating toast, thinking her charge occupied with a book.

"Miss Josephine Black, please come out of there immediately," she ordered.

Josy came out clutching the patient cat who dangled by its neck. "Yes, Miss Tweed?"

"What on earth have you been doing, child? Put down the cat, please. You need washing and changing." She had to laugh for Josy was black as a miner, coal dust from head to toe. "What on earth were you doing in the coal bin?"

"Blacky was in there hiding from me and I couldn't find him."

"Oh lovey," she had to smile, "The cat goes into the coal bin to get away from you. You never leave the poor thing alone."

"He's my friend, he likes me," she said, smiling up at them. Josy was a happy child now her mother was gone, she laughed at the silliest things and made them all laugh. "Anyway, I had to get him out in case he got dirty."

Angela had the stable man hitch the trap and took a drive over to Hillshead. She did not, however, find a welcome there either.

Valerie was hanging out nappies when she arrived.

"Hello, Valerie. Where is everybody?" she asked looking around. The men were out in the fields and only Valerie and the baby were at the house. Joyce, now married to a farm hand and living in a tied cottage, was in the dairy sorting eggs.

"Working," she said shortly, taking in Angela's fussy ribbon trimmed gown and feathered hat, "To what do we owe the honour of this visit?"

"I thought I'd pay a call. I don't often get to Mayhurst these days. How is Eddy?"

"Fine."

"And your father-in-law?"

"Fine."

"How is the crop this year?"

"Fine."

"Can you say anything but 'fine', do you think?" Angela snapped. "You're not being particularly hospitable."

Valerie looked at her before she turned back to the washing line. "I wasn't expecting company and I have a lot of work. This is not a Sunday day of rest, you know, this is a working day. You can help me iron some of these nappies if you like."

Angela almost stamped her foot. "What way is this to treat a relative?"

"A relative?" Valerie turned and looked at her. What was she up to now?

Angela narrowed her eyes and stared slyly, wanting to catch Valerie's expression when she heard. "Yes, your father-in-law is my father. Oh, didn't you know that?" She grinned widely at the look of shock on Valerie's face. "Well, I don't suppose he's made too much of it. I was born out of wedlock, you know."

Jeannie looked at her suspiciously. Apart from the shocking revelation about her and Clifford, Angela was being sweet, too sweet. Something was afoot since she only did things for her own benefit, or so Eddy had told her. What was she after, she wondered?

She picked up the clothes basket and made her way to the kitchen with Angela following.

"Shall we have a cup of tea?" Angela said sitting at the table.

"I don't have time," Valerie snapped. "If you want tea, make it yourself."

Indignant, Angela took the kettle to the pump and filled it. She put it over the fire and then poked at the coals to make a blaze. In her mind she contemplated what she would say to her father and half-brother.

It was almost four before Clifford came into the kitchen. He stood at the door, took off his boots and slipped his feet into a pair of old backless shoes.

When he saw Angela his eyebrows rose. "Well, this is a surprise," he said, "Mrs. Angela Black sitting in my kitchen drinking tea. To what do we owe this honour?"

He did not sound welcoming either, Angela thought. What was it about these country people? Their voices were all so sarcastic somehow.

"I thought I'd come home . . . Father," she said quietly.

Clifford stopped dead in his tracks and his face became stony and white. "What did you say?" he hissed.

Uh-oh! He was not pleased, she could see that. Still, in for a penny, in for a pound.

"I have left John Black, so I need a place to live," Her expression was of happiness, and she raised her chin. "Why not here? You have lots of room and surely you could not turn away your own child."

"What? My own child? You are no more my child than Valerie here," he said sharply.

She smiled knowingly, and glanced at Valerie who stood against the sink. "You have to admit, though, that you are my father," she said waspishly.

"Aye, if we're going to speak the truth, I sired you, but that doesn't mean you're any daughter of mine. I never saw you until you were at least eight and then didn't know you were mine." He moved closer and looked down into her fat face. "Listen to me now. I don't want you as a daughter as you are the nastiest piece of work I've seen in a long time. You have no home under this roof, Mrs. Black. Go to your brother."

"Freddy does not want me to stay with them." Her voice rose to a whine. "What am I going to do?"

"I don't know, and I don't much care." Cliff glanced at Valerie. "How dare you come waltzing in here claiming I'm your father? It might be biologically correct, but it's morally wrong. If I were you, I'd be ashamed to be a bastard, and as for myself I've lived with the shame of siring you since I found out. I've never been a father to you, nor do I wish to be one. You're not staying here. Go back to your husband and act like a proper wife for a change."

Valerie cuddled the baby as she listened to this exchange. Who would have thought, eh? Clifford, Angela's father. She could not see much of him in her, at least as far as personality, for he was a kind man, a caring man, whereas Angela was all grab and take.

"I can see you don't want me here," Angela said as she grabbed her reticule and stood. "How could you do this to me? How could you turn me away in my hour of need?"

She was dramatic, theatrical, Valerie thought, smiling, then unable to resist, said, "Thank you for asking after the baby, Angela. He'll be thrilled to know he has such a caring aunt."

Angela looked at her with narrowed eyes. Who cared about the baby? Who needed another puling child? Valerie did not like her; she was making it obvious, had done so since she arrived. All that fuss about giving no warning. Relatives didn't need invitations, nor did close friends in polite society.

She smiled, though it was forced and did not extend to her eyes. "What's his name?"

"Nathaniel."

"How very biblical," Angela said, pulling down the corners of her mouth.

"That's a book you'd do well to read, my girl," Clifford said acidly. "It's about time you acted like a decent human being."

She turned on him. "The Bible probably also says you should not turn away a person in need, but you don't care, do you? You'd see me out on the street or in the workhouse before you would help me."

"Aye, that's right and I'll confess it to God when I go to church. Now are you going? I want my tea in peace." He turned to Valerie. "That gypsy was right and she did put a curse on this house. It proves it when this bad tempered, unmannerly shrew shows up demanding house room."

Angela drove back to Mayhurst, seething with indignation. Her birth father didn't want her as his daughter, but she *was* his daughter and as such was entitled to certain things. When he died, she should get something from the estate . . . and while he lived, he should house and feed her.

She drove the trap to the stables and left it standing while she went into the house. It did not occur to her to unhitch the horse.

"You were gone a long time," Margaret said as she looked up from her darning. "Jane needed help in the dairy and I had to do it. Sorry, no dinner today, I didn't have time, but I expect you had your dinner while you were out."

"No, I didn't. I would like something now."

Margaret looked at her sharply. "You know where the kitchen is, make it yourself. I've got to get this lot darned and then it's time to start supper."

"Well!" Angela spat as she turned on her heel. Having to make her own meals, that was asking too much of anyone.

As she clumsily sliced bread and cheese, she thought about Clifford Wright. He would not get away with it. She must not allow him to treat her this way. Clifford was her father and soon everyone would know about it, absolutely everyone, for what had she to lose now? At church this Sunday she must let it slip, although she supposed lots of people already knew: not much got past the villagers.

Yet what was all that about a curse? Strange, this was the first she had heard of it, but she could bet the older locals knew the details.

Margaret took her time over the darning, refusing to fetch and carry for Angela, no matter what. Already she and Freddy had argued over her unwelcome intrusion. Thank God the boys were away at boarding school, although she was sad about that. Their rambunctious presence would have shifted Angela faster than anything else.

CHAPTER FORTY-EIGHT

It never occurred to Angela that she acted irrationally. To her, it seemed common sense to attain vengeance against Clifford Wright. The man had money, lots of it and a huge house, yet had turned her away. He was going to pay for that action, and hour after bitter hour she sat plotting his downfall.

The loquacious village postmistress told her about the gypsy, how her curse caused the death of old Eddy, then caused the end of Liz from a disease that ate her away from inside. The curse was also responsible for the death of Albert and Adele Stockton for they had accepted money from Clifford. The gossips foretold all manner of horrible things for the Wrights and the Stocktons, so much so that Angela felt a cold shiver.

To the postmistress she professed to consider the story the ravings of an overactive imagination and said there many plausible explanations. Still, she became nervous thinking about the many deaths, even while managing to convince herself that it was foolish to give the stories credibility. Clifford Wright's blood ran in her veins and nothing bad ever happened to her. Her estrangement from John was John's fault. The accident that had almost killed her was Freddie's fault and she had survived anyway.

She turned her thoughts then to her husband. He would soon learn he could not treat her in such a cavalier manner. In his case, she needed to take precautions because she must consider Josy. Already she had formulated a plan to cause John's buildings to burn to the ground.

As for Clifford, she mused, what would hurt him more than anything? What would cause him the most heartache?

The hammering at his front door awakened John Black. Mrs. Higgins, recently widowed and now living in, was suddenly running up the stairs calling, "Master! Master!"

In two hours it was all over. The fire reduced his shop and four adjacent buildings to rubble. Three families who lived over the shops were homeless and a falling beam had killed one volunteer fireman.

The disaster was totally unexpected as the shops and flats were well maintained. The town engineer had lately inspected and found John's building to be within all bylaws and regulations. Since the fire seemed suspicious in origin, the authorities instigated an investigation. John did not mind. He could always rebuild as his insurance coverage was more than adequate. It was the homeless that bothered him because they had no insurance, nor did two of the destroyed shops owners. He offered temporary lodging to one family of four at his house.

The local paper carried drawings and blurred photographs of the blaze and these were picked up by the national dailies. When Angela read the report in the Manchester Guardian, she laughed delightedly. She had done it, she had put John Black right out of business. Already she had begun a suit against him claiming support, and was in the process of demanding access to her child. It was wonderful how destructive she could be when she put her mind to it. Nobody could say she was stupid, could they?

Clifford sat in the parlour as Nathaniel played at his feet. With the onset of a damp autumn, his arthritis worsened and sometimes he found it painful to move. Valerie did her housework as he watched the child.

Nathaniel, or Nat as they called him, was a happy baby. He rarely cried and if he did it was for good reason. Already with a full head of dark curly hair, he was the spitting image of Valerie, although he had his father's eyes of the brightest cornflower blue.

"Is he being a good boy?" Valerie said as she brought Clifford a mug of tea.

"Aye, he is an' all," Clifford said, "Thanks, lass. Not a peep out of him apart from a few chuckles. He likes my boot laces, loves them in fact, loves them enough to chew on them."

"Oh Dad, don't let him do that. Them laces have been through muck and mire more times than I care to think about."

Clifford smiled. "He's going to come to no harm. Look at him, he's a healthy little lad, and we all have to eat a pound of muck afore we die."

Jeannie laughed, "Yes, but not before we're a year old." She picked Nat up and cuddled him. He grabbed at her hair and pulled hard. "Ouch, don't do that, son. Here, Dad, have him on your knee for a while. He'll play for hours with your watch chain."

Clifford took the baby and sat him in the crook of his arm. Nat looked up at him and chortled. He loved his granddad.

Jeannie straightened the couch cushions and plumped them. "Could I leave him here with you a while longer? I'd like to see to the bedrooms and I can't watch him then."

"Go ahead, lass, take your time. Me and Mr. Nosy here will be all right. That's until he pees on me, of course."

"Of course. Never mind, he's not been changed long so I guess he'll hold it until I've finished."

She left and went upstairs. Strange that, about Dad. He liked to play with the child until Nat wet himself, then wanted nothing to do with him.

Clifford sat and dozed as Nat sucked on his watch chain. Soon Nat also nodded off to sleep in the quiet parlour.

Angela peered in the front window and saw them. So Clifford liked his grandson, did he? He obviously liked that brat more than he liked her. Well now . . .

As she opened the door, Valerie was going up the stairs and, thinking it was Eddy, turned with a smile that vanished the moment she saw Angela.

"What do you want?" she snapped as she came back down.

"How gracious a hostess you are, Valerie," Angela said as she removed her gloves.

"Well?"

"I came to see my father," Angela said sticking her nose in the air.

"Does he know you're coming? He told you to get out the last time you came calling."

"No need to be nasty, Valerie, but I suppose we must put that down to your lack of education. The village school isn't renowned for turning out scholars."

Valerie glared. She stood in the centre of the passage, arms akimbo, so Angela rudely pushed past her and went into the parlour.

Eddy and Valerie heard the rumour that Freddy had forced Angela to leave and thought she might have found herself lodgings in town, but here she was large as life and twice as ugly.

She stood in the parlour and looked at Clifford and the child as they slept in the armchair. If only she had a gun, she could have shot the pair of them. Yet no, they'd hang her for murder, and if it was to be murder, then she must plan it so as not to implicate herself.

Clifford snored himself awake and opened his eyes to find Angela looking down at him. At first he thought he was dreaming and knuckled his eyes, but she was still there.

"What are you doing here?" he asked in a sleep thickened voice.

"I came to see you, Father," Her voice was sweet, so very sweet.

Valerie came in, took the sleeping Nathaniel from Clifford and left the room. Soon, she knew, the voices would rise in anger.

"Came to see me?" He coughed up phlegm and spat into the fireplace, as she recoiled with distaste. "You must think I'm thick to think you had any fellow feeling for me."

"I heard you were ailing and came see how you were."

"Aye, and I suppose you read it in the Guardian, did you? You never knew whether I was well or sick for the past twenty-four years, yet you come in here now saying you wanted to see how I was? There's something missing in you, girl, something wrong with your head. Get out of my house, and don't come back."

Angela threw herself to her knees. "Please, you've got to help me. I need money. John has not paid me any support and I have no money of my own. I need to pay for lodgings, for the necessities of life. You've got to help me. You're my last resort."

Clifford regarded her with distaste. "Aye, well, that's too bad. You can always go to the workhouse. Might set you right, that might. At least you'd lose some weight. Go on, get out of my house."

"How could you do this to me?" She broke into ugly racking sobs. "How could you? Please let me have some money, or give me a roof over my head. You're my father. Please, please."

Clifford looked at her. All he felt was sorrow that he had sired such a child. Look at her, all fat, frills and feathers, pleading for support. Who'd want her? He didn't blame John Black one little bit and thank God, John had kept the child. A lovely little lass, Josy.

"Please, Father, please help me."

Clifford looked at her. With her face wet with tears, her eyes swollen and red, she looked ugly. He sighed. What should he do? It was not in his nature to refuse anyone who needed help, but if he as much as gave her an inch she'd take a mile.

Her voice keened, full of anguish. "Please help me, nobody wants me and I have nowhere to go. Please, please help me."

Against his better judgement and knowing the angry words he'd hear from Eddy and Valerie, and even Joyce, he said, "You can stay for a week. That's all, one week, seven days. Do you understand?"

Her face lit with a wide smile. "Yes, oh yes, Father. I'll find something soon, I know I will. I'll help around the house, too. You'll see."

"Aye, that's as maybe." He said sceptically. "You'd better go and tell Valerie, but don't blame her if her nose is out of joint. She doesn't need this, doesn't need the upheaval and the bother of having you here."

Angela wiped her face on her handkerchief and stuffed it up her sleeve. "I know, I do know. I'll not be any trouble, I promise you that, and I thank you for this, Father."

"Do me a favour, Angela, don't call me Father. I'm not your father, nor do I *want* to be your father. Call me Mr. Wright or Clifford."

"All right, Fa . . . Clifford." She smiled through her tears and wiped her eyes with the back of her hands. "I'll go and tell Valerie."

Clifford slumped back in the chair as she left. What *had* he done? Still, he could not turn away a lost dog, never mind a human being. Served her right, it did, the way things had turned out for her. She had masterminded her own dismal future, and dismal it was, for who'd want her now?

Valerie felt so furious that she couldn't speak. She said not a word to Clifford for days and made Eddy's life a misery when they were alone. Angela she ignored completely, not even setting her a place at the table. Eddy, miserable and completely flummoxed, said little to anyone, apart from saying good morning or goodnight, and never spoke to or looked at Angela. Then Joyce laid into Clifford, but he was intractable.

All in all, Angela felt like a leper. The men ignored her, Joyce and Valerie would not speak to her and Valerie refused to let her hold the baby and this was the unkindest cut of all. She missed Josy so much and often cried when she thought of her. Nobody understood her, she moped, cursing them, nobody knew how much she needed love.

In her search for revenge, everything that happened in and around the house came under her scrutiny. She missed nothing and her active mind stored away many insignificant details for, who knew, they might come in handy.

Each day Valerie made breakfast at five thirty, cleaned the kitchen, worked in the dairy for three hours, then made the noon meal. Clifford, his joints painful, looked after the baby. Afternoons were spent in household chores, baking, darning or mending, washing or ironing.

Never was the house was empty, so Angela never saw a time when she could rig up an accident.

On market day she rode in the cart to Weatherly. Once she would have been too proud to have people see her in such a conveyance, but now she sat in the back with Valerie and the child as Eddy drove, his father beside him. Today she'd buy her needs and this time next week she could return to Wigan. She felt furious that Clifford Wright had denied her, his true daughter, a home and an inheritance. He had denied his paternity, the bastard, even as she stood in front of him, denied her birthright.

"A woman was involved, you say?"

"That's right, sir, we have a witness who saw a woman coming out of the back alley. Out of your yard gate."

"Have you apprehended her?" John asked.

"No, sir. We have many thousands of women in Wigan and it could have been any one of them. We're continuing our investigations and when we have anything definite, we'll let you know."

Detective Pearson tucked his notebook back in his packet and put on his hat. "How soon do you think the new store will open, sir? People miss your emporium, and everyone is asking."

"Less than a month now." John smiled, glad at the publicity the fire and erection of his new building had generated. "We should open at the beginning of October. We'll have lots of opening specials. Why don't you buy yourself a new bowler, lieutenant? We'll have them at half price for one day."

"Might well do that, sir. I'll look forward to the event and if I can't make it in because of duty maybe you could hold one for me? Size seven and five eighths."

"I most certainly will, officer."

John mused on this latest snippet of information. A woman coming out of his back gate, eh? Only one person he knew had it in for him, and that was Angela. He felt sure that bitch would laugh as she burned down his shop.

He decided to withhold the information until he felt it might aid their search. If they dropped the line of investigation, he must see to it that they opened it again with her as the chief suspect. To him, she was surely the cause.

CHAPTER FORTY-NINE

"Valerie, where's Dad?" Eddy asked as he came into the kitchen from the yard.

"I thought he was with you," She looked up from the dough she was kneading. "Since he felt good and it was a nice day, he said he was going to the top field to help supervise the harvest."

"Well, he's not there and I haven't seen him at all day."

Valerie put the dough to rise, went to the window and looked out, wiping her hands on her apron. "It's not like him to be late home for his dinner, is it? I wonder where he's got to? Look, you sit down and have your dinner and I'll have a look around the buildings." Stooping to the rug, she picked up Nathaniel and took him with her, straddling her hip.

Angela sat at the table end, looking into space. She ate her dinner slowly, chewing each mouthful a full thirty times.

"You don't have much to say for yourself these days, Mrs. Black," Eddy blurted out, uncomfortable with the silence and her staring bulging eyes.

Angela swallowed her last mouthful and wiped her lips on her handkerchief. "I have nothing to say."

"How long are you staying? I thought Dad told you only a week." Time and again he had wanted to ask her about Josy, yet was reluctant to ask because of Valerie.

She sighed deeply. "Yes, I shall be leaving soon."

Eddy felt uncomfortable with her. To think at once he had been desperate for her body. Ah, but then she had been slim and graceful, full of joy, and her face was that of an angel. Now she was another person altogether, a fat, ugly, miserable woman.

Valerie came in shaking her head. "No sign of him anywhere. I'm worried, Eddy."

Angela sat still and smiled behind her hand. The old man was finished, at least she hoped so.

Eddy wiped his mouth on the back of his hand and, going to the door, put on his boots. "I'll take the horse and see if I can find him. I mean, how far could he have walked with his rheumatics?"

Angela sat at the table for another hour or so, completely idle, waiting for them to fetch the bad news. Valerie and Joyce were so upset that Valerie left Nat in Angela's care while she joined in the search.

"Nice baby, such a nice baby," Angela crooned as she held Nathaniel. He did not like her and struggled to be free. "No, no, baby stay with Aunty Angie," she said as she held him tighter. "Aunty Angie loves the little baby."

"What are you doing?" Eddy's voice made her jump and she quickly put the baby on the chair.

"I was holding him, that's all," she said defensively.

Eddy picked up his son. "You were holding him far too tightly. Nat never grizzles like that. What were you doing?"

"I told you," she snapped. "He was crying and I picked him up to comfort him."

Eddy looked at her. She was lying. He knew her and her ways. Why would she want to hurt his child? Angela was an evil person these days, and nasty with it as well.

"So?" she asked sharply. "Did you find your father?"

"No, I came back to make sure he wasn't in the house. Did you look in every room?"

"I sat here as you instructed," she said sharply. "I have looked nowhere. I must say it seems like a whole lot of fuss when he's probably gone for a stroll."

"My Dad never goes for a 'stroll' as you put it. If he isn't here, he'd let us know where he was going. This isn't like him."

"I think it's nonsense, all this running around shouting for him." She craned her neck to see out of the window. "He's a grown man, not a little boy."

"This house is cursed," Eddy said grimly. "Still, I'm sure you've heard the stories. My grandfather walked out of the house and disappeared into thin air, and I don't want that to happen to my Dad."

"Gypsy curses?" Angela put back her head and laughed. "Time you read a few books, Eddy, got an education. Gypsy curses do not exist. It's all in your mind. Bad cess comes from addled brains. You've been listening to those old soaks down in the village."

Eddy made a sound like a snort and walked out of the house carrying Nat. No way could he leave his son with her, because she was off her head these days. Maybe it was because John Black had thrown her out, or it could be that she missed her child. Whatever, she acted peculiar; the way she stared, her eyes like marbles, her manner of talking.

She was sly, that's what it was, crafty. Something told him to be on his guard, for she was up to no good. That his father had allowed her to stay at the farm was strange in itself and, too, Dad would brook no argument. Yet his Dad refused to converse with her and while they occasionally exchanged remarks about mundane matters, no friendship lay between them.

To where could his father have wandered? Not far surely: his arthritic knees would prevent a journey of any length.. Yet why would he have gone out without telling Valerie where he was headed, and *when* had he gone? For hours they searched unsuccessfully as Angela sat in the parlour reading and, smirking. Valerie came back to help Joyce in the dairy and Nat played at their feet.

Angela sighed. It was boring, dead boring, not knowing whether they had found him.

"So you see sir, we think this woman might have had something to do with the blaze," Inspector Murray said, "It was suspicious enough that we informed the insurance company detectives. I thought I should warn you, as I'm sure you'll be hearing from them."

John's heart sank into his boots. He had thought it all over with and looked forward to his new emporium. The new building was much brighter and larger, the windows were huge and held lavish displays of merchandise that promised to attract even more customers. He had thought the fire a blessing in disguise.

"Er, from the description we received, sir, it is conceivable the woman seen might be Mrs. Black," Inspector Murray was uncomfortable even saying it. "I have to ask you some further questions in that regard, sir."

John felt a cold hand clutch his heart. He had rebuilt his shop using the insurance money and they could now snatch it away from him because of Angela. If they could prove she had set the fire, they might think it collusion. Things like that had happened before. Oh God, let it not be she, he prayed, knowing it was exactly what she would have done to get her revenge.

Still, surely she would realize that if he had no income, then he could not support her. Angela wanted money, as much as she could get. She possibly still had the money Freddy paid her, but he did not know how much that was, although it was enough to purchase a small house. On the other hand, if she ruined him, she might possibly get her child back. He didn't doubt that she loved Josy.

Miserable, he accompanied the detective to the station and sat in a cold white tiled room as two detectives questioned him about Angela and their nuptial relationship.

How degrading to air their dirty linen to strangers. No, he had no idea where she had gone. Yes, she left of her own free will. It had been a simple family argument. No, he did not have a mistress. From being the injured party, it sounded to his ears as if he were the prime suspect, but he dared not ask. He wanted to yell that, yes, she was a bitch who would stoop to anything for her own purposes, and yet he did not want people to call him a fool, for a fool he surely was. He trod the middle ground and thought he succeeded in making her sound nothing more than a typically neurotic, dissatisfied wife.

The insurance company investigator read the reports and made a report to his superiors. Until they apprehended the woman, they would watch Mr. John Black closely. Until they found actual proof that pinned arson on a person, his claim was suspect.

Angela booked a first class carriage on the train to Southport. She decided to rent herself a small bungalow on the coast. A place she could call home until her plans were complete. In her purse were the twenty gold sovereigns she had stolen from the farmhouse, Clifford's money. Her penchant for snooping had paid off in a big way. Too bad she couldn't take the lot but they were too heavy to conceal. Eddy and Valerie would discover the loss sooner or later, but it would be too late.

Her main aim in life was to get back her child. Josy was her baby, hers alone. How was she doing, she wondered, and who was looking after her? John was out at business all day and someone had to see to her. John surely had kept on the nanny. Thinking of another woman looking after her child, infuriated her.

Her income was small, but she believed John would send her a quarterly allowance as he promised. Fool that he was, he was still a gentleman. This allowance, the sovereigns and her interest income should allow them to live well; not as well as she would have liked, but she could afford a cook and a maid. She could look after Josephine herself.

The first thing she must do was ingratiate herself enough with John to see Josy. Access that once granted, he could not remove.

Angela thought of herself as coming into her adulthood, beginning to realize her full potential. Suddenly her mind became crystal clear and she felt conscious of every tiny nuance of her thoughts. She knew now that John Black had taken advantage of her when she was merely a child, as had Eddy Wright. In fact, all men were her enemies.

Clifford Wright, her real father, had turned her away. The bank manager who looked after her investments was continually taking money from the account for things he had not done. She stewed on that. Oh yes, a mere woman, he probably thought, what could she know of business or life as it should be lived? We'll let her have it, take her child, take her money, deprive her of love, that's what we'll do, and nobody can fault us for this is the way of the world. Yes, that's the way men thought, and now she knew it.

Completely paranoiac, the more she dwelt on these matters, the larger their importance grew in her mind, and she looked askance at any male who crossed her path.

She withdrew her gaze from the passing scenery to look at the man who sat reading a newspaper in the far corner. After she stared at him for some time, he felt her eyes and glanced at her. He blinked and went back to his paper wondering what her problem could be. Did she feel ill, he wondered?

Angela huddled into the corner. Surely that man in the corner seat was eyeing her too strangely. Was he going to attack her? They were alone in the carriage. What would she do if he approached? She sat, a quivering mass of nerves, unable to take her eyes off him for a second.

Jack Atherton, uncomfortable under the woman's scrutiny, did not like what he saw. She stared, stared with eyes that looked as though they might pop right out of her face. Hugely fat, she dressed in so many frills and flounces that she resembled an unmade bed. As she stared, she clutched at her purse, arms trembling, her knuckles white.

After ten minutes or so, he felt discomfited. Her strained expression irritated him and he felt perplexed because if he as much as cleared his throat, she gave an almighty jump as if terrified. Nervous, yes, that much was evident, but her manner seemed so peculiar that he decided to get out at the next stop and move into another carriage.

As he moved restlessly in his seat, she twitched. Oh lord, what was he going to do? Quickly she clutched her purse to her chest, thinking he planned to rob her.

"Is anything wrong, madam?" he asked, his voice soft.

It was an educated voice, she noted, an upper class voice. Why would such a man be riding a train, she wondered? Surely he had his own carriage. Was he a rapist, a killer, or a man who enjoyed hurting women? Oh, they all enjoyed that, did men, liked inflicting physical and mental abuse on the female sex.

When she did not reply, he asked again. "Excuse me, madam, but is there a problem?"

She shook her head, shook it so hard that her hat slipped to one side.

"Could I be of any assistance?" he asked, rising to his feet.

Angela's eyes raced around the carriage. She felt like a small animal in a lion's cage. She saw no escape. A small shriek issued from her lips as he moved toward her.

"My dear lady, please may I be of assistance? You appear to be most upset," he said approaching, one hand outstretched.

Angela jumped to her feet, her head whipping from side to side, seeking escape. How could she get away from the monster? What was she going to do? She looked at the door, her only way of escape. Yes, she'd open the door and jump onto the line as they passed through open farmland. Yes, that was it.

Jack Atherton attempted to grab her as she flung herself onto the line, but her cloak came away in his hand and he had to grasp the door frame to save himself. What on earth? Quickly he pulled the emergency cord and the train's brakes slammed on, squealing and groaning as they shuddered to a stop.

The verdict was: "Death from suicide while the balance of her mind was disturbed," and John felt such relief. The insurance investigation had not found the mystery woman who might have set the fire and the constant questioning ceased. His stores were doing well, better than expected. Josephine bloomed under the care and tutelage of a governess and a nanny. She was now an intelligent five.

As he watched her practising the piano and murmured words of encouragement, he thought back over the last few years, the years since he married Angela. Was it his fault that Angela had become paranoid and unstable? He did not think so. Whatever had caused her to destroy herself was a mental deficiency. That being so, and he must watch Josy closely in case she showed any of her mother's tendencies.

If Josy was the daughter of Eddy, as he suspected though never proved, and since both Clifford Wright and Angela had committed suicide, then it was evident the slightest deviation from normal activity needed analysing, for hadn't Clifford Wright's father had also wandered away, never to be found?

Josy was delightful, vivacious, full of animation, filled with joy at the slightest thing. Yes, if anything ever happened to Josy, he didn't know what he would do.

CHAPTER FIFTY

Freddy sat atop his horse watching the men harvest the last of the corn. It had been a good year, and this bountiful harvest came because of books he had read and the advice of Eddy Wright.

Too bad about Eddy's Dad, he mused, poor old chap, practically crippled with arthritis. No wonder he had thrown himself down a mine shaft.

What nobody knew, or ever would know, was that Angela had drugged Clifford. The resulting euphoria had led him to walk further than he normally did. The cessation of pain made him feel like a young man and he walked to the top of the nearest hill where he could overlook his land. It was only when he reached the top and stopped for breath that he began to feel dizzy, and stumbling across the hummocky grass, had tumbled down an old shafts, one of the many that were unmarked as nobody walked up here now it was private land.

The body was found two years later, two long years of distress for the family who did not know what had befallen their patriarch. They buried the body with full honours in the village grave yard and life resumed its normal course.

Eddy ran Hillshead, which became the pride of the county. Valerie gave birth to twins and now their family had two boys and a girl.

Eddy and Clifford's sage advice to Fred proved itself correct and now Fred was almost out of debt. Surely the curse had passed and was no longer effective, though the locals still muttered in the pub, still foreseeing more grief to both families whose lives it intertwined. Yet others felt convinced the curse had left the land because of the abundant crops.

As he sat his grey, he saw a carriage crest the hill and head toward Mayhurst. Curious, he galloped across the stubbly field, made his way to the house and went in through the kitchen.

They stood in the parlour as a plump, tall man got down from the carriage. Taking off his hat, he mopped his brow and regarded the front of the house.

Margaret and Fred peered through the window from behind the lace curtains. Neither knew the man and could not imagine what he wanted.

"The way he's looking at the place you'd think he wanted to buy it," she hissed.

"We own it and it's not on the market. I wonder who he is?" Fred said, scratching his head.

"We'll soon find out. He's coming to the door," Margaret said, pulling at her blouse to set it straight.

"Good morning. Is this the Stockton residence?" The man asked, and then laughed. "Well, of course it is, I should know as I was born in this house."

Margaret gaped. What did he mean?

Fred moved to open the door wider. "Won't you come in, sir? I'm Frederick Stockton and this is my wife, Margaret."

The man moved into the parlour. "You've opened this up, haven't you? I like it better this way. It were cramped. Aye, and the new windows make a pile of difference, let more light in here."

Margaret sat on the couch staring at the stranger. Freddy stood by the fireplace, his arm on the mantel.

"Excuse me, sir, but who are you?" Freddy asked. He looked the man over closely, noticed his custom tailored suit, hand-made shoes. Whoever he was, he was rich, the carriage was the finest, and the horses of good blood lines.

"Albert Stockton's the name, Albert Stockton, junior. You must be the lad my Dad adopted after I left."

Fred felt like someone had hit him on the head with a sack of coal. His knees became like rubber, and he sank onto a chair before he fell down. Margaret gasped and put her hand on Freddy's arm.

"Well now," Albert said beaming jovially, "I've made a pile of brass, own two mills and a foundry and decided I want my old home back. It should have come to me, anyroad, because I'm the eldest son of the marriage, and my parents adopted you."

"What?" Fred and Jeannie gasped in unison.

"You can't come here and demand that we give up our home and our livelihood." Freddy said, his voice shrill. "Father's will was most specific. This place was left to me. You were left money, as was your brother."

"Aye, well. I've decided I need land in the country now. Oh, I know I could buy a place but you can't blame me for wanting my old home. I was happy here as a lad. I can remember . .,"

"No, you can't have it," Margaret shrieked. "What are we supposed to do? Leave and let you take everything? The law is on our side, isn't it Freddy?"

Freddy felt stunned and his mind raced for a way to get the man out of the house. "Yes, it is, and don't doubt for one moment that I will not start action against this claim when you leave." His voice shook.

Albert laughed. "Oh dear, I hate to tell you lad, I can get the best solicitors and barristers money can purchase. I've got more money than you can imagine, Frederick. More money than you'll ever see in a lifetime."

Fred stood. "Please leave my house, Albert. Your money cannot buy this place and I have no intention of selling. Return to your home and consider buying a gentleman's estate. Leave us alone."

Margaret cried softly. All she could see was the loss of her home, a home that she had come to love though she had hated it at first. Her parents could lend them enough money to fight for their rights, she was sure, although Albert must be wealthy.

Albert stood and brushed down his jacket. Maybe these two pitiful creatures were right. He didn't need this dump, the few hundred acres that produced only enough to support the family. "These your sons?" he asked pointing to a framed picture of Neville and Frederick.

"Yes," Fred said.

"Away at school, I suppose? I'd have liked to have met them. They're relations of a sort."

Fred lost his temper. "I'm sure my sons would not like to meet you, the man who wants to steal their inheritance, to turn them out of the only home they have ever known. How dare you come here and make these outrageous demands?"

Albert stuck his thumbs into his waistcoat pockets and smiled on them. "Now, now, lad, don't get all twisted out of shape. I'm sorry. I can see what it means to you and your wife. I'd thought you'd have a manager in here and live in town. It never occurred to me that you'd actually be farming. Let's forget I said anything."

Margaret heaved a sigh and her face broke into a smile. "Thank you, Mr. Stockton," she said.

"Nay, now lass, Albert, we're kin."

"All right, Albert." Margaret, happy the crisis was over, said, "Won't you stay for a cup of tea? You must have come a long way."

Fred glared at her but she raised her eyebrows and quelled him.

"Aye, maybe I will," Albert's entire attitude had changed. He was all *bon hommie* now. "You can tell me about the nippers."

CHAPTER FIFTY-ONE

1910

Seven year old Josy Bradley sang a solo in the school concert. Tiny, her red-gold hair hanging to her waist, wearing a long gown of pink muslin, she looked and sang like an angel.

John, thrilled at the way people looked over to him as she took her bow, felt his heart swell with pride. His daughter was the head of her class both in intelligence and physical endurance. She ran faster than the others, could jump higher, her exam results were excellent. By some quirk of genetics, she had inherited both brains and beauty. Never had he ever worried about her mental or physical stability.

"Did you see me, father? Was I all right?" she asked as the youthful entertainers joined their parents after the show.

"You were wonderful, darling, wonderful," he said as he hugged her.

"Mr. Bradley," the head mistress said as she approached. "Let me congratulate you. Your daughter is a credit to the school and to your family. I understand she also plays the pianoforte and I do think we should include that in her curriculum. It will cost a small amount extra, but I'm sure you will want the best for her."

While it gratified John to hear his daughter was so well thought of, he resented the proprietary tone of Miss Watson. It was at her urging that Josy took ballet lessons, fencing instruction, ballroom dancing and now had more clothes for more purposes than he had dreamed necessary. Shoes for this and that, dresses and gym clothes, summer and winter outfits for all occasions. It was just as well John had no female interest, for his money would have vanished like the morning mist.

"I don't think Josy would want to spend so much time indoors, particularly during the spring and summer months. Maybe she could take lessons in the autumn and winter. What do you say, Josy?"

"Oh Daddy, I don't like the piano, all those scales. They won't let you play tunes. Gladys told me . . .,"

"Miss Bradley, remember your manners, please," Miss Watson said, raising her pinz nez to her eyes.

"Yes, Miss Watson. I'm sorry, Miss Watson," she said, eyes downcast.

"Come along, darling. Shall we have some ice cream?" John said taking her hand and turning to move away. "Thank you, Miss Watson. We'll talk about piano lessons later in the year."

Mollified, Miss Watson moved to corner another parent. They needed money for roof repairs, so she and her staff had an active campaign under way to sell as many unnecessary courses as possible to unsuspecting parents.

"She's horrible, is Miss Watson," Josy said with a great deal of satisfaction. None of the pupils liked her, perhaps because she was a disciplinarian.

"Now, darling, she has your best interests at heart. I don't think you're being nice."

"Well, I don't want to play the rotten old piano. Not if they won't let me play tunes. I can play lots of tunes, you've heard me at home. Miss Scott taught me an awful lot, and she didn't make me play boring scales all the time."

John smiled. Miss Scott, the governess, was one in a million; a compassionate woman possessed of such tenderness that her charge worked hard to please her. Josy had forgotten the long hours of scales now, only thinking piano playing was easy. Well, she'd had the grounding, so maybe a course in the fall semester might do some good.

"I think you'll find it is not all scales, darling, but scales are important to gain flexibility in your fingers so you can play intricate tunes with panache."

"I suppose." She didn't sound convinced. "Look there's Gladys and her parents. Shall we join their table?"

That was the first time John met Phyllis, the woman whom he would marry. She was with Mr. and Mrs. Glover and their daughter Gladys.

After the introductions (Phyllis was Mrs. Glover's sister), the group sat chatting about the entertainment and the school in general and all the time John's eyes were drawn to Phyllis. She wore a lavender afternoon gown with a matching hat. Her hair was red gold, like Josephine's, and she was a genuine lady. As she gazed around, taking in the hurly burly of the open house, she smiled pleasantly, not at all upset at the high pitched, excited shrilling of young girls.

Her poise made John experience a sense of calm and he moved his chair closer so they could talk.

"Did you enjoy the concert, Miss Glover?" he asked.

"Indeed I did, Mr. Black. Your daughter was delightful and you must be proud. Such poise for a seven-year-old."

"I *am* proud. Especially since fate has deprived her of a mother for many years now."

So it was that Phyllis learned that Mr. Black was a widower. His wealth was apparent from his attire and she felt a surge of excitement. Not for ages had she met a man to whom she felt attracted, and here, when she least expected it, and at a school function, he had popped up.

By the time John was ready to leave, he had made a date with the fair Phyllis and arrived back in Wigan with a song on his lips.

Albert Stockton became a good friend of the Mayhurst Stocktons. Margaret was thrilled when Albert Junior took them to visit his own family in Newton-le-Willows, transporting them in a grand carriage drawn by four matched blacks. When passers-by stared, she felt like a queen.

They travelled down to London with the Stockton's when Edward VII died and saw the grand parade through the city streets. They even saw King George V who had the family resemblance.

Albert's wife, Millicent, was a down-to-earth motherly type who welcomed them with open arms. A warm caring woman, their new found wealth had not destroyed her inherent unselfishness. Margaret felt at home in the grand mansion and took to Millicent as if she had known her all her life.

Fred accepted Albert's friendship for a different reason. He admired the man for his hard work and skill in turning a job as a garage mechanic into an empire of mills and factories. Albert had lately purchased a blacking factory and a pottery in Liverpool.

Fred nurtured the relationship as he could see something in it for himself somewhere down the line. As for Margaret, she saw nothing but the hand of friendship.

That month the four were invited to attend a play at the town hall in Chester by a Shakespearean troupe who were the latest rage. Margaret was in a dither of excitement. To think they'd rub shoulders with the cream of County society, and meet the mayor and his councillors. Fred thought it a nuisance but, to placate Margaret, agreed to attend.

In her new grey and yellow striped silk gown and with a tiny rhinestone tiara at the front of her piled up hair, Margaret looked beautiful. She was agog with excitement as the coach, which had taken them from the Stockton mansion to the town centre, slowed at the steps. A vast crowd of spectators stood to each side, ogling and eyeing the invited guests.

Once inside the vast building, they congregated in the lobby to drink, mingle and drink punch. Fred spotted John Black, and felt both amazed and surprised when he saw the beautiful woman at his side.

"There's John Black," he said to Margaret, gesturing with his glass.

"So it is. Who is his companion? She's beautiful, and looks very young."

"I don't know, but we can soon remedy that. Come, we will stroll over and speak to them."

So Phyllis was John's new fiancee. What a surprise. John was obviously in love with her, and even Freddie gazed entranced.

"She looks as though she could be Josy's mother. Doesn't she?" Margaret said as they made their way back to Albert and Millicent. "How wonderful that he found such a lovely woman and one who resembles his daughter."

"Yes, fate has been kind to John." Although Fred had not much liked his sister Angela at the time of her death, he felt John looked far too happy about his current situation. He was jealous, he thought with surprise, he was jealous of John Black. How incredible that he should feel such a emotion because Angela had been a petty spiteful person and John deserved some happiness.

"It looks like John's life is back on track and Josy has a mother again," Margaret said as they rode home the next day after staying overnight at Albert's.

"I'm glad for him, though don't forget he was married to my sister."

"Oh, Freddy, what does that matter? We both know now that Angela had lost her mind. I'm glad you were only her adopted brother."

"We'll never know, will we? I know that Clifford Wright was her father and Jenny Bradley was her mother. Strange that Josy looks so much like young Eddy Bradley, isn't it? It goes to show that one's genes do pass through the generations."

"Hmm." Margaret was not so sure. Something told her that Angela had been in a relationship with Eddy, but nobody would ever know the truth.

John Black married Phyllis Grover and they built a grand new home in Southport. They did not have any children.

Josy Black went on to become a concert pianist and a painter of some renown. At the age of twenty-two, she left the concert stage and married her manager, Derek Platt. They were supremely happy.

No one knew that Derek was the bastard son of Albert Stockton junior.

Valerie and Eddy raised a large family at Hillshead. The curse seemed to have lifted, but Valerie always treated gypsies with respect and paid each of them to remove the original curse. Eddy said she was wasting money. She gave birth to twin girls, Edwina and Nancy, then later had two more boys. Sadly, when he was ten, Nathaniel died from tetanus. From then on Valerie watched the children more closely. When an outbreak of foot and mouth disease depleted their herd of cattle, they asked each visiting gypsy to remove the curse. None could.

Fred and Margaret doted on their sons but when they were in their twenties, aided by Albert Stockton, both left home to work in the city. At the age of fifty, Fred sold the farm to Eddy, and he and Margaret returned to Leeds where they lived a quiet life.

For them, the curse was finished

-end-